HEART AND SOUL

HEART AND SOUL

Maeve Binchy

First published in Great Britain in 2008
by Orion Books
an imprint of the Orion Publishing Group Ltd
Orion House, 5 Upper St Martin's Lane, London, WC2H 9EA

An Hachette Livre UK Company

1 3 5 7 9 10 8 6 4 2

A CIP catalogue record for this book is
available from the British Library.

ISBN 978 0 7528 7336 7 hb
978 0 7528 9750 9 tpb

Typeset at The Spartan Press Ltd,
Lymington, Hants

Printed and bound by
Clays Ltd, St Ives plc

The Orion Publishing Group's policy is to use papers that
are natural, renewable and recyclable products and made
from wood grown in sustainable forests. The logging and
manufacturing processes are expected to conform to the
environmental regulations of the country of origin.

www.orionbooks.co.uk

In memory of my dear younger sister Renie.
And with great love and thanks to Gordon who makes
the bad times bearable and the good times magical.

Prologue

S ome projects take forever to get off the ground.

One of these was the disused storage depot that was owned by St Brigid's Hospital. It was an unattractive cluster of warehouses around a yard. Once it had held supplies for the hospital but it was in an awkward place; new traffic regulations meant that it was a long and cumbersome journey through the Dublin streets to get from one place to the other.

It was a part of Dublin that still had its old workers' cottages, and factories which had been transformed into apartment blocks. This part of the city was 'going up' as the property people described it; soon speculators would look at the storage depot and make St Brigid's an offer for it, the kind of offer they could not refuse.

That's what Frank Ennis wanted. He thought of himself as the financial brains behind St Brigid's, and this was exactly what they needed. A large lump sum, a huge financial injection on his watch.

Frank Ennis could see it happening.

Of course every year when the planning committee met at the AGM there was always some problem and distraction or other. Something that stopped Frank getting this white elephant sold and investing the money in the hospital. One year there was the rheumatology lobby; they wanted a rheum-atism clinic. There was a pulmonary wing too which wanted to set up a day centre for chest patients. And the increasingly vocal heart faction which claimed that there was sufficient evidence to prove that patients could be kept out of hospital, thus freeing up hospital beds, if they had someone to provide back-up support. The cardiologists were like a dog with a bone: they wouldn't let it go.

Frank sighed as they faced in to yet another afternoon in the close, stuffy boardroom. The members were sitting around the table. Frank looked at them without great pleasure. There was the usual collection of people who might have sat on any hospital board. There was what he would describe as a plain-clothes nun. St Brigid's had once been run entirely by nuns; now there were only four of the sisters left. No new vocations. There were senior officials from the health authority; there were important business people who had proved themselves in other walks of life. There was that good-tempered American philanthropist, Chester Kovac, who had set up a private health centre miles away down in the country.

The plain-clothes nun would always open the window, then the papers would fly around the table and someone would close it again. Frank had been through this many times. But on this occasion he felt that victory was in his corner. He had a written offer of a huge sum from a property developer for instant possession of the much discussed and wasted land around the storage depot. This was money that would make everyone sit up and take notice.

Then would come the argument about how the money should be spent: would it go to new state-of-the-art CAT scan machines? Or to changing radically the front of the hospital? Like many buildings of its time, which was the early twentieth century, the hospital had entirely unsuitable stone steps lead-ing to the entrance hall. A ramp would be appropriate or some more satisfactory way of getting into the hospital for the lame and frail.

There was always a need for more beds in women's surgical, there was always a call for isolation units. A lot of pressure had come from the HDU section. They wanted to be raised from high dependency to intensive care and this would need money being spent.

Well, at least they would be able to reply to the property developer today, accept his offer and stop wasting time on the various special interests who all wanted to enlarge their empires.

Coffee and biscuits were served, the agenda was distributed and the meeting began. But from the outset, Frank knew that something was wrong.

The board members had been foolishly influenced by some statistic recently published that seemed to prove the Irish had more than their fair share of heart failure. Possibly connected with lifestyle and diet, with drinking and smoking undoubtedly playing their part in it all. They were all discussing methods of giving heart failure patients more confidence. How great to be at the forefront of a battle against heart disease. A day clinic that would help patients to manage. Frank Ennis could have cursed the organisation which had published these figures just days before his board meeting. For all he knew it could even have been done deliberately – there was something very arrogant about those cardiologists in St Brigid's. They thought they were omnipotent.

He looked for support to Chester Kovac, usually a voice of sanity in such situations. But he had read it wrong. Chester said that this was an imaginative idea and he would be happy if St Brigid's were at the forefront of such a move. After all, the alternative was only money.

Frank fumed at this. It was easy for Chester to say

something was *only* money; he had plenty of money himself. Certainly he was generous, but what did he know? He was a Polish-American with an Irish grandfather – he was the victim of the last person he had spoken to.

Frank seethed with rage.

'It's not *only* money, Chester. It's *huge* money, going into St Brigid's to improve it.'

'Last year you wanted to sell that land for it to be a car park,' Chester said.

'But this is a far better offer.' Frank was red in the face with the effort of it all.

'Well, we would have been foolish to accept your suggestion last year, Frank, seeing the way things turned out.' Chester was mild but firm.

'But I spent weeks raising this guy's offer . . .'

'And last year we all agreed that we didn't want a car park.'

'So this is *not* a car park. It's superior housing – of the highest specifications . . .' Frank said.

'Not what a hospital is necessarily about,' Chester Kovac said.

'If we're sitting on this piece of land we should use it,' said one of the captains of industry.

'We *are* using it, we are going to get a small fortune for it and invest that in the hospital!' Frank felt that he was talking to very slow learners.

The plain-clothes nun spoke primly. 'We *would* like something within the spirit of the original order who once ran the hospital.'

'Housing is hardly against the spirit of the order is it?' Frank asked.

'Expensive housing of the highest specification might not be what the good sisters wanted.' Chester spoke gently.

'The good sisters are all dead and gone, they died out!' Frank exploded.

4

Chester looked at the face of the plain-clothes nun. She was very hurt by this. He needed to be a peacemaker.

'What Mr Ennis means is that the nuns' work is completed here, their work is done. But they have left their legacy. This is a community that needs more health care and fewer expensive apartments which will each be host to two cars, thus clogging up the roads still further. What it needs is a good positive system set up, something that will go on helping people to make the most of their lives after the initial set-back of cardiac failure. And to be very frank, when it comes to the vote, that's what I would most like to see and that's where I will place my choice.'

There was something dignified about the way he spoke.

Frank Ennis was crestfallen. The place would not be off their hands as he had so confidently hoped this morning. Now it was back on the table. The cardiologists had won. There were going to be months and months of agreeing costs and building work and furnishing and equipment. They would have to appoint a director and staff. Frank sighed heavily. Why did these people not have any sense at all? They could have had so many of the items on their wish list if they had any understanding of how the world worked. Instead they were complicating everything.

He sat through the meeting, moving on automatically from item to item. Then it came to the vote for the change of use of the premises owned by St Brigid's and known as the former storage depot. As he expected it was unanimously agreed that a heart care clinic should be built there.

Frank suggested a feasibility study.

He was voted down immediately. They were not in favour of this – they would be another six years debating the issue. If they had agreed to do it then they had agreed. It was feasible.

It would however need an Extraordinary General Meeting,

once costs had been agreed, tenders received from builders, numbers of staff agreed with cardiology.

They consulted their diaries and fixed the date.

Frank had wanted it in six months' time. Chester Kovac said that surely a matter of a few weeks would be enough to get the submissions in. Builders must be so anxious to get work. The representative heart specialist said that cardiology in St Brigid's would be so grateful they would set out their requirements speedily.

'Requirements!' Frank Ennis snorted.

'And of course the post of director will have to be advertised,' the plain-clothes nun said.

'Oh, yes indeed. I suppose he's out there waiting in the wings for a nice easy number,' Frank muttered, still bitter in defeat.

'He or *she*,' the nun said firmly.

'God – I'd forgotten the women,' Frank said under his breath. He was a man who had often forgotten women. At the golf club he was always outraged when there was a Ladies Day delaying his round. He had even forgotten to get married along the way. But that had all probably been for the best. 'He or *she*, of course,' he said aloud. 'I am stuck in the old days, Sister.'

'Bad way to be, Mr Ennis,' said the plain-clothes nun as she opened the windows and let some fresh air into the room once more.

Chapter One

They had told Clara Casey that there was a small budget to furnish her new office. A tiresome administrator with a loud voice, tousled hair and irritating body language had gestured around the dull, awkward-looking room with its grey walls and ill-fitting steel filing cabinets. Not the kind of room that a senior consultant would consider much of a prize after thirty years studying and practising medicine. Still, it was never wise to be negative at the outset.

She struggled for the man's name. 'Yes, indeed . . . um . . . Frank,' she said. 'It certainly has a lot of what might be called potential.'

This was not the response he had expected. The handsome, dark-haired woman maybe in her forties, wearing a smart, lilac-coloured knitted suit, was striding around the small room like a caged lioness.

He spoke quickly. 'Not unlimited potential, Dr Casey, not financially speaking, I fear. But a coat of paint here and a piece of nice furniture there, a feminine touch will do wonders.' He smiled indulgently.

Clara fought hard to keep her temper.

'Yes, of course, those are just the kind of judgements I would bring to decorating my own home. This is entirely different. For one thing I can't have a room hidden miles away down a corridor. If I am to run this place I have to be in the centre of it and run it.'

'But everyone will know where you are, your name will be on the door,' he spluttered.

'I have no intention of being locked away in here,' she said.

'Dr Casey, you have seen the funding, you were aware of the set-up when you took the position.'

'Nothing was said about where my desk would be. Nothing at all. It was left to be discussed at a later date. This is the date.'

He didn't like her tone. It was definitely like the tone of a schoolmistress.

'And this is the room,' he said.

She was tempted to ask him to call her Clara, but remembered he would have to recognise her status here if she was to get anything done. She knew his type.

'I think not, Frank,' she said.

'Can you show me where else you could be placed? The dietician's room is even smaller, the secretary has just room for herself and the files. The physio has to have his room laid out with equipment, the nurses need their station, the waiting room must be near the door. Can you kindly inspire me as to where we can find you another room if this perfectly serviceable place doesn't suit?'

'I'll sit in the hall,' Clara said simply.

'The hall? What hall?'

'The space when you come in the glass doors.'

'But, Dr Casey, that wouldn't do at all.'

'And exactly why not, Frank?'

'You'd be at everyone's beck and call,' he began.

'Yes?'

'There would be no privacy, it wouldn't look . . . it wouldn't be right. There would only be room for a desk.'

'All I need is a desk.'

'No, Doctor, with respect, you need much more than a desk. Much more. Things like a filing cabinet,' he finished lamely.

'I can have one of those in the secretary's office.'

'A place for your patients' case histories?'

'In the nurses' room.'

'You'll need some privacy sometimes to talk to patients.'

'We can call this room that you like so much the consultation room, we can all use it when needed. You could paint it calm, restful colours, get new curtains; I'll choose them if you like. A few chairs, a round table. Okay?'

He knew it was over, but he gave one final bleat.

'That was never the way before, Dr Casey, it just wasn't the way.'

'There never *was* a heart clinic here before, Frank, so there is no point in trying to compare it with something that didn't exist. We are setting this place up from scratch and if I am going to run it then I'm going to run it properly.'

Clara knew that he was still looking at her disapprovingly from the door as she walked towards her car. She kept her head high and a false smile nailed to her face.

She zapped to unlock the car and swung herself into the driving seat.

After work today someone would certainly ask Frank what she was like. She knew just what he would say. 'Ball-breaker, big-time.'

If pressed he would say that she was power-hungry and couldn't wait to get into the job and throw her weight around. If only he knew. No one must ever know. No one would know just how much Clara Casey did *not* want this new job. But she had agreed to do it for a year. And do it she would.

She pulled out into the afternoon traffic and felt it safe to let the false smile fall from her face. She was going to go to the supermarket and buy three kinds of pasta sauce. Whatever she got one of the girls objected. The cheese was too strong, the tomato was too dull, the pesto too self-consciously trendy. But out of three they might find something that would suit. Please may they be in good humour tonight.

She couldn't bear it if Adi and her boyfriend Gerry had yet another ideological disagreement about the environment or the whale or battery farming. Or if Linda had yet another one-night stand with some loser who hadn't bothered to call her.

Clara sighed.

People had told her that girls were terrible in their teens but became fine in their twenties. As usual Clara had it wrong. They were horrific now at twenty-three and twenty-one. When they had been teenagers they hadn't been too bad. But of course that bastard Alan had been around then so things had been easier. Sort of easier.

Adi Casey let herself into the house where she lived with her sister and her mother. *Menopause Manor*, her sister Linda used to call the place. Very funny, really humorous.

Mum wasn't home yet. That was good, Adi thought, she would go and have a nice long bath, use the new oils she had bought at the market on the way home. She had also bought some organic vegetables; who knew what kind of shop-bought thing Mum might bring home next, filled with additives and chemicals.

To her annoyance she heard music from the bathroom. Linda had beaten her to the bath. Mum had been talking about a second bathroom. Shower room, anyway. But there had been no mention of it recently. And what with Mum not getting the big job she had hoped for, this wasn't the time to mention it. Adi gave a little at home, but she didn't earn much as a teacher. Linda gave nothing. She was still a student but it never crossed her mind to get a part-time job. Mum ran the show and was entitled to call the shots.

Before Adi got to her room, the phone rang. It was her father.

'How's my beautiful daughter?' he asked.

'I think she's having a bath, Dad, will I get her?'

'I meant you, Adi.'

'You mean whoever you're talking to, Dad, you always do.'

'Adi, *please*. I'm only trying to be nice, don't be so cross over nothing.'

'Right, Dad, sorry. What is it?'

'Can't I just call to say hello to my—'

'You don't do that, you ring when you want something.' Adi was sharp.

'Will your mother be at home this evening?'

'Yes.'

'What time?'

'This is a family, Dad, not a facility where people check in and sign books.'

'I want to talk to her.'

'So call her then.'

'She doesn't return my calls.'

'So turn up.'

'She doesn't like that you know. *Her* space and all that.'

'I'm too old. This game between you has gone on too long. Sort it, Dad, please.'

'Could you and Linda be out tonight, I want to talk to her about something.'

'No, we will *not* be out.'

'I'll treat you to supper somewhere.'

'You'll pay for us to go out of our own home?'

'Try to help me on this.'

'Why should I? You never tried to help anyone anywhere along the line.'

'Why won't you do this small thing?'

'Because Mum has arranged to cook us a supper to celebrate taking a new job. Because it's long planned and I am not cancelling it now. Sorry, Dad.'

'I'm coming over anyway.' He hung up.

Linda came dripping out of the bathroom wrapped in a damp towel. Adi looked at her without pleasure. Linda, who ate junk food, who smoked and drank, looked just beautiful, her long wet hair as good as anyone else's would look coming from a salon. There was no fairness in life.

'Who was on the phone?' Linda wanted to know.

'Dad. Like a bag of weasels.'

'What did he want?'

'To talk to Mum. He said he would pay us to go out tonight.'

Linda brightened. 'Really? How much?'

'I said no. No way.'

'That was very high-handed of you.'

'You call him and renegotiate if you want to, I'm not going out.'

'I suppose it's the big D,' Linda said.

'Why should they bother to get divorced *now*? She didn't throw him out when she should have. Aren't they fine as they are? Him with the bimbo and Mam here with us?' Adi saw no reason to change things.

Linda was shruggy. 'Bet she's pregnant, the bimbo, bet you that's what he's coming to tell her.'

'God,' said Adi, 'now I wish I *had* agreed to take his bribe if that's what it's all going to be about. I think I'll call him back.'

In the end she sent him a text: 'House will be daughter-free from 7.30 tonight. We have gone to Quentins. Will send you the bill. Love, Adi.'

*

'Alan? Alan, the phone is a bit fuzzy. Can you hear me? It's Cinta.'

'I know it is, darling.'

'Have you told her?'

'I'm just on the way to her house, darling.'

'You won't bottle out like last week?'

'That's not exactly what happened . . .'

'Don't let it happen again *please*, Alan.'

'No, darling, you can rely on me.'

'I'll need to, Alan, this time, I need to.'

Clara let herself in. The house was suspiciously quiet. She would have expected both girls to be at home. There were wet towels on the bathroom floor. Linda had been home having a bath. There were leaflets about recycling plastic on the kitchen table, so Adi had been back too. But no sign of them now. Then she saw the note on the fridge.

> *Dad is coming round at 8 to talk to you; he sort of implied he wanted this to be a one to one. Without us being there. He implied rather heavily as it happens. Actually, he offered to pay for a meal out for us, so we're going to Quentins.*
> *Love from us both,*
> *Adi*

What could he want tonight of all nights? At the end of a long, tiring, disappointing day which had involved seeing the place without a soul which was going to be the centre of her work for the next year?

At the end of hours of role-playing and attitude-taking about territory with a tiresome bureaucratic hospital official. After hunting through three different delicatessen sections to get pasta sauces for her picky daughters. And now they were both going out to a fancy restaurant and Clara had to face

13

Alan and whatever cracked scheme he had worked out to take something back from their financial settlement.

Clara put the food away; there would be no sharing of anything with Alan. Not any longer. Those years were long over. She took two bottles of fizzy water out of the fridge. She put the two bottles of Australian Sauvignon Blanc at the very back of the fridge behind the yoghurts and low-fat spreads. He would never find them there. And she might well need them badly after he had gone.

At Quentins restaurant Adi and Linda settled down happily.

'You could run a small country for a week on what they're paying at that table over there.' Adi was disapproving.

'Yeah, but not with any sense of fun,' Linda said.

'I wonder are we really blood sisters?' Adi asked.

'You've always wondered that.' Linda slowly sipped her Tequila Sunrise.

'What time do you think he'll go?' Adi wondered.

'Who, the guy at the table?'

'No, Dad, you fool.'

'As soon as he gets what he wants. What makes him different to any other man?' Linda caught the waiter's eye. Another Tequila Sunrise and she would be ready to order.

Clara had intended to change into home clothes but the phone never stopped ringing so there was no time. Her mother wanted to know what the new office was like.

'Do you have a carpet on the floor?' Her mother was down to basics.

'It's sort of modern flooring throughout the whole place.'

'You don't then.' She could see her mother's mouth closing like a trap. The way it had when she had got engaged to Alan, got married to Alan and got separated from Alan. There had been many closed-trap moments.

Her friend Dervla had called to know what the mood of the place was like.

'Mushroom and magnolia,' Clara had told her.

'God, what on earth does that mean?'

'That's the colours it's painted in at the moment.'

'But you can change all that.'

'Oh yes. Definitely.'

'So it's not really just the colour scheme that's upsetting you.'

'Who's upset?'

'I can't imagine. Did you meet any of the people you'll be working with?'

'Nope, it was tombstone city.'

'It's a question of nothing will please you? Am I right?'

'As always, you are right, Dervla.' Clara sighed.

'Listen, Philip is out at a meeting and he won't be baying for food. Would it help if I were to bring round a bottle of wine and a half kilo of sausages? Used to work in the old days.'

'Not tonight, Dervla. That bastard Alan has paid the girls to go out to Quentins because he wants to tell me something, ask me something. What's left to ask at this stage, I ask myself?'

'I was at a meeting yesterday and one of the items on the agenda said TBA. I actually thought it meant That Bastard Alan because you never call him anything else.'

Clara laughed. 'What *did* it mean?'

'I don't know. To Be Agreed, To Be Arranged, something like that.' Dervla wasn't very certain.

'No one would ever know you had a brain, Dervla, you always put on this vague fluffy act.'

'For all the good it does me.'

'I wish I had your know-how. I don't know *what* he wants but whatever it is I don't want to give it to him.'

'If it doesn't matter to you then give it to him. Make a big deal out of it of course, but if you don't care then give it and walk away.'

'But what can it *be*? He can't have the house. He doesn't want the girls, they're big enough anyway to go wherever they want and they hardly go near him.'

'Maybe he has a touch of angina and wants an examination.'

'No, I never treated him. I always made sure from the start that he went to Sean Murray.'

'Maybe he wants to marry the young one, and needs a divorce.'

'No, he's running headlong from marrying her.'

'How do you know?'

'The girls tell me, *he* even tries to tell me when he thinks I might listen to him.'

'And will you listen to him?'

'Not much. I know you all think I should have finished this totally ages ago. Who knows? I might. I might not.'

'Good luck, Clara.'

'I wish we *were* having those sausages and wine.'

'Another night, Clara.'

Then there was an email from the paint shop saying that she could pick up a colour chart next morning; a text from her cousin in Northern Ireland to say that there was going to be a Ladies Club Outing to Dublin and could Clara suggest somewhere good value where they could park a bus and lunch, buy souvenirs and get a bit of country air at a reasonable price; a neighbour came in to ask for support about banning a pop concert which would deafen them in three months' time. And then it was eight o'clock and Alan was on the doorstep.

He looked well. Annoyingly well. Much younger than his forty-eight years. Under a dark jacket he had an open-necked, lemon-coloured shirt. Easycare, Clara noted. No careful ironing of collars and cuffs for the bimbo. He was carrying a bottle of wine.

'More civilised, I thought,' he said.

'More civilised than what exactly?' Clara asked.

'Than sitting glaring at each other. God, you look well, that's a lovely colour. Is it heather? Or mauve?'

'I'm not sure.'

'Oh yes, you are, you were always great with colour. Perhaps it's violet or lilac or . . . ?'

'Perhaps it is, Alan; will you come in.'

'Girls out?'

'Yes, you paid for them to go to Quentins, remember?'

'I said I'd stand them a bite of supper. I didn't know they'd go upmarket. Still, that's youth today.'

'Yes, well, you'd know all about it, Alan. Come in and sit down since you're here.'

'Thank you. Shall I get the opener?'

'This is *my* house. I will get *my* opener and *my* glasses when I am ready.'

'Hey, hey, Clara, I brought you a pipe of peace, well, a wine bottle of peace. Where's all the aggravation coming from?'

'I can't think. I really can't. Could it have anything to do with your cheating on me for years, lying to me, promising things were over when they weren't, leaving me, fighting me through all the lawyers in the land?'

'You got the house.' To Alan it was simple.

'Yes, I got the house I paid for. I didn't get anything else.'

'We have *been* through all this, Clara. People change.'

'I didn't.'

'But you *did*, Clara, we all did. You just didn't face it.'

She suddenly felt very tired. 'What do you want, Alan? What do you actually want?'

'A divorce,' he said.

'A what?'

'A divorce.'

'But we *are* divorced, separated for four years, for God's sake.'

'Not divorced, though.'

'But you said you didn't want to remarry. That you and Cinta didn't need any bonds like that.'

'Nor do we. But you see, she's gone and got pregnant and so, well, you see?'

'I don't see.'

'You *do* see, Clara, you just won't admit it. It's over. It's been over for a long time. Why don't we just draw a line in the sand?'

'Get out, Alan.'

'*What?*'

'Get out, Alan, and take your wine of peace with you. Open it at home. You really picked the wrong night.'

'But it will happen anyway. Why can't you just be gracious, decent, I wonder?'

'Yes, Alan, I wonder too,' Clara said, standing up and sliding his unopened bottle back across the table to him.

She wished she felt a sense of closure about it all. It was unsatisfactory leaving it up in the air like this, but Clara was not going to play along, doing things according to *his* time-table. Was it possible she thought it wasn't entirely over?

So even if it was unfinished, that's what she wanted just now. She stood there long enough for him to realise that he really did have to go; and so he went.

'Cinta? Darling?'

'That you, Alan?'

'How many other men call you Cinta and address you as darling?' His laugh was tinny.

'What did she say?'

'Nothing.'

'She must have said something.'

'No, she didn't.'

'You didn't go.'

'I *did* go.' He was stung by the injustice of it.

'She can't have said nothing.'

'She said, "Get out." '

'And you did?'

'Love, it doesn't make any difference.'

'It does to me,' Cinta said.

Clara had always been a great believer in putting worries out of your mind. Years back they had a wonderful professor of general medicine who had managed to inspire them all. He was Dr Morrissey, her friend Dervla's father.

'Never underestimate the curative powers of being busy,' he had advised them. He said that most of their patients would benefit from having more rather than less to do. He had achieved a near legendary reputation for curing insomnia simply by advising people to get up and sort out their tape collection or iron their table napkins. What would he say now? Kind Dr Morrissey who had been more of a father to Clara than her own remote, withdrawn father ever had been.

Dr Morrissey would have said, 'Tackle something that will absorb you. Something that will put that bastard Alan and his divorce and his infantile girlfriend way out of mind.' Clara poured a glass of wine and went upstairs. She would fill every corner of her mind with this bloody centre which she had signed on to run.

In Quentins Adi was watching her sister with disapproval. Linda was twining her long blonde hair around her fingers and smiling at a man across the room.

'Stop it, Linda,' Adi hissed.

'Stop what?' Linda's eyes were big, blue and innocent.

'Stop attracting his attention.'

'He smiled. I smiled back. Is this now a hanging offence?'

'It could end up being complicated. Will you *stop* smiling, Linda!'

'All right, prune-face. Whatever happened to being pleasant?' Linda sulked.

At that moment a waiter bristling with disapproval came to their table. 'Mr Young's compliments and would the young ladies like to choose a *digestif* with his compliments.'

'Can you please tell Mr Young no thank you very much,' Adi said.

'Please tell Mr Young that I'd love an Irish coffee,' Linda said.

The waiter looked helplessly from one to the other. Mr Young, from across the room, had seen the situation and materialised at their table. A tall man in his late forties, in a well-cut suit and with the appearance of being a person who could manage most situations.

'I was just thinking about how life is so short and how sad it is to have to spend it talking business with men in suits,' he said, a practised smile on his suntanned face.

'Oh, I do agree,' Linda simpered.

'So do I,' Adi said. 'But we are the wrong people to waste the rest of your life on. Mr Young, my sister here is a twenty-one-year-old student. I am a twenty-three-year-old teacher, we're probably not much older than your own children. Our father has paid for us to have a nice dinner here while he tells our mother that he wants a divorce. So you see it's a fraught time. And really you would probably find it more fun with the suits.'

'Such passion and strength in one so young and beautiful.' Mr Young looked at the elder girl with admiration.

Linda didn't like that at all.

'Adi's right, we *do* have to go home,' she said and the

waiter's shoulders relaxed. Problems didn't always sort themselves out so easily.

'And you just actually got out because she said "Get out"?' Cinta was disbelieving.

'God, Cinta, what did you expect me to do? Take her by the throat?'

'You said you'd ask her for the divorce.'

'And I did . . . I did. We'll get it eventually. It's the law.'

'But not before the baby is born.'

'Does it matter when we get it, we'll both be here for the baby? Isn't that what counts?'

'So no wedding?'

'Not yet, you can have the biggest, best wedding in the world later.'

'Okay, later then.'

'What?'

'I said all right, it's hard for you. *I'm* not going to nag you. Why don't you get that wine you were going to give her and we'll open it now.'

'I left it there.'

'You gave her the wine, and left without the divorce? What kind of clown are you, Alan?'

'I really don't know,' Alan Casey said truthfully.

Clara had met Alan when she was a first-year medical student and he had been working for his first year in a bank.

Clara's mother said that there were very few people in the world who did not make money while working for a bank. Alan Casey, however, was one of these. He placed rather too much faith in the more speculative and wilder aspects of investment. They never had much material comfort. Alan was always being pipped at the post for some house or some really great property. Clara just saved steadily from her salary. She closed her ears to the unasked-for advice from her mother and her friends. This was her life and her decision.

Alan had always been the ambitious one: enough was never enough and there had to be more. That came to include women as well. For a time, Clara pretended it wasn't happening. But then it became too hard and she faced it.

When Clara and Alan had split up officially, Clara made sure that each of the three bedrooms should be furnished with shelves and desks. This way they could all work in their own space without interfering with the others. Downstairs was meant to be a more general area. Clara's room was cool and elegant. On one side of the room were her bed, dressing table and large fitted wardrobe. The other half was a work station with filing cabinets, but it looked like quality furniture rather than cheap office supplies. She had a comfortable leather chair and a good light. She opened a drawer and took out a large box file called Centre. For three weeks she had been avoiding looking at it. It brought home the realisation of all she had lost and the small consolation that had been offered in return. But this was the night she would attack it. Maybe after she had watched the nine o'clock news.

When there had been a special offer on television sets in the huge warehouse, Clara had bought three sets. The girls had said she was behaving like some mad exhibitionist millionaire, but Clara had thought it well worth the investment. It meant that Adi could watch programmes about the planet being in decline, Linda could see pop shows and she, Clara, could relax with costume drama.

She reached around for the remote control but she remembered that Dr Morrissey had always said that we found excuses to put off doing something that would take our minds off our worries. It was as if we didn't *want* to lose the luxury of worrying. So she opened the large box and looked with some small degree of pleasure at her neat filing system. There was the documentation about the whole nature of the heart clinic, what it was meant to do, how it would be funded, her own role as its first director. There were her own reports of educational visits to four heart clinics in Ireland and three in Britain and one in Germany. Tiring visits all of them, wearying hours touring facilities which would not be appropriate or relevant to her own centre. Note-taking, head nodding, murmuring approval here, asking questions there.

She had seen money scrimped here, money wasted there. She had observed no planning, excessive planning, making do with what was already there. Nothing to inspire her. Some idiotic decisions like placing a heart clinic on a third floor in a place without proper elevator access. Like the casual attendance of staff on no regular basis. She had seen duplication of files and reports. She had seen trust and hope among patients who felt that they were learning to manage their disease. But surely you could get that in any good GP's office or an outpatients department.

Clara had taken notes on what she had liked and hated in two different coloured pens. It would be easy to summarise her findings. Then she saw a file called Personnel. The pool on which she was allowed to draw, for assistance. She would need the services of a dietician, and a physiotherapist. She would need at least two trained cardiology nurses, the services of a phlebotomist for taking bloods. They would have to have a houseman or woman working there for six-month periods, a system of referral from doctors and the general hospital. They would have to get a campaign of public awareness going, arrange interviews in the national press and on radio.

She had done it all before. When she had been at the forefront, and that was when she was going somewhere. Or thought she had been. Still, it had to be done, and she would do it right. What else was she in this for if it weren't that?

She started to look through the files.

Lavender. What a name for a dietician. But she had a good CV, she said she wanted to specialise in healthy eating for the heart. She sounded lively, young, dedicated. Clara put a tick beside her name and reached for the phone. Might as well start now. Okay, so it was nine o'clock at night, but this was the girl's mobile phone. She would no doubt be surgically attached to it.

'Clara Casey here, Lavender. I hope it's not too late . . .'

'No, of course not, Dr Casey, I'm delighted to hear from you.'

'Perhaps we could have a chat tomorrow if you could come to the centre. There's a sort of conference room there. When is best for you?'

'I'm working from home tomorrow, Doctor, so any time is fine.'

They fixed a 10 a.m. appointment.

Now she needed a physio but she didn't know how many hours a week. She went through the applications to see who was available for part-time. A big bluff face came through the photographs. Square, reliable, not handsome, looked like an ex-boxer, but there was something about his story that she liked. He did a lot of work in inner-city clubs, he had been a late student; the word 'mature' didn't really apply to him. He had a lopsided grin. Great, she thought, I'm choosing staff on their pictures now.

He answered his mobile first ring. 'Johnny,' he said.

Clara Casey explained and, yes, he could make eleven o'clock, no sweat. It was going well. She lined up two nurses and got the name of a security man as well. Tim. She rang his mobile phone. A slightly American accent told her that he would get back to her. If she was going to start to tear this place apart tomorrow she would need someone to keep the building safe.

To her surprise she heard the key in the door and the sound

of her two discontented daughters returning. They came in to her room without knocking. That was something else that annoyed her these days.

'What did he want?' Linda asked.

'Who?'

'Dad.'

'A divorce, he wants to get married again.'

The girls looked at each other. 'And?'

'And I told him to get out.' Clara seemed unconcerned.

'And he went?'

'Well, obviously. And did you have a nice night? No? Well, he left you some wine downstairs. You could kill that, I suppose.'

Linda and Adi looked at each other, confused. Their mother's phone rang.

'Oh, Tim, thank you for getting back to me. No, of course it's not too late. Could you come in tomorrow to discuss a small security job? I am going to knock down a lot of walls and leave a place wide open for a few days, so that will be full-time. After that it will just be on regular routine patrol. Fine. Fine. See you then.' She smiled vaguely at her daughters.

They were uneasy. It had not been a hugely successful dinner at Quentins, their father was going to marry a girl of their own age, and now it appeared that their mother had gone raving mad.

The next morning flew by. The interviews went remarkably well. Lavender turned out to be trim and businesslike. She was realistic about the number of hours needed to give dietary advice. She suggested a weekly cookery class, and said it had worked well when she had been in a clinic in London. A lot of the patients had no idea how to cook vegetables properly or make a healthy soup and were astounded at the possibilities. Lavender was a no-nonsense person, a single woman in her forties. She took two months off in January and February every year and went to Australia but would arrange a substitute herself. She would help Clara to set up the kitchen and could start work in two weeks' time.

Clara found it very reassuring.

Johnny the physio was indeed big and bluff but seemed to have huge reserves of patience. He said that heart patients had seen too many movies where people clutched at their chests and died in seconds on the floor. This made them terrified of taking any exercise in case they over-exerted themselves and brought on the heart attack that would kill them. Instead they allowed their muscles to waste. He enquired whether Clara would be able to wire the patients up to an ECG so that their progress could be monitored.

'Doubt if they'll give me the equipment,' Clara said.

'We could make a case for it,' Johnny said and joined the team.

Tim the security man had lived in New York for two or three years. He had done a lot of hospital work there, so he knew just what was needed. He could give it his full time for the next couple of weeks as he was hoping to go into business on his own and needed a couple of major satisfied clients. But he didn't want to tread on any toes.

'Why aren't you using the existing hospital security?' he asked.

'Because I want to run my own show.' Clara was equally direct.

'And will they pay for it?'

'Yes, if you give us what those guys in the offices might consider a fair quote. They love to think they're saving money. It's all they care about.'

'Same everywhere,' Tim said pragmatically.

'You came back from America?'

'Yeah, everyone I knew out there worked fourteen hours a day. All the people I knew here were wearing designer suits and buying property in Spain. Thought I'd come back and get a bit of that for me. I'm really no better than the men in suits.'

'Glad to be back?'

'Not totally sure,' he said.

'Early days yet.' Clara was practical. She felt at ease with this quiet man.

The first nurse she interviewed, Barbara, was exactly the kind of person she would have hand-picked. Outgoing, direct and very much on top of the subject. She answered the routine questions about heart medication, blood pressure and stroke.

The second woman was older but not at all wiser. Her name was Jacqui and she spelled it twice in case there should be any misunderstanding. She said that she was applying for the job so that she would have no evening or shift work. She said that existing holiday arrangements would have to be honoured. She said she would need an hour and a half for lunch to walk her dog who would sleep peacefully in her car once he knew that an extended 'walkies' was included in the day. She said that her present job was like working in the Third World. Most of the time was making yourself under-stood to foreigners. Clara knew in moments that this woman would not be part of the team.

'When shall I hear from you?' Jacqui asked confidently.

'Many, many more people to interview. I'll let you know in a week.' Clara was clipped.

Jacqui looked around her without much pleasure. 'You'll have your work cut out for you here,' she sniffed.

'Indeed, but isn't that where the challenge lies?' Clara felt the smile stiffen on her face.

*

27

What Clara really needed, she discovered next morning, was an extra pair of legs. Someone who could run and find this form, leave in the other form, get the hospital building team and the electricians to gather for discussions. But nowhere had this pair of legs materialised. She would have to find her own. By chance she found them in the car park. A thin girl with long, straggly hair, carrying a chamois cloth, offered to clean her windscreen.

'No thanks.' Clara was pleasant but firm. 'This isn't really a good place to get business, mainly staff who don't care what their cars look like or patients who are too worried about themselves to notice.'

The girl didn't seem to understand her properly. She was straining to get the meaning of the words.

'Where are you from?'

'*Polski*,' the girl said.

'Ah, Poland. Do you like it here?'

'I think yes.'

'Do you have a job?'

'No. No job. I do some things.' She indicated her cleaning cloth.

'What else? What other work?'

'I go to houses to wash the cups and to clean the floors. I put the leaves from the trees into big bags. I see little boys clean car windows. I think maybe . . .' Her face was pale and peaky.

'Do you get enough to eat?' Clara asked.

'Yes, I live up the stairs in a restaurant so I get one meal a day.'

'Do you have friends here?'

'Some friends. Yes.'

'But you need work?'

'Yes, madam, I need work.'

'What's your name?'

'Ania.'

'Come with me, Ania,' Clara said.

There were lengthy and wearying conversations with builders. The foreman told Clara that she'd never get all these changes past administration. They hated change, administration did, they feared open spaces, loved small individual rooms where people could talk in private. Clara chose fabrics for the curtains which would divide the cubicles, as well as blinds for the windows. She looked through office furniture catalogues marking desks and cabinets. The time flew by.

She sent the little Polish girl scampering all over the place as she dealt with officialdom. Clara had typed out a letter explaining that Ania Prasky was the temporary assistant to Dr Clara Casey and put in every initial and qualification that she possessed. They weren't going to get in the way of this battery of achievement.

It was four o'clock in the afternoon and she hadn't even thought about lunch. Ania must have had no lunch either. She came running at Clara's command.

'Lunch, Ania,' she said briskly. Across Ania's face went a shadow of anxiety.

'No, madam, thank you, but I work,' she said.

'A nice bite of lunch and good strong coffee and we will work even better.'

The anxiety left Ania's face. Clara was going to pay for lunch. A day's wages wouldn't be broken into. She looked just like a happy child.

Clara knew that when Adi and Linda had been travelling the world when they were eighteen kind people had often put them up for the night or given them a good hot meal when they needed one. It was a kind of currency, you were kind to other people's young, they were kind to yours.

'Come on, Ania, this will put hair on our chests.'

'It will?' Ania was startled.

'No, not real hair. It's a figure of speech. Do you know what that is?'

'Not really, madam.'

'Well, I'll try to explain it to you over lunch,' Clara said, reaching for her jacket.

Frank couldn't believe that this woman had taken on so much and so quickly. His desk was filled with forms, requisitioning this, that and the other. It was a day's work to get through his in-basket. Now he had an additional problem. He had heard that a small Polish girl with large worried eyes had been seen running around at least half a dozen times carrying more information. This Clara Casey seemed to be taking her new premises apart brick by brick. Each request or explanation was accompanied by a personal note from her on her own headed notepaper which she must have had printed practically overnight. She referred back to 'our conversation' or 'our agreement'. She was effectively making him part of her expansionist plan. He would have to stop her now before he was dragged down with her. Or else he could let her go ahead. Not the kind of woman he liked, a real ball-breaker, but as a hospital colleague intent on getting things done, she was unbeatable.

Frank decided to give her a day or two before stepping in. Surely in the next forty-eight hours she would exceed her brief so spectacularly it would be a case of self-destruct. In the meantime he would write her a cautious meaningless letter covering his back saying that all the plans would of course have to be sanctioned by the board.

Barbara sank her teeth into the big hamburger. She had been on a diet for six weeks and lost only six pounds. She had promised herself a treat if she got the new job in the heart clinic. She *had* been thinking of new shoes or a big classy handbag. But it had been a long day and she hadn't the energy to go to the shops. She was meeting her friend Fiona for a celebration.

Fiona was envious. It sounded just the kind of job she would have liked.

'But you didn't apply.' Barbara was furious with Fiona. 'You'd have got the job and we could have worked together but no, you wouldn't fill out any forms.'

'I didn't know she was going to be nice, that it would be open plan, that you'd have so much power. I thought it would be a "Come Here, Do That" sort of job.'

'Well, it's too late now, she's probably hired some awful battleaxe that I'll have to work with just because you wouldn't fill in a form.'

'What's she like?' Fiona asked.

'Dark-haired, groomed, sort of good-looking in an oldish way. A bit like that woman at the table over there. Hey, wait a minute, that *is* her.' Barbara's hamburger remained poised in the air.

'She's eating *here*?' Fiona was open-mouthed.

'Yes, and that's a girl from the centre, a foreign girl called Ania, with her. How extraordinary!' Barbara shook her head in disbelief.

'The woman has to eat somewhere I suppose . . .' but Fiona was already heading towards Clara.

'Come back,' Barbara hissed, but it was too late. Fiona was already talking.

'Dr Casey, please forgive me interrupting your meal but I am Fiona Ryan. I work with Barbara over there who is going to start working with you next week. I meant to apply for a job there but I thought it would be a bit routine. Barbara has been telling me all about it and it sounds brilliant. I was just

31

wondering was it too late to send you my CV. I could leave it in tonight if you haven't picked anyone else yet.'

Clara looked and saw a pretty girl in her twenties with a broad smile. She radiated confidence and encouragement. Exactly the kind of person she wanted working with her. In the background she saw Barbara trying desperately to discourage her friend, but Fiona was having none of it.

'Barbara is embarrassed but I thought if I didn't ask you now I'd never know.'

She looked bright and alert. It wouldn't hurt to read her CV.

'Sure,' said Clara. 'Leave it in as soon as you can and a phone number where we can get you. This is Ania by the way.'

'Hi, Ania. I'll leave you both to your food. Thank you very much.' And she was gone, back at the table with Barbara who was babbling abuse at her.

'Nice, isn't she?' Clara seemed to be treating Ania as an equal.

Very flattered, Ania agreed. 'She has a big smile. Will you employ her, madam?'

'Definitely,' Clara said. 'Now, Ania, will we have an ice cream, do you think, or should we get back and get our clinic up and running?'

'We go back now, madam,' Ania said. Lunch was good but they must know where to draw the line.

At seven o'clock Clara paid Ania her day's wages. 'See you tomorrow at eight thirty,' she said.

Ania's face was split in half by her smile. 'I work again tomorrow?' she said, clasping her hands.

'Sure, if you'd like to. I mean you're trained now. But you may have to do some cleaning and hauling furniture about. I'll help you of course.'

'Thank you, madam, with all of my heart,' Ania said, 'and for my beautiful dinner too. You are a very kind lady doctor.'

'That's not what they say about me at home,' Clara sighed. 'They say I am barking mad.'

Adi had brought her boyfriend Gerry home for supper. They were eating soup and a salad at the kitchen table when Clara came in. Adi got up to get some for her mother but Clara waved it away.

'Just a coffee, love. I had a huge meal in the middle of the afternoon. Burger and chips.'

Gerry sent out waves of disapproval. 'Meat! Very bad. Very bad indeed.'

Adi was surprised. 'That's not your normal speed, Mum.'

'No, but things are far from normal these days,' Clara said, taking her coffee upstairs. She knocked on Linda's door.

'Come in.' Linda was in bed and wearing a face-mask. She looked like a mime artist or a child dressed up as a ghost for a fancy dress party.

'Sorry, I didn't think you'd be in bed this early,' Clara said.

'No, this is just getting ready to go out. I'm off clubbing around eleven, there's a new place opening tonight and I want to be in the whole of my health for it.'

Linda looked at Clara as if expecting some rebuke or mention of keeping anti-social hours. Surely her mother would say *something* about the lack of books and study. But you could never second-guess Clara.

'When will you actually be earning any money, Linda?' she asked mildly.

'I knew you'd start to grizzle.' Linda's face under the mask was moving with annoyance.

'Who's grizzling? It's just a simple question.'

'Well, in a couple of years, I suppose,' Linda said grudgingly.

'Don't you qualify next year?'

'Mother, what *is* this? Do you want to let this room or something?'

'No, I'm quite happy for us all to live here. It's just that today I met a lot of builders and electricians and plumbers—'

'And you're going off to live in a commune with them,' Linda interrupted.

Clara ignored her. 'And I was thinking of having a second bathroom built. But your warm, generous father is unlikely to want to support this project, and I was wondering how to finance it. Adi could give a little and I was hoping that next year you'd be in a position to contribute too.'

'I was thinking of a gap year before settling down to work.'

'A gap between what and what exactly?' Clara asked.

'Don't take it out on me if you've had a bad day.' Linda looked mutinous.

'I haven't had a bad day; actually, as it happens, I had a very good day. I employed a girl who was about your age, she worked from 9 a.m. until 7 p.m. like a little slave. I asked her to come in and do the same tomorrow and she cried with gratitude.'

'Bet she wasn't Irish,' Linda said.

'She will be one day, but at the moment she's Polish.'

'Aha!' Linda was triumphant.

'Oh, Linda, shut up, you don't know the first thing about work of any kind and here you are bleating on about gap years. You don't know how lucky you are.'

'I don't think I'm lucky at all, not even a little bit. My parents hate each other. My father is going to marry someone of my age. Think how that makes me feel. My mother is a workaholic, bellyaching about the fact that I'm not out there slaving for a living even though it was *agreed* I'd be a student. I was here minding my own business having a sleep and you come in and unload all this on me. Why not tell me about all

34

the starving orphans in China or India or Africa as well as the Polish girls who are *your* slaves?'

'You are a truly horrible girl, Linda,' Clara said and banged the door on her daughter's bedroom.

'What's all that shouting upstairs?' Gerry asked Adi.

'It's the real world, Gerry,' she said. 'It's the world of people not getting on, not making allowances for other people, not seeing anyone else's point of view.'

'It's all that red meat,' Gerry said. 'No good could come from eating a dead cow in the afternoon.'

Next morning Clara was gone by the time Adi came down to breakfast. There was no sign that she had eaten anything, and no note left about evening plans. All that shouting last night must have been more serious than it sounded. Adi went to wake Linda who was not best pleased.

'You only need to close your eyes in this house and someone barges in roaring and bawling,' she complained as she struggled to wake up.

'What's wrong with Mum?'

'God, how do I know? She was like a bag of weasels last night, complaining that I wasn't Polish, that I wasn't financing a new bathroom, that I was still a student. She nearly took the door off its hinges. She's coming unstuck I'd say.'

'What was it *about*, Linda?'

'I have no idea on earth. Maybe she's upset about Dad wanting to marry Cinta.'

'She doesn't love Dad any more.'

'How do *we* know who she loves, she's totally deranged. Now will *you* go away and let me sleep.'

'What about your lectures?'

'Oh, for God's sake, Adi, go away and poison young minds, will you.'

Linda was back snuggled down again, deep in her bed. Adi shrugged and left. There was no further information for her here.

Little Ania was sitting outside the door of the centre.

'You did mean it, madam?'

'Indeed I did, Ania. I'll get a key cut for you today, so tomorrow you can be in before me.'

'You will give *me* a key to this place?' Ania was astounded.

'Sure, then you can have the coffee ready when I get here.'

'We will have a coffee machine?' Ania said, excited.

'Yes, it will arrive today, meanwhile here's some money. Go get us two huge coffees down in the precinct, and whatever you think we should have for breakfast, something full of sugar to give us energy: a croissant, a doughnut. Whatever. One each.'

'This is a wonderful job,' Ania said and trotted off obediently.

The day flew by again, the builders were a cheerful crew and they worked fast. Soon the place was beginning to resemble Clara's plan. Her own desk was out in the centre keeping an eye on all that happened. The nurses' station was waiting to be fitted out from General Medical Supplies. The treatment beds had arrived; small cubicles were erected with curtains made from the material Clara had chosen. The waiting room was painted and fitted with racks that would hold information about heart care. There would be a water filter for patients and a coffee urn.

Lavender's room had been prepared for the dietician; her weighing scales would arrive later in the day, together with one for the nurses' station.

The physio room was suitably bare; the equipment depended on what Johnny and Clara could winkle out of the establishment. Clara was pleased with progress so far. She would show that Frank what she was made of. She was surprised when Ania delivered her a salad sandwich at lunchtime and another coffee.

'Let me pay you for this,' she said.

'No, madam, you gave me much money yesterday. Today I get *you* lunch.'

She looked so pleased and proud it wrenched Clara's heart and made her even more annoyed with her own lazy daughter who at this moment was probably sleeping off the effects of last night.

'Have you everyone you need now, madam?'

'No, Ania, I still need an office manager. Someone who will keep the payments in order. Someone who will cover my back.'

'Cover your back?' The phrase was new to Ania.

'Yes. Keep me out of hot water, out of trouble.'

'Will this be a secretary?'

'Sort of, but they want me to have a young girl. That's no use to me. I need someone who can stand up to monsters like Frank Ennis and his gang. You can't expect a child to be able to do that.'

'Do you think that you will win, madam?' Ania's eyes danced with excitement.

'If I find the right person we can get her installed before they are aware of it. The trouble is finding her.'

'You will do that, madam. I know.'

'You have more faith than I do, Ania.'

'Where would we be in life without faith?' Ania asked as she went for a brush to sweep up cheerfully after the carpenters and make them mugs of tea.

When the first week was nearly finished Clara knew that she must go and meet the local pharmacist. She knew him to be

Peter Barry, a fussy sort of man of about fifty who had a chemist's shop in the shopping precinct very near the centre. He would be filling prescriptions for her patients once they started. She must check that he was up to speed with the various heart and blood pressure medicines that she would be prescribing. She need not have worried.

Peter Barry was certainly on top of his work. Fussy or not he had read all the recent research on new drugs and contra-indications. Clara felt briefly that she was back at medical school being lectured to all over again.

'I wish you every success in the centre,' he said formally. 'It's badly needed, something that will make people realise they can control their own heart problems.'

'Oh, yes indeed, it's long overdue,' Clara murmured. It was the usual polite response she gave when told what a worth-while job it was. No one must suspect how much she resented this backwater where she had ended up. She would do her job as well as possible and then leave, but her smile was bright.

'You're right. If you could see patients clutching at their little bottles of pills terrified that they haven't understood which little magic potion will keep them alive. I try to be reassuring but often they need to talk, to ask and learn, and there just isn't the time.'

Clara was impressed. This man had more humanity than she suspected.

'It's a lot of work, I agree. Do you have an assistant here?'

Peter Barry became prim again. 'There is always a qualified pharmacist on the premises, Dr Casey, I assure you. But my assistant is part-time. I had hoped, you see, that my daughter Amy would join me in the business. But then, daughters!' He shrugged.

Clara was sympathetic. 'What did Amy do instead?'

'Finding herself apparently. It's a long search.' Years of disappointment were in his voice.

'Mine is talking confidently about a gap year. Another year of being supported and having to make no decisions.' Clara knew she sounded bitter. She hoped that her mouth was not cold and hard like her own mother's was. But then maybe her mother had every reason to be disappointed with Clara. What had she achieved in life? Two sulky daughters, a broken marriage, failure to get the cardiology job that everyone said was hers. Possibly her mother was as disillusioned with her as she was with Linda and as this man with his glasses on his head felt about *his* daughter.

Peter Barry wasn't letting the topic go. 'What would you do if you had your time all over again?' he asked.

Clara knew exactly what she would do. She would not have married Alan. But then those two girls would never have existed, and that was unthinkable. True, they had their difficult moments but they were her children – she remembered so well the day that each of them had been born. They could be very good and loving; they were funny, too, and tender. She wouldn't wish their lives away. And yet – if she hadn't married Alan, she would have the cardiology post which was rightfully hers. But Clara had spent many years hiding her true feelings and disguising her reactions. She wasn't going to let down her guard and discuss it with this man now.

'Lord, it's hard to know. What would *you* have done?' she asked, putting the ball firmly back in his court.

Peter Barry had no hesitation. 'I would have married again and made a proper home for Amy,' he said simply. 'Her mother died when she was four. She has never known a family.'

'It's hard to find someone to love and marry just like that.' Clara shook her head. 'It's so much luck, isn't it?'

'I don't know. I really don't know. I think there are a lot of people in the world who would make perfectly suitable mates, companions, spouses, if we just put our minds to it.'

Clara murmured her agreement and left. She saw she had a text message from Alan on her phone but didn't read it. Her mind was already full with things that needed to be done or worked out or avoided. She didn't need to think about Alan as well. But at the end of the day she was ready to read his message. She had achieved more than she thought possible. The appalling Frank Ennis had come on an unexpected visit expecting to find disarray and confusion and found instead a near completed job. The floor covering had arrived, the builders were cheerful and enthusiastic, the furniture was on order and Tim, the security man, proudly showed off the system he had chosen. The two nurses, Barbara and Fiona, were busy planning their nurses' station.

Lavender had brought in her posters about healthy food. Johnny had set up his exercise machines. And, best of all, Clara had found her assistant.

She was called Hilary Hickey and she had come in to enquire was there any part-time work. She was a qualified nurse, phlebotomist and worked in hospital administration. She was forty-nine, widowed, with one son. Because of home circumstances she needed to be around the house a bit these days so could not commit to full-time work. Before they had finished talking Clara knew she was perfect for the job. But she must curb her automatic response which was to jump in with both feet before asking any practical questions.

'Are the home circumstances connected with your son?' she asked.

'No, my mother. She's elderly and she lives with us. She needs an eye kept on her. Someone to put a head around the door and make sure she's all right.'

'Sure, sure. How is her health?'

'Sound as a bell. She'll outlive us all. She gets a bit confused sometimes, but nothing to worry about.'

Hilary was full of energy and could turn her hand to anything. She helped Ania, Clara and Johnny carry in a huge machine that looked like a bacon-slicer but he assured them was an arm exerciser. Hilary got on easily with everyone who was there. And she was there when Frank Ennis arrived on his tour of inspection. Clara could not have wished for a better ally. She introduced them.

'Miss Hickey.' He nodded and shook her hand.

'Frank, how are you?' Hilary said cheerfully and Clara had to put up a hand to hide her smile at the look on Frank's face. He was so accustomed to being Mr Ennis and having huge respect.

Frank looked with some mystification as Ania refilled his coffee mug. 'And you are . . . exactly?'

'I am *exactly* Ania Prasky,' she said.

He glared at her, but it was clear she did not intend to mock his form of speech. It was obviously unfamiliarity with the language. 'And are you employed here?'

Clara intervened. 'I pay Ania from petty cash. I would prefer to have it on a more regular basis,' she said.

'You pay her as what?'

'As a carer.' Clara didn't let her glance flicker.

'But there are carers in the wards to help the nurses, not here.'

'We find that there will be a great need for a carer here. Some patients will need wheelchairs, some will need assistance to and from the bus stop, there is a need for coffee, for general cleaning, making the place acceptable and attractive to those who come here. We will need someone to go to and from Mr Barry's pharmacy for those unable to make the journey. We constantly need someone to go to and fro to the hospital to collect X-rays and to do general messages. There is work every minute of the day, I assure you.'

'Oh, I'm afraid it will be quite impossible to get the hospital to agree to that,' Frank began.

Clara saw Hilary's eyes narrow slightly. The fight was on.

'You see, Dr Casey, you already *have* Miss . . . er . . . Hickey here to help you. We can't expect to provide a bottomless pit of employees—'

Hilary interrupted. 'But, Frank, a persuasive man like yourself would have the hospital eating out of your palm in no time and you needn't think that my knees are as young as Ania here and that I'd get down and clean the floors, nor would I spend the time when I could be helping to run the place, so I am sure you'll see to it that Ania stays with us.'

It felt like ten seconds but Clara knew it could only have been three at the most. Then he spoke. 'How much do you pay her?' His voice was more like a bark.

'The minimum wage, but now that she has had a week on-the-job training I would have thought—'

'Minimum wage!' he snapped and left.

Ania hugged them both and brought out the chocolate biscuits. After all this goodwill Clara was able to face Alan's text message. He wanted to meet her. He suggested a drink after work, a meal even. She texted him back. He could come to her house but he must bring no wine, they would talk for an hour, there would be no rows, the girls would not be dragged into it. If he agreed to that then he could come to the house at seven.

Her mother rang just then to know if Clara would come around and help her decide between fabrics for curtains. Clara knew that this would be an unsatisfactory endeavour. Her mother relished indecision. Nothing would be agreed, nothing would be chosen.

'I can't, Mother, I have to meet Alan,' she said.

'To get rid of him finally, I hope,' her mother said crisply.

'Perhaps and perhaps not. We'll see.' Clara was mild.

'We *have* seen,' her mother snapped, 'and we haven't liked what we saw.'

'Sure, Mother.' Clara hung up wearily.

Hilary looked at Clara who worked so hard and hoped that she had planned a good evening out. But she was surprised when she enquired.

'My tiresome ex-husband is coming around to the house to ask, yet again, for a divorce,' Clara said simply.

'I'm sure you'll say yes and get rid of him,' Hilary said, as if it was the most obvious thing in the world.

'Why should I make things easy for him?' Clara wondered.

'Because hanging on to him only makes things worse for you. I must rush. Lord knows what my poor mother will have got up to.' And she was gone.

Clara's friend Dervla phoned as she was driving home. 'He's coming round again this evening,' Clara explained.

Dervla had never liked Alan but she was usually reticent. Not this time, she spared no feelings when she heard the news.

'I have been hearing that he's coming round or that he hasn't come around for twenty-five years; Clara, give him the bloody divorce. Get closure on the thing, for heaven's sake.'

'Thanks, Dervla,' Clara laughed.

'Have you thought he might be tiring of the new broad and wants to come back to you?'

'No. I'm too old and hatchet-faced.'

'Would you have him if he *did* want that?'

'That's like talking about white blackbirds,' Clara said. She wasn't going to go down that road.

At home Clara was relieved to find the house empty. It would make things easier. She had a shower and washed her hair. She had just dried it and put on a fresh pink shirt when she heard him ring at the door. She offered him coffee and poured it out for him. Black, as he always took it.

'Just a chat, Clara, like old times,' he pleaded.

'Not like old times. Old times were mainly a screaming match if you remember.'

'Well, the very old times then.' He had a nice smile. She would have to agree to that. He held his head on one side as if he were convincing you to see things his way, which of course she had done for years.

'What did we talk about in the very old days?'

'Work, the children, each other.' He found the answers easily.

'Well, work is the safest. How's yours?'

'It's all right. It's tiring of course. Banking has changed. There's just so much more pressure these days. And yours?' He really did sound as if he wanted to know.

She told him about the Polish girl, Ania, and the new assistant, Hilary Hickey. About the two cheerful nurses, the physiotherapist, Lavender the dietician and Tim, the security man. She even told him about the dreaded administrator Frank and Peter Barry the pharmacist. And yes, he did seem interested.

Suppose he hadn't met this terrible girl Cinta. Could they possibly have had a normal sort of life together? She tried to get the thought out of her head. It wasn't going to happen. And anyway, there had been others before Cinta and there would be more after her.

He asked her questions about the people she described. Questions that showed he was paying attention. She remembered that about him. It had been easy to discuss her work with him. Alan was a good listener. She had missed him when she had to go it alone through the humiliation of being passed over for the job. She refilled his coffee cup.

'You might meet someone in this new job,' he said softly.

'I must have met a hundred people this week,' she sighed.

'No, I meant *meet* someone. You know, I meant get together with someone.' He was smiling enthusiastically. Wishing her well in the great big frightening world of relationships. She looked at him in bewilderment. Sometimes he could be impossibly insensitive and thick.

'I don't think we should spend any time wandering around that remote possibility. It's nice of you to wish me well but actually I find it unbearably patronising.'

'Patronising? Me to you? You have to be joking! Clara, you've always been the brainy one. You *know* that.'

'Leave it, Alan. Next thing, you'll be saying you married me for my fine mind!'

'I did in many ways but also because you were and are one of the loveliest women in the world.' He leaned over and stroked her cheek. The sheer unexpectedness of it made her flinch away.

'Alan, *please*.'

'Now don't tell me that you don't feel something for me. You're just lovely, Clara. Your hair is so fresh and shiny. You smell like a flower. Come here to me. Let me hold you.'

Because she was so startled, Clara didn't fight him off as quickly as she might have and there he was holding her face in his hands and kissing her before she could struggle away.

'Are you mad?' she gasped. 'It's been five years.'

'Since you threw me out, but I never wanted to go. I never went in my heart.'

'Are you telling me that Cinta has thrown you out too?' She was looking at him in disbelief.

'Not at all, but she has nothing to do with this. With us.'

'There *is* no us, Alan, get off me.' She struggled but he held her all the more firmly.

'This reminds me very much of the old days, Clara,' he said into her ear.

She finally got away from him and ran across the kitchen, putting a chair between them.

'What do you mean nothing to do with Cinta, you *live* with her. She's having your baby, for God's sake. You're here to ask me again for a divorce so that you can marry her.' Her eyes were blazing with rage. 'What are you *at*?'

'I'm trying to get you to relax. You're so tense and strung up. Why can't you unwind and let me make you happy like I used to. For old times' sake.'

He smiled at her, handsome Alan who was always used to getting his own way. He hadn't changed. Alan who was already as faithless to Cinta as he had been to her. Suddenly like a focus in binoculars, everything became clear. This was a man worth spending not one more minute thinking about, second-guessing or trying to understand.

'Right,' Clara said briskly. 'It worked. You can go home and tell little Cinta that she has the divorce and the prize of you as a husband. And that you did it as you usually do by suggesting that you screw me.'

'That's not the way I'd actually describe it,' he began to bluster.

'That's the only way it can be described and will be described.'

'You're not going to say anything to the girls.' He was frightened.

'Adi and Linda will be only slightly more embarrassed by the news than they already are by you having a child with a girl who is the same age as they are.'

'Please, Clara . . .'

'Go, Alan. Go now.'

'You're just locking yourself away. You're still a fine-looking woman . . .'

'Go while you are still able to walk.'

Clara made a gesture with the chair as if she were going to

use it as a weapon. He backed out of the door and was gone. She didn't feel outraged or insulted. She didn't even feel patronised any more. She felt empty and foolish and ashamed that she had spent any small moment hoping this worthless man would tire of his mistress and come home to her.

Tomorrow she would start the divorce process.

What her mother, her daughters, her good friend Dervla and her new assistant Hilary had not been able to make her do, Alan had done himself. By his clumsy attempt to make love to her, by his casual assumption that she would welcome it, he had actually achieved what he wanted – a divorce. Or maybe didn't want. But she would never know or care. She had more important things to think about. And for the first time since she had embarked on this new job, Clara felt it was in fact the most important part of her life.

She would put Alan totally out of her mind and think instead about what lay ahead tomorrow. She would be meeting the new doctor and welcoming him to the clinic. He seemed a very nice young man, good CV, red hair, a calm manner – everything in fact you need for heart patients. His name was Declan Carroll and Clara had a feeling he was going to be very good.

Chapter Two

It was useless trying to tell his mother that it was a run-of-the-mill posting in the heart clinic. Molly Carroll was telling everyone that her son had a huge new job as a head cardiologist. Declan gave up trying to change her take on it all. Anyway, her friends and family *wanted* to think that he was a boy genius. It would be downbeat, pedantic and tedious to explain that as part of his training in becoming a GP he would need to do a stint in cardiology.

He had already done the six months in an accident and emergency department, and the same in a children's hospital, and when this heart clinic was over he would do a further half-year in geriatrics. Only then would he be considered experienced enough to join a general practice.

He never knew whether his father understood the system. Paddy Carroll was a quiet man who went to work in the meat department of a supermarket, who had his pint every evening and his three pints on a Saturday. He always said that it was a miracle that young Declan had done so well. 'Your mother must have slept with a brainbox for us to get you,' he'd say admiringly.

Declan hated it. He wished his father wouldn't put himself down so much. It would have made him much happier if only his father had realised that Declan had got so far simply because he had worked so hard.

Molly was cooking a breakfast that would kill an ox. 'You never know when you might get to eat again, Declan,' she fussed. 'They'll all be consulting you all day and asking your opinion.'

'Or showing me the ropes and telling me what to do,' Declan said, looking dismayed at the huge plate of food in front of him.

Paddy Carroll looked meaningfully at Dimples, the big sleeping dog. 'You won't forget to walk that dog before you head off to work, Declan,' he said.

Declan got the message. He wasn't to upset his mother by refusing the monstrous breakfast, but Dimples would make short work of the sausages and black pudding. His mother came round to give him a hug before she rushed off to open up the launderette.

'I'm so proud of you, I could burst!' she said.

'Aw, Mam, sure it's all down to you and Dad, doing overtime and saving for me.'

'I wish I could tell everyone who comes in today that my boy is starting work as a heart specialist,' she said, her face glowing with happiness.

Declan Carroll knew that she *would* tell everybody who came in. She might even show them all a photograph of his graduation, Declan in full gear, his freckles and ginger hair making him look like an impostor, he always thought. There were enlargements of this picture in three rooms of their little house.

Dimples, who was partly Labrador and partly something unspecified, was delighted with the unexpected breakfast. It was fanciful but Declan thought that even the dog was proud of him this morning. Just as well that none of them knew how anxious he felt about his first day as a new boy. He must be there in good time. It would be a very bad beginning to arrive late. He patted the overfed dog on the head and got on his bicycle to head off for the heart clinic. As he rode his bike through the busy early morning traffic he wished there had been someone just leaving the post, someone who could have marked his card. But this was a new outfit. He would be their first houseman, registrar, dogsbody. Or as his mother was telling everyone already . . . senior cardiologist.

Declan locked his bicycle outside the clinic. He had been asked to be there at nine thirty but he was half an hour early. That rather cool, groomed woman, Clara Casey, had shown him around when he came to discuss the position. It was open plan. She had stressed no hiding away in offices. He would have a desk of course and a filing cabinet but the emphasis would be on getting the patients to manage their own condition and to have everyone in the team involved.

She was good, Dr Casey; he had heard her spoken of as a possible successor for the big cardiology job in the hospital earlier this year but it hadn't happened. Maybe she didn't want it. One thing she certainly had going for her, she wasn't afraid of the hospital authorities. That would be a great asset, Declan thought. He wondered would he himself ever be courageous like that. Probably not. He was cautious by nature and his parents were so humble it made him even more afraid of putting a foot wrong. He remembered when he was back in A&E and a young motorcyclist had literally died in his arms. When he got home, still trembling, he was telling his mother and father about it.

'They can't blame you for that, Declan,' Molly had said firmly.

'There's no one can point the finger at you, son.' Paddy was bursting with loyalty.

Neither of them seemed to understand that he didn't

remotely think himself responsible for the death of a drunken joy-rider. He just wanted some sympathy for holding a nineteen-year-old as he breathed his last breath. He wanted them to grip his arm and say, 'You are a fine fellow, Declan, and you'll make a great doctor one day . . .' But instead they had worried in case he was somehow at fault. It was hard to be courageous and gutsy when all you had known at home was fear that the supermarket might close its butchery depart-ment and Dad would be unemployed or the launderette might want someone younger and prettier than his mam.

But Declan was a good listener. He would soon get the measure of this new place.

He hoped that he wasn't *too* early. It might look too eager, too anxious. But the girl who opened the door seemed de-lighted to see him.

'I am Ania. I'm just getting your name label ready. You can tell me how you like it.' She had a big broad smile and a foreign accent.

'I suppose just my name,' he said, surprised.

'But I am about to write it, would you like Celtic lettering or just bold print?'

'Are you the clinic calligrapher?' he asked.

'Please?'

'Sorry, are you a writing expert?'

'No, but Clara liked the badge that I did for myself and she suggested I do one for everyone. She said they looked nicer than the boring ones the hospital does which are too small for older people to read anyway. She got me these special pens for thick and thin strokes.'

'I'm sure the hospital loved that,' Declan said.

'No, they did not but Clara doesn't mind.' Ania seemed very proud.

'Right. I'd love Celtic lettering please, Ania.'

'*Right*. I'll do it now and by the time the others come in you can have it on your chest. They'll know who you are.'

She seemed to be happy and enjoying her work. He had no idea if she was a secretary, a nurse or a cleaner. It was a good sign that she didn't see any need to explain. It meant that she was part of a team. Declan relaxed and watched her confident strokes as she drew out his name. DR DECLAN CARROLL. His mother would just love it; maybe he could put it on the photocopier and give it to her.

And one by one, the rest of the team came in.

Lavender the dietician, who congratulated Declan on choosing to be a GP. Too many young men now wanted a showy career as a consultant. Fine lot of help that was to ordinary people who, like Kitty Reilly, needed a good doctor.

Barbara, a nice lively nurse, who said that this clinic was a great place. It had only been up and running for two weeks and yet you felt at the end of the day that you had done some good, which was more than a lot of people must feel if you were to judge by their faces. Barbara said that she started each week with three resolutions: this week she was going to lose four pounds' weight, she was going to frighten this barking patient Kitty Reilly into learning the names of her tablets and she was going to a charity do at a very smart golf club, because she and her friend Fiona heard there were going to be some unmercifully gorgeous men at it.

Hilary Hickey, who said she was Clara's assistant, welcomed him and said he would be very happy here. There was a kind of magic about seeing people who thought they were finished and for the high jump when they had heart attacks come round to realising they could cope with it after all.

There was a security man called Tim who said he only came in for a short time each day, mainly to see that things were functioning all right. He wanted to check if Declan would have any drugs in his filing cabinet because if so there would have to be extra precautions and lists and locks. Declan said he thought it was highly unlikely. He might prescribe drugs but people would go to the pharmacy to collect them.

He met Johnny the physiotherapist who told Declan that he had high hopes for this place. That woman Clara had more balls than most men in the business. There was absolutely no money for machinery and she had gone and ordered it all. Johnny had been almost afraid to unwrap it, so quickly did he think that bollocks Frank what's-his-name in administration would have repossessed it. But no, the cunning Clara had given a press conference saying that it was all state-of-the-art equipment and thanked the hospital publicly for its great sense of commitment. Frank, the bollocks, now had no way out.

Declan noted that they all called the director of the clinic by her first name. That was certainly different to his last posting where people had been *Mr* this and *Dr* that and a huge amount of pecking order and distinction was the norm.

'How about the patients?' he asked Hilary. 'Do we call them by first names too?'

'We ask them how they like to be addressed. Clara says they all want to be on first name terms but often their children get sniffy and think we are being too familiar.' It made a lot of sense to Declan.

At that moment Clara came in, tall, dark and very groomed. The first thing you'd notice about her was that she took care of herself. The second was her smile. She made you feel that you were the one person in the world that she had been looking forward to seeing.

'Declan Carroll. Welcome. Welcome. I'm so sorry I wasn't here to greet you. I had a meeting with some Neanderthals up in the hospital. You have to go to these meetings or they'll decide something ludicrous behind your back. Anyway, I'm here now. Have you met everybody?'

'Oh, yes, yes indeed.'

'And you're ready to start?'

'Yes, absolutely.' He wondered would he ever have the confidence and polish of this shiny woman.

'Good. Off we go.' And she turned to the left where there were three treatment cubicles. Each one was brightly lit with cheerful curtains separating each area and giving some privacy. There were reclining chairs which turned into beds should the doctor need to make the patient lie down. They stopped at the first one, where an elderly woman peered at them suspiciously.

'This is Dr Declan Carroll, Kitty. And Declan, this is Mrs Kitty Reilly. You'll see her chart here. She's in fine shape and needs to come in to see us every three weeks. Declan will listen to your heart and breathing, Kitty. I'll leave you in his hands.'

'What happened to the other doctor, the fellow who was here last time?'

'That was Sulong. He was only filling in until we got Declan,' Clara explained.

'Was he a qualified doctor, did he train properly out where he came from?'

'Yes, indeed, he was very highly qualified in Malaysia. But he was just helping until Declan was able to come to us.'

'How are you, Mrs Reilly, or will I call you Kitty? Tell me which you prefer.' He felt rather than saw the look of approval from Clara.

'Well, since you are going to be feeling my vest and everything I think you should call me Kitty,' she said almost grudgingly.

'Yes, Kitty, and what medication are you on?'

'Lord, you're as bad as that bossy nurse Barbara, she's always asking me do I know which tablet this is and which that is. I suppose I'm on whatever this place put me on.'

'It's useful for *you* to know what you're taking, Kitty.' Declan had a persuasive smile.

'I don't see why.' Kitty Reilly's face showed someone

looking forward to a lengthy argument. 'That's the clinic's job, isn't it? Mine is just to take them.'

'Ah yes, but suppose you were feeling short of breath and rang us up, we might say take a diuretic, a water pill, you know, but it wouldn't be any use if you didn't know which was which.'

Kitty's scowl had lessened a little. 'Learning the tablets is actually for *me* then?'

'It certainly is, Kitty. Here, show me your pill box. I'll go through them with you, if you like.'

'You won't make me learn them like a child at school?' Kitty looked defensive and for a moment a little frail and vulnerable.

'Of course not. Let's put them out on the table.'

'This won't take away from the time listening around my vest?' She wanted to make sure she was getting value.

'Not at all, there's all the time in the world,' Declan said, the soul of reassurance.

'One thing though.' Kitty's eyes were bright. 'Where do you stand on Padre Pio?'

'On what?' Declan asked, bewildered.

'You *must* have heard of him, he had the stigmata.'

Dimly, Declan remembered his mother talking about this priest in Italy somewhere who had wounds like Our Lord in his hands and feet and side.

'He was a truly great gentleman,' he said.

'I'm not sure he was a gentleman.' Kitty would fight with her shadow.

'But he was gentle. Surely he was a gentle person? Now let's have a look at all these pills, every colour of the rainbow here.'

Clara left the cubicle. She had a smile on her face. This Declan Carroll had been a good choice, he had the makings of an excellent doctor, and she would enjoy teaching him a lot about cardiology while he was here.

In the next cubicle, Barbara was taking Mr Walsh's blood pressure. He was 'Mr' because his wife had said that she found it offensive and patronising to hear young girls addressing her husband as 'Bobby'. Mr Walsh was a patient man. He had always wanted an easy life, he told Barbara, he was happy now that he was retired. He had a son, Carl, who was a school teacher and very happy in his work. Bobby did a little painting, mainly watercolours, he went fishing, he spent long happy hours in the library. His wife wished they would entertain more but mercifully the heart specialist who had referred him to this clinic said that he was to stay quiet. Barbara sighed. Good, decent gentlemen like this were always married to dreadful old rips like Mrs Walsh. It seemed to work that way. Sometimes it did in the opposite direction too. Think of all the time and tears her friend Fiona had wasted over that loser Shane, who was now in jail somewhere for drug dealing. Fiona never gave a backwards glance, mercifully. Still, it had been fairly horrific at the time.

Barbara had never really been in love. Well, not in the sense of settling down for life with someone. But that would all change when they went to this glamorous gathering at the end of the week. It was a celebrity auction. Really famous people were going to come to it and you could bid for a well-known singer to come and do a number at your party, or a chef to cook you a dinner, or an artist to paint your house or your garden.

Barbara had heard that the style was going to be something out of this world. She had got two free tickets from a patient of hers, a young fellow who worked in a bank. She told some of this to Mr Walsh who said that these young men would have to be blind and mad not to see how beautiful Barbara and Fiona were. Fiona and Barbara were going to knock them all dead, he said.

Fiona was not at the hospital today: Clara had thought it a

good idea to send her to a pharmaceutical conference. Some firm was having those involved in cardiology to a lunch at one of the big hotels. She called just as Barbara was back at her desk and thinking about her.

'Are you busy?' Fiona asked.

'Not really, just lying down, feet on the desk, sipping a Tequila Sunrise,' Barbara said.

'Okay, you're between patients. Who have you got?'

'Let me see. Nice Mr Walsh, mad Kitty, a few new people. That nice woman with the yapping dogs rang, she's coming in tomorrow.'

'Oh yes, that's Judy, but isn't she better to have the bloody Jack Russells than to have nothing?'

'I'm not sure,' Barbara said broodily.

'And how about your resolutions?' Fiona said.

'I only had an apple for lunch. But you won't believe this: remember I was going to teach Kitty Reilly her tablets today or take her by the throat?'

'Yeah, and did you?'

'No, the new doctor had got there first. She knew which were beta-blockers, which were heart medicine. She pointed out the diuretics to me as if I were soft in the head.'

'He must be something, the new doctor.'

'Nice enough fellow. Declan is his name.'

'Well, I'll see him tomorrow. Got to go now. They're serving lobster with lunch. I don't want to miss out on it.'

'Lobster?' Barbara cried. 'Does it have a big creamy mayonnaise? Or hot butter? God, I'd love lobster.'

Declan was passing by, and heard her. 'No you wouldn't, Barbara, you'd hate it, rubbery texture, swimming in grease, think of your resolution.'

'God, who was that?' Fiona whispered.

'The new fellow, you'll meet him tomorrow.'

'Can't wait,' Fiona said and hung up.

Declan cycled home. His route took him through some of the fastest-changing areas of the city and he never ceased to be surprised by some new aspect that he hadn't ever noticed before. He passed an open market which used to sell cabbages and potatoes, but now where people from faraway lands sold Indian silks and exotic spices; then there was a huge block of luxury apartments that had suddenly sprung up on the site of – what? He couldn't remember any more. He felt the usual triumph at having moved faster than the almost stationary traffic; and then he was home, back in St Jarlath's Crescent.

His parents were delighted to see him back and sat at the table asking questions about his day. To please them he made his role seem more important than it was. He asked his mother about Padre Pio. She told him much more than he needed to know. He asked his father about his day at the meat counter. Paddy Carroll shrugged his shoulders. It had been just like any other day, he said, big rush with a crowd wanting attention one moment, and then a valley period where there would be nobody. Declan ate his two lamb chops and tinned peas. He thought about the laughing nurse and her friend talking about lobster. He wished that he had a more exciting social life. He looked down a road where he and his parents would live here forever with only one change. He would eventually make the meals for the three of them because they wouldn't be able to do it any more.

Next morning, Declan cycled to the clinic again. This time he was looking forward to it without anxiety and today everyone knew his name. The patients were filing in and chatting away in the bright, cheerful waiting room.

His first patient was a woman called Judy Murphy who told him that she had no worries whatsoever about herself. She would be fine, just fine, but they wanted her to go into hospital for three days' observation. The problem was the dogs. She had two little Jack Russells and who would look after them? She couldn't afford an expensive kennel and anyway the dogs would pine. Her neighbour would open tins of dog food twice a day but wouldn't take them for a walk. The dogs *needed* their walkies. She couldn't go to hospital. Perhaps she could have stronger medication. She was fine. Her thin, worried face looked at him as he went through her notes. Persistent angina attack, wild fluctuations in blood pressure. Declan Carroll's eye fell on her address. Judy Murphy lived a few short streets from where he lived himself.

'I'll walk them,' he said.

'You'll what?'

'I'll take them for a walk every evening. I take our dog, Dimples, for a walk, we'll go together.' He saw some hope return to her face.

'Dimples?' she enquired.

'A huge, lovable, neutered near-Labrador. Your fellows will love him. He's like an enormous pussycat.'

'Doctor, you wouldn't, would you?'

'Declan,' he corrected her. 'I'll start tonight.'

'But I'm not going to hospital tonight, surely?'

'No, Judy, but you should go tomorrow and this way they get to know me and get to meet Dimples. I'll come round to your place at eight o'clock. Now you go and check in with Clara, then Ania will get in touch with admissions and you'll be as right as rain.'

'You're the very best, Dr Declan,' Judy said.

Clara was delighted with him too. 'I've been bringing that woman in here three times a week just to keep an eye on her. Now you've got her to do what the rest of us couldn't. Is there a St Declan by any chance? If not, you could be the first.'

'There's meant to be a St Declan but I didn't ever find out

much about him. In the dictionary of saints it goes straight from David to Demetrius so I sort of gave up on him. Anyway, my mother had me baptised Declan Francis to be sure, to be sure.'

Clara laughed. 'Well, she's right to cover all options,' she said. But Declan wasn't listening. He was looking at the girl in the dark trousers and white jacket which was the clinic's uniform. A girl in her early twenties kneeling down beside an elderly man, helping him fill in a form. She had long lashes and a perfect smile. She was the most gorgeous girl he had ever seen. For the first time in his life Declan Carroll felt what he had read about and sung about and dreamed about. He ached to get to know her properly, this beautiful Fiona. For the first time since he was fourteen he wished he was tall and dark and broody-looking, rather than square and red-haired and freckled. Who in their sane senses could fancy him?

Fiona looked up from filling in Lar Kelly's form and saw Declan with his brown eyes looking right at her. She would have had to be blind not to have noticed the admiration in his look. This must be the new guy, the one who had got Kitty to learn her tablets, the one who had made Judy agree to go into hospital. What kind of guru was he?

'Declan,' she said, 'welcome to the asylum.'

'Is this an asylum?' Lar looked up anxiously. He was a small, round man with a bald, egg-shaped head and a bow tie.

'Sorry, Lar, of course it's not, it's just a disrespectful way of talking about our workplace. Declan, this is Lar Kelly. He is a fund of information. He tells me something new every single visit. I want him to come in every day.'

'What did you tell Fiona today, Lar?' he asked.

'You know who I am?' She had totally forgotten she was wearing a name badge.

'Indeed, I do. I know what you had for lunch yesterday. You had lobster,' he said.

'Aren't you great.' She seemed pleased.

'You didn't tell me you had lobster.' Lar was aggrieved.

'No, I hadn't got round to it. There was only very little actually, a bit cheapskate, I thought.'

Declan wanted to talk forever. 'So what was the new thing today?'

'Lar taught me the offside rule in soccer,' Fiona said.

'You know the offside rule?' Declan's jaw fell open in admiration. Hardly anyone could explain that to you.

'Lar said that it's in order to stop players hanging around the goal of their opponents waiting for a long ball to come to them. You're offside if when the ball is passed to you, you're nearer the goal than the ball and the second last defender.'

'You should be a sports commentator,' Declan said, awe-struck.

Lar joined in. 'Her memory isn't all that good. You wouldn't want to test her on terms like URL or html. I don't know how she works a computer at all. Our lives in their hands, it would frighten the wits out of you.'

Fiona wasn't at all put out by this. 'I *did* remember what a vole was. I never knew when I came across them in books were they good or bad. I don't think we have them in Ireland. But anyway, Lar said that vole was a name for any number of blunt-nosed, short-eared mouse- or rat-like rodents.'

'Is that good or bad?' Declan asked.

'Very bad, I would think. Come on, Lar, we'll never get this form finished.'

'I like to read documents carefully,' Lar said.

'Yes, but it's an X-ray form, Lar, and this question, it's asking are you pregnant?' Fiona's eyes danced at the two men.

'You can't be too careful,' Lar said.

With a great effort Declan dragged himself away.

*

Declan realised that Fiona was utterly enchanting and that he didn't stand a chance with her. He looked at himself in the mirror of the clinic's cloakroom. A great round face looked back at him with a topping of awful ginger hair. Maybe if his hair wasn't so terrible he might have some hope?

Yesterday, cycling home, he had passed a row of smart shops which had included a very expensive hair salon. Today he would call in there and discuss his hair. It couldn't do any harm.

The place was full of black marble and chrome and glass.

'Could I have a consultation?' he asked.

'Sure, you can consult me. I'm Kiki, one of the stylists,' said the girl with the long black hair, heavy white make-up and dark purple nails.

'Thanks, Kiki, should I sit down or something? What could I do with my hair?' he asked.

'What do you *want* to do with your hair?'

'That's why I need to consult. It can't stay like this.'

'Why not?' Kiki yawned a terrible yawn showing the back of her throat.

'Well, it's desperate,' said Declan.

'Is it falling out or something?' Kiki asked.

'No, it's not falling out, but it's like a pot scrubber or something. It's desperate.'

'I don't see anything wrong with it,' Kiki said.

'It's ludicrous.'

'Naw, it goes with your face. It's fine.' Kiki said she thought the consultation was over.

'I thought you were meant to attract business, not turn it away,' he said.

'Mister, you're fine. What's the point in my suggesting some kind of treatment or colour or streaks or frosting or something that would set you back hundreds of euros when you're *fine* as you are. How often do I have to tell you?'

The manager, not liking the sound of raised voices, edged over slightly. 'Everything under control here?' he asked.

'Yes. Kiki has been very helpful. I'll come back next week,' Declan said, moving for the door.

Kiki went and held it open for him. 'Thanks,' she said. 'It's just I hate them making money out of people like you. People who haven't a penny to their name.'

Declan unlocked his bicycle. Did she think he was poor because he was riding a bike? His mother thought he was a heart consultant. Neither of these things mattered very much. What mattered was what Fiona thought he was. And the other thing that mattered was that she wouldn't meet anyone at the charity gathering on Friday, anyone who would take her fancy.

Judy Murphy's little Jack Russell terriers were no trouble. They got on very well with Dimples, who ignored them loftily and pretended he wasn't with them at all. Declan talked to the dogs as he brought them to the park. Told them about Fiona and how beautiful she was. How sharp and funny. She had travelled too, lived in Greece once, even. She shared a flat with Barbara but she went to her parents' house a lot as well. She *seemed* to like him, Declan told the dogs, but you never knew with women. The problem was if you spoke too soon you might make an eejit of yourself, if you spoke too late she might have met someone at this terrible charity do. Declan told them that it was much easier being a dog if they only realised it. The Jack Russells agreed with him in supportive barks. Dimples looked disdainful. Then Declan heard a shout.

'Glory be to God, there you are talking to that pack of hounds and there's not a word out of you at home.' It was his father. Paddy Carroll was on his way to the pub for his evening pint. 'Come on and join me, and bring that troop of huskies with you, we can sit outside on the footpath.'

'I don't want to be going in on top of you and your friends, Dad.'

'Sure, aren't I proud of my son, the Dog Walker.' His father laughed. 'And maybe you could tell me about this girl you fancy.'

'What girl?'

'Decco, I know that fifty-seven seems very very old to you, but I haven't forgotten what it was like. I was all over the place like you are now when I first laid eyes on your mother.' Declan hoped his father wasn't going to tell him anything embarrassing or intimate. He couldn't take it just now. But Paddy Carroll seemed to be taking a pleasant trip down memory lane. 'It was 1980 and the real hit song was "Your Eyes are the Eyes of a Woman in Love", and I saw your mother. She had a red velvet skirt and a white blouse. And when we had been dancing for the whole night and I knew this was right, this was the real thing, I said, "Are they?" and she said, "Are they what?" and I said, "Your eyes, Molly, are they the eyes of a woman in love?"'

'And what did Mam say?' Declan was engrossed, in spite of himself.

'She said that they might be, that only time would tell, but hadn't we plenty of time. Do you know, Declan, I couldn't sleep for a week, and how I didn't cut off my full set of fingers at work I don't know.'

'How soon did she know about whether she was in love or not?' Declan could hardly believe he was having this conversation.

'Eight weeks,' his father said.

'And did you play hard to get or anything?'

'No. I'd be no good at that sort of thing. I have too open a face. And if you want my advice, for what it's worth, Decco, neither would you. I think honesty is our long suit. Decency, you know, reliability in a world of sharks.'

'I'm sure you're right, Dad.' Declan had never sounded so unconvinced.

'Declan, to celebrate finishing your first week here and surviving it, will you have a drink with Hilary and me tonight?'

Declan was pleased but he had kept hoping that in some way he could have wangled himself a ticket to this charity do. He had even found a dress hire place that stayed open late so that he could grab a tuxedo if it were called for. He knew it was foolish but he had the most awful foreboding that Fiona was going to meet the love of her life at this golf club. And he had loved her since Tuesday. Yes, it was love like his father had felt for Mam. Something that had developed in a short time because you knew it was right.

'That's very kind of you, Clara, can I just call my dad and ask him if he'll walk the dogs for me tonight?'

'Do you still have Judy Murphy's awful little things every night?' Clara was admiring.

'They're not too bad when you get to know them. They're deafening, of course, but that's their way.'

'You're a very tolerant young man,' Clara said approvingly and they both went back to work.

Barbara and Fiona had been to the hairdresser's during their lunch hour. When Declan saw them at the staff meeting that afternoon he longed desperately to curl his fingers around the little ringlets beside Fiona's ears. He pulled himself together sharply. He must be going mad. He cleared his throat three times before he felt confident enough to wish them happy hunting at the gala tonight.

'We'll hear all about it on Monday,' he said, hoping that the yearning wasn't obvious in his voice. She must not know how desperately he wanted her not to go.

'I'll be able to report first hand,' Tim the security man said. 'I'll be working there tonight and I'll have chapter and verse about what went on.'

Declan wondered for one mad moment if he could beg Tim to ensure that Fiona came home early, safely and alone.

'So can I report,' Ania laughed. 'I will be taking in the coats there.' Barbara and Fiona were delighted with this news and jumped up and down with excitement.

'Maybe you'll meet someone too,' Barbara said.

'Not in the cloakroom, I fear.' Ania was realistic.

Somehow Declan got through the rest of the day. With a heavy heart he went out to join Clara at her car.

'Hilary had to cancel at the last moment. She's got some crisis to do with her mother, but let's you and I go anyway,' Clara said. They folded his bicycle away and she drove off to a smart wine bar.

'This is very kind of you,' Declan said, trying to drag his attention to this amiable woman sitting opposite him.

'No, on the contrary, I am grateful to have a pleasant person to talk to on a Friday evening rather than going home to an empty house,' she said.

Clara ordered a fizzy water, followed by one glass of white wine, then another fizzy water. Declan had three glasses of claret. Clara told him of her daughters, Adi and Linda, of Adi's difficult boyfriend and Linda's difficult lifestyle. She told Declan how she now had rules in the house, for their own good as well as hers. They must realise that they could not walk forever over people.

'I don't expect you walk over your parents, Declan,' she said unexpectedly.

'I have probably taken all their sacrifices for me very much for granted,' he admitted. 'I think we all do. Did you?'

And there she was again, talking away about her remote

father who never seemed at all interested, her difficult disappointed mother who snapped out a series of criticisms rather than having a conversation.

'What one word would you use to describe her?' Declan asked.

'*Regretful*. That's the word. She always regrets something. Like that nobody has any manners any more, or how expensive everything has become, or that I married Alan or that I left Alan, that Adi *has* a boyfriend and Linda *doesn't* have a boyfriend. Whatever state there is, it's wrong. I didn't realise it before.' She looked surprised.

'Maybe I should be a psychiatrist,' Declan joked.

'Don't you dare. You're just the kind of GP we used to read about but never met. Stick at it, Declan.'

'I will. I wish I weren't so dull and plodding though.'

'I don't think of you at all like that. You've helped a lot of patients very significantly in under a week. You actually like people and it shows. What's dull and plodding about being that sort of person?' She sounded sincere.

'Women prefer rats, bounders, merciless people.' He kept it light.

'Yeah, they do for five minutes, not when they grow up.'

'I hope you're right. I'm not much good in the merciless stakes.'

'I'm right. Trust me.'

'Let me get you one for the road,' he offered.

'No, Dr Carroll, and you remember this, never encourage a driver to have a drink.'

'I forgot,' he said, shamefaced.

'Okay, and I think after all that claret I shouldn't leave you in charge of a bicycle, I'll drive you home.'

On the way back he saw his mother locking up the launderette. Molly had two late evening shifts and the money was still going to a fund to buy a place in a practice for her son.

'That's my mam,' he said, 'can we give her a lift home?'
And Declan sat in the car while his mother told Clara Casey,
his boss, what a wonderful cardiologist he was and how he was
destined for great things.

On Monday, while Declan was examining Bobby Walsh he
asked about his painting. Did he prefer watercolours or oil?
Apparently Bobby Walsh liked watercolours.

'Why is that?' Declan asked.

Lar was listening from the next cubicle. 'You should train
your mind to learn something new all the time,' he said
reprovingly. 'Even that young Fiona, and she's only a brainless
little nurse, *she* manages to get new facts into her head all the
time.'

Declan burned with resentment about Fiona being dismissed as a brainless little nurse. But he didn't show it. It was
early in the day. Too early to get upset. Soon, only too soon,
he would hear how they had fared at the charity function.

'Wonder how the girls got on at that do,' he said to Bobby
Walsh as he took the man's blood pressure.

'My wife was there. She said the place was swimming in
alcohol,' Bobby Walsh said, glad to be of service.

Declan moved on to Jimmy, a small, foxy man from the
west of Ireland. He had come up to Dublin for a football
match, had a heart attack and been taken into St Brigid's.
They had asked him to have follow-up treatment when he was
discharged. Jimmy was a very shy, private person who pre-
ferred to come the whole way across the country to attend this
clinic rather than let any of his neighbours get to hear that he
had heart problems. Declan could hear Fiona two cubicles
away talking to Kitty Reilly.

'Well, Kitty, you're the sharp one. I'll have to watch out for
my job here. You know more about your medication than I
do. Now I imagine the doctor will want to talk to you about

68

that breathlessness, but it went when you took the right tablet, didn't it?'

'I had a word with Padre Pio as well, it wasn't *just* the tablets.'

'No, Kitty, it never is. There are so many other factors out there.' Fiona was the soul of diplomacy.

Declan tried to learn something from her tone. Had she spent the weekend in some playboy's penthouse? Had it all been a washout? Impossible to guess. Kitty was in full flight.

'Still, I'll listen to that nice young doctor with the ginger head on him. Is he a family man, would you say?'

'Oh, bound to be,' Fiona said, 'the nice doctors always are. Married to ruthless shrews with spectacles and research projects.'

Declan's face broke into a huge smile. She thought he was one of the nice doctors, she thought he was married. Ah, dear Lord, there might be a hope for him still. At lunchtime he asked her out. Declan Carroll, who had never asked a girl out properly on a date because there was never enough money or time or confidence.

'Would you like to come out and have dinner with me one night this week?' It sounded quite a normal thing for a person to say, yet it echoed in his ears as if he were in some huge cavern. Maybe she would laugh and tell him to have some sense. Maybe she would say no, that she had a new relationship but thanks all the same.

'That would be great,' she said and sounded as if she meant it.

'Where would you like to go?'

'Take me somewhere *you* like,' Fiona said.

Declan's mind went blank. Where did he like? He didn't *know* anywhere. He went home to his mother's kitchen table for supper in the evening. How sad was that. He had seen an article in one of the papers recently about a place called

Quentins. It was *'über elegant'* they said. *Über? Over* elegant? Maybe that meant pretentious. Still, it was the only place he could think of.

'Quentins?' he suggested, amazed that his voice sounded normal. In his own ears it felt like a screech.

'Gosh,' Fiona said, impressed.

'That okay then?' He *must* sound casual.

'And there's no Mrs Declan is there?' she asked.

'No. No, there'll be just the two of us,' he stammered.

'I didn't think you'd be inviting her to dinner,' Fiona said.

'No, no, of course not. I mean there isn't one, a Mrs Declan. Lord, no.'

'Good,' said Fiona and went off to sort out some blood test results that should have gone to the warfarin clinic but had turned up here instead.

Declan cycled home that day on a route which took him past Quentins. It looked very imposing. Declan wondered was he quite mad to have suggested this place. With any luck they might be full and he could honestly tell Fiona that he had tried. But no, when he called them on his mobile from round the corner it turned out that they could easily find a table for two. So he booked it, with a very heavy heart. Perhaps he should go in and examine it, give himself *some* hint of the familiarity he had claimed with the place. He pushed the door open. It was quite busy. There was a good value 'Early Bird' dinner there for people on their way to the theatre.

A handsome, middle-aged woman, who seemed very much in charge, approached him; she was about to find him a table, but Molly Carroll's shepherd's pie would be shortly on the table at home.

'No, excuse me, I was just coming to have a look. You see, I have never been here before, but I have invited someone to dinner . . .' He realised that he sounded like a madman coming in from the street. This woman would probably ask him to leave and never allow him to be readmitted. What a *fool* he had been to come here and see the lie of the land. But she seemed to accept his behaviour as normal.

'Of course you want to have a look at the place. Let me take you on a quick tour. I'm Brenda Brennan, by the way, my husband Patrick is the chef here. We'd be delighted to show you around.'

'I'm Declan Carroll,' he said, hardly daring to believe that he had been reprieved.

'Yes, of course, Mr Carroll, you rang a few moments ago; let me show you the table I had in mind for you.' Dazed, he followed her from the oyster bar, with all its crushed ice, to the dessert display, with its fruit cascades tumbling from little pillars. She pointed out the rest rooms, and took him into the kitchen to meet Patrick and his brother with the odd name of Blouse. Stunned by it all, he thanked her and said how much he was looking forward to Thursday.

'You are very kind, Mrs Brennan, to take me on this tour. I am afraid that I'm not what you'd call experienced at all this fine dining.'

'Few of us are, Mr Carroll, but even fewer have the sense to admit it. Is this a big occasion on Thursday?'

'It is for me. I have asked a most attractive girl out for the first time, I hope it will be a success.'

'We'll do our best to make sure it is.' Brenda Brennan saw him off at the door as if he was a regular and honoured client. She saw him getting on his bicycle and heading off happily into the traffic.

'Very nice young fellow,' she said to Patrick in the kitchen.

'Is he a doctor by any chance?' Patrick asked.

'Don't think so. He'd have said, they always do. Anyway, he doesn't have the sort of over-confidence the medics have. Why do you ask?'

'Oh, remember Judy Murphy said there was a young red-headed doctor on a bike who was walking the awful hounds for her. Could be the same guy.'

'I'd say Dublin is full of them,' Brenda said and they got on with the evening ahead, but she thought she might check with Judy next time she saw her.

Declan sat down to his supper. Molly watched anxiously as he attacked the huge mound of food.

'Tell me things that happened today,' she begged.

It wasn't much to ask. Not after a lifetime of denying herself everything so that he could get this far. But tonight Declan didn't feel able to fill the room with aimless prattle about his day as the white-coated Medicine Man. He answered a few questions and seemed restless.

'Mush, mush, mush,' his father said unexpectedly.

'What do you mean, Dad?'

'I was wondering do you and your team of huskies want to walk over and meet me at the pub later for a pint? That's what you say when you're driving a dog sledge.'

'Aw, Paddy, don't be bringing the boy into awful shabby pubs like that. It's hotel lounges and wine bars for our Declan from now on at least.'

Declan looked at them helplessly. He could *never* let either of them know that he intended to spend what his father would take nearly a week to earn on one meal in Quentins on Thursday night and that he had been in there examining the Native Oysters and the Pacific variety so that he would be able to make an informed choice when the time came.

If he only knew what had happened last Friday. He didn't like to ask either Barbara or Fiona in case it made him sound like an old woman. Maybe Ania, the Polish girl, would tell him. Or Tim, who had been doing security for the function.

Ania said she didn't have a good time.

'Bobby's wife was there, very bad-temper, and I say hello to her by name. So stupid. She was very angry, she said, "My goodness, the Poles are everywhere these days, they're taking over the country." '

'God, what a terrible woman, Ania, I hope you don't meet many like that.' Declan was sympathetic but he still ached to know more. 'Did Fiona and Barbara have a good time?'

'No, I don't think so. No, I *know* they did not. There was something that was badly understood by two sides. What do you call that?'

'A misunderstanding?' Declan suggested.

'Yes, I think that was it. A serious misunderstanding.' But he heard no more.

When he found Tim, he learned that there was a very snorty crowd there, lots of drugs. He had gone into the Gents at one stage and saw a whole stack laid out for people to buy as if it was an open market.

'What did you do? You were meant to be security.' Declan thought that other people had very complicated lives.

'I went to the top security guy and he told me to shut my face and look the other way. So I did, Declan. I'm not a one-man mission to clean up the country.'

'And Fiona and Barbara? Did they . . . I mean, were they . . . ?'

'No, they hadn't anything to do with anything. They left early. They asked me to get them a taxi in fact.'

'Because of the drugs?'

'No, because the organisers thought they were party girls. That's what he had expected, wanted, ordered when he gave them the tickets. Jesus, what a night.'

Declan felt insanely cheered by this. It had all been all right. He breathed deeply and that night the dogs seemed to sense that he was more at peace with himself than he had been before.

On the Thursday morning of the date, Declan woke excited. Everything about this day was going to go well. He would be positive and strong from the moment he got up.

He began at breakfast. 'I won't be home for supper tonight, Mam,' Declan said.

'Who'll walk those animals then?' Molly asked to cover her disappointment.

'Judy Murphy is out of hospital today, and Dad can take Dimples to the pub.'

'And what are *you* doing that means you can't come home for your tea?' Molly wasn't letting it go.

Declan had thought about this for a while. If he lied and said there was a meeting, he was only putting off the day when he had to tell them that he had found a girl. There was nothing odd or unnatural about it. In fact it had been un-natural for a man of twenty-six *not* to have gone out on dates regularly.

'I'm meeting a girl from work. We're going out for a meal.'

'A girl from work,' his mother said grimly.

'Yes, Fiona Ryan, she's a cardiology nurse in the clinic.'

'A nurse,' Molly repeated.

'And is she a nice girl, Declan?' Paddy asked.

'Very nice.' He knew he sounded clipped but it had to be done.

'And where are you going?' Molly was taking no prisoners on this one.

'Oh, somewhere around, we're not fussy,' he lied, hoping it didn't sound as unlikely as it sounded to him.

'Well, I hope you have a nice time. I have to go. *Some* of us have work to do.' Molly went away, her stiff little body showing the intense disappointment and hurt that she was being relegated to very much second best.

Fiona said that she would meet him at the restaurant. Declan wondered should he have suggested that he call for her in a taxi. Was he being cheapskate? But Fiona said that the bus went straight to the door of Quentins from her flat. 'It's not often they get a customer coming off the bus,' she had said.

'Well, they got me getting off a bike on Monday,' he said and could have killed himself.

'You go to Quentins *twice* in one week!' Fiona's eyes were round with amazement.

'No, no. I just went in to book.' He was shamefaced.

'I'm just dying for it,' Fiona said with the same enthusiasm that she had been dying for a coffee break, or lunch, or something on television, or last week the big function that had never been mentioned since.

How great to live life at such a high level of excitement, Declan thought. He hoped that he wouldn't be too dull for her. Too plodding. But then she didn't *have* to go out with him.

Somehow he got through the day. Declan had never known time to drag before but this day it did. He wondered did Fiona feel even one little bit of anxiety about the evening ahead? He was waiting outside the door of Quentins when Fiona got off the bus. He had never seen her dressed up before, only in the white and black hospital outfit. She wore a sparkling sequin-covered jacket over a rose silk dress. She looked stunning.

Brenda Brennan welcomed them in as warmly as if they had been captains of industry, ambassadors or international politicians. She offered them a glass of champagne on the house and wished them a pleasant evening.

'How did she get to be like that?' Fiona whispered in wonder.

'Women are better at it,' Declan said admiringly.

'Not all women. I wouldn't be able to do it in a million years.'

'She wouldn't be able to do what *you* do every day. You're terrific with people.' He was full of genuine admiration.

The waiter wondered would they like oysters. Fiona had seen how much they cost and said that she thought she would prefer a small salad to start.

'Do have the oysters if you like, Fiona.' He was so eager that she enjoy herself.

'Honestly, I only tasted them once and I thought it was like drinking a bit of sea,' she said.

Declan smiled with relief. The oysters were astronomically expensive. He could breathe again now.

Brenda Brennan had supervised their meal from afar. She never interrupted their conversation but she was always nearby to refill the water glasses, the coffee cups, the bread basket.

When Declan paid the bill, Brenda Brennan said, 'Thank you, Dr Carroll.'

'She knows you're a doctor.' Fiona was impressed.

'I didn't tell her, honestly,' he said.

'I know you didn't,' said Fiona. 'You're far too nice.'

The meal was over before they realised it. Declan said he would get a taxi to take her home, but Fiona said it would be pure madness. The bus still went to her door. She said she had loved it and asked him would he come to supper at her mum and dad's next week.

'Won't you have to check with them first?' Declan thought about the sheer impossibility of ever inviting a guest to his own home in St Jarlath's Crescent.

'No, why would I? Please come. Then you'll see me as I am and if you like me we can go on going out.'

'I like you very much,' he said.

'And I like you too,' said Fiona.

Declan could see Brenda Brennan observing them with a pleased smile on her face.

They were up at home when he got back. His dad's friend Muttie Scarlet was with them.

'There's Declan coming in now.' Paddy Carroll was pleased. Dimples raised his head from his paws in greeting.

'Declan was taking a young lady out, a nurse,' Molly sniffed, still resentful and disapproving.

'Ah, isn't that grand now!' said Muttie.

'And what did you eat?' his father asked.

'We had a salad and some fillets of sole.'

'You must be starving,' Molly said, looking as if she was going to get the chip pan out.

'No, no. We had lots of bread.'

'You could have had *that* at home.' Molly's hurt was plain to see.

'And maybe one day we will. I'll ask Fiona to one of your nice suppers, Mam. I'm sure she'd love that.'

'She would indeed,' his father said.

'I'd want plenty of warning before you even considered bringing her back here.' Molly went red with excitement. 'This kitchen has to be painted for one thing. We have to get a new surface for the worktops and maybe we should think of opening up the front room and making it a dining room.'

'No, Mam, we'll eat here, like we always do. It's absolutely fine.'

'Excuse *me*, but who will be putting the meal on the table? I will. And I say the place has to be done up before we bring strangers in here.'

The three men sighed. This is the way it was going to be.

Next morning, Jimmy arrived on time after a three-hour train trip from Galway. He was looking very grey when Declan brought him into the cubicle.

'Any pain at all?' Declan asked.

'Well, the usual, you know.'

Declan looked at his chart: there had been no mention of pain anywhere in Jimmy's notes.

'Like sharp is it?'

'Like as if someone had a very tight belt around me and was pulling tighter.' Jimmy was wincing.

'I'll be back in a minute,' said Declan, beckoning Fiona who was nearby. 'Is Clara here?'

'No, she's having one of her confrontations about funding. She won't be in until after lunch.'

Declan spoke quickly and quietly. 'I'm getting an ambulance over here from A&E. Can you close the door of the waiting room when it arrives so that everyone in there doesn't see what's happening. And can you go in and talk to Jimmy. You'd reassure anyone, but try to find out who we should contact back home over in Galway, will you?' He noted that she sprang into action. Apart entirely from the fact that he was mad about her, she had been a very good choice by Clara.

Jimmy died twenty minutes after they got him a bed in the hospital. Clara had miraculously appeared. She was full of praise for Declan and Fiona. They had done everything perfectly. Fiona had even managed to get details of a nephew and his severe wife who were after his farm, and the information that he had made a will and they would be unpleasantly surprised. She had held his hand and soothed him, travelled with him in the ambulance and was there for the whole business.

Clara asked them both to come back to her office with her.

She would have to write a report on why a man who was attending their heart clinic had suddenly gone into cardiac arrest on their premises. She knew that everything that should have been done had been done but these hospital people would need endless back-up and details.

Ania went out and brought them soup and sandwiches. She was about to leave them alone to discuss it.

'Please stay, Ania, you are as much a part of this team as anyone,' Clara said. And Declan saw the little Polish girl's face pink with the pleasure of belonging.

Jimmy's funeral was on Tuesday in a tiny village on the rugged coast of County Galway. Clara suggested that Declan and Fiona go and represent the clinic there. They were, after all, his only friends in Dublin. They took the train to Galway City and a bus to Jimmy's home. It was an easy journey. They felt as if they were old friends. Fiona had brought sandwiches in case there was no refreshment car. They were happy to have the day off and to watch the countryside changing as they crossed the River Shannon and approached the west where the fields were smaller, where the walls were handmade stone and where the sheep looked up with interest as the train snaked by. They talked about Jimmy and wondered why he had been so secretive. Yes, of course he qualified for free train travel, but really, all this distance just to avoid prying eyes.

There was a respectable crowd in the little church. Fiona and Declan were objects of interest as the only strangers. They met the nephew and his harsh wife who was exactly the way Jimmy had described her.

'And how did *you* know Uncle Jimmy?' the sour-faced wife asked Fiona.

'Oh, you know the way it is' – Fiona was wonderfully vague – 'it's an extraordinary world, isn't it, the way you run into people here and there.' They would get no more from her.

Their train back wasn't until six o'clock.

'Let's go back to the house,' Fiona suggested.

Declan had hoped they could stroll together in the woods nearby and go and walk the cliffs of Jimmy's neighbourhood. But Fiona was determined. 'We got the day off to come here. We must do him proud.'

'But we're *not* doing him proud, Fiona, we're not telling people that he was at our clinic.'

'No, we can't do that, he was so determined it should be a secret. Still, I'd like this crowd to think he had some friends from elsewhere.'

And Declan agreed.

They had ham and tomatoes in the cottage which had once been Jimmy's home. He had never married and had lived alone in this little place; there were no pictures, no keepsakes, no personality. There was a small front parlour which was obviously rarely used. Fiona and Declan talked to everyone while giving nothing away about their own connection with the deceased. They learned that once he had his sights set on this woman called Bernadette, but nothing came of it because his holding was too small a place and he was never going to amount to anything.

Then they announced the reading of the will. Declan and Fiona made vague efforts not to take part in this. They weren't family, they said. They would go and catch a bus to Galway, but by this stage everyone had talked to them and they were very much part of everything.

Fiona's eyes danced with anticipation as she thought about the will reading and the shock the cold nephew and his harsh wife were going to get. It turned out that Jimmy had applied for planning permission in his little small-holding. It had been granted so the land was now much more valuable than anyone had thought. The nephew and niece could barely contain their excitement. Then it was read that he had left his entire estate to be divided between a heart clinic in Dublin and the lady Bernadette whom he had admired so much in his youth. He wanted her and her family to know that he really *had* amounted to something in the end.

Declan decided they should get out of here fast. Certainly before anyone knew they were connected with a heart clinic. They were out on the road before the shock had dawned properly on the niece and nephew and before the conversation had reached the level of a roar. They hitched a lift to Galway and spent magical hours looking at an art exhibition, touring a bookshop and having a coffee in the open air.

On the way back to Dublin Fiona fell asleep with her head on Declan's shoulder and as he saw the sun setting he told himself that he never remembered feeling quite so happy before.

He was hugely nervous of meeting Fiona's parents but she seemed utterly casual about it. And when they went together on the bus he hoped that he had done the right thing buying her mother an orchid in a pot. Fiona said she'd love it but then Fiona thought everyone would love everything. She wasn't used to the atmosphere in St Jarlath's Crescent, where everything was analysed and examined for days on end.

He dreaded the day that Fiona would come to visit his parents. That was if the day ever arrived.

Fiona's father Sean was a very easy-going man. 'Lord, you've really raised the bar bringing an orchid to this house,' he said to Declan. 'There'll be no getting away with a bunch of flowers from the petrol station for Maureen from now on.'

'I hope it wasn't the wrong thing to do,' said Declan fearfully.

'Not at all, lad, it was a grand thing to do.'

Fiona was relaxed and at ease. Nobody was fussing or

insisting that people wash their hands or take the best chair like would happen in his house. Fiona was putting the salad and bright coloured table napkins on the table. Her mother, Maureen, called the younger children to the table and served a big bowl of chilli and rice. They hardly seemed to notice that he was there. Once more he thought of the interrogation that Fiona would get whenever she came to his house. He shivered. *Why* couldn't Paddy and Molly Carroll be like this normal, relaxed family instead of grovelling with inadequacy like his father or raking the conversation for a slight or an insult like his mother?

'Do you think they liked me?' Declan asked anxiously as they went to the bus stop.

'Sure, they loved you. But they would have anyway, you know.'

'What do you mean?'

'Well, compared to the last fellow I brought home, you are like an angel with wings,' she said, as if that explained everything.

Declan put off the business of inviting Fiona to St Jarlath's Crescent.

It was all going so well, why ruin it now? He had also put the whole matter of sex on hold. There had been fond kisses goodnight and on the evening he had supper with Fiona in her flat, Barbara had been out. Perhaps that could have been an opportunity, or indeed an invitation, but he hesitated. He cared so much about her and wanted it all to be perfect. Was he a fool in this regard? Fiona was a normal girl.

Declan had had sex before. Not enough of it, of course, but he knew how much he had enjoyed it. And possibly Fiona might too. But he must be certain. Maybe they could go on a little holiday together. By now they were seeing each other almost every evening after work.

The days flew by at the clinic. He learned a great deal from Clara who taught him without appearing to do so. They would have case conferences where she would ask as many questions as she answered. He got to know his colleagues. He was now a legend among the patients because he had minded Judy Murphy's dogs while she had gone into hospital for a procedure. Judy had bought a wonderful bowl with Dimples painted on it for the big soppy Labrador. Declan's mother said that Judy was *much* too old for him and he mustn't get notions about a woman like that who could be his mother. Paddy raised his eyes to heaven, begging Declan not to engage on the subject.

'I'll take very good notice of what you say, Mam, as always,' Declan said.

He had become very friendly with Hilary in the clinic. She had asked him to cover for her one lunchtime. She simply had to go home. The neighbours had phoned to say her mother was out in the garden in her nightdress. Like everyone, Declan had suggested that Hilary's mother might be ready for residential care. And, like everyone, he was gently refused. Nobody could begin to understand what this woman had done for Hilary. She was not going to be tidied away in the twilight of her years just in order to give Hilary a less complicated lifestyle.

'You'll have to give up work soon, Hilary,' Declan said in his calm voice.

'No, no. My son Nick is a great help. He's there a lot. He's composing music, you see, and he keeps an eye on his gran.'

Declan thought that it wasn't much of an eye if the old lady was out in the garden in her nightdress. But agreeable as ever, he said he would mind the desk during lunchtime and take any calls.

That evening Fiona was going to a hen party so Declan had dinner at home with his parents. His mother had to go through a scene of pretending to be surprised to see him home. He listened patiently while Molly said she was glad the place was good enough for him tonight. She then produced a steak and kidney pie with a carefully fluted edge.

'Does your young lady make a pie like this?' Molly asked.

'Don't you know she doesn't, Mam.'

'And are we ever going to meet her, do you think?' Here it was, his opportunity.

'I'd love to invite her to supper, Mam. Maybe you could make her a pie like this.'

'I will not make a pie. If there are guests coming to this house, they'll get a proper roast,' Molly said.

'So can we pick a night?' Declan begged.

'When your father has painted this room,' Molly said.

'That's a coincidence. I thought I'd do it this very weekend,' Paddy Carroll said. And Declan looked at his father's face and saw the same look of love that had come there when he first saw Molly at the dance in her white blouse and her red velvet skirt.

It took them two days to empty the room and three hours to choose the colour for the walls. Paddy thought magnolia white, Molly wondered about lime green, Declan said that he really loved a peachy colour called Indian Summer.

The date of the dinner party was fixed and then Declan asked Fiona.

'Sure,' she said, as if it was something normal. 'I'd love that, Declan. Thank you *and* your mother too.'

'She will be delighted with you,' he said in a very uncertain tone.

'Am I better than your ex then?'

'I have no ex. No ex I brought home anyway,' he said, flustered.

'I'm sure the place is littered with them,' Fiona said cheerfully. 'What will I bring her? My ma just loved the orchid.'

'Maybe a small tin of biscuits,' he said, thinking hard. Was there *anything* that Fiona could buy that would not be criticised? Very unlikely.

When Declan was doing his rounds, Judy Murphy surprised him by saying that she worked part-time as a bookkeeper in Quentins. She did the VAT for them once a week and they told her that the nice young doctor, who sounded like the one who had walked her dogs, had been in for a meal with a beautiful fair-haired girl.

'Was it our friend?' Judy nodded down the room towards Fiona.

'Yes, it was actually. How did you know?'

'Everyone knows,' she said.

'God!' Declan was alarmed.

'She's a lucky girl,' Judy said, as if she meant it.

Barbara was going to a wedding in Kilkenny. She would be away all night. She told this to Declan twice in case he hadn't understood it the first time. He approached Fiona who was with Lar.

'Have you a moment?' he asked.

'I have indeed.' She seemed eager.

'Thanks,' she said when they left the cubicle. 'I'm meant to know four of the major cities in Tennessee. I can't remember any of them. Is there a Tennessee City by any wonderful chance?'

'I don't think so, but there's Memphis and Chattanooga and Nashville,' he offered.

'One more *please*, Declan.'

'Isn't that where Knoxville is too?'

'I love you,' she said and kissed him on the nose.

'*Wait!*' He caught her by the arm. '*Wait* one moment. I was wondering, Fiona, since Barbara will be away tonight, could I maybe, you know, stay over, in the flat?'

'I thought you'd never ask,' she said and he heard her reciting the Tennessee names out to Lar as she took his blood pressure and reassured him that he would indeed live to see all these places if he spent less on the horses and more on building up his travel fund.

Declan went to phone his parents and tell them that he had to be on duty tonight. That's the way it was . . .

They were nervous of each other at first and making little jokes almost putting off the moment. Eventually Fiona took the lead.

'We could always take our glass of wine into the bedroom,' she suggested. And after that it was all right. As he lay there afterwards, Fiona asleep with her head on his chest, Declan knew that the happiness he had felt on the train had only been a very faint preparation for the happiness he felt now.

They woke late and had to scramble for the bus. They thought that everyone in the clinic knew what they had done. Though this could not possibly be so. Declan didn't care if they did know. He would be proud for them to know. And in two days' time Fiona was coming home with him to meet his parents to have supper in St Jarlath's Crescent. What could go wrong with life now?

Molly had got a new perm for the occasion and she had warned Paddy a hundred times that he was to wear a jacket and tie for the meal. She had ironed the table napkins which had been a wedding present when they married and hardly ever used since.

Tim the security man had told Declan that he would give him the loan of his car for a few days.

'Am I insured?' Declan wished that he weren't always so cautious.

'Sure, you're on my insurance, and have my permission to drive the car. Anyway, you're not a maniac driver, I'd say!' Tim laughed.

Declan rehearsed the journey so that he wouldn't be a complete amateur. On the day of the big meal he saw that Fiona had fixed her hair and had brought smart clothes into work. A cream silk dress and jacket. Her best outfit. Possibly too smart. His mother would find fault with that too. Back home, Dimples had been washed and brushed and refused permission to sit on his favourite chair. Dad's friend Muttie Scarlet had been warned not to call in and ask Paddy out for a pint. Declan's mother was wearing lipstick at breakfast. She told them she was breaking it in since she didn't normally indulge. He wanted to hold her newly permed head to him and tell her that she was marvellous and he loved her and that he would never abandon them, but of course he did nothing except grin foolishly and say it would be a wonderful evening.

The day seemed endless. Bobby Walsh had been having chest pains and his wife said he was not going into that ward where everyone from all parts of this country and the Lord knew what other countries were gathered. Whatever he came in with he would be much, much worse when he came out.

Declan wished that their son Carl was with them. He would be able to calm his mother down.

For the second time since he had gone to work there, Declan found himself watching the clock. Finally it was time to leave and he opened the door of Tim's car proudly for Fiona. His girlfriend. They drove cheerily through the traffic, Fiona chattering happily about the day that had just ended. What a marvellous man Lar was, his mind so full of information. How Mrs Walsh, Bobby's awful wife, had sighed and groaned at Lavender when she was giving her a diet sheet for Bobby.

'At least you're Irish. I suppose that's one thing that can be said about you,' was how she finished.

'Right in front of Ania. Really, the woman is a monster!'

After a while she noticed that Declan wasn't responding. 'Am I talking too much? I'll be quieter when we get there,' she promised.

'No, don't be quiet, please don't. Just be yourself. But you will realise that they are themselves too.' He looked very sad.

'But they're your mam and dad. I'll love them. They produced you. What's not to love about them?'

'They're awkward and shy. They're not normal and casual like your parents.'

'Ah, God, Declan! Would you come on! No one's parents are normal. It will be fine.'

Back at St Jarlath's Crescent, Molly and Paddy were ready. The kitchen was glowing with its peach-coloured walls and gleaming white paintwork. The melon was sliced and each piece had a glacé cherry on top. The beef was cooking away in the oven, beef chosen carefully by Paddy Carroll, master butcher, that day. Was there anything else that should be done?

'That dog will want to have a wee the moment the girl arrives,' Molly declared.

'Right, I'll take him out now,' said Paddy Carroll who thought this night would never be over.

'But be back in time!' Molly screamed.

Paddy put the big dog on the lead and marched him out, but at the gate Dimples saw a cat slinking along the road. He didn't like it. He growled. Paddy took no notice. He didn't realise how serious the growl was. Then the cat streaked across the road and Dimples was after her with his lead dangling behind him. Paddy watched as it all happened in slow motion. The car coming down the crescent, trying to swerve to avoid the dog, and driving straight into the lamppost. He heard the sound of glass breaking, metal buckling and saw the blood of his only child all over the windscreen.

He had never felt so powerless or shocked in his whole life. And as he stood rooted to the ground Dimples came back penitently and licked his hand.

And from the passenger seat in the car emerged a beautiful fair-haired girl, her face and dress covered in blood.

'Call an ambulance,' she shouted, '*quickly!* Tell them that there are head injuries.'

Paddy realised that this was her, the nurse, the girl that Declan had said was really special. And she had been coming to dinner tonight, except that now Declan was dead. He looked at the angle of the boy's head. His neck must be broken.

He moved like a robot into the house, pushing past Molly who had come out to see what was happening. 'Come back inside, Molly, I beg you,' he said, and picked up the phone. But she didn't and as he was giving the emergency services the address, he saw his wife with her hands to her face looking in disbelief at the car where Fiona was kneeling in the broken glass and talking in the driver's window. She was assuring Declan that help was on the way. And she was telling him that she loved him.

Dimples knew something was wrong but he didn't know what it was. He sat down sadly beside the range and with a great degree of interest smelled the beef that was cooking.

Paddy had brought out a rug and people had gathered in the street. Fiona was completely in charge.

'He can't hear us,' she was saying to Molly. 'Please believe me, he's unconscious. They'll be here any moment.' And amazingly they were.

The ambulance men were very relieved to see a nurse in charge of everything. Fiona held the crowds back, spoke reassuringly and took complete control. She assured them that she had only surface wounds in her forehead and she would see to them once they had Declan on the way to A&E. She wanted to go with him as they lifted his body from the front of the car, but she knew that his parents needed her more.

'Anything?' she asked one of the men.

'A weak pulse,' he said.

'Better than nothing,' she said with a watery smile and then turned to the police who had turned up in a Guards car and were beginning to take statements.

'Could we have the discussion inside?' she said. 'These are Declan's parents and they must want to sit down in their own home after the shock.' She helped Molly back into her own house, got a rug for her knees and rubbed her hands for her. She got a nip of whiskey from a man called Muttie to bring some colour back to Paddy Carroll's face. And she turned off the oven where an enormous joint of beef was cooking away. And then they began the interminable business of the dog who had seen the cat and had run out on the road, and the son of the house who had seen the dog and swerved to avoid it and hit the lamppost.

Several times Fiona left to call a friend in the hospital, a friend who would be able to tell her more than the enquiries desk. The news was reasonable. He was on a life support, but everything seemed to be working well enough. A fractured skull, a broken arm, but no internal injuries in the rest of his body. He would not be able to be visited by anyone until the next day.

At 11 p.m., five hours after she had arrived in St Jarlath's Crescent, Fiona spoke to both her friend and enquiries for the last time that evening. They were both able to say that Declan would live. And so they took the beef out of the oven and the three of them sat and ate it with slices of bread and butter. And she stayed the night with them in the same house where Declan had been born and brought up. And she actually managed to get some sleep as she lay in his bed.

And in his hospital bed Declan Carroll slept a normal sleep and dreamed about the clinic. He was on the floor trying to reach up to the desk and Hilary kept telling him to rest where he was and let nature take its course. Eventually after a few failed attempts he decided to do that. Hilary was usually right.

Chapter Three

Hilary Hickey caught sight of herself reflected in a shop window and paused in shock. She was not only very old-looking but she also looked quite eccentric. Her hair stood up in spikes and her clothes seemed to have been thrown on at random. Is this the way people saw her? Hilary was surprised. She had thought she looked quite different. If she had been asked to describe herself she might have said small, neat, trim, fit, with a nice broad smile, the smile that so many years ago had made Dan Hickey leave his wealthy fiancée at an art gallery opening and come to her side.

No one would leave anyone to come to her side nowadays, Hilary thought ruefully. They might cross the street to avoid her. She looked into the shop further and realised it was a hairdressing salon. Perhaps this was a sign, a message saying that it was time she did something about her unkempt head. She would go inside and see if they had anyone free to do her hair now. If they had, then it was definitely a sign. The young girl at the desk was called Kiki.

'Sure,' she said, 'I can do you now.' She looked dangerously young and rather over made-up for Hilary's conservative thinking.

'But what about the . . . um . . . reception desk?' Hilary asked nervously.

'Oh, that looks after itself,' Kiki said, getting towels and directing Hilary towards a basin.

Kiki talked incessantly about a new club that was opening next week.

'My son may well be going to that,' Hilary said cheerfully. It sounded the kind of thing that Nick would like, noisy and colourful and opening its doors at midnight. She often met him returning home when she was heading off to the clinic. But she had learned not to comment.

In many ways Nick was a perfect son. He was a talented musician who gave music lessons in the afternoon when he taught the clarinet and kept an eye on his grandmother. In as much as he could. But of course if he had to go out to a school or to visit a pupil at home then there was no cover, no one to look after Hilary's mother.

Hilary bit her lip and thought about it over and over again. She didn't care *what* the so-called experts said. Her mother Jessica was not going to go into a home for the bewildered. She would *not* put her mother away.

Hilary had been an only child with parents who had been absolutely devoted to her. Her father was a very handsome man who sold cars in a showroom. He loved cars. Hilary remembered how he had stroked them and almost purred at them. He would promise that one day he would have saved enough to buy them a beautiful car and all three of them would go driving in the countryside on a Sunday.

But before that could happen Hilary's father met a lady with very blonde hair and a black leather coat. The lady was buying a car and needed a lot of test drives. During one of the test drives it turned out that Hilary's father and the lady in the black leather coat were meant for each other and would go and live in the south of England, and have their own family.

Hilary had been eleven at the time.

'Will I be going to the south of England to see them and to spend holidays?' she had asked. Her mother thought not. Better not to build up any hopes. Better to work hard and get a good job. That's what Daddy would have liked to see.

So why didn't he stay to see it? Hilary wondered. Her mother never answered this; and so her life was never quite the same afterwards. She only saw her father once a year; her mother went out a lot. She helped people in their gardens and she made cakes for her friends. She always encouraged Hilary to invite friends home on a Friday evening and they now had so much room in the house without Father that they let two rooms to paying guests. These were two mousey women called Violet and Noreen who worked in a bank and lived very quietly. Hilary's life fell into a routine. Home from school, glass of milk and a homemade biscuit, then homework.

Then Violet taught her bookkeeping, and Noreen taught her to type on an old machine where the letters had been covered with sticking plaster. By the time she left school, Hilary had achieved what they apparently wanted for her, a good education and some steps down the road towards being a secretary. She would have loved to have gone to university like some of her school friends, but by the time she was eighteen she realised that the money just wasn't there. Her mother wasn't doing gardens and cake-making out of friendship for people. She was doing it to earn a living for them both.

Hilary went to a secretarial college and because the two paying guests had helped her so much, she learned everything she could in a very short time. She got the Certificate of Merit from the college and was ready to earn her own living in a few short months. She started in hospital administration and this is where she stayed. She had concentrated too much on her work to consider men and marriage. Until she met Dan Hickey.

All her friends warned her against him. He was too good-looking, they said. He was unreliable. If he left his fiancée for her, he could do the same thing again. He didn't have a real career. He was a gentleman. He needed a rich woman to support him. Only her mother agreed that Dan was wonderful. Anxiously, Hilary ran her friends' concerns past Jessica.

'Suppose that he *is* too good-looking for me, Mother?' she had worried.

'Nonsense, Hilary, you are a fine-looking young woman, *and* you have a good career, *and* you have a house to offer him.'

'He can't come to live here.' Hilary was aghast.

'Where else would he live? I worked long and hard enough to keep this house for you. We have no paying guests now. Make me a small flat beyond the kitchen and we are right as rain.'

'But it's putting you out of your own house . . .' Hilary began.

'No, it's not. I'm not really able for those stairs anyway. This way I have company *and* independence. What could be better?'

'But will we be able to afford to build an extension?'

'Certainly we will. I have been saving like a squirrel. I've been waiting for this day.'

'It hasn't come yet. He hasn't asked me.'

'He will. Just have an open mind,' Jessica had advised.

Dan asked her to marry him the next week.

'I'm not much of a catch,' he apologised.

'You're the only catch I wanted,' Hilary had said and he seemed delighted. He was also delighted that he didn't have to think of finding a family home, and after their quiet wedding he moved in seamlessly.

Dan was always seeing someone about an opening or talking to someone about a possibility. But in the twelve years of their married life he never earned one single penny. Instead, Jessica returned to her garden pruning and cake-making, and added dog walking as well. Hilary took on private bookkeeping jobs for clients, small companies or wealthy individuals, which paid well.

When Nick was eleven, exactly the same age as Hilary had been when she lost her father, Dan went out of their lives. But he did not disappear to the south of England with a woman in a black leather coat. He was drowned in a deep, dark lake when he had gone to the Irish midlands to meet a chap who might be able to give him a job. The Guards came to the door to tell Hilary and her mother and her son. They were very kind. They came in and made tea for the stricken family and left knowing as little about the man who had drowned as they had before, except that he had left three broken people behind.

There had been a small insurance policy. Jessica insisted that they have an elegant funeral for Dan Hickey. He would have wanted it that way. Hilary was too shocked and angry to care. *Why* had he gone swimming in an unfamiliar lake? *Why* had he gone before his son grew up to know him properly?

Looking back on it all afterwards she was deeply touched at and grateful for her mother's insistence the funeral be done right. The delicate sandwiches in the posh hotel, his many friends and acquaintances, none of whom had delivered a job, a contract or an introduction, but who were all happy to turn up for the reception. It had indeed been exactly what he would have wanted. She had not one moment of regret.

And after that Hilary had set about making Nick's childhood as good and happy as Jessica had made hers. When he showed an interest in music, she paid for private lessons. She never fussed. She knew that his friends envied him his crazy house with two old women in it. To boys of that age, Hilary knew that she must seem the same generation as her mother. And the years went by. Hilary never found anyone else remotely attractive enough even to consider an involvement. She wasn't short of offers of company, a hardworking young widow with her own home, a good income, an easy-going, grown-up son who composed and taught music and a cheerful mother tidied away downstairs in a granny flat. She had a lot going for her. Or had, at one time.

But since her mother had become more frail, more forgetful and less able to cope on her own, Hilary had given little attention to her appearance. It was just to do with getting older – it was beyond belief that Jessica would lose her fine mind, her generous nature, her grasp on everything.

But in her own way, Jessica guessed what was happening. Realising what the future might hold, she wrote a letter. It was a short, typed note:

> *As I am getting older I am becoming more forgetful; and it is possible that one day I might not know where I am or who I am and, even more importantly, who you are. So I wanted to say a nice, clear-headed goodbye and thank you to everyone while I still do have my wits, or at least some of them, about me.*
>
> *I have had a very good life and I hope you won't be offended if I am confused later on. The real me, inside here, remembers you well . . .*

Then she wrote a few words to each person. To Hilary she wrote:

> *You are simply the best daughter in the whole world. Never forget that. Do what you have to when the time comes. I'll love you anyway . . .*
> *Mum*

Her mother was giving her permission to put her away. How generous was that? And how sane? There was no way Hilary could do it.

She looked at her reflection in the mirror without much pleasure. 'What are you going to do with it?' she asked Kiki.

'I'm going to give it some shape. You want it shorter and glossy, yeah?'

Short and glossy was what Hilary had thought it was until she had seen herself in the window.

'Yes, not too short.'

'Trust me,' Kiki said and huge showers of Hilary's hair seemed to cascade on to the floor.

Hilary wondered why she had trusted this girl with huge, dark-rimmed eyes and green nail polish. There must have been a reason.

Clara gasped with admiration when Hilary came back to the clinic. '*Where* did you get your hair done, Hilary? You look ten years younger. I'm going there at once.'

Hilary showed her the card. 'Ask for Kiki. She's got green nails.'

'Well, there's nothing wrong with the way she cuts hair. You look terrific. I think you and I should go out on the pull one night.'

'I'd hate to think what we might reel in,' Hilary laughed, but there was a strain around her eyes.

'No use asking how things are at home. It's more of the same, isn't it?' Clara was sympathetic.

'No, it's slightly worse. She was out in the street last night asking anyone who passed by what time it was.'

'And what time *was* it?' Clara asked.

'It was 4 a.m. but she thought it was 4 p.m. and said I would be home for my tea soon.'

Clara was silent.

'Go on, Clara, say it.'

'No, *you* say it, Hilary. You know what has to be said as much as I do.'

'You think she should be put in care,' Hilary said.

'It's not what I think that matters.'

'I'm sure you know the perfect place for her. If I were to ask you, you'd have the name and phone number . . .' Hilary bit her lip.

'It's your decision, but if you *were* actually asking about somewhere, there's a very good place called Lilac Court. The woman who runs it is a sort of friend of mine, Claire Cotter. I've known her for years. She makes a very pleasant life for the people there.'

'Can't *do* it. Not yet.'

'Sure, sure.'

'Don't put me down, Clara. You don't know what that woman did for me. I can't tidy her away.'

'It might be kinder.'

'It might be easier but it would never be kinder. Even if I have to give up working here and stay at home.'

'You do, more and more.'

'I know, you probably think that I take too much time off . . .' Hilary began.

'No, it's not that at all. You make up for every hour you take. Don't I see you working through your lunchtime or staying on after work if Nick is around. You do your full job here, believe me.'

'If it were *your* mother, Clara?'

'I'd have her into the first place that would take her and walk away.'

'You say that.'

'I mean that. My mother was and is a discontented, trouble-making woman who sees the worst in everyone and every situation. Your misfortune is that yours has been decent and

99

kind-hearted throughout and it's blinding you about doing what's best for her.'

'It wasn't a misfortune,' Hilary said.

'No, indeed it wasn't, it's the greatest thing that could happen to anyone who didn't have it and I sure don't think I'm giving it either. My girls are so pissed off with me, they haven't a good word to say about me, I know.'

They were interrupted by Barbara, collecting for the 'welcome back' present for Declan. It wasn't a tough job – Declan was very popular with staff and patients at the heart clinic. The two women each took out large euro notes.

'I went in to see him last night,' Clara said. 'He's getting on fine. He'll be into a convalescent home next week.'

'I'd love to have gone to see him,' Hilary said.

'One day you'll have time for the rest of your life, but not yet.' Clara was comforting.

'Ooh thanks.' Barbara was pleased with the donations. 'You know that nice guy Tim has just given me a big note too. He said that good people like Declan should be made into national treasures. Imagine!'

'Maybe he keeps a romantic poet's heart in his tool bag,' Clara suggested.

'Do you think? Well, he certainly keeps a Polish phrase book and he's been practising some phrases, *tak* and *Dzien dobry*, over and over.'

'What do they mean?' Hilary was interested.

'No idea.'

'Maybe he's interested in Ania,' Clara wondered.

'No, I think it's her flatmate,' said Barbara, who always made it her business to know what was what.

Ania was having her English lesson from Bobby Walsh's son Carl in the waiting room. Their heads were close together as

Ania struggled with giving somebody directions from this hospital to the centre of the city.

'You go first along the main road and take the signs to Trinity College and then you will see the university on your left. You keep walking on then you see a big bank that was one time a parliament house. You could turn right here if you wanted to go into O'Connell Street. If you want to go shopping you should turn left past the front gates of the university and then you will find Grafton Street for the shopping . . .'

'Just "shopping", not "the shopping",' Carl corrected gently.

'Why don't I just say, "I'm Polish, I don't know where anywhere is!"?' Ania asked, laughing.

'Because it's not true – you *do* know where everywhere is. I'm only aiming for perfection!' They laughed out loud when they realised that Barbara had observed the squabble, and they both gave a contribution.

'Your father gave already.' Barbara wanted to be fair to Carl.

'No, no, I'm happy to contribute. Declan's marvellous.'

'I will make a big banner to say "Welcome Back",' Ania said, and Barbara thought she'd caught Carl looking at the little Polish girl with affection.

Hilary knew that something was wrong as soon as she turned the corner into her street. A small crowd of neighbours had gathered outside her house and there was smoke coming from the kitchen window. At first she found herself almost paralysed with shock and certainly unable to move her legs. Then she was running to the house shouting, 'Mother, Mother!'

Neighbours and friends held her back.

'She's fine, Hilary. She's fine, not a scratch on her. Look at her over there in a chair.' And Hilary saw her mother surrounded by well-wishers drinking a mug of tea while neighbours went in. The fire was out by now but they had called the Fire Service just in case. As she approached her mother, Hilary glanced at the damage. The curtains were gone, just torn shreds hung down, the kitchen wall through the broken window looked black. Her mother could have been engulfed in flames here. She could have burned to death in her own house.

Hilary knew that she must thank God that she had somehow escaped. Jessica was completely unfazed by it all.

'I can't understand the fuss,' she said, over and over.

'But, Mother, you could have been killed. You could have died in there!' Hilary was so relieved she was shouting now.

'But I did it for Nick. He said he would love a plate of chips like the old days. I said I'd make them. He went out somewhere and then the pan caught fire.' Hilary knew that Nick would never have allowed his grandmother near a chip pan.

'No, Mother, you can't have understood him properly,' she began and then she saw the figure of her son running down the road carrying two portions of chips. He had gone to get them for his grandmother who said it would bring her back to the old days. Only then did Hilary let herself cry.

Later that night, when the window had been replaced and most of the burned shelves and scorched utensils thrown out, Hilary and Nick sat down to talk.

'I suppose we'll have to decide what to do,' Hilary said.

'Well, the carpenters are coming in the morning. I'll take Gran for a walk while they're here . . .'

'No. I mean long term, Nick.'

'How long term?'

'Well, she's not really able to cope, is she? She thought you meant her to *make* chips!' As if.

'You're always the one who says she's perfect, Mam. You go for anyone's throats if they dare to say otherwise.'

'Yes, well, maybe I've dug my head up from under the ground.'

'My mother, the ostrich.' Nick was affectionate.

'I know. I wonder why no wise young ostrich didn't tell the older ones that it just didn't work as a policy.'

'They probably tried but the elder ostriches said, "Nonsense, nonsense," so they gave up in the end.'

'Have you wanted to say something to me about Gran?'

'No. I don't see a thing wrong with her. You're the one who is always whining and shuddering when Gran says something off the wall. I love it. I think it's cool.'

'You didn't know her when she was as sharp as a stick.'

'She still is in lots of ways. Here she is in bed with a mug of drinking chocolate and you and I are in here fussing ourselves to death over her. Who's sharp here, I ask?'

'I hate to see her losing it.'

'She's a really old ostrich, Mam. She's entitled to lose bits here and there.'

'At work they tell me that I should—'

'We can manage, Mam. I'll take more home tuition and go out less.'

'I can't ask you to put your life on hold.'

'Is it on hold? I have a great life at night.'

'Do you meet any nice girls?'

'I meet lots of girls, certainly, Mam, whether they are nice or not . . . now that's the question.'

'But is it a good place to meet them, in late-night clubs? I only ask out of concern for you, not because I'm interfering.'

'You never interfered, Mam, you were always terrific.'

'But you still can't spend all your daylight hours looking after your grandmother,' she said.

'Not all daylight hours, but a few more of them than I have been. I wouldn't walk away from the house and leave her on her own again.' He looked ruefully around their burned kitchen.

'Will we get any insurance, do you think?' Hilary wondered.

'Don't know. Those insurance companies are monsters about defending their own. They'll say Gran is a liability. I don't think we should even think about approaching them, to be honest, for fear of what we might draw on ourselves.'

'Like your gran being put into care, you mean?'

'Well, that's up to us to decide, not some faceless insurance company to insist on. And the time hasn't come yet.'

Hilary felt flooded with relief. She had been so afraid that Nick would turn on her and ask her to be realistic, tell her that for everyone's sake Gran should be looked after properly. And now it appeared that he was just as desperate as she was that Jessica should stay at home.

Hilary looked around the kitchen and smiled. What was it really but a few cupboards here and a lick of paint there. She could take on some extra bookkeeping work to pay for it. The main thing was that Mother had not been hurt or frightened.

She felt like jumping up and giving him a great clinging hug, but he would have said, 'Get off me, Mam, you're mental you are.' Instead she kept the conversation light. 'You see your generation is so lucky. You can more or less do what you like. We were all buttoned up and peculiar. Everything you ever read about us all back then was true.'

'It was just different.' Nick was forgiving. 'You were obsessed by sex because you didn't get any. Now that it is all round the place, people are much more easy-going about it.'

'And it *is* all around the place, I imagine?' Hilary asked mildly.

Hilary bought Ania a bright-coloured scarf as a thank you gift.

'Why do you thank me, Hilary?'

'Because you are doing so much of my work for me and you never complain. You are so bright, you know, you could do anything.'

Ania was pink with pride as she stroked the scarf as if it were the finest fabric in the world. 'Tonight I write to my mother. I will tell her all about this gift,' she said.

'You write every week?'

'Yes, I tell her about the new land where I live and all the people I meet.'

'And do you tell your mother about your love life?' Hilary wondered.

'No, but then I don't *have* any love life. I had too much love life when I was in Poland, but not now. Now I work so much I have no time for love.'

Hilary smiled. 'That would be a pity. You know the expression about love making the world go around.'

'Yes, but it turned my world upside down. I think perhaps I am wiser without it. Make money now and find love later.'

'But suppose he came along. What would you do? Ask him to wait ten years?' Hilary asked.

'Not ten, surely. Five, maybe. I want to buy my mother a little shop with a place to live up the stairs and a place to work down the stairs. She is a dressmaker you see. If she had a name over the door and some garments in the window then she would have respect, then the people in the town would not pity her.'

'I am sure they don't pity her now, Ania.'

'They do. They pity her because of me. I was so foolish. If only you knew. I made her such a disgrace in our part of the world. She could not lift up her head and look people in their eyes.'

'Lord, what did you *do*, Ania?'

'I believed a man who told me lies. You see I thought if he said "I love you" he meant it.'

'There's women all over the world doing that all the time. Men too,' Hilary said.

'But in your case your husband *did* love you.'

'Yes, yes, but that was different, years and years ago. The world has changed so much now. You know, last night I was talking to my son about how much sex there is all around the place. Imagine!'

'I imagine you would be a good person to talk to about such things. My mother never mentioned sex. Never once to me. She was much too upset.'

'And your sisters, did they talk to you?'

'No, because when it happened they were all so ashamed of me. They had married when they were seventeen or eighteen, both of them. They married the children of neighbouring people. I had to love a man who came from miles away. A man who had come to our town to start a business.'

'And did he?'

'For a while, yes. But he needed money, so he married the daughter of a rich man.'

'Instead of you?'

'A dressmaker's daughter with no father alive? But I thought he loved me.' The girl's eyes were very sad.

'Possibly he did, in his way. People love in different kinds of ways.' Hilary was trying to console her.

'No, Marek never loved me. He told me that later. He said he had been laughing at me and his friends had laughed at me.'

'My friends thought I was mad to marry Dan. Several of them told me. Even on the night before the wedding.'

'But you were sure?'

'Yes, I was sure. And what's more, my mother was sure, which is why I can never let her go into a place with strangers. You do see that, don't you?'

'Of course you can't. And I will do all I can to help you,' Ania promised.

As Hilary went home at lunchtime she wondered how she could take Ania up on her offer. Maybe the girl would come one evening a week and sit with her mother. Or possibly go and make her lunch from time to time. Hilary could find the money that Ania badly needed to buy the little house with her mother's name on it. The business premises which would give her respect.

When she got home a carpenter was already installed in the kitchen, sawing and hammering. Nick and Jessica were in the front room going through a photograph album.

'That was your mother's wedding day, Nick. Look how well he looks. It was one of the best days in our lives. In fact it was *the* best day until you arrived.' There they sat companionably turning the pages, her mother making sense and Nick content in her company. Hilary breathed more easily. What was she worrying about? Her mother was fine. She didn't need Ania or any carer. She certainly didn't need to think about residential care.

Four days later her mother packed a bag and phoned a taxi to take her to the railway station. Nick had left just as Hilary came in so there was nobody to ask what had brought this on. There was a lot of confusion when the taxi arrived and had to be sent away again.

'Where are you going, Mother?'

'To the south of England to get your father to see sense and come home to us. He has a fine son here, Nick. It's time he got to know the boy properly.'

'Mother, Dad died. You remember. It was ages ago. He died and *she* married her next-door neighbour.'

'He must come back to his son.'

'Nick is his grandson, Mother.'

'No, that's not so. Don't you think I know my own family?'

'Nick is Dan's son. You remember Dan? My lovely Dan who died in a lake.'

'Stop telling me about all these people who are dead. I never heard of Dan.'

'You did, Mother, you loved him. You were great to him. You told Nick that the day I married him was the second best day in your life.'

'You're very emotional, Hilary, I don't think this job suits you.'

'Don't leave me, Mother, please.'

'Well, I can't very well, can I? You've dismissed the taxi.' Her mother looked very put out.

'Hold on a bit, Mother. I have to make a call.' She went into her bedroom and found Nick on his mobile phone.

'What happened, Nick?'

'What do you mean?'

'Your grandmother. Did anything happen to upset her?'

'No, she was fine when I left. Is anything wrong?'

'She's completely confused, she was going to go to England in a taxi.'

'That would have cost a bit.'

'Be serious for a moment. She's babbling. She thinks you're her son, not her grandson.'

'Do you want me to come home?'

'Where are you?'

'I'm in a coffee shop having a cappuccino with a friend of mine. We were going to catch a movie and then I'm going to play in a club.'

Hilary suddenly realised there was nothing Nick could do. He had done enough. She was flooded with guilt that she had bothered him.

'Listen, Nick, I'm sorry,' she began, 'have a good time. Everything here is just fine.'

Back in the kitchen, her mother was sitting watching her. Her eyes were far away.

Hilary didn't sleep a wink that night. At breakfast the next day she apologised again to her son.

Nick shrugged. There was nothing to apologise for, he said. He would be at home all day with his gran. Of course Jessica was now absolutely calm and all was as normal.

At work in the clinic, Hilary knew she looked tired and indeed Clara mentioned it, in a roundabout way.

'I think everyone's tired these days, it must be the weather and the thought of all that Christmas fuss ahead,' she said conversationally.

'I know, Clara, you don't have to play games with me. There isn't enough under-eye concealer in the world to wipe out the lines and blotches on my face.'

'Is it your mother?' Clara asked.

'Of course it is. She has periods of complete confusion and then long days of perfect sanity. It's a nightmare.'

'What about a day centre, Hilary?'

'Nick and I can manage.'

'Just take her to the doctor for an assessment – Hilary, you know that's what you should do.'

'Offload my problems and decision-making to someone else? I don't think so.'

'Look, I was telling you about my friend Claire Cotter and her place, Lilac Court. The residents there are very happy—'

'You mean they don't know where they are?'

'Not so. It has a lovely garden and very good food. The people who stay there feel safe.'

'Even if they do know where they are.'

'They do indeed. Have a look at it, Hilary, before you dismiss it completely.'

'I'm only dismissing the idea that I'd put my mother *anywhere*.'

'This time I'll write down the address,' Clara said.

Two days later, Hilary arrived home from the hospital to find her mother behaving very oddly and apparently trying to get Nick out of the room. Nick realised, and left without protest.

'What is he doing here?' Jessica hissed.

'Who? Nick? He was getting your lunch ready while I was at work.' Hilary's heart felt heavy.

'But who *is* he? What's he doing in this house?'

'He's your grandson, Mother, he's Nick, my son.'

'Don't be ridiculous, Hilary, you have no son. But what's that tinker boy doing here?'

'Mother, don't you remember Nick?'

'I'll tell you what I remember, I remember that he slit a hole in my handbag and took out all my money. There's hundreds of pounds gone.'

'Mother, we use euros now and in any case, you don't have hundreds of pounds *or* euros,' Hilary protested.

'I don't *now*,' agreed her mother.

So Hilary pulled out the address and phone number of Lilac Court and arranged to go and inspect the place. It looked fresh and clean, as she was greeted at the front door by Claire Cotter. She was smartly dressed and full of warm smiles as she took some details; she put Hilary at ease straight away.

'I want the families to feel every bit as happy and secure as our residents,' she said. 'Please look around, Mrs Hickey, and go and see our facilities. We'll show you an empty bedroom, you'll see what we have to offer and then you can come and talk to me.'

Hilary passed a big, airy dining room where a number of elderly people were already having lunch. The tables had vases of flowers; some of the very elderly or infirm had helpers to assist them with their food and there was a cheerful atmosphere and a buzz of conversation. She inspected a couple of bedrooms, each with its own bathroom, then toured the bright sitting room, large enough to hold concerts but full of little alcoves where friends and family could sit and chat in privacy. There was even a small gym where they held exercise classes . . .

Hilary went to have a cup of tea with Claire Cotter. Again, she was put at her ease, though she noted that while Lilac Court was comfortable for the residents, Ms Cotter's own office was very simple. No smart furniture, no luxury carpet, just a practical place with filing cabinets and bookshelves.

Claire Cotter saw that Hilary was taking it all in. 'We prefer to spend what we have making our residents comfortable and reassuring their families,' she observed.

Hilary allowed her first real smile of the day to escape.

'And we do know that it's never easy, Mrs Hickey, there's never what seems a right time.'

'How do other people know?' Hilary was honest.

'When they know it's better for the other person,' Claire Cotter said gently. 'No one else can tell you, and no one else should put any pressure on you.'

'You see, most of the time, she's perfectly fine.'

'And what does her doctor say?'

'I haven't really discussed it with him yet. It's only come on significantly over the last few months, you see,' admitted Hilary.

'I see. Why don't you let him talk to her? It might make us clearer about where we are.'

'Thank you, I will,' Hilary agreed.

This woman had calmed her down. It was possible to deal with this terrible business. She wasn't alone in the world.

*

The next day, her mother was calm and doing a jigsaw when the doctor arrived. He'd see no symptoms and would probably think she was as sound as a bell.

Jessica thought that Dr Green had come to see Hilary.

'She fusses too much, Doctor,' Jessica confided. 'Worries about work and about me and about things that will never happen. She was always the same.'

Hilary looked up sharply. Something in her mother's voice had changed and she was slipping out of her normal, rational self. She knew the signs now.

She was right.

Hilary sat and listened as her mother told the doctor how sad it was that Hilary had never married. Too choosy, she had been, and too serious.

'And what about young Nick?' Dr Green asked mildly.

'Nick? Nick? You mean that young traveller, the tinker? Let me tell you what he stole from me – I don't know why Hilary gives him the run of the house . . .'

Dr Green's report was clear. Hilary's mother had severe dementia and was going to need round-the-clock care.

The following weekend, Hilary took her mother to visit Lilac Court. Claire Cotter was there, as reassuring as ever. She read the doctor's report, then the three of them toured the premises.

Jessica, in a voice as clear as it had ever been, said that she was grateful for the tea and the tour, but could she go home now, please, because she'd seen enough of this place and its strange old people. She wanted to go home now.

From that day onwards, Jessica was never in the house alone.

Between them, Hilary and Nick and Ania were on duty at all times. And Gary and Lisa, the nice couple who lived in the house next door, also kept an eye out for her. Nothing could happen to her now.

Hilary began to breathe easily again. She didn't have to do what so many other people did, put a much-loved mother into an institution because there was no place for her any longer at home.

Two weeks later, Hilary woke to hear a door banging. She got up to investigate: her mother's door was closed and the bathroom door was closed also.

It was the hall door, wide open and hitting off the heavy marble door-stop. Her throat narrowed. Mother couldn't have opened the door, surely? They always locked it at night and the key was always kept in a vase on the hall table. With a shaking hand she picked up the vase. The key was gone.

She opened her mother's bedroom and bathroom.

Empty.

'Nick, *Nick!* Your gran has got out!' she called. But Nick wasn't home, it was only 3 a.m. He had a gig and a club and it would be in full swing now. Hilary flung on a pair of warm trousers and her coat. *Please God* may her mother not have got too far.

She was nowhere in the street, so Hilary ran through the freezing night air towards the main road. Who were all these people driving around at this time in the morning? As if it were a normal time to be out. She stood still and watched the traffic. Which way might her mother have gone? Impossible to know: she looked up and down the street, bewildered.

Then she saw it in the distance, the flashing lights and the Guards out on the road waving traffic past. There had been an accident.

She felt dizzy and leaned on a parked car for support. It didn't have to be Mother. There were accidents all over the place.

She began to walk with leaden feet towards the scene. A crowd had gathered and the ambulance was expected. A middle-aged couple were sitting in chairs that had been brought out of someone's house. The man was shaking all over.

'She came from nowhere, just stepped out in front of me in her nightdress. I saw her eyes, they weren't focused. She didn't know where she was. My God – can someone tell me if she's still breathing?'

The faces of the people around were offering no consolation. Hilary moved silently forward.

There was a rug over her mother's body but she could see the familiar slippers peeking out the end. She held a Guard's arm to steady herself.

'It's my mother,' she said. 'I know it is. Those are her slippers.' Then she felt herself slipping down to the ground.

When Hilary came to, the crowd were still there. The ambulance had arrived and she saw her mother's body being lifted inside. Then a variety of hands helped Hilary in as well. She was to be treated for shock, they said.

Before they drove away Hilary said, 'Could someone please tell that poor man it wasn't his fault, my mother has been suffering from dementia, he has nothing to blame himself for . . .' Then she took a seat in the ambulance beside the lifeless body of her mother.

They had driven along this road two weeks ago to visit Lilac Court. Why had she not listened to everyone and put her mother in there? Jessica would have been alive and safe and none of this nightmare would be happening. It was all Hilary's fault.

She knew that she would by haunted by the thought for the rest of her days.

*

Declan's father organised a welcome home party in St Jarlath's Crescent on the day that his son was eventually allowed home. They had painted the outside of the house in his honour, although Fiona knew that Declan would hardly notice all the hard work that had gone into it. She would be sure to brief him properly; he must admire the window-boxes that Muttie Scarlet had planted, the smart new curtains that his mother had been sewing every night for three weeks.

'You're very good to go round there so often.' He held her hand as they walked the hospital corridor together. He was off his crutches now and only needed a stick.

'But don't I love it, Declan? Your ma and I are the best of friends. I mean it – we are.'

'She fusses so much, I was afraid she'd drive you crazy.'

'No, how could she drive me mad? Haven't we one thing in common – we're both mad about you!' laughed Fiona.

'She means so well, but I go crazy when she tells people how important I am.' Declan was struggling to be fair.

'Oh, I put her wise on that ages ago, I told her you were a great useless waste of space at the centre.'

'You didn't?'

'Of course I didn't, you eejit. I told her the truth, which is that you are a great doctor and they are all aching for you to get back.'

'My successor hasn't stolen your hearts away then?' Declan asked, knowing well that this was not the case. The locum had been a smart aleck of a fellow whom none of them liked much.

'Stop fishing and walk straighter, you'll have to make an entrance tomorrow. Oh, and don't forget to notice that your mother has a new outfit in honour of the occasion.'

'She actually spent something on *herself*?' Declan was astounded.

'Well, I got it for her, actually, in a thrift shop, she gave me the money.'

'You didn't go to a thrift shop?'

'I did too!' But Fiona wasn't a good liar. 'Oh, all right, I went to a shop but there was a sale on. It looks terrific on her. She wouldn't take it unless I said it was from the Vincent de Paul.'

'Who else is coming?'

'People from the clinic, some of your mates, your father's friend Muttie, his wife and those children or grandchildren who speak like aliens.'

Declan laughed. 'They were always great kids. They must be about sixteen now.'

'They're seventeen. They are saving up to go abroad during the spring break; they offered to be waiters and Muttie nearly beat the heads off them asking your ma and da for money. So they're going to help for free now.'

'We can't have them doing that. I'll slip them something. They're a great pair those two, they're no relation of Mutti's and Lizzie's at all, you know.'

'I didn't know. What are they doing there then?'

'God knows – lost in the mists of time, somebody couldn't keep them and they were cousins of Cathy's first husband . . . I think.'

'Cathy?'

'Now she *is* Muttie and Lizzie's daughter, I know that much. Is she coming to the party?'

'No, she's doing a big catering job for some boy band somewhere. Let no one say that St Jarlath's Crescent isn't the heart of the universe!'

'I'm exhausted already and I'm not even home yet,' Declan said.

'Then let's get you back to bed,' Fiona said.

'I wish . . .'

'Not at all – you're as frail as a day-old chick. You'd be no use to me,' she said. But she said it affectionately and as if she thought the days of total recovery were not far away.

Ania had made a great banner with *Welcome Home Declan* on it and it was strung between the two bedroom windows. The neighbours were all at their gates looking on and Paddy waved them in.

'The lad would love to see you,' he begged.

Declan's mother was resplendent in a dark purple dress with a lace collar. Her hair looked different and for once she didn't seem to be fussing. Declan could hardly take it in. There was no racing around asking people to sit here or there, she was relaxing with a glass of wine. He shook his head in disbelief.

Maud and Simon were like a courteous committee, almost as if they were representatives of another civilisation. Fiona was spot-on to say they spoke like aliens: that was exactly what they did, with one starting and the other finishing every sentence.

'Everyone in St Jarlath's Crescent wants you to feel very welcome . . .' Maud beamed.

'Back to your home after your great ordeal,' Simon continued.

'And to say how much the accident was regretted . . .' Maud added.

'Particularly by the family that owned the cat . . .' Simon looked very solemn.

As people often did talking to the twins, Declan felt increasingly disconcerted.

'The cat?'

'The cat that attracted Dimple's attention and made him run away from your father.' Maud spoke as if Declan might be now deranged as well as limping.

'I'd forgotten the cat,' Declan said truthfully.

'Oh well, she *will* be pleased to know that,' Simon said. 'She was afraid to come in to welcome you back . . .'

'The lady who owns the cat, that is. The cat herself has no memory of it at all,' Maud explained.

'Listen, I gather you're giving a bit of a hand with the party. I wanted to thank you.' Declan rustled for some euros in his pocket.

'Oh no, Declan, thank you but the matter of finance was raised . . .' Simon said.

'And turned out to be very inappropriate,' Maud finished.

'No, no, we can't have you working for nothing, everyone gets paid for their work,' Declan protested.

'It's a neighbourly gesture, not a job,' Maud said firmly. And that was that.

Declan looked around the small house in St Jarlath's Crescent in bewilderment. His mother seemed quite at ease entertaining the people from the clinic. She seemed to have had a personality change in the time that he had been in hospital. He listened as his mother told Clara Casey all about how hard Declan studied when he was young, but there was no fantasy about his being senior cardiologist any more. Molly was nodding her head eagerly with Lavender the dietician about the amount of protein there was in good lean meat, and she was offering Ania some hours in the launderette if she needed them.

Everything had changed since Mother and Fiona had got to know each other. What he had been trying to do for years, Fiona seemed to have achieved in a matter of a few short weeks. He looked at her proudly across the room, laughing and at ease, her curly hair tied up with a green ribbon that matched her eyes. Her friend, Barbara, helping her with everything including keeping Paddy Carroll's pint glass well topped up.

He wished he could spend some time alone with her, but Fiona had put her finger on his lips and said there was plenty of time for all that.

Later, when most of the guests had left and Maud and Simon were busy clearing up, Declan and Fiona asked them about their plans. They explained that they were going to Greece for the spring holiday; they hoped to get jobs in bars or restaurants.

'Do you know any Greek?' Fiona wondered.

'Not yet but we were sort of thinking . . .' Maud began.

'That we could pick it up as we went along,' Simon finished.

'I have a booklet I could give you, it's a help to know a few basics in advance,' Fiona offered.

'What did you work at when you were there?' Simon asked.

'Well, I didn't really work there . . .'

'It was a holiday?' Maud said.

'Sort of . . .' For once the confident Fiona looked less than comfortable. 'Here, you don't want to go through all the silly things I did. What you do want is a bit of advice and even a couple of introductions.'

'We'd love some advice,' said Maud.

'Could you sort of mark our card?' Simon asked.

'I think you should go to a small place, somewhere that hasn't become a big international tourist area. Then you get to know the people, and the place.'

'And would we just turn up . . . ?'

'With our words in basic Greek?'

'I'll tell you what I'll do. I'll write to a friend of mine in this lovely place on one of the islands and tell her that you might need a job.'

'Would you?'

'Is it a restaurant?'

'Well no, she runs a craft shop, but she has a great friend Andreas and he runs a taverna.'

'*Taverna*,' the twins repeated solemnly.

'The island is called Aghia Anna – look, find me a map and I'll show you . . .'

Declan's heart nearly burst with pride as the twins ran back home for their map of Greece. Knowing Fiona she would indeed be able to set them up.

He looked across at her as she traced her finger across the map. This was the road from Athens to Piraeus, which was the harbour town. Then they were to walk along the line of ferries heading out for the Greek islands. They must write down the name Aghia Anna in Greek letters so that they would recognise the words when they saw them. She was as enthusiastic as if she were going with them. He felt a catch in his breath. She wasn't just a girlfriend, not just a pretty nurse and part of a hospital romance. This was something totally different. As he watched her push the curls out of her eyes and behind her ears he realised that he couldn't live without this girl.

It was part of his life that she should be there, reacting and smiling and pealing with laughter. He needed her approval and her courage. He had to know what she thought about everything. She looked up suddenly to know were they boring him and caught him staring at her.

'What is it, Declan? Am I droning on too much?'

'You couldn't drone on. It just isn't in your vocabulary.' His voice sounded thick suddenly, as if he had a cold.

'Hey – I'm meant to be looking after you,' she said anxiously. 'Are you developing a wheeze?'

'No – it's something else entirely.'

'Like what exactly?'

'Like *emotion*, if you push me. You know, the way they say in books "His voice was husky with emotion" . . .'

'Oh, *Declan* – aren't you a scream!'

'I mean it,' he said simply. 'I was just looking at you and realising how precious you are to me.'

Maud and Simon pretended to study the map with huge intensity.

Fiona came over and kissed Declan lightly.

'And you to me,' she said. 'But I'll have to borrow your laptop. There have to be cheaper flights than the twins have found.'

He still held her hand a little and didn't take his eyes off her face. It was as if he was looking at her for the very first time. Nothing mattered as long as he could be with Fiona, at St Jarlath's Crescent, her parents' house, the flat she shared with Barbara, by the seaside. Anywhere. Suddenly it was clear to him. She was quite literally the centre of his life. And soon he would be back in the clinic working with her all day and he would see her every night.

When Declan came back to work in the heart clinic everyone was very supportive and he caught up on all the news surprisingly quickly. He had been away when Hilary's mother had died, but he knew the whole story from Fiona and he took the first opportunity to tell Hilary how sorry he was.

'She's at peace now,' he said to Hilary.

'Thank you, Declan. Another way of putting it is that I wouldn't be told, I wouldn't listen and she was killed by a car as a result.' Her voice was very flat.

'Don't think like that, it wouldn't bring her back.'

'No, but if I had listened to other people she wouldn't be dead. I can't forget that. I am allowed to feel ashamed and sad about it.'

'You loved your mother, what's bad about that?'

'You are very soothing, Declan, but we must not be bland.'

'No, I agree, I have a tendency to go down the bland route, but can I tell you something. If I hadn't had the accident, Fiona wouldn't have got to know my family so well, and they love her now. If it had just been a dinner, a roast that night, we would still be playing games and dancing round each other. Am I mad to think we were meant to be together? Is that too bland or is it just being grateful for how it turned out?'

'It hasn't turned out well for me.'

'Yet,' Declan said. 'A day will come when you are glad that she didn't spend years lost in a fog. Not yet, but believe me it will come.'

'She's a lucky girl, Fiona,' Hilary said.

And she watched Declan move towards his patients with their notes in his hand and a smile of reassurance on his face.

'Well, Joe, you're looking fit and well, I hope you feel as well inside. No palpitations?'

And it was as if he had never been away.

Hilary and Ania watched him, delighted to see him back.

'He is so important to this clinic,' Ania said in a solemn little voice.

'As are you Ania. This place couldn't function without you,' Hilary said with such sincerity in her voice that Ania's eyes filled with tears.

Chapter Four

It had been like a personal intervention of the Mother of God when Ania met Dr Clara Casey and got a job in the heart clinic.

Ania was the youngest of her family. She could not remember her father because she had been only three when he was killed in an accident. It had been a terrible day when poor Pawel had reversed his new lorry, which had been his pride and joy, into a deep quarry. He had only made the first payment on this truck which was going to change their finances. Papa would work all the hours that God sent and the family would be wealthy in their happy home. His daughters would marry men of substance in the area, his son Józef would join him in the business. Their name would be known all over the countryside as people who could be relied on.

Ania heard all this later. Because the story was so often told in her family she sometimes believed that she remembered that day, the day they brought the news home Papa was dead and the lorry had not been paid for. Two pieces of almost equally bad news, the way it was told.

So there was no wonderful family home, there was her poor mother, her Mamusia, who worked all the hours in the day to put food on the table. Her brother Józef joined no family company; instead he went north looking for work in Gdansk. At first he wrote and said he was in the shipyards and doing well and he sent Mama a little money. But then he met a woman from Gdynia and with the expense of setting up a home for himself and his new bride, soon the money stopped coming.

Her two sisters worked in a factory where they met men and married them. There was nothing for them at home now, better to start lives of their own. They would come by from time to time, complaining about their in-laws and how hard they worked.

'Stay single as long as you can, little Ania,' they warned. Not that this was hard for Ania to do: she was still very young and when she came home from school each day there was little enough time even to do any studying. Not that she was such a good student; but she had to help her mother while she lived at home. It was her job to get the irons ready to press the clothes that her mother mended. And it wasn't a matter of lovely, easy electric irons like now, with steam irons like today. Ania had learned to iron with great heavy things that warmed on the stove, and always with a damp cloth to protect the material. Woe betide anyone who left a scorch mark.

Mamusia always said that if you returned the clothes steamed and pressed to people when the alterations were done, they really appreciated the garment looking much smarter than it had before. It would encourage them to bring their skirts to be let out for a matronly figure or a school uniform adapted for a younger child.

Some other girls in her street went to the carnival when it came to town, and the circus, and they would meet for coffee and fizzy drinks in the café beside the bridge. But not Ania. There was always too much to do.

Mamusia was always cheerful and full of hope.

'We have our good name, little Ania, we have our standing here among these people. Your father was a respected man. We have managed to pay off what was owing on his lorry. We are people of honour. Nothing can bring us down.'

But Mamusia didn't know what was in store that would change everything.

When Ania was fifteen, Mamusia made her a birthday present of a little jacket trimmed with dark green velvet. A customer had bought too much and Mamusia had carefully put aside some of the small pieces that she snipped off.

Ania was delighted with her finery. Her dark hair looked very shiny and she thought that in fact she might not be that ugly after all. She had always seemed so scrawny and awkward compared to other girls, she hadn't known that she would look so well when dressed up.

She saved her little amount of money to go to the café with her best friend Lidia, to show off her new style. The other girls were very admiring and all the time she was aware that a dark-haired man was looking at her with some interest.

Eventually he introduced himself.

'I'm Marek,' he said. 'And you are very beautiful.' Nobody had ever said anything remotely like this before to Ania. She felt a lovely thrill of excitement. This man really thought she was beautiful – little Ania, Mamusia's little kitchen help.

'Thank you,' she said softly.

'What a pity they don't have a juke box here, we could dance,' he said.

'I'm not a good dancer.' Ania looked at the ground.

'I could teach you,' Marek said. 'I love to dance.'

'I might see you again . . .' Ania looked at him innocently.

'Yes, you might, but not in a dull, dead place like this. In the next town there is a good café called Motlawa. I go there most afternoons.'

And little Ania, who had never told her mother an untruth in her life, wove a long story about a friend at school whose mother had died and the funeral was in the next town. Her mother gave her the money for the bus fare and Ania set out alone for the Café Motlawa. She had washed her hair and put the juice of half a lemon in the rinsing water as Lidia had told her this made it shiny.

As she left the house her mother pressed a coin into her hand, to light a candle in the church for the poor soul who had died. Ania had never felt so guilty in her whole life. She spent the extra money on a lipstick and hoped against hope that this would be an afternoon that Marek was dropping in to the café.

She saw him immediately and there was music playing. He came straight over and stretched out both his arms. Soon they were dancing. It seemed as natural as anything to lean against him and feel his arms around her. They didn't talk much. They didn't need to. And then when she said she had to go to catch her bus, he walked her to the bus station.

'You look so beautiful in your green jacket,' he said. 'Like something from a forest, a nymph maybe.'

'It's my only good coat,' she admitted. 'You may get tired of looking at it.' Then she realised how forward she had been. 'I mean, that is if we were to see each other again . . .' She was full of confusion now.

He lifted her chin and gave her a gentle kiss. She could feel it on her lips all the way back on the bus, while she tried to make up some story about the funeral she was meant to have attended and to think up an excuse to go to the Café Motlawa again.

*

Love always finds a way.

Ania had read that and it was true. The local school teacher was having several outfits made but she needed smart buttons, much better than the local shop provided. Ania said that she remembered she had passed a shop that day when she had gone to her friend's mother's funeral. Perhaps she could go and spend a day in that town and see what she could find. Again, she felt overcome with guilt at her mother's gratitude.

'What a good daughter you are, Ania. I was truly blessed with you,' her mother said. 'When my Pawel was killed, when my Józef went away to Gdansk, I knew I could rely on you. Thank you, my daughter, thank you again.'

Ania found a shop in minutes which sold the right buttons. The old man told her to help herself from the box. He was short-sighted and couldn't see properly.

Ania had pocketed half a dozen tiny pearl buttons before she realised what she was doing. It would mean that she now had spending money. She was wearing her old navy blue jacket, which was very shabby but could easily be dressed up. So when she left the old man with the buttons in her pocket, she spent the extra money on a pink and white enamel brooch to pin on her jacket.

Marek said that she looked beautiful, and they danced together all afternoon. She saw people looking at her admiringly. None of them knew that she would spend the evening ironing the alterations her mother had been doing all day and then sewing on little pearl buttons that she had stolen.

'What do you do for a living, Ania?' he whispered in her ear.

So he didn't know she was a schoolgirl. 'I help in my mother's dress designing and tailoring business,' she said.

'And do you make much money doing that, little Ania?'

'No, very little.'

'You'd like money to buy beautiful things?'

'Oh yes – but wouldn't we all?'

'I love good clothes too, so I work to make money to buy them.' He was so handsome with his white teeth, his snowy white shirt, his black leather jacket and his dark grey, fine wool trousers. Just to look at him you would think he was a very wealthy man. And yet if he was why was he able to hang around cafés and dance for the afternoon instead of going to work?

It was a mystery.

So she asked him.

'I am waiting until I can afford a place of my own, Ania, a really good place. I don't like working for other people. It will happen one day. Meanwhile, I look and learn . . .'

Ania managed to find excuse after excuse to bring her to town and three months had gone by when he suggested that Ania miss the bus back to her village.

'I couldn't do that!' Ania said, shocked.

'You could stay with me for the whole night, we both want it . . .'

'But Mamusia?'

'Your Mamusia will be told you have missed the bus, you are staying with that friend whose mother died – remember? You will go back on the bus tomorrow morning . . .'

'No, Marek, I cannot.'

'Right.' He shrugged and already she could see that he was emotionally saying goodbye to her.

'I could do it next week,' she said hastily.

And he smiled his slow wonderful smile.

One of the reasons she had said no was because she was wearing such shabby underwear, an old grey slip, washed so many times it was shapeless and almost threadbare, a tired bra that had belonged to both of her sisters. If this were to happen, then she would be prepared.

For a week she sewed in her own room, adding lace here,

little rosebuds there. She also worked hard for her mother to lessen her guilt when the time came. It was an endless week, she missed a lot of classes at school and brought her sewing to the school bicycle shed to make sure that she finished the garments for her mother.

On Saturday, dressed from the skin out in her best, Ania got on the bus trembling. She was going to have sex for the very first time tonight. She was going to spend the whole night in Marek's arms. Her heart was beating so fast it made her dizzy.

'Be careful, little Ania,' her mother called.

For one moment, Ania wanted to run back and weep on her mother's shoulder, tell her everything. But the moment passed and she was on the bus.

By now, she knew some of the people in the Café Motlawa. They nodded at her and welcomed her as a regular.

Marek was waiting, leaning on the counter.

'*Dzień dobry*, Ania,' he greeted her formally.

'*Dzień dobry*, Marek,' she responded, shyly.

Then she was in his arms dancing to the music. Like always. Except that this time she was not going home to her mother.

Please, *please*, may it all be all right . . .

She had never stayed late like this before, so she saw them putting candles in bottles and watched the great romantic shadows flickering on the walls. Then she went to the telephone and called Mrs Żak who ran the corner shop back home.

Mrs Żak was horrified that Ania had missed the bus. 'Where will I tell your mother that you will stay, Ania?'

'With my school friend, Lidia, Mrs Żak, I will be home tomorrow.' Eventually, after what seemed an age, Mrs Żak hung up.

As Ania turned around she saw Marek was looking at her.

'You are beautiful Ania, and I love you,' he said.

'I have never done this before. I might not be very good at it,' she began.

'You will be wonderful and we will be very happy,' he said, putting his arms around her. They went to a room upstairs where there was a mattress and a rug on the floor. There was a jug with flowers in it, placed there by Marek. It wasn't wonderful but she felt very happy as she fell asleep in his arms. Next morning he went and got her a breakfast of coffee and rolls.

Nothing had ever seemed so magical.

Then, smiling at the whole world around her, she got the bus home.

Her mother suspected nothing when Ania got back. Her two sisters called that day and there was talk that one of them might be pregnant and a lot of excitement about the news. Ania was miles away in her mind, back in the Café Motlawa. There had to be a way that she could go back to Marek's town again, but it had been such a performance missing the bus once, she could never try that again.

She sewed and mended and ironed, her heart heavy at all that was nearly within her grasp but could so easily be snatched away.

The following day, when she went to Mrs Żak's shop to buy bread and vegetables she heard that the café on the bridge was for sale. The long thin miserable man who owned it had decided there was no future in selling coffee and cakes that were too expensive for the older people while the younger ones travelled on the bus to the next town for cafés that had music. So he was selling it as soon as he could.

'Let's hope nobody buys it who is going to make it a noisy place,' Mrs Żak said.

'Oh heavens,' Ania said.

'Because whoever does buy it may well want to have it as a bar.'

'That is true. Mrs Żak, can I also buy a stamp?' Ania asked.

Dear darling Marek,

You know the café on the bridge in our town? Well, it is now for sale. I remember you said you wanted your own place, so perhaps you could buy it and then I could see you every day. I would like this so very much.

Your loving Ania

The very next day he arrived. He brought his brother and another friend and they talked for hours to the man with the long, sepulchral face who ran the café. They explained they wanted a quiet family business, and that he would not find it easy to get buyers in such an out-of-the-way spot. There was a day of talking and small cups of coffee; and by late afternoon, a deal had been agreed. Marek, his brother and their friend would buy and refurbish the Bridge Café.

Marek and his partners had acted quickly and got a good price. By the time any other buyers had heard of the sale and shown some interest, it was over and done with. The next step was to apply for the liquor licence.

He knew better than to go to Ania's house when the business was concluded; her Mamusia sounded a force to be reckoned with. So instead he waited. He knew she would find him and she did.

Her eyes lit up as she saw him sitting on the bridge.

'Marek! You got my letter!' she cried.

'What letter?' he asked.

'I wrote to tell you about this café, it's for sale.'

'Not any longer, we bought it. Three hours ago!'

'Oh, Marek, how wonderful! This is what I prayed and prayed would happen . . .'

'And your prayers were answered, little Ania.'

'But how did you hear about it?'

'I heard,' he said.

She was disappointed for a moment, she had wanted to be the one who had steered him in the right direction. But she was so happy that he would be here it didn't matter.

'Imagine – we both had the same idea.'

'You had the same idea?'

'Yes, yes, I thought it would be wonderful, I wanted you to hear before anyone else. My letter will arrive tomorrow, and now it's already decided!' She clasped her hands with excitement about it all.

'You had the same idea? That you should come and work for us at our new café?' He sounded disbelieving.

Ania bit her lip. She hadn't thought of this – but why not? It would mean she could see Marek every day. But there was another hurdle to be overcome. Mamusia wouldn't hear of it. She would say Ania was too young to leave school. She wouldn't like her being associated with a café that sold alcohol to young people.

But she would think about all that later.

'I didn't put that bit about working for you, in my letter,' she began.

'But you will? You will, Ania?'

'Yes, of course I will.'

He could never have known how hard it was for her but Ania knew that Marek thought life was simple. You wanted to do something, you did it. He didn't have people like Mamusia, Mrs Żak, her sisters, her teachers. But better not to list the problems now. She would wait until the time was right.

The time became right sooner than she might have thought.

Marek had endeared himself to the formidable Mrs Żak, throwing himself on her mercy and saying he wanted a nice young girl from a good, honourable family who lived with her parents but who could work in the new café and attract a nice wholesome type of clientele.

Mrs Żak immediately told Ania's Mamusia.

'What a pity you are still at school,' Mamusia said. 'It would have been a wonderful job for you so near to home.'

'About school,' Ania began slowly. This was the most important moment of her life; she must not handle it badly. 'About school, Mamusia, the teacher was telling me only last week that she didn't see much purpose in my studying any more . . .'

'She said this!' Mamusia was stricken.

'Yes and at first I was upset because I could not see a way that I could earn a living and still help you, Mamusia. But now, possibly . . . who knows?'

'Do you think he might give you a job?' Mamusia's eyes were full of hope.

'We can only see,' Ania said and ran down the road to the café.

For the first few days Ania wore a blue and white check blouse and a dark blue skirt. She served coffee and cakes to people like Mrs Żak, her own Mamusia, two of the priests in the parish, the local doctor and some of the older neighbours. It was a deliberate attempt to win support and fight back any criticism. Ania's sisters said she was lucky to have found work so near home. Her sixteenth birthday came and went and she made no fuss of it, mainly because she didn't want Marek to know that she was still so young.

There was a small apartment above the café and Marek and his brother Roman and their partner Lev each had their own rooms. Ania secretly made curtains, cushions and a quilt for

Marek's room. She bought a picture of flowers in a field for him at a local auction, she found an old chest of drawers out in the back and sanded it and polished it for him. Soon she had Marek's room looking like a little palace.

She longed to come and live with him there. How happy she would be all day, going to get the bread and milk in the mornings, dealing with the deliveries, maybe visiting her mother once a day for an hour or two to help with the sewing and to chat.

But this was impossible.

Ania spent the first hours of the day sewing; then she went to the Bridge Café, helped to tidy up after the night before, aired the place and made herself useful while Marek, Roman and Lev drank coffee and talked about how to bring in more customers. One day they planned their big buy of a juke box. It would be expensive but soon it would pay for itself.

Not, of course, if Mrs Żak and Ania's Mamusia and their like were their only customers. Soon they would make a push to get in the younger generation.

The machine arrived and they stood around it in wonder, and when it sprang into life and into music all four of them danced around in celebration. Ania had never felt so happy and part of something marvellous.

Then they had to attract the young people. For one thing Ania must dress differently: right now she looked like a prim little schoolgirl. People would come to the Bridge Café to forget school and work, hoping to be transported to somewhere more exciting, and magical. Ania should wear a frilly black skirt and a low red top.

'Where would I get those kind of clothes?' Anna gasped.

'You are a dressmaker, you could make them,' Marek said and he sounded impatient. So she made them. Then Marek said that she should dance to give the others the idea of dancing too.

'You mean I get paid to dance with one of the bosses. This is okay!' she laughed happily.

'Yes, with me and, of course, with anyone else who asks you,' he said.

'But, Marek, I don't want to dance with strangers, I want to dance with *you*,' she protested.

'And I want to dance with you, Ania, but work is work, business is business. When they have all gone home we can dance together.'

'But I can't stay late, I have to go home after work,' Ania said with a trembling lip.

'Ania, are you beginning to nag and complain?' he asked. She dreaded hearing him talk like this. There was an edge of impatience in his voice. It would be followed by a lack of interest.

'Me? Nag? Complain? Never!' she laughed.

Marek rewarded her by putting his arms around her waist. 'That's my girl,' he said.

It was torture having to dance with clumsy men who groped her, watched by those who waited for the number to end so that they could do the same.

'We don't have enough girls coming here,' Marek complained. 'Can you go up to that school where you used to be, Ania, and tell the girls what a great place it is.'

So Ania went to the school and outside the playground gates she told the girls about the fun in the Bridge Café. Her best friend, Lidia, was wary at first, but promised to bring some of their old classmates along. Slowly they came to try it out. Nervously they came in, unsure, not knowing what to expect. Marek, Roman and Lev welcomed them warmly and danced with them. It was even worse torture to see Marek dancing with other girls, particularly that bossy girl Oliwia, whose father owned a large bakery. A girl always full of self-importance at school and now queening it over the café.

Marek laughed when Ania complained.

'She has plenty of money, Ania, she treats her friends to coming here. Is it not wise to encourage her?'

Ania thought Marek was being far too encouraging. She saw Oliwia's flushed face when she left the dance floor and there was no time for Ania to have those beautiful, soft, slow dances where she folded into Marek's arms so naturally. And she couldn't stay the night with him. They were able to steal a few hours in the early afternoon when business was slack and they could sneak up to Marek's room but it wasn't very satisfactory. They were always listening for one of the others to call upstairs to them.

Still Mamusia suspected nothing. One of Ania's sisters told her that the place was beginning to have a bit of a reputation. The word was out: young people were there drinking too much.

Ania said that simply couldn't be. Mrs Żak went there every day for her morning coffee. She would have been the first to complain if there were anything wrong, but she went in regularly. Ania didn't say that she had to be sure to have the place shining for her, with no sign of the previous night's bad behaviour. They had boxes by the back yard where they stacked the bottles. Then once a week they drove them in Roman's van to a recycling place. Nobody must be allowed to see just how many had gathered there.

One afternoon when they had a secret hour to spend together, Ania found a woman's hairpins in Marek's bed. The shock hit her like a physical blow as she held them up in horror.

'I don't wear any hairpins, Marek, where could these have come from?' she cried.

'Oh, I often curl my hair,' he laughed.

'Be serious, Marek. Have you had another girl here?'

His face was very hard. 'How *dare* you ask me that? How *dare* you accuse me like this? You know I love only you.'

'Well, how did they get here?'

'How do I know? Maybe one of the others brought a girl here. We are not policemen, we don't examine each other's movements . . .'

'The others have rooms of their own. This is our room.'

'Yes, well, whatever . . .' Marek said dismissively.

Ania sat shivering.

'Come on, Ania, we haven't much time,' he encouraged her.

But Ania got up and dressed quietly. She went downstairs and stood behind the bar.

'My, that was quick,' Roman said.

'Can you please pack your van with bottles? There are far too many of them cluttering up the yard.'

'Right, okay, peace,' he said.

'Have you ever slept in Marek's and my room, Roman?'

'I have my own room.' He looked indignant.

'I thought that was the case,' she said.

Roman realised he might have said the wrong thing.

'Maybe, perhaps I made a mistake – like, some night, you know, late. It's possible. I could have . . .' he said lamely.

Ania prepared the little *uszka* and *golabki* they served at lunchtime; she worked away steadily at the dumplings and the cabbage parcels and when Marek appeared disgruntled and complaining she took no notice. She talked instead to the customers.

'Ania, come here and listen to me,' he begged.

'It's business. You told me to make the customers happy. This is what I am trying to do.'

'Roman could have managed this – there are only four people here.'

'There will be more later.'

'Where *is* Roman?'

'Filling his van with empty bottles. I asked him to.'

'You're making a silly fuss over nothing, Ania.'

'I have worked for five hours. My arrangement here was for eight hours a day. When would you like the other three?'

There was something like respect in his face. 'Believe me, it's only you I love,' he said.

'There are ways of showing love and taking another girl to bed with you, a girl with hairpins, is not one of them.'

'I love no girl with hairpins. I love you.' His eyes were so big and true. He hadn't said he loved her for a long time now. She softened a little but not totally.

'So, which three hours, Marek?'

'It's not like you to look at the clock and count hours.'

'No, it's not. Which hours?'

'Come back at seven and we can dance together,' he said, giving in at last.

So Ania went home and helped her mother.

'You are very quiet today, Ania, normally you chatter and chatter.'

'I am a bit tired, Mamusia, that's all.'

So her mother nattered instead about the new baby who would be here soon and they must make clothes to welcome it, what would be best and how they could thread in blue or pink ribbons when they knew whether it was a boy or a girl.

After dinner, Ania walked back slowly to the Bridge Café.

'Come and sit with me,' Marek said.

'It's my working time,' Ania countered.

'No, it is not. Just come with me and we will look at the river together.' He held her hand and told her that he had never loved anyone but her. He stroked her gently, and whispered in her ear.

'I came to live in your town, I let you go home to your Mamusia every evening when I want you here with me. I dance with other girls to get business for the café, you dance with men for the same reason. What does it mean to you? Nothing at all except that it is building up the business. What does it mean to me? Nothing except that the day you and I can be together all the time comes a little nearer.'

She said nothing for a long time, and still he spoke and still he stroked.

'You know I love you?' he asked.

'Yes,' she said simply.

'So why the sad face?'

She managed a watery little smile. He still hadn't explained the hairpins in the bed. Or denied that there had been anyone there. With a dull ache in her heart she wondered who it was. Perhaps that Oliwia. The pushy girl whose father was a wealthy man. Lidia had mentioned something, but Ania hadn't paid any attention.

'Where is Oliwia tonight?' she asked, catching him by surprise.

'Oh, she doesn't come in every night,' Marek said.

'No, no, of course . . .' Ania stood up and went to the coffee machine. She put on a bright smile for the customers and out of the corner of her eye she saw Marek raise his thumb in the air as if to say 'good girl'.

Roman and Lev exchanged glances of relief. The crisis was over.

Oliwia was staying on at school until she was eighteen, and then she would go to university – or so she had told the crowd at the Bridge Café. But her plans changed. A few months after the Bridge Café had opened, Oliwia stopped talking about university. She said university was overrated and after all there was everything anyone could want nearer home.

Ania meant to discuss it with Marek but he was away a lot on business, trying to get some more investment in the café. The juke box hadn't paid for itself, the coffee machine hadn't paid for itself and even the wages they paid from the till every Friday were smaller.

She hoped he would find an investor soon. Roman and Lev seemed very unwilling to talk about it; possibly they were more worried than they let on about the debt. Still, she would know soon enough.

Mamusia had been in bed with a very bad cough and so Ania tried to fit her working hours around looking after her mother. She had come home to make fresh bread and prepare soup; Mamusia was looking a little stronger now and Ania decided to sit with her for a couple of hours.

'You are so much better now, Mamusia, you will be well in no time,' Ania said cheeringly.

'All I ask God and his mother is that I should live to see you settled with a good man and a home of your own. Then I will be happy to say goodbye to this world.'

Sometimes Ania wished she could tell Mamusia just how well settled she was, and that she had a home already waiting for her in the Bridge Café but she and Marek had decided not to tell anyone until they could be together openly. She walked back to the café. She could see immediately that there were plenty of people there, which was a relief. Marek would be pleased when he came back this evening.

Oliwia was there, the centre of attention; she was showing off her engagement ring, a small diamond which flashed around the café. Part of Ania was pleased with this development. It would mean that Oliwia would no longer come in and lounge around the place hoping that Marek would dance with her. But then, would he miss the business she brought to the place? Would Oliwia and her new husband still come to this café or would she be too busy furnishing some huge house bought by her father?

She was about to join the group admiring the ring when Marek came in the door.

'*There* he is!' cried Oliwia, and as if it were all in slow motion, Ania saw Oliwia run to his side and put her arm around his waist. And, impossible as it was to take in, Marek was smiling and accepting the congratulations and applause.

She felt faint. There had to be a mistake. Maybe they were doing this as a joke? Then everyone would laugh at her innocence and the fact that she had believed it. But it didn't look like a joke.

The room started to go around a little bit and she heard Marek's voice. He was speaking to his brother.

'Roman, take her outside *now*.'

She felt strong arms urging her out of the café into the yard and around the corner out of sight. She sat on an iron chair and looked at the little garden she had tried to plant here. The flowers she had watered and little stone rockery she had built. One day they would open a garden café here, they had agreed. For families and children. There would be swings and a see-saw.

Well, Ania had agreed this, Marek had just gone along with it. And now it wasn't going to happen. She saw that Lev had brought her a small glass of śliwowica. The smell of the strong plum brandy made her retch slightly, but the hot, burning taste seemed to bring her to her senses. This couldn't be happening. Marek could not do this to her.

She tried to stand up to go back into the café, but strong, gentle hands were pushing her back. She could hear Roman saying, 'Stay here, it is best. He will be coming out to you in a minute . . .'

She heard another cheer from inside the café.

'Why, Roman?' she asked him. 'Why did he do this?'

'Shush, shush . . .' Roman wiped away her tears with his grubby handkerchief. He put the glass of spirits to her mouth again but she pushed it away. Then she felt the hands loosen their grip on her.

Marek had arrived.

She looked up at him, her face tear-stained, as Roman and Lev went back into the café.

'Little Ania.' Marek knelt beside her and held her hand.

She said nothing, just stared past him at the flower bed which had once been a gutter until she had dug it and planted it and fed it, and got rid of the slugs and insects which had gathered to celebrate her little garden.

'Ania – this changes nothing,' Marek was saying over and over.

She looked at him eventually. 'How *exactly* does it change nothing?'

'We will still meet. You are the one I love. You *know* that.'

'I'm sorry?'

'But you know that what you and I have is special. Nothing can replace that.'

'You are going to marry Oliwia,' she said dully.

'Yes – but that makes no difference to us. We will still work together, have our room to go to for loving.' He was looking at her as if nothing had happened.

'Why are you going to marry Oliwia?' she asked.

'You know why,' he said.

'No. I don't. Why?'

'Because she's pregnant of course,' he said, as if it were the most normal thing in the world.

'I don't believe you.'

'Well, that's what happens.' He shrugged.

'And it's your baby?' Her eyes were huge.

'It's not a baby yet . . . and nobody's saying anything about that. But you did ask.'

'Of course I asked, Marek. I may be silly but I'm not a total fool. Of course I ask why the man who says he loves *me* and is going to marry *me* has made *another* woman pregnant and is going to marry *her*. Why should I not ask? And what do you *mean* nothing will change?'

'Nothing *needs* to change, Ania – it's up to you.'

'But if you're married to her . . .'

'She will be at home, her father is building her a big house. We can go on as before.'

'You are mad, Marek. You are cruel and mad.'

'I am a man who just got engaged to the daughter of a rich man in order to keep our café afloat. It has all to do with business and nothing to do with love. If you don't believe that then I am lost.'

'And so am I. Lost. Totally lost.'

'What will you do?'

'I don't know yet. Maybe I will die, maybe the river will close over my head.' She spoke very calmly.

'No, no – you can't think like that.'

'Nothing to live for now.'

'You will see, Ania, everything will be the same as before,' he said.

'I will go home now.'

'You'll come to work tomorrow?'

'I will see.'

From inside the café she heard them call, *'Mar-ek, Mar-ek!'*

'I had better go back,' he said.

'It was her hairpins in our bed.'

'It was business. It had nothing to do with love.'

'In *our* bed.'

'It will never happen again,' he said.

'No, of course, she will have her own marriage bed from now on,' Ania said bleakly.

Ania couldn't remember the weeks that followed. Only little incidents that happened here and there.

Her mother got well and strong again. Her sister's baby boy was born so Ania went to the trimmings shop in the next town and bought blue ribbons. The old man with the poor sight was there.

'You don't come here so often now,' he remarked.

'No, my reason for visiting here changed,' she said.

'And are you happier now?' he asked unexpectedly.

'No. I'm not happy. I don't see any reason for going on.'

'I felt like that once when my eyesight started to go. I wanted to go up to the north and swim far out to sea in the cold water and not come back. But then I thought perhaps I will have happiness even without good sight.'

She remembered the little pearl buttons she had stolen from him on her first visit.

'Oh, I realise I took extra buttons by mistake the first time I came to see you, I always forgot to tell you about them. I must pay for them. I can do so now. It was six little pearl buttons . . .'

He smiled a relaxed smile. 'I knew that one day you would remember.'

'You knew?' Her face burned with shame.

'And now you have.' He was pleased and vindicated in the goodness of people.

'Have you been happy since . . . since everything?' she asked.

'Yes, little one, very happy. What a waste it would have been to swim out into the North Sea.'

'I'll remember that,' she said. But she didn't remember much else.

She didn't remember whether she worked all the time in the Bridge Café and if Oliwia came in, and if Ania and Marek went up to the room that she had prepared so lovingly for them and their life together. She didn't remember the builders coming to put on the big extension, the long-planned dining room over the river. But they must have come. And people must have delivered furniture. Marek, Roman and Lev must have hired a chef and more waitresses.

And Oliwia must have gone into labour and had a baby daughter, because Ania did remember a big christening party at the Bridge Café and the little girl who was baptised Katarina. Ania must have met Oliwia's father but had no memory of him whatsoever. And she didn't remember why Lev had an argument and left, saying it was a family concern now and he was better out of it.

All she remembered was feeling numb; and occasionally Marek's lips on hers while he told her over and over that she must believe that she was dearly and deeply loved by him.

If she had heard this story about someone else Ania would have said that the woman must have been completely mad. And perhaps that's what she was: mad.

That was what her family thought. Her sisters each took her aside and said there had been serious gossip. People were saying that Ania was having an affair with Marek, a married man.

When Józef heard about it he decided that it was time to bring his wife down from the north to pay a visit. He spoke to Ania the first night they arrived. All they had left was their good name, he told her. Fortunately, no one had told their mother about what was going on. It must cease immediately.

Ania didn't remember much of Józef's visit. His wife Zofia went to visit the café.

'I can easily see why you fancy him,' she said, having inspected Marek. 'He's a handsome man, but he's only playing with you.'

Ania found herself asking her why she said that.

'He's a married man,' Zofia answered baldly.

'But he doesn't love her,' Ania explained.

'I know, I know, I'm sure that's true, you know. But he doesn't love you either. If you understood that you would be free.'

'I don't want to be free. I want to be near him all my days,' Ania said, visibly distraught.

'One day you will love someone else. You will be glad we spoke like this.'

'I am not upset that we spoke but I will never love anyone else and nobody else will love me . . .'

'I do wish you well,' said Zofia softly. 'If ever you want a holiday, come and see Józef and me. He is very silly, the way he puts things, but he is so fond of you. He's always telling me stories of you as a little girl.'

Ania supposed she cooked their meals for them, it was hard to recall. They were always thanking her for this meal or that. Her Mamusia was smiling and was of course overjoyed to see her son and she got on so well with his bride, Zofia.

'It's lonely without them,' Mamusia said sadly when they left.

'But they say they'll come back every year,' said Ania.

Mrs Żak told Ania that people were so shocked at her behaviour that they were going to take their work away from her mother.

'Will you leave my mother as well, over what they call my behaviour?' Ania asked.

'No, because I am your mother's lifelong friend. She has been a good, hardworking woman since your poor father died so tragically. It's not her fault that you can't respect other people's marriage vows.'

'Maybe other people will think as you do, Mrs Żak.'

'I wish I could agree. I am a business woman, a practical person. A lot of the other ladies here have no work outside the house. Too much time to gossip and make judgements. Mark my words – she will lose work over this . . .'

'Unless?'

'Unless you give up your foolish ways, Ania.'

'Thank you, Mrs Żak.'

She must have spoken to the shopkeeper again on many occasions; but there were months and months of a fog and she couldn't recall.

Then one day she saw her friend Lidia. Lidia was going to work in Ireland. There were huge opportunities there if you were prepared to work. Possibly Ania would come too? They could find adventures, a new life and earn money. Irish people were Catholics like here in Poland, so it wouldn't be so much of a change. Lidia had heard they were friendly there and made strangers welcome.

'Oh, but that's all right for you, Lidia, you studied English, you will be able to speak to them. I would be lost.'

'I'd help you in the beginning,' offered Lidia.

'No – I would hold you back.'

'You just don't want to leave him – isn't that it?'

'No, it's not that.'

'Of course that's what it is, Ania.'

'I'm not ready to leave yet.'

'So I'll give you my address there, and when you are ready you come to me.'

'You seem very sure I will come.'

'You will one day,' said Lidia confidently.

'It might not sound like love to you, Lidia, but it is,' said Ania sadly.

'Suppose he had somebody else?'

'But, Lidia, he does have somebody else, he has a wife and a daughter.'

'No – I mean as well as that.'

'Don't be ridiculous!'

'He does, Ania, believe me,' urged Lidia.

'Why should I?'

'She's a friend of my sister's, she says it's love. Just like you do.'

'It's not true.'

'Why would I tell you if it were a lie?'

'To make me come and work abroad with you, for company. I can't go. I can't leave Mamusia, or this place, or my sisters . . .'

'Or Marek,' Lidia ended for her. 'But you will one day, so I'll give you my address when I get there.'

'What's her name?'

'Who?'

'Your sister's friend?'

'It's Julita.'

'Right,' Ania said.

After that things became a bit clearer. It was as if a camera had come into focus. Ania remembered the weeks after she had heard about Julita. She had done nothing with the information, of course, except file it at the back of her mind in an area that was rarely disturbed. But Mamusia had started to complain that some of her old clients were finding what seemed like excuses for not coming to her any more. Her two sisters said that she was by now the talk of the town. The nice young priest asked her if anything was troubling her because he always had a good listening ear even if he might not be much help.

Ania met Lev, who worked in an ice cream factory now that he had left the Bridge Café. Ania had gone there to see if she could get a contract for her mother to make their overalls and uniforms.

'How is the café going?' he asked.

'It's going well I think. You know Marek, he doesn't tell us much.'

'He should have told you more, I always said that.' Lev shook his head. 'After all it was you who found the place for us.'

'No – I wrote to him but he already knew.'

'He didn't know, Ania, he just didn't want you to think that you had found it for him.'

'I'm sure it was some mix up . . .' she said.

And eventually she received a letter from her sister-in-law in Gdansk.

Dear Ania,

I don't know why I am writing this letter, but I liked you straight away when Józef and I came to visit.

A couple of weeks ago, we went to a trade fair, where people buy fittings for restaurants. We saw Marek there. He was looking at very expensive pancake-making equipment, what they call a creperie. We spoke to him but he didn't remember us at all so we didn't explain exactly who we were. He was with a very young girl called Julita.

Whatever you do in life I wish you luck and happiness.

Józef thinks we should leave well alone and say nothing, but I felt you should at last have this information to help you make your choice.

Love,

Zofia

'Where was Marek last week?' Ania asked Roman casually.

'Oh, he went to this trade fair, saw all kinds of great stuff there. I expect he ordered all kinds of stuff as well.'

'Can he afford it all?' They had long stopped calling it 'our' café, it was Marek's now and everyone knew it.

'Well, he has a fair amount of support from his father-in-law,' Roman said.

'Yes, as long as he keeps his nose clean,' Ania said.

'What do you mean?' Roman looked anxious.

'I don't know,' Ania said truthfully.

Marek came in that evening. She heard Roman warning him that she was in an odd mood, so he was very charming when he approached her.

'Lovely Ania, how well you look. Will you dance with the men tonight, make them thirsty, make them spend their money?'

'So that the creperie machine will soon pay for itself?' she asked.

'How do you know about that machine?' he asked suspiciously.

'Oh, me? I can see into people's souls. I see you have been interested in having a pancake machine.'

'Oh, and do you see that you are going to lower your frilly blouse and get those men dancing?'

'No, I don't see that. Oddly . . .'

He left her and went back to Roman. 'You're right, she is in a funny mood,' she heard him say.

Ania wandered out into the yard and picked some flowers. She arranged them in a glass and was about to bring them upstairs.

'Where are you going?' Marek barred her way.

'I've arranged some flowers for you. I was just taking them—'

'No, don't go up, the place is very untidy.'

'So what makes it any different from usual then?'

'Are you all right, Ania?'

'Yes, I'm fine.'

'Good. So I'll take them upstairs later.'

'Shall I stay tonight?'

'Well . . . perhaps not tonight.'

'I see.'

'Do you?' He was troubled.

'Yes, possibly Oliwia is becoming suspicious, and you will need her father to be your friend to pay for all the things you ordered at the trade fair.'

'How do you know I was at a trade fair?'

'You told me you were going to it, don't you remember?'

'No, I don't.'

'Oh, but you did, and Roman told me that you were there too. Why?'

'Nothing.'

'Am I right about Oliwia's father?'

'Sort of.'

'Weren't you lucky to hear about this place, Marek?' she asked him.

'Yes, yes, I was.'

'And who exactly did you hear it from?'

'I can't remember – it was all long ago now.' He was very uneasy now. It was so strange to see him like this. Always it had been Ania who had been apprehensive but not to-night.

She worked late, no dancing but a lot of serving and waiting on tables. Then she put on her jacket and began to walk home. Marek ran after her.

'Is something wrong, Ania? You have been very strange tonight,' he asked.

'No.' She carried on walking.

'I mean you know the situation. We are into Oliwia's father for so much money, you and I can't make any move at this stage. And of course little Katarina is getting older and sees things so she can't be around the café so much, which means I have to be up at the house more. But you know all that.'

'Yes.' Ania didn't break her stride.

'And you do realise that I love you and only you?'

'Sure.'

'So what's all the attitude about?'

'Go back, Marek, back to the café. Julita will wonder what has happened to you.'

'Julita?' He stopped as if shot. 'You mean Oliwia.'

'No. I mean Julita; she will be in a good mood because she has a lovely vase of flowers but she will wonder why you are not coming upstairs to see her.'

'I don't know what you're talking about,' he blustered.

'Goodbye, Marek.'

'What does this mean?' He was starting to look defeated.

'What it says. Goodbye.'

'You are leaving the café.'

'I have left.'

'But you can't do that, what about your wages . . . and . . . everything . . .'

'I have taken my wages from the till. I left a note.'

'What are you going to do?'

'I don't know.'

'You'll get over this – it's a silly fit. It's nothing.'

'No, I won't.'

'You got over my marrying Oliwia. You came back to my bed after that.'

'I know. Wasn't it extraordinary?' Ania said.

They were nearly at her house now and he realised he wasn't going to get any further tonight. 'Tomorrow, when all is calm, we will talk. There is a phrase, "Morning is wiser than night". Perhaps it's right.'

'Yes, perhaps.'

'See you tomorrow, Ania.'

'Goodbye, Marek.'

She did not close her eyes that night, which was just as well since there was a lot to be done. She finished a great mound of her mother's sewing work and left the garments neatly ironed, folded with labels on each one. Then she sat down and wrote a long letter to her mother. Once she got the first few lines, it was easy to write.

Dearest Mamusia,

I have been a poor daughter to you and I mean to make it up. I have been so very, very foolish, Mamusia, seeing love where there was no love, believing words which were not true and making myself into such a fool.

I have to go away. I will make it up to you, Mamusia, believe me, I will. I will go to Ireland with Lidia. But first I will tell you the whole story. No more lies, Mamusia. Just the whole sad stupid story . . .

Then it was simple. In fact Ania wondered why she had never told her before. She packed a suitcase to take with her and placed the rest of her clothes in a cardboard box in case they would be of any use to her sisters. She left the green jacket on top, the one her mother had trimmed with velvet. The outfit she had worn to attract Marek.

She left the pink and white enamel pin that she had bought to hold his attention, in a little box for her mother. Just before dawn she brought her mother breakfast in bed. Warm bread and honey and milky coffee.

Mamusia sat up in bed, delighted.

'It's not my birthday, Ania. Why did you do this?'

'I have to catch the early bus, Mamusia. Take your time getting up. Everything's done downstairs.'

'You are the best daughter in the world.'

'Go back to sleep, Mamusia.'

'See you this evening, little Ania.'

'Goodbye, Mamusia,' she said.

She had tidied and emptied her bedroom, and left the envelope of her savings on the kitchen table for Mamusia to find. She looked around the house for the last time and pulled the door after her.

From the next town she took a train to the city and a plane to Dublin; she had hardly any money left when she arrived. She owed it all to Mamusia who would now have to face life without her. She, Ania, would start saving all over again.

This was a rich, rich country with jobs everywhere. Lidia had been pleased when Ania telephoned that morning and had given her an address to go to. Her apartment was upstairs over a Polish restaurant and Ania would arrive late in the evening. If Lidia wasn't there, Ania could wait downstairs and have a coffee. Lidia would tell them she was coming.

Sitting in the bus leaving Dublin airport, she looked openmouthed at all the huge motorways, all the new buildings, the tall craggy cranes reaching up into the sky. As they drew nearer the city centre, she saw big houses, apartment blocks and buildings all lit up in the night sky. There were hundreds of young people moving around the wide streets and elegant squares. Had she arrived on a festival or during a carnival?

She showed the handwritten address to people and they waved her in the right direction. Soon she was in the Polish restaurant having a bowl of soup and talking to the friendly people who worked there.

Lidia would be back soon, they said. She worked in several bars and restaurants; they did not know which one it was tonight. And then Lidia came in and there were hugs and tears and the people who owned the restaurant offered them some plum brandy.

'Where are you going to work, Ania?' one of the waiters asked her.

'I don't know yet – I still feel I am in Poland,' she smiled.

'Maybe you could wash and iron our clothes here!'

'Oh, I would be very happy—'

'She would be very happy to see you well-dressed and smart,' Lidia interrupted.

'But why won't you come to work for us? Both of you?' the man said with a huge smile.

'Because if we had wanted to work for Polish no-hopers who drink a bucket of beer each a night then we wouldn't have come all this way. Plenty of those back home,' said Lidia cheerfully and she propelled Ania upstairs.

The apartment was small and poky. They had a tiny bed-room each.

'You didn't get a flatmate?' Ania asked in admiration.

'No . . .'

'You knew I'd come eventually?'

'When you were ready,' Lidia said.

It wasn't hard to get work in Dublin if you were prepared to clean floors, wash dishes, look after old people or stack shelves. But Ania's English was not good.

'Don't go where there are a lot of other Polish, you'll never learn English if you do that,' Lidia warned.

'Maybe I could go to an agency?'

'No, then you meet other immigrants all day, and the agency takes most of the money in any case. All we will do is ask around. They won't take you in a pub – not until you can work out what's a half one, a half and half, a black and tan – you could write a whole dictionary on the names of drinks,' Lidia said.

'And thank you for not asking questions, Lidia.'

'I'll hear eventually,' Lidia said.

Every week Ania wrote to her mother. She asked for news about Mamusia's health and about the baby nephew. She asked how Mrs Żak was and if the uniforms for Lev's ice cream factory were going well. She never mentioned the Bridge Café and its occupants. She told stories about Dublin, the wealth all around, the beautiful clothes; the handbags in stores costing a fortune, the young people who had cars that they parked at school and university. It was like the movies, it was just like Hollywood, she said over and over.

She got letters back that made her homesick even though her mother never mentioned Marek, and the occasional post-card from her sisters. She often longed to be in a small place where she would know everybody who passed by.

She got a short letter from her sister-in-law Zofia.

> *Well done, Ania. You are a young woman of great courage. I am glad you made this decision and I hope it works out well for you. I am sure that it will.*
>
> *And now I will tell you a secret. Before I met your brother I was involved with a man like Marek. He took and took and gave nothing. Only when I have found a good man do I see how bad the first one was. It will be the same with you. Good fortune in a strange land . . .*
>
> *Zofia*

And for the first few weeks, it was indeed a strange land.

Ania cleaned offices early in the morning: it meant getting up at 4 a.m. She also worked at a hairdresser's, washing the towels and sweeping up the floor. But these were just filling-in jobs when someone was on holiday or off sick. She had yet to get a job of her very own. She longed to approach a dressmaker or even a dry cleaner's and offer to do mending and alterations, but her English was still very poor. Who would want to pay someone who could only say *Please? Sorry? What did you say?*

She studied hard with a phrase book and went to English classes in a church centre. There she met Father Brian and made curtains for his club, and eventually did his ironing for him. She never missed Sunday mass.

Naturally she agreed to do the ironing for the people who ran the restaurant downstairs.

Lidia shook her head. 'They will just use you, they have no money themselves; they won't pay you . . .'

But they paid her in meals, so she was never hungry and she kept the euros she earned in a box under her bed. But now she had this really wonderful job in the heart clinic. Once there she had come on amazingly. She was a person of authority now, a member of the team. She had new friends who all helped her to speak English. She begged them to correct her if she got a word wrong, for how else would she learn? And Clara had taken her out to a restaurant to lunch the very first day and many times since then. She had become a friend of the nurses Fiona and Barbara and went to the cinema with them from time to time. Dr Declan's mother had got Ania some hours working in her launderette. Poor Hilary, who had lost her mother so tragically, was also a friend. Ania had helped her carry bag after bag of her late mother's clothes to charity shops. Hilary had a warm, friendly son called Nick, who was a great support to her; week by week she seemed to grow a little stronger.

She told Ania that she was a peaceable person to have around the house.

'Peaceable!' Ania repeated the word a few times.

'Don't mind me – I will only teach you mad English.'

'I like this word "peaceable",' Ania said. 'It's what I would like to be.'

And soon the letters Ania wrote to her mother were more about people than about the great wealth and glitter of a capital city. She was no more on the outside looking in; she was part of it all now. She wrote how she had helped Judy Murphy to wash her funny Jack Russell dogs, how she had met a great Polish priest called Father Tomasz who had invited them all to have a picnic at a shrine to St Ann in Rossmore. She wrote about Dr Declan and his terrible accident and how he was now back at work again.

She mentioned a very nice man called Carl, who was the son of one of the patients at the clinic. He was giving her English lessons and teaching her about Ireland at the same time. Carl was a real teacher in a real school and he had taken her to see a nativity play up there. Wasn't it amazing that all over the world children told the story of Baby Jesus in the same way?

'You might be even a little proud of me, Mamusia, if you saw me,' she wrote. 'I have learned to hold my head up high and greet people and I am never without work. I am saving and in about a year I will come back to Poland and give you all I have saved.'

Mamusia wrote back saying that she was always proud of Ania and it had nothing to do with saving money. Ania should spend money on herself. Go to a theatre maybe, buy a nice outfit and a piece of jewellery – that's what Mamusia would really like for her daughter.

And as Ireland became more and more real to Ania, Poland began to fade away. Apart from Mamusia's letters, the chat in the café downstairs and the girls she met at the church centre, she did not think or talk in Polish any more. In fact she told Lidia proudly that she even dreamed in English now. Which made it such a huge shock the night she came back home late and discovered Marek in the café.

Waiting for her.

She was tired. It had been a long evening and there hadn't been as many customers where she was working which resulted in even fewer tips. She had been thinking of taking a sandwich and a big milky coffee up to bed.

This was absolutely not what she wanted, her first confrontation with Marek after all this time.

'What a surprise!' she said in English.

He replied in Polish. 'How good it is to see you again. Oh, Ania, I've longed for this moment.'

'Yes,' she said, still in English, 'yes I'm sure you must have longed for it.'

He gave in and spoke in English too. 'And tell me – do you feel the same?'

'I feel tired, Marek. That's all.'

'Are you not pleased to see me?' He couldn't bring himself to believe the coolness of her response.

'Oh, everyone is always pleased to see you, Marek. Oliwia, yes, and Julita?'

'Julita is not around any more.'

'I am sure she has been replaced,' Ania said bitterly.

'You know there was never anyone but you.'

Ania smiled a tired smile. 'Oh, I know that,' she agreed. 'Where did Julita go?'

'I was sure that busybody Lidia told you all about the whole business, what happened at the café.'

'No, Lidia and I never talk about the café,' she said simply.

'As if I believed that . . .' he said.

'Go home to your wife, Marek.'

'No, Oliwia is not around either. There was a lot of trouble, her father got to hear about things, he was very angry.'

'That is sad, but it has nothing to do with me,' Ania said.

'It has, I want to start again. All over, from the beginning.'
He had a yearning look in his face.

'Are you mad?' she asked.

'Well, you did come back to my bed after I married Oliwia,' he said, aggrieved at her reaction.

'Yes, I did, and I have no idea why. It's a mystery to me. It's I who was mad at that time.'

'You were there because you loved me,' he explained, as if to a small child.

'Is this a holiday in Ireland?' she asked, changing the subject suddenly.

'No, I hear there's plenty of work here and with two friends I am going to open a club.'

'You are leaving the Bridge Café?'

'It's no longer mine to leave.'

'And your little daughter, Katarina?'

'She will not want to be bothered with me, she has her mother and her rich grandfather.'

'And why do you come to me?'

'When we have this club, I want you to come and work with me, it will be like before.'

'They don't have cafés like that in Ireland,' she said.

'It's going to be a lap-dancing club; they have those everywhere. And you, Ania, you dance so well . . .'

'But I don't dance naked around a pole or at people's tables in front of their faces.' She was appalled.

'You would be so good. You still look lovely, you haven't got fat and puffy like Oliwia has.'

'Goodnight, Marek.' She made a move to go upstairs, but he put his hand on her arm.

'Let me come with you.'

'Go home, Marek, go back, clear up the mess you made.' This time he held her arm more firmly, stopping her from leaving. Behind him, she could see the waiters come closer. Protectively.

'It's all right, he's going,' she said to them.

'You owe me – we owe it to each other to finish the dream.'

'That's what it was – a dream. On my part. On your part – I don't know. You never loved me. Never. Do you know what a relief it is for me to know that? For such a long time I thought you had loved me and I had somehow done some-thing to lose your love. This way it's much better. I have no fear of you any more. No fear of displeasing you . . .' She was aware that Lidia had come in, and was standing silently, sup-portively, at her side.

'Well, go on, bitch, why didn't you tell her?' Marek spat at Lidia.

'I didn't tell her because I didn't want her to find some excuse for you, to feel pity. I was afraid she still loved you and might find something to say in your defence.'

Marek reached towards Ania, but she pushed him away. She could hear the restaurant owner asking, 'What do we do now?'

Lidia was wordless. It was Ania's call.

It took her ten seconds. Then she said, 'He will go away.' She stood tall, as she had told her mother she did. She met people's eyes. She had nothing to apologise for.

It was a moment when they all recognised this, particularly Marek. He shrugged off the hands that been about to restrain him.

'It's all right, I'm going,' he said angrily. Then he turned back to Ania and said roughly, 'I did love you for a bit. Truly . . .'

'Goodbye, Marek,' she said, as she had said all those months ago, the night before she left Poland. But this time she really meant it.

She felt that she had been given a fresh chance, a new start.

It was as if she had been cleansed, the way she had felt when she went to Confession a while back. Her English was nearly good enough to go to Confession now in this country. Perhaps she could see that nice Father Flynn. She would do it this week.

Chapter Five

Brian Flynn hadn't known what to expect when the new Polish priest arrived in Rossmore. He certainly didn't expect that he would have a new best friend.

Tomasz was a cheerful, optimistic young man eager to do anything to help in the parish. He was the kind of priest that Brian thought he himself used to be twenty years back. Someone who believed that anything could be done if there was enough goodwill. Brian didn't really believe that any more. People didn't seem to *need* the Church these days, so what was he doing trying to be a bridge between God and the faithful?

Apart from a few elderly folk there was hardly anybody at his daily 10 a.m. mass. Once it had been the start of the day for women who went about their shopping afterwards and shop workers who used to slip in to his church for a quarter of an hour during their break. Schoolgirls praying for a good career or a handsome boyfriend came in to light a candle. The parents of sick children came in to seek help, the anxious and disturbed came looking for peace.

Where are they now? Either up at that Holy Well talking to St Ann or just getting on with life according to their own resources. Father Brian Flynn knew that if this was true and that people *were* managing on their own, then he should be pleased for them, and God would be pleased too. Why keep an empty ritual going if nobody needed it?

But then this way heresy lay. The next step would be to think that the Church had *no* role to play in salvation. And this was a road that Father Flynn did not want to travel. So he watched enviously as young Father Tomasz laboured on, organising processions which hardly anyone supported, and festivals that were largely ignored.

The days went on. Every morning he visited his mother who stayed in Neddy Nolan's house, a happy home where Neddy and Clare with their baby girl managed to combine looking after not only his mother but also the aged canon, and two confused brothers who used to work in a garden centre before the bypass came and changed the town. They had now totally transformed Neddy and Clare's garden and made it the envy of all Rossmore. Meanwhile, Clare was still teaching at the local convent school.

These were the kind of people who had replaced the Church, Brian Flynn would sometimes say to Tomasz when they played a game of chess at night. Tomasz said people like the Nolans hadn't replaced the Church, they had just added to it and wasn't it something to be celebrated rather than sighed over?

Tomasz learned three new words every evening. He particularly liked the word '*eejit*'.

'What does it signify exactly, Brian?' he asked.

As so often these days Brian Flynn felt at a loss. 'That fellow's an old eejit. It means he hasn't a great brain.'

'Is he mentally ill? Does *eejit* mean mentally ill?'

'No, no, it doesn't, it means that he behaves kind of foolishly.'

'Like he is going through a breakdown?'

'No, it's in his nature to do something sort of eejity. No, that's not much help. He's a bit of a gobdaw.'

'*Gobdaw!*' Tomasz cried, delighted. 'What a wonderful word! What is a *gobdaw*?'

It was a relief to turn to talk about the conference in Dublin, the day of lectures and seminars about the Church and the New Irish, the reaching out to immigrants, policies which were now becoming relevant to parishes all over the country.

Brian and Tomasz took the train to Dublin for the meeting. During the day the bishop approached Brian and explained that there was a great need for hardworking, energetic priests in Dublin's inner city.

'Oh, Your Grace, please don't take Tomasz from me now. He's such a livewire, such a force in Rossmore,' Brian begged.

'Who said anything about Father Tomasz? I was talking about you,' the bishop explained. And it was as simple as that. The process had begun. In a matter of three months Father Brian Flynn was transferred to a Dublin parish.

Nobody seemed to mind where he lived. The days were gone when the priest's house was a matter of concern and importance, but it was expected that he find somewhere to live fairly speedily. He had asked around and Johnny, a big, bluff guy with the looks of an all-in wrestler, said there was a flat going in the house where he lived. Not elegant, mind, but convenient, good pub round the corner, late-night shop up the street. The landlord didn't live on the premises which was always an advantage but of course come to think of it Brian wouldn't be throwing many wild parties. Anyway, the negotiation was done swiftly and Father Tomasz hired a van to bring Brian Flynn's few possessions up to Dublin.

'Take that nice warm rug, Brian, it might be cold here in the winter,' he begged.

'No, no, that rug belongs to the priest's house.' Brian struggled to be fair.

'*Jaysus*, you're like a pair of auld ones dividing up the assets after years of marriage,' Johnny said. Johnny had strong views about matrimony, all negative. 'I don't know what all this fuss is about clerical celibacy,' he would say, shaking his head in amazement. 'You're well out of it, I say, steer far away.'

'You only say that because you haven't met the right girl,' Brian would counter.

'There is no right girl, they're all the same. When I see fellows, normal fellows, wiping sick off their shoulders, changing nappies, being tormented by things going *wa-wa* for hours on end, I wonder has the world as we know it gone mad?'

'Well, if we were to follow your line of thinking, Johnny, the world as we know it would die out completely because no one would procreate at all.'

'No harm either,' Johnny would mutter.

Johnny's flat on the first floor was full of exercise equipment. The only books were fitness manuals. His fridge had health drinks and there was always a bowl of fresh fruit on his window sill. He was an easy-going, good-natured lad and very generous with his time and skills. He gave several exercise classes a week at the social centre and encouraged people to run with him in the parks, Brian included.

'We'll have to get that clerical stomach off of you, Father,' he would mock. 'If you're going to survive in the city you must be a much leaner lad.'

Tomasz had taught Brian some helpful phrases in Polish. He was far better at explaining the words of his language than Brian was about English and as the weeks went on Brian found that his work was much more in the nature of a social worker than the tradition and ritual of the priesthood.

This was no bad thing. If, at the end of the day, you had helped with housing or child support, or intervened to ensure that the minimum wage was being paid, it was often a better feeling than having offered prayers to God for something that would surely never happen. If he had the joyful attitude of Father Tomasz he would have seen virtue and value in both approaches.

He took a train to Rossmore every week to see his mother but as time went on she recognised him not at all. Neddy said he must have no worries, he would call Dr Dermot instantly if anything were to happen and in the meantime Mrs Flynn was content living in her early girlhood and hoping that the nice young man she had met on a day trip to the Isle of Man would get in touch.

'Was that your father, Brian?' Neddy asked kindly, always looking for a happy ending.

Brian knew his father had never been to the Isle of Man but kindness was a higher law. 'It was indeed,' he said and he saw Neddy's smile broaden.

Brian heard regularly from Neddy on matters such as his mother having developed a liking for St Ann's Well; and from his sister Judy, who had married Skunk Slattery; and sometimes parishioners wrote to him to thank him for what he had done in the past and to update him on miracle cures for drinking husbands, reconciliations in loveless marriages, successes of once wild children who had returned to their studies. But more usually credit for this was given to St Ann and her mad well.

Brian learned more about Dublin in his runs with Johnny than he had ever found out anywhere else. As he paused for breath he would find little known statues, memorials, that had escaped him. He discovered too that even in this big, wealthy, shiny city which was full of lights and bustle, there was intense loneliness. His heart went out to the young Eastern Europeans who clung to each other for company in this strange land. He learned to eat all kinds of strange, spiced foods; he had made discoveries about cabbage and meatballs that flabbergasted him. Brian Flynn, who used to be a two slices of meat, two boiled potatoes and carrots man, was now much more adventurous. And it was not hard to make friends.

Johnny had introduced him to Ania, a Polish girl who worked in the heart clinic where Johnny did physical exercises with the patients. Ania made curtains for Father Brian's flat and said she didn't want money because it was an honour to do a small service for a good father. Brian reminded her that Our Lord had said the labourer is worthy of his hire, and Ania had told him that God was indeed good. She had met a lady doctor in a car park who had given her a job with huge money and great importance and now she felt she could do anything, be anybody that she wanted. Sometimes she came to the evenings that Brian organised where he invited various Irish personalities to talk about the country to the newly arrived residents.

Ania explained that people loved these evenings on different levels. Some were really interested in the country where they had come to live, others were hoping to meet people who would give them jobs. A lot of them were cold and lonely and relished the thought of a warm room and company. Brian built on this last reason for attendance and arranged that there should always be something to eat and an urn of tea at the ready. He even introduced a log fire, which they loved, and decorated the hall with pictures of Irish treasures or castles or beauty spots. He worried that they all worked too hard to earn money and didn't get to know the country where they had come to live.

It was on New Year's Eve that Brian met Eileen Edwards. Eileen had heard about the social centre and wanted to be part of it. Gently, Brian told her it was really a drop-in and welcoming place for recently arrived immigrants, but Eileen insisted.

'I've heard you mention it at mass, Father. I am one of your parishioners and I would like to be involved, if you see what I mean.'

Brian didn't really see what she meant. She was in her mid-twenties, a good-looking blonde with long curly hair, well dressed in leather jackets. She lived in one of the very up-market apartment blocks nearby. She told Brian that she was a freelance writer, but her real problem was that she had an allowance from her father so she wasn't *hungry* enough to write, if he knew what she meant. Again, he didn't really know what she meant. To him it was simple, you were a writer or you weren't a writer. But then what did he know? Here she was, a kind parishioner wanting to help. He must find her something to do.

Gradually, Eileen Edwards became part of life around Father Flynn's social centre. She helped to teach English conversation classes. She was often there, pouring out the great tea urn. Always dressed as if she was going out somewhere very smart. Sometimes she let the girls in the centre try on her jackets. She told them about her apartment where she had a special closet just for shoes.

'She's slumming it, Brian, that's what she's at. She's only here looking for a bit of rough!'

'Ah, Johnny, always the hard word,' Brian said, shaking his head.

'But what else could it be, Brian? Hanging round here looking everyone up and down.'

'And has she hit on you yet?' Brian asked with interest. 'I mean she couldn't get a better example of rough than yourself. Broken nose and all.'

Johnny took no offence, he thought about it seriously. 'No, she hasn't come on to me at all. She'd get short shrift if she did. No, I think it's *you* she fancies.'

'Me?' Brian Flynn was astounded. 'A fat, middle-aged priest!'

'Of course you'd give up the whole priest business and be normal like the rest of us,' Johnny suggested.

'Normal? You? You're insane, Johnny, that's what you are.'

'I think I might be, all right,' Johnny agreed. 'The only cure for insanity is a pint.'

'I don't know why you drag me on these punishing walks then fill me up with beer again,' Brian grumbled.

'Someone's got to look after your social life before we let that lulu drag you down,' Johnny said.

Brian laughed at him. Johnny was a man who saw drama everywhere and predatory women round every corner.

But he wasn't the only one who took against Eileen Edwards. Judy Slattery, Father Flynn's sister, had taken against her, too.

Judy was married to a man back in Rossmore whom everyone else called Skunk, but she always addressed as Sebastian. She had found her husband through St Ann's Well and would hear nothing against the saint or the so-called superstition surrounding her shrine. She was obsessed with trying to get her husband's name – which was and had always been Skunk – changed to Sebastian. Skunk had turned out to be not only the name of an offensive and smelly animal, but also some horrible drug. Sebastian must not have such connections.

Sometimes her conversations with Brian could become quite sharp. Skunk Slattery was a great peacemaker.

'Will you leave the poor man alone, Judy, isn't he only a confused cleric who doesn't know whether he's coming or going. Let him have his little rants and raves about St Ann. It makes him feel adventurous.'

There was no Skunk around to keep the peace when Judy dropped in to see her brother in Dublin.

'What do you have that troublesome girl hanging round here for?' she asked.

'She helps. She's a volunteer.' Brian was vague.

'I'd say there isn't much *she* wouldn't volunteer for.' Judy was disapproving.

'Why don't you like her, Judy? She's harmless and possibly a bit lonely.'

'Hmm. I don't like the way she refers to you . . . Oh, I'm teaching Brian to text message; oh, I think Brian must learn the email; oh, Brian's doing *such* a good job with these people.'

'Mimicking someone is always very cruel.' Brian was cross now. 'She can't help it if she speaks in a posh accent.'

'I'm not *talking* about her accent, I'm talking about what she says.' Judy was spoiling for a fight.

'Well, that's all true. She *is* teaching me how to use email. She *has* taught me to text. All of this is very useful.' You could hear Judy's snort at the other side of the Liffey.

A few days later Eileen turned up at Father Flynn's ground-floor flat.

'Hello?' he said, surprised.

'Well, I thought you sounded lonely in your email.'

'My email?' Brian was bewildered.

'Yes, the one you sent a couple of hours ago,' Eileen said.

'No, I didn't send any email, Eileen.'

'But you *did*, Brian. Look . . .' She produced a sheet of typed paper from her handbag.

'I need my glasses,' he said.

'Then invite me in rather than leaving me to stand at the doorway.' Unwillingly he asked her into his simple place. When Eileen saw it she screamed in horror.

'*Brian*, you can't live with that carpet, it's ancient!'

'I didn't notice,' he said.

'And there's not a matching chair in the place, it's like a

first-year student's flat. And that lumpy, bumpy sofa. Really, Brian, you deserve better than this.' She shook her head.

'I'm fine here, thank you, Eileen,' he said and she seemed to notice the hint of resentment in his voice.

'No, I didn't mean to criticise, I just wanted you to know how *valuable* you are to everyone here. You should look after yourself more, give yourself a little comfort. I bet you haven't even got a proper kitchen . . .' Without being invited, she went into his kitchen and looked around it sadly, tutting and clucking to herself. 'Look at all those uneven surfaces, look at that cold floor, that torn lino . . .' And before he could stop her, she had gone into his bedroom, seen his tousled bed, the clothes rail on wheels which served him as a wardrobe. The walls were covered with soccer posters hastily stuck up to cover damp or stained portions of wallpaper.

Quite.

As he loosened his collar with his finger, Brian felt very uneasy. Could there possibly be anything in what Johnny had suggested? Then he pulled himself sharply together. Eileen Edwards was a beautiful twenty-five-year-old girl, he was a fat middle-aged priest. Was he going mad thinking she might fancy him!

Eileen had got out a notebook and was beginning to make a list. Brian knew that this must be cut short immediately. 'It's very kind of you, Eileen, and I know you mean well but actually you're not helping me at all. I am blind to my surroundings really and this carpet and this place are just fine with me. So I'll have to ask you to let me go my way.'

'But, Brian, your shirts aren't even ironed. I mean, really.'

'They're drip dry,' he said plaintively.

'No, they're not. They're all wrinkled and crushed. You need a nice, kind girl to do your ironing for you every week.'

'Please, Eileen.'

'No, be serious, when you were a priest in Rossmore did someone iron for you there?'

'Anna, who was married to Józef. They did ironing, I suppose.'

'You suppose! Imagine, you don't even know!' She professed to be amazed.

'Well, it didn't seem very important.'

'It *is* important if you meet people, people of substance, who might help you and the centre. What will they think if you turn up looking like a hooligan? Who would advance you money or support then?'

He was anxious that she should be gone. 'I won't keep you any more, Eileen, and as I say I thank you for your interest. I *will* think about it all, I promise, but I couldn't have you doing my ironing for me . . .'

Eileen gave a scream.

'*Me?* You thought I was offering to do your ironing? Oh Lord, what an idea!'

He felt his face and neck redden. 'I'm sorry, I thought you said I needed a kind girl to do it.'

'I didn't mean that *I* would do it. The centre is full of girls who go out to clean houses, they'd do it quick as look at you.'

'Yes, of course. Sorry,' he mumbled.

'And I wouldn't have come round at all only that your email seemed to suggest that you needed company.'

'I didn't send any email, Eileen, I told you I didn't.'

'What's this then?' And Brian Flynn found himself reading a sheet of typed paper which indeed did purport to come from him. It said that the evenings were long and lonesome and that a bit of pleasant company would never go amiss.

'What was I to think?' Eileen opened up her china-blue eyes in puzzlement.

'I'm sorry, Eileen, I didn't write it,' he said.

'Well, it's got your name, your email address.' And, true, it did say it was from Father Brian which was his email name.

'Okay, Brian, so the moment has passed,' she said, forgiving, understanding, all-knowing.

'There was no moment to pass,' he said despairingly.

She just looked down at the sheet of paper again. It was as if she rested her case.

Brian Flynn didn't sleep well that night. He examined all the possible explanations. None of them seemed reasonable or good. He said mass next morning and shook the hands of those who had come to pray.

'It would be wonderful if you had a Polish priest to give us a sermon some time,' little Ania said. She and Lidia were there as usual and Ania always spoke to Brian as she left the church. Suddenly the thought came to Brian that he would invite his friend Tomasz to preach once a month. Tomasz would love it, the people here would love him. His tired face lit up with pleasure thinking of how he would arrange it.

'Oh and Father, Eileen was telling me you needed someone to do your ironing. It would be an honour for me—'

'No, Ania, Eileen got it wrong.'

'But she said she was in your flat last night having supper and you said your clothes looked crumpled and not like the clothes of a man who dined with gentlemen and she wondered would I—'

'No, Ania, many thanks but no. And Eileen did *not* have supper in my flat last night or any night. She called with some cracked email that I was meant to have written to her.'

'She says you are very good at the email now, that you write her many letters.' Ania wanted to give praise where it was due.

'I have written her *no* letters. But, Ania, why am I shouting at *you*? This is all a misunderstanding that's all.'

'I know, Father Brian.' The girl's grey eyes were kind and

sympathetic. They were not the cold, china-blue, slightly mad eyes of Eileen.

Brian Flynn got on with his day, a heavy feeling of dread around his heart.

Tomasz was very excited by the chance of speaking to his fellow Poles. He wondered where he could stay in Dublin, everywhere seemed too expensive to him. 'You could stay in my place for free,' Brian offered. 'There's a lumpy sofa but with a few cushions it should be all right.' Tomasz thought that was a great idea and they fixed a date.

Tomasz emailed him a few lines in Polish saying what he was going to talk about. Brian picked it up at the internet café. Out of interest he asked the proprietor was it possible to send an email pretending to come from someone else.

'Only if you knew their password,' the man said.

So that was that. Brian knew that nobody knew his password. So what could have happened? Had he in fact in a moment of madness really written that letter to Eileen? Was he losing touch with reality?

Father Tomasz loved the old cobbled streets and tiny restaurants in Brian Flynn's part of Dublin. He had a half-pint with Johnny and a mate of his, Tim, the security man at the heart clinic. He did a tour of the centre, discussed the next day's mass, and came back via a cheap Indian restaurant to Brian's place.

'It's lovely, Brian, haven't you everything you need here,' he admired. Brian got a lump in his throat. This was what he had wanted to hear, not that he was a pitiable loser. The men sat and talked happily about Rossmore, the canon, Neddy Nolan, Skunk and Judy's new bookshop and the goings-on up at the Ferns and Heathers.

At midnight Brian Flynn got a text message. 'No, Brian, it's too late tonight, it wouldn't be wise to come and see you. We'll meet tomorrow. Stay cheerful, try to sleep and don't contact me again like a good lamb.' It was signed, 'love, Eileen'.

Brian showed the text message to Tomasz. 'The only thing is that I *didn't* contact her,' he said with a sad face like a bloodhound.

They talked late into the night. Tomasz was full of theories. Maybe Brian's kind manner had given Eileen some sort of false encouragement? But that couldn't explain these emails and text messages that she claimed to have got from him. Possibly she was a reformer, someone who had to change other people. That might be why she felt free to walk through his house commenting and criticising.

Yes. But it still didn't explain the messages.

'Perhaps she is a mad person,' Tomasz said eventually.

'Yes, I think that must be it,' Brian agreed sadly.

They had another mug of tea and sighed over it all.

'Maybe you could get in touch with her family?' Tomasz suggested.

'I don't think she is close to them. She talks about her father giving her an allowance. She never says anything about them. Any of them.'

'And does she live alone?'

'Yes, I think so.'

'You don't know much about her, Brian?'

'You're right, Tomasz, I hardly know anything about her at all.'

Johnny was in the heart clinic doing cardiac exercises with a group of patients. The group included Kitty Reilly, who kept insisting that any good health or improvement was due to the direct intervention of some saint or other and blamed the world in general for ignoring this saint whenever she was not feeling great. There was the kindly Judy Murphy who was now so fit that she was like an assistant to Johnny, helping the

wild, flailing limbs of people like Lar to stay some way contained. Bobby Walsh with his anxious, sad face, said that he
would do anything to get more strength in his arms, so Johnny
had put him for a sustained period on the arm machine.
Everyone was getting along fine at their various stations when
Clara came in.

'An urgent phone call for you, Johnny,' she said.

Johnny was surprised. Who could be ringing him at the
heart clinic? His mobile phone was on answer. He could have
got the message later.

'I'm sorry, Clara, I don't know what it's about.'

'It's a priest, a Father Flynn, he sounds very distressed. Go
and deal with it, Johnny, I'll supervise the class here.'

'Oh good, we can relax a bit now that the sergeant major
has gone,' said Lar with some relief.

'Oho, you haven't seen me in action. I'm a devil for the
treadmill,' Clara Casey said. 'You'll be praying for Johnny to
come back, believe me.'

'Hello, Brian, how's tricks?'

'Not good, Johnny: that Eileen came up to me after the
Polish mass today and said I'd asked her out tonight and that
she was buying a slinky black number.'

'What?'

'A dress, I think she meant.'

'I know that's what she meant. But you didn't ask her out,
did you?'

'Of course I didn't. So what am I to do, Johnny?'

'I think it's a sign you should give up being a druid once
and for all. That's what it's saying to me.'

'I'm serious, Johnny.'

'So am I. If you can pull good-looking birds while you're
inside the system *think* what you could do when you shake
yourself free.'

There was a silence.

'I'm sorry, Brian, she's a nutter, that's all.'

'Probably, yes.'

'So treat her as one, ignore her.'

'That's hardly the way to deal with disturbed people.'

'No? Then get yourself a slinky black number too and hit the town.'

'Sorry for having interrupted your work.' Brian's voice was clipped.

'Jesus, Brian, I'll buy you a pint at lunchtime, try to put old loony tunes out of your mind.'

'Sure. Fine,' said Father Brian Flynn and hung up.

Ania watched Johnny as he too put the phone down.

'Does poor Father Brian have problems?' she asked.

'Yeah, he does a bit.' Johnny didn't want to tell any secrets and start gossip.

'He is such a kind man and he lives so simply. I iron a few shirts for him. I see how little he has in his flat.'

'Would you iron *my* shirts, Ania?'

'Yes, but you would have to pay me. To do work for a holy priest is an honour, a privilege, not for a gymnastic person like you.'

'Your English is getting better every day, Ania,' Johnny said.

'Well, if you lived in a place where they only spoke Polish you too would learn the language,' Ania said to him.

'Oh no, I couldn't learn your language. It's all Ws and Zs.'

'Sorry for that.' Johnny came back to the exercise room. Bobby hadn't fallen over anything and some of them were moving at a brisker pace.

'Your friend, the priest, is he all right? He sounded very stressed,' Clara enquired.

'He's stressed all right, he has a stalker, a mad one

178

altogether. Keeps claiming that he's asking her out. Poor Brian wouldn't do that in a million years. He must be the only one in the Church who has always kept the rules.'

'There are a few, certainly,' Clara agreed.

'He wants to know what to do,' Johnny said.

'Only one thing he can do.' To Clara it was simple. 'He has to go to the Guards.'

'Are you out of your mind? Go to the Guards?' Brian said to him in the pub as they had a pint and a sandwich.

'They'd stop her antics. What's she doing now?'

'She's showing everyone these text messages and emails that I am meant to have sent her.'

'But they weren't sent on your phone?' Johnny was bewildered.

'Apparently they were. She showed me. It was my mobile number on the top. I don't know how it works. Could she have transferred it or something?'

'I don't think so. Could she have found your phone and borrowed it, so to speak?'

'I don't see how. I nearly always have it on me.'

'And about the email?'

'It came from the internet café down the road where I *do* send emails from.'

'And would she have known your password?'

'No. She made a great play out of telling me to keep it to myself when she was teaching me. She said she would look away when I was putting it in.'

'Maybe she didn't look away at all. Brian, she's unhinged. We *do* need to tell the Guards.'

'I can't land in on her like that. I'd have to tell her first. It's only fair.'

'She hasn't played fair with you.'

'No, but that's different.' As usual Brian found excuses for people.

'Because she isn't playing with the full deck?'

'Something like that. I will have to warn her, then maybe it will stop.'

'And maybe we'll see little pink pigs flying over the Dublin Mountains,' said Johnny, who was not of a naturally optimistic frame of mind.

It wasn't hard to find Eileen Edwards. She was having a coffee at the social centre, talking animatedly to the girls, telling them about a new handbag she had bought. There were only thirty-six of them in Ireland. She had stood in line and queued for it in Grafton Street. The girls listened, fascinated. Eileen came from another world. A world they were dying to join.

'Can I have a word, there has been a mix-up about arrangements?' Brian said and sat down at a table in full view of all the others. Eileen was not going to claim that they had a secret meeting or anything.

'Oh well, if it's *private*,' she simpered at him.

'No, it's not private. It's just that you made a mistake. There was no arrangement to meet you this evening.'

'I have your text message.' She flashed her phone at him triumphantly.

'Well, that's what I mean. Somebody must be playing games because I didn't write that message you showed me this morning.'

'It came from your phone, Brian,' she said, her eyes dancing.

'That's what we are going to have to investigate. The Guards will help us find the solution.'

'The Guards?' Her eyes widened.

'Yes, they have people who can trace these calls and emails. We have to find out what's happening.'

'And you are willing to let the Guards know all about our . . . relationship.'

'We don't *have* a relationship, Eileen.'

'No? They might be surprised how I know all about your bedroom and the posters for Real Madrid and Sunderland on the walls, the bathroom with the big, old-fashioned water heater, the lumpy sofa in the sitting room. How could I know all these things if you haven't invited me in to your flat?'

'Eileen!' His big, honest face was aghast at her cunning.

'No use saying my name like that, Brian. You told me that I was special, that you would get released from your vows to marry me. You introduced me to your friend James O'Connor who was an ex-priest . . .'

'I introduced you because you came and stood by us for so long in Corrigans I had to do something. Listen to me, Eileen, stop this thing, whatever it is, before it gets started. You're a beautiful young woman. You can have a life of your own, *should* have a life of your own.'

'You always tell me I am beautiful,' she said dreamily, 'but that's not what I want to hear. I want to hear *when* we can be open about what we have.'

'What we have? We have *nothing*, Eileen. Come to your senses, for heaven's sake.'

'You've committed yourself to me, there's no way you are wriggling out of it now.'

'You know this is nonsense—' he began.

'Well, tell the Guards then, see if I care.' She looked very young and vacant as she spoke.

'I will tell them, Eileen, for your sake as well as mine. You need help.'

'Not from the Guards I don't. Anyway, they won't believe you. Just another priest with a panic attack. That's what they'll think.'

'Suppose they do believe me and give you a caution,' he said.

'Then I'll go to the newspapers. The way I was treated here is shameful. Building up my hopes, promising me the sun, moon and stars and when you had your way with me, just backing out.'

'Eileen, I beg you, you're not well . . .'

'No, of course I am not well if you throw everything back in my face, and take away my future.'

'But your parents, Eileen. Your family, what would they say? Can't they help you? If I could meet them and explain.'

'Nothing you would say would make any difference to them. They would see you as a priest who abused your position. So, what time are we meeting tonight and where are you taking me?'

'We are not meeting. I am taking you nowhere.'

'Oh well, have it your way, but if they find my body in the Liffey, you can be quite sure they'll find the whole explanation in my apartment. Details. Pictures. Everything.'

Brian sighed, 'Eileen, the Guards wouldn't *give* that kind of thing to the tabloid papers. It's just the ravings of someone who is a bit upset. Disturbed even.'

'Oh well then, I had better go straight to the papers,' she said cheerfully.

'There's nothing between us, Eileen,' he began.

'You're right. There's not now. Only a lot of hurt and disappointment,' she said.

'There never *was* anything. Anything at all.'

'Yes, I can see. It's all tidied away for you and you expect the same from me.'

He spoke gently now. 'There was nothing *to* tidy away. I beg you, think back, think clearly.'

'I'm very clear, thank you. Crystal clear. You've moved on, found someone else. But I owe it to her and the many others to go public on this.' And she picked up her new handbag and flounced out of the coffee area.

Brian went back to his flat. He was deadly tired. He needed to lie down and rest. Maybe an idea would come to him. He sat at his table and thought for a long time. Wasn't it sad to have lived this long and have no one to turn to? His own mother didn't recognise him. His sister would only say, 'I warned you!'

He couldn't ask the bishop as His Grace would undoubtedly think that Brian had been somehow inappropriate.

He thought suddenly of James O'Connor who had been ordained with him all those years ago. James was always so definite and certain. He had wanted to be a priest, missionary even, then he met this woman and he wanted to be a married man. Once he knew that was what he wanted, he set about it without a backward glance. He even managed to convince his parents that what he was doing was right. James was the man to consult.

And Johnny, who was always such a great, solid mass of common sense. Johnny had no time for nonsense. He once told Brian that he had never dreamed, he actually didn't know what people were talking about when they said they dreamed of this or that. He might well know what to do. Maybe they would be able to find a way out. As he was considering calling him, Brian got a phone call from Neddy Nolan.

'The most extraordinary thing, Brian. You know the way your mother often has a problem remembering who people are.'

'Yeah, I do. Mainly Judy and myself.'

'Well, she's convinced that you have left the priesthood and got married. She said she got a phone call telling her that your wedding is in Dublin next month and she wants to go to the wedding.'

'God Almighty.'

'Well, I'm only telling you this, Brian, because she told Father Tomasz and he hit the roof. I tried to explain to Father that poor Mrs Flynn had trouble sorting out fact from a kind of dream world but I didn't do a good job. Father Tomasz has been here all morning asking me who could possibly have telephoned your mother. Then he kept saying "bad bad woman" and assured me he did not mean your mother, so I didn't know what to do, you see . . .'

Brian Flynn could see poor Neddy confused and trying to do what was best.

'So I asked Clare and she said I should call you myself. If you *were* getting married then you wouldn't mind us knowing and if you weren't then you'd know what to do.'

'The answer is *no* to everything, Neddy. No, I'm not getting married and no, I don't have any idea what to do.'

'Tomasz?'

'Is that you, Brian? You heard?'

'Did she really ring and ask to speak to my mother?'

'Yes, she must have. The carer answered the phone and brought it in to Mrs Flynn. This can't go on.'

'I know it can't.'

'Are you ready to talk to the police yet?'

'I'm ready,' Brian said. But he wasn't ready to go alone. He needed an ally. And yet he himself was meant to be a priest of God, a man with strength and confidence. Where was it when he needed it most? And to think he had once thought it was hard and complicated living in Rossmore.

He took the train to visit his mother. He held her hand in his and said that once a priest always a priest. The lady on the phone was just confused. It was a lady, wasn't it?

'Yes, a lady called Eileen. She said she was going to marry

you, that you had got your papers from Rome and didn't want to tell me in case I would be upset.'

'And what did you say, Mother?'

'I said I was happy to see you well out of the priesthood. But I pointed out that you were engaged to *me*, had given me a ring and that she was to get any ideas of *her* marrying you out of her head.'

Brian Flynn realised with a sense of defeat that within one paragraph his mother had slipped from knowing who he was to believing he was his father. There would be no further details about the phone call from Eileen. All was resentment now. Eileen was the enemy. The threat who might take his long dead father away from the marital home.

Wearily he came home, back to Dublin and let himself into the flat. There was a light on in the bedroom. He opened the door of the room and there on the bed was a bunch of red roses. And a note. The note enclosed a picture of Eileen lying there among those cushions with the football posters on the wall in what was undeniably his bedroom. Her letter said simply:

Thank you for letting me be part of your life, your heart and your bed. I had always looked forward with hope and happiness to our future together. Perhaps it will still come to pass.
Love always,
Eileen

There was no longer any time to wait for allies. Brian Flynn left his flat and walked purposefully to the Guards Station. It wasn't going to be easy but it had to be done. He was right in that it wasn't going to be easy. The desk sergeant was a small, foxy-looking man who had seen it all in his time. Priests wandering from the straight and narrow was part of the territory nowadays, he said. Often it was no more or no less than a vocation having ended, a new phase of life having begun.

With a very short fuse Brian listened to this man spouting nonsense.

'But where do you stand, Sergeant, when there isn't one word of truth in these allegations? This woman has told my friends, she has told everyone at the social centre where I work and now even my mother, who is suffering from partial dementia down in Rossmore, that she and I are a number, an affair, even an impending marriage. *Not one word* of this is true.'

The sergeant glanced at the photograph of Eileen Edwards in the priest's bed. The email he was alleged to have sent to this woman, the list of names and addresses: Father Tomasz, James O'Connor and Johnny Pearse.

The glance said everything and hinted that despite the filing of a report, nothing was going to be done. The glance said this was a priest who had had a fling and had now changed his mind. For no reason Brian Flynn felt as if he were going to cry. He hadn't cried for a long time. But now everything seemed to be beyond him like a swimmer heading for shore. Shore was too far away. He might not make it. Perhaps he *had* encouraged this woman. A tear fell down on the sergeant's desk.

The sergeant was not entirely unfeeling.

'Maybe you should just go home now. Think about it and if it's still preying on your mind, then you should get a lawyer and write to the young lady in question . . .'

Brian scooped up all his belongings and stored them in the canvas bag he used for his shopping. It had a logo on it: 'Take Care of the Earth'. Brian thought to himself that he was doing his best but it wasn't working out very well.

*

'Ania, will you come for a pint in Corrigans tonight?' Johnny asked when Ania came into his cardiac fitness room with the forms the patients were meant to fill out every session.

'Not if you want me to talk to Father Brian,' she said.

'But why, Ania? He's such a good guy, for a druid, well, by any standards really.'

'A druid?' Ania asked, puzzled.

'Forget it. It's just a sort of insulting word for a priest.'

'Right, good. A druid, is that it?'

'No, that's not important, the bit you are to remember is that he's a good guy.'

'He's not a good guy, Johnny. I thought he was, but he is not.'

'Why do you say that? Did somebody say something against him?'

'No, but I saw his girlfriend in his bed, lying there as bold as bronze.'

'Brass,' Johnny corrected.

'What?'

'You say as bold as brass, not bronze. Did she speak to you?'

'Of course she did.'

'And was it Eileen Edwards, the one we call Goldilocks?'

'You know that it was. You all protect him. You're as bad as he is.'

'But it's all lies, Ania, every word of it.'

'Not what I saw. That wasn't lies. She was lying in his bed, Johnny.'

'How did she get in?'

'He gave her the key.'

'He swears there's only one other key and you have it,' Johnny said.

'He surely is not saying that I let her in?'

'No, but could she have taken your key?'

'No, she could not do that. It's in my handbag.'

'And she couldn't have got at your handbag? She's very mad, you know.'

'No, she would not have been alone with my bag . . .' Ania stopped. 'Unless of course . . .'

Johnny leaped at this. 'Unless what?'

'No, it was impossible. She called in one day when I was doing the ironing. Father Brian wasn't in. She asked me to make her a cup of tea . . .'

'And you left your bag . . .'

'Only for a small moment.'

'But you did leave it in the same room?'

'I was not expecting that she would open my bag . . .'

'No, none of us were expecting this . . . and she probably put it back in your bag next day at the centre when she had made a copy.'

'She was very much at home there in Father Brian's house.'

'In her mind she was, Ania. She is really mad, you know.'

'I know that she is dangerous,' Ania said.

'That too,' Johnny agreed. 'Please come tonight. Brian needs his friends.'

'I was going to have an English lesson,' Ania said.

'Sure, don't you speak better English than any of us. Come to Corrigans, *please*,' he said.

And Ania said that she would ring and cancel her English lesson. Carl would understand.

'I have learned one new word anyway today,' she said cheerfully.

'What's that?' Johnny asked.

'Droo-id, a word for priest,' she said proudly.

Johnny put his head in his hands.

That night they all sat open-mouthed in Corrigans while Brian told the whole tale, showed the photograph and eventually had a cry with big, heaving shoulders. Johnny ran to get him a brandy. This had gone beyond pints. Ania cried with him at the unfairness of life and out of shame that she had ever doubted him. James O'Connor said the one thing about being a school teacher was that you knew the first thing to do with anything was to make a list of what to do now.

They dried their tears, sipped their drinks and planned what to do. Could they get a private detective to follow Eileen to see where she went and perhaps to find her family? That way they might find out a bit more about her.

How would they find one? In the classified directories? Maybe the security man who worked with Johnny and Ania at the heart clinic might know someone in that line of business. James wrote down 'Ask Tim for contact'. But then it might cost huge money which none of them had. They couldn't follow her themselves as she would recognise them.

'The girl I share a flat with, *she* could do it,' Ania offered. Her name was Lidia. She worked in a bar, was very confident, Ania said enviously. Lidia could cope with anything that life threw at her. James wrote down 'Discuss matter with Lidia'. There were further options: 'Talk to bishop', 'Go to someone higher in the police force', 'Set up a petition', 'Get a journalist to tell Father Brian's side of things', 'Tell everyone she's mad and ignore her'. None of their ideas seemed very good. The best hope was Lidia.

Lidia was bemused when little Ania came in to her pub with three men in tow. She was even more astounded when she took her break to sit with them and realised what they wanted her to do.

'Is this some kind of a joke, Ania?' She spoke in English out of courtesy to the others, but Ania answered in Polish to show how serious it was.

'This is our only hope to save a good man, you must help us, you must.'

'But suppose it's not what you think—' Lidia began.

Brian interrupted, 'Please believe me, Miss Lidia, this is a lot to ask you but without your help we have no hope at all.'

'But the government, the Church, the law? They cannot punish you if you are innocent.'

'If it were only as easy as that, Miss Lidia, then believe me we would not be here wasting your time.' Brian looked very defeated.

'What do I have to do?' Lidia asked.

The first thing the little committee asked her to do was to follow Eileen back to the big apartment block where she lived. She had told tales of how wonderful the commissionaire was, a real sweetie, she said, who would do anything for you. Eileen had said she was friendly with a lot of the people and sometimes went to their little drinks parties.

She had described the beautiful view right across the Dublin Mountains; the place, she said, was very well kept. Cleaners came at 4 a.m. to do the stairs and landings and they were very quiet. She had told all this to the hardworking girls, many of whom might actually *be* part of the 4 a.m. cleaning force. Eileen saw nothing incongruous about describing her privileged lifestyle to those who had such a small income. She said they loved to hear stories about her fairy princess lifestyle.

Lidia couldn't help wondering why Eileen would seek out the company of immigrants, of people considerably less fortunate, as she put on her jacket and jeans and pulled a soft, dark hat over her face. She would have to look anonymous if she were to follow this woman and not be recognised.

The very first night Lidia followed Eileen home, she saw her go up to the porter at the gate, rather than go up to the main entrance of the building. She looked so beautiful and very well dressed. Lidia liked clothes and she knew that Eileen Edwards's outfit cost a small fortune. What was she doing with her life? And what could she have in common with the rather bullet-headed-looking boy who let cars in and out? To her surprise, Lidia saw Eileen empty her handbag and put the contents in a plastic bag. The porter put the expensive handbag down under his desk. Eileen ran quickly away and hailed a bus on her side of the road.

Where was she going?

Lidia threw herself across the road and just caught the bus before it left, nearly killing herself in the attempt.

'Yes?' said the weary-looking driver.

Lidia didn't know where to say. She had no idea where Eileen would get off the bus. 'The end of the line. The terminal station, please,' she said.

'Are you from Lithuania, by any chance?' the driver asked.

'Why do you ask?'

'I met a gorgeous Lithuanian girl at a club. I really liked her. I wondered did you know her.'

'This is a very big city,' Lidia said.

'Don't I know. I walked this area here as green fields when I was a lad.'

Lidia sat and looked out the window at the rows of houses that had sprung up where the driver had once known green fields. She watched the reflection of Eileen, carefully ready for any sign that she might be about to get up and leave. Eventually she did. She looked around her as if anxious that she would not be spotted.

Lidia got out after her and went deliberately in the opposite direction. Then she took off her black hat and wrapped her red scarf around her head so that hopefully she looked totally different and turned to follow Eileen Edwards. She walked for five minutes and saw Eileen stop in Mountainview Road, a very shabby street outside a particularly dilapidated house. Again, she looked up and down the street and let herself in.

Lidia took a picture of the house with Johnny's phone which she had borrowed for the occasion, then she caught the bus back to the apartment block and photographed the man

191

in the porter's office outside the apartment block. And, exhausted, she went back to the flat she shared with Ania over the Polish restaurant. Ania was sitting up in bed, studying the English book that Carl had given her.

'They were very religious here in Ireland, back in the old days,' Ania said.

'Well, they aren't these days,' Lidia said, taking her shoes off and rubbing her feet.

'Did you get anything?'

'Yes. Eileen is *such* a liar. Not one thing she has said to anyone is true.' Lidia showed the pictures.

'Let's call Father Brian.' Ania was excited.

'But it's late, it's surely too late.'

'He won't be asleep, poor man, and he will be so happy to discover we have some proof.'

'Hang on, what do we have proof of, Ania? That she went to a house in a poor area? That is not a crime.'

'It's proof that she tells lies,' Ania said happily as she telephoned Brian's number.

His response was muted.

'Are you not more pleased, Father Brian? Now we *know* that she is a liar.'

'You see, I always knew that,' he said sadly.

The Friends of Brian Committee arranged for different people to follow Eileen in order to find out more. Johnny had asked Tim the security man to help. Tim said that he would enquire about the porter at the gate, find out if anyone knew anything about him. He would also follow Eileen on one of her shopping trips. Tim was a quiet man, a bit of a loner, but used to long hours and hard work; he said he was happy to do this for the priest.

He talked to a few colleagues who had jobs as store detectives in other security firms. He barely needed to show the photograph. They all knew Goldilocks. She was banned from city centre shops and shopping malls. Goldilocks, a known shoplifter, who had got away with it several times in court by claiming that she was only taking the garment or item outside to see it in daylight. She had put up such a good performance that magistrates, district justices and even tough solicitors had been fooled.

No, their job was just to prevent her getting *in* to the stores. Goldilocks had smiled at them forgivingly as if they were just doing some crazy job. They told Tim she was a minx from a tough family. Her father was known to be violent. Tim kept the last piece of information to himself.

Brian Flynn was a decent kind of fellow who was sorry for people. He might even stop the whole thing if he heard about a violent father. In Tim's opinion Goldilocks should be locked up. Now.

James O'Connor was next on the list to do his bit. He was going to run into Eileen accidentally, remind her that they met in Corrigans and invite her for a drink. He would find out more about her and deliver the news to the committee the following night. The more information they could give to the Guards when applying for a restraining order the better. James managed it very well and Eileen remembered him clearly.

'You were with dear Brian that night in the pub,' she said.

'Yes, poor Brian's going through a bad patch at the moment.'

'Isn't he just!' Eileen was sympathetic.

'Did you and he *really* have a thing?' James asked.

'You *know* we did and do, James. He's just not able to face it.'

'He does deny it, certainly.'

'Well, think how it makes me feel? It was difficult enough in the first place to believe him that his religious vows weren't important. That *our* vows to love each other forever were what mattered.'

'He said that?' James was wondering and admiring.

'Oh yes, you know what a hopeless romantic he is. And now, for some reason, he wants to cut me out of his life. Utterly unbearable.'

James looked at her round face, her innocent blue eyes. How terrible if this girl had taken a fancy to *him* and told his wife and children that they were deeply involved. Who would have doubted her? He shivered slightly at the prospect.

'I wonder, should you move on, Eileen? Forget him, just get on with your life.'

'Well, of course I would, James. That's what I would advise anyone to do, but it's not as simple as that. You see I'm pregnant. It's not only myself I have to think about. Yes, Brian and the child as well.'

James told Brian when the two of them were alone.

'I didn't think you'd want me coming out with that lot in front of everybody. You didn't, did you?'

'James, my friend, you think it might be true and that's why you told me privately.'

'No, I did *not* think that.' James was indignant.

'So why the secrecy then? Why can't the others be told how absurd this woman is? You are all so helpful to me, why shouldn't the others know the extent of her madness and delusion?'

'Of course, Brian, I'm sorry, I didn't think.'

'You did think, but you thought the wrong thing. If that girl *is* pregnant, it has nothing to do with me. *Nothing.*'

'Look, it even might be to our advantage,' James said, anxious to make amends. 'You know, blood test, DNA, that sort of thing.'

'Thanks, James, really, I mean it, thanks.' But Brian's face was grim. He was disturbed that James would doubt him like that. Even for a minute.

At the heart clinic, it was Hilary's day off, but she had trained Ania very well in the routine. Ania went about her work confidently, noting and filing and confirming appointments. She checked that there were suitable chairs ready in the waiting room.

Rosemary Walsh was there with her husband Bobby; she was sighing as usual. Bobby, on the other hand, was smiling as always and both cheerful and polite. It was striking how like his father Carl was and how very unlike his snobby mother. Ania sighed. This was no time to think of Carl. Maybe she shouldn't be thinking of him at all. She was such a poor judge of men – look at the fool she'd made of herself over Marek. She must not do that again.

There was a ring at the clinic door. It must be a new patient: everyone else knew to walk straight in. Ania went to answer it.

She saw an elderly woman in her seventies, clutching a thin coat around her. She had straight, matted hair and big, frightened eyes. Then the woman gave her name: Kathleen Edwards, 34 Mountainview Road.

She filled in carefully the name of Mrs Edwards's family doctor and of her cardiologist, and took a photocopy of the discharge sheet from the hospital.

'I have to put in your next of kin, Mrs Edwards. It's just a formality, you know hospitals! It's in case you didn't feel well one day and we needed to get in touch with someone. Shall I put your husband's name?'

'No, pet, he'd be no good to God, man or the devil,' Mrs Edwards said sadly. 'He'd be bound to be drunk or in a temper about something. Put my daughter's name.'

'And that is . . . ?'

'Eileen Edwards. I'll give you her mobile phone number. That's the best way to find her.' Ania wrote it down carefully on the form.

'Where does she work, your daughter?' She hoped the woman couldn't hear her heart thumping as she asked the question. Mrs Edwards looked at least twenty years older than the age in her file.

'She works for a big advertising company in an old Georgian house. They give her beautiful clothes to wear. She has to look smart, you see, to meet the public.'

Ania realised that none of the clothes that Eileen had stolen, none of the money she had made by selling on stolen handbags, had come to this woman. She felt a lump in her throat. Maybe that's what mothers did, believed fairytales about their own daughters. Like her own mother back in Poland telling everyone how well young Ania was doing in Ireland and how she visited big stores and tried on coats that cost twenty weeks' wages!

Ania was miles away in her head when she realised that Rosemary Walsh was talking to her. She seemed to be offering her a cleaning job of some sort.

'Because Bobby is literally able to do *nothing* around the house I will need someone for a couple of hours each evening, washing, ironing, cleaning. I won't ask you to do the silver. You wouldn't be used to good silver, you might ruin it, but basic stuff.'

'When, Mrs Walsh?'

'As soon as you can. Tonight if you like.'

Ania wondered should she take it. It would mean that she would see more of Carl, be in Carl's home, maybe even have her English lessons there. But wait a moment. Mrs Rosemary Walsh would not consider her son and heir cavorting with the cleaning staff, the *Polish* cleaning staff. Worse still! She must say no immediately. Why had she ever said in front of this woman that she was anxious to make money?

'Sadly, Mrs Walsh, I already have too many jobs. I could not give you good attention. I can suggest a friend of mine, Danuta? Or another called Agnieszka. What do you say? Shall I ask them to call to your house?'

'That is, of course, if *they* have the time. If *they* haven't swept up all the other jobs in Dublin.'

'We work very hard, Mrs Walsh, and we are glad to be here. It is good to know we are so welcome in this land,' she said, trying to hide the tears of rage and humiliation.

To her astonishment, Mrs Edwards reached out her hand and clutched her arm. 'Good girl,' she said, 'good strong girl. Where did you get the courage?'

'I don't know,' Ania said, truthfully.

'You would never let a man beat you like I did.'

And Ania, for the first time in her life, confessed as she had never confessed to anyone before, 'I did once, Mrs Edwards, but not any more.'

When the committee met at Corrigans bar that night they were staggered by the news about Eileen's mother.

'A smart ad agency where they *give* her the clothes. Huh!' said Johnny. The man in the porter's hut outside the up-market apartment had, according to Tim, turned out to be a known fence, dealing in only top-of-the-market goods. James said that maybe Eileen kept all her things in Mountainview Road if they could only get in there. Ania said she knew she was being irritating, but she felt very uncomfortable using this poor woman who was, after all, a patient in the clinic where she worked, as a trap to catch Eileen.

'It would break her old sad heart into little pieces,' she said.

They were all silent. Only Brian Flynn seemed to under-stand and sympathise.

Nothing happened for a week. Father Tomasz came up from Rossmore and was brought up to speed on what was happening. He said it was like a story but nobody knew the end. Eileen came in and out of the social centre as usual, but more fleetingly. She said no more about Father Flynn, just a few mysterious remarks that everyone would know in time. In a short while they would see for themselves.

And then, on her second visit to the heart clinic, Kathleen Edwards walked out of the clinic without looking where she was going and tripped over a loose paving stone. Fortunately, it wasn't too serious. The A&E department treated her for shock and a graze on her forehead, but what was to happen now? They asked the clinic for details of her next of kin. Johnny was there when the request arrived.

'Why don't I take her home? I have something to do up that way, near Mountainview Road,' he said.

'How do you know where she lives?' Clara had Kathleen Edwards's file in her hand.

'Oh, I think Ania mentioned it. Look, it's Ania's lunchtime, why don't we both take her home?'

Normally Clara was loath to make anything easier for Frank Ennis and the mandarins, as she called them, in the hospital, but this did seem sensible. 'And you'll contact the daughter, okay?' she checked.

'Absolutely, we'll ring the advertising agency,' Johnny said.

In 34 Mountainview Road they found a very shabby, ill-kept house. Two windows had been broken and were filled in not with glass but with plywood.

Ania went off to make a cup of tea and Johnny looked around. 'You'll need a rest. You've had a shock,' he said.

'Yes, well I'll lie down on the sofa,' Kathleen Edwards suggested.

'No, let's get you into a bed.'

'He might come home. He wouldn't like to find me in bed.'

'Well, is there another bedroom?' Johnny asked.

'Only Eileen's, we never go in there. It's locked, you see.'

She looked to a door across the corridor from the kitchen/ living room. Johnny ran at it with his shoulder. The door splintered.

'It's not locked now,' he said.

They looked in. Two clothes rails stood there with jackets, coats and dresses on them. Some in plastic bags. Handbags and shoes were lined in the alcove beside the window and down one wall were shelves holding a series of sweaters, blouses and jeans. Kathleen Edwards stood, her hand holding her throat.

'You broke down her door,' she gasped.

'It was an emergency,' Johnny said, 'she won't mind. Let's call her on the phone and tell her about everything.'

Eileen answered immediately.

'Your mother had an accident. She's fine and we've got her home but she will need someone here to keep an eye on her.'

'If she's fine and you're with her, then she doesn't need anyone else.'

'*Come back here, bitch. Come back this minute,*' Johnny said slowly.

'Who *is* this? What on earth is this about?'

'It's about you, Eileen, I'm standing in your bedroom. Come home at once.'

'*You can't be!*' Her voice was a gasp.

'Want me to read out the merchandise to you? From left to right?'

'Are you the Guards?' Her voice was shaky now.

'I'm one step, one phone call from the Guards. Let's say ten minutes from the Guards.'

'I can't be home in that time, the buses are—'

'Take a taxi.'

'Whoever you are, I can't afford taxis.'

'Yes, you can. Use some of the money you got from the porter up at the apartments when you sold him your hand-bag.'

'*Who are you?*' It was like a whisper now.

'Come home and find out,' Johnny said.

Together Ania and Johnny calmed Mrs Edwards down. They reassured her that her heart was fine, her blood pressure almost normal and all she was feeling was shock. They wanted her out of the bedroom and all it contained, so she sat at the kitchen table and told them how frightened she was that her husband would come home drunk. He was two men, her husband, one in drink and one sober. Trouble was you never knew which one was going to come in that door.

'Don't worry, I'll be here.'

'He'll be very upset about that door,' she warned.

'I'm great with upset people,' Johnny promised.

Ania looked up with huge anxious eyes. 'You won't do anything . . . you know.'

'I won't,' Johnny promised. 'And now it's time for you to get back to the clinic.'

'Oh, I must stay here and look after Mrs Edwards.'

'You're not a nurse, Ania, get back to Clara.'

'But how will I know?'

'We'll meet later on in Corrigans.'

'If my poor mother knew that I go to a public house every single night!' Ania grumbled, but Johnny was right. She had to go back to her job.

The taxi drew up outside 34 Mountainview Road and Eileen got out. Johnny noticed that she wore a smart, lilac-coloured jacket, and a black skirt and lilac-coloured boots. She must do her shoplifting with a colour-coordinated plan. Around her neck was one of those very expensive silk scarves that ladies often wore at the races. That's where Eileen Edwards would be more in place than letting herself into this broken-down house where the presence of a violent father and a nervous mother sat side by side with a locked room full of stolen goods. Johnny hardened his heart. No sympathy, no pity. This woman was totally prepared to destroy Brian Flynn, one of her few decent friends left in the western world.

Kathleen Edwards looked up fearfully when she heard the key turn in the lock. She seemed relieved that it was only Eileen.

'You didn't have to come home. I'm fine,' she began.

'I did have to, apparently. Where is he?'

'In your room. He says he'll repair the door.'

'He'd better. Who is he?'

'I don't know. He was there just after the accident.'

From the next room as he listened Johnny realised that the girl had not offered one word of sympathy to her mother. Eileen came into her bedroom and saw Johnny sitting casually on the bed. She recognised him at once, as a regular at Corrigans, a man who had occasionally come to help at the centre. He had a flat in the house where Brian lived.

'I might have known that it was his doing,' she said as she looked at the splintered door.

'He has no idea we are here.'

'We?'

'Ania and I. We brought your mother here after the accident. She's going to be fine, actually, if it's of any interest to you.'

'What will be of interest to *you*, Johnny, is what my father will do to you when he comes back and finds you've broken into his house.' Her voice was level. She had shown no fear, no panic at the situation.

'Of course, he will also find a house full of Guards, his daughter arrested for theft and himself brought down to the Guards Station for domestic violence.'

'She'd never say a word against him.' Eileen looked scornfully towards the kitchen and the weak mother who had never stood up to violence before and would not do it now.

'She already has,' he said casually, almost lazily, as if he didn't really care.

'I don't believe you.'

'She's made a statement to Ania and myself. She'll talk to the Guards this time.'

'In your dreams.'

'Who else has she in this house that will listen to her?' Johnny asked. There was silence.

'What do you want, Johnny?' she said eventually.

Michael Edwards was on his way back from the pub where he had spent lunchtime. A very odd thing had happened. A message had come to the pub that he had to pick up some wood and bolts and a heavy-duty lock at Finn Fitzgerald's Builders Providers shop. They had been paid for because there were some urgent repairs to be done at home. It was very puzzling. Michael didn't remember any fracas at home last night. And when he went into the shop, Finn Fitzgerald had the stuff ready and had indeed been paid for it. 'What's the story here, Finn?' he had asked.

'I'd get home as soon as you can, Mick. I didn't like the look of that fellow who was in here earlier with your daughter. Some kind of weightlifter.'

'And he paid?'

'No, your daughter paid. Real money. It's all kosher, Mick. Get back there soonish.'

He came into 34 Mountainview Road with his usual bluster and flung the wood and locks in the hall.

'What is this about?' he began.

'Your wife had a bit of a fall, Mr Edwards. Fortunately her injuries are minor, but she is of course in a state of shock. She's in the kitchen if you want to check things out.'

'Who are you to be telling me to check things out in my house?' Michael Edwards had a red, angry face.

'Who am I? I am a friend of your daughter's and I also happen to work in the clinic where Mrs Edwards was attending. That's who I am.'

'And why are you still here? She's home. She's all right. What's your business here?'

'To help you repair a door that unfortunately got broken in the course of things.'

'What?'

'Yes, I thought if we started now we could get it done together.'

'Well, you thought wrong. I'm having a pint, minding my own business and I get a message shouting the odds at me.'

'We could start by pulling the broken wood out,' Johnny said.

'How did the wood get broken?' he asked.

For the first time, Eileen spoke. 'Do what he says, Dad. I mean it. It will be better for all of us in the end.'

'I won't be talked to like that in my own house—'

'It's Mam's house, Dad, she got it from her father. Remember?'

'Same difference,' he said.

'Not now. Things have changed.' Eileen was crisp.

'For you they may have if you want to put up with the manners of your fellow here.'

'He's not my fellow.' The sentence came out like bullets.

'Well, it's got nothing to do with me.' Mike Edwards looked as if he was heading back to the pub.

'Dad, have sense. She's telling the Guards. Finally.'

'She hasn't an ounce of proof.'

'She has. This nosey parker, she has Ania the Polish girl, and she has me.'

'But you're not going to open your trap.'

'This time I am.'

'Why on earth?'

'It's my get-out-of-jail card.'

'And what about mine?'

'Mend the door, Dad, and then Johnny wants to talk to you.'

'And what will *you* be doing, I ask?'

'Making Mam some soup and toast.'

'But you never do that.'

'I'm going to be doing it from now on, it seems.' She looked balefully at Johnny.

Mike Edwards took off his jacket. Whatever this was about it was serious. He looked into his daughter's bedroom. Rugs covered rails of clothes. He couldn't see what the clothes were even if he was interested. 'This isn't going to look great, a door sort of nailed together,' he grumbled.

'The windows don't look all that great either. Eileen is going to a glazier next week to get those restored, aren't you, Eileen?'

'I am,' Eileen said glumly.

It took an hour to get the makeshift door mended and put on the lock. There were two keys. Eileen got one and Johnny kept the other.

'I'll be back in a week so we will see how the decluttering is getting on,' he said. 'New windows might even be in?'

Mike went back to the pub having cleared up the hall under Johnny's supervision.

'I hate a mystery,' he said over his shoulder to Johnny, 'and you're one real mystery man, so you are.'

Kathleen Edwards was very unaccustomed to being fussed over and looked after. 'Don't you need to get back to work, Eileen?' she asked anxiously.

'No, Mam, I have the rest of the day off.'

'And most of this week,' Johnny added helpfully in case she had forgotten. Eventually Kathleen Edwards went up to her bed. And left Johnny and Eileen in the kitchen. He poured himself another mug of tea with the ease of a regular visitor, an old friend.

'You're not going to get away with this,' she said.

'I have,' he said simply. 'I made you an offer, you accepted it. That's all.'

'You didn't make me an offer, you blackmailed me.'

'I asked three things. You move all this stuff in your bedroom on to charity shops, that your mother is made safe and comfortable in her own home and that you tell Brian the charade is over.'

'And you tell him all this?' Her lip trembled.

'Not if you do your bit.'

'And if I don't you get the Guards.'

'I have a great friend, a desk sergeant, he'd be down on you like a ton of bricks.'

'It's not going to be easy getting that stuff, as you call it, into charity shops.'

'You'll manage. You got it out of posh shops.'

'If my father gets drunk again I can't be held responsible.'

'I've given your next-door neighbour my phone number, told him I was a welfare worker.'

'He won't believe you.'

'I gave one meaningful look at that pit bull terrier with a muzzle that he has in the house. He believes me.'

'And Brian?'

'Tonight in Corrigans at seven o'clock. The snug at the back.'

'I'm not sure I'll be able for it.'

'I think you will. It's Corrigans or it's my mate the desk sergeant at the Guards Station.'

'But if I can't say it?'

'We've been over it twice. Let's do it a third time to make sure you're word-perfect.'

They filed into the back booth in Corrigans: James O'Connor, Father Brian Flynn, Johnny, Tim, Ania and Lidia, and Father Tomasz who had taken the bus up from Rossmore for the occasion.

Brian thought it was just an ordinary meeting. He was surprised that James didn't have a clipboard and paper to take notes. James bought a drink for everyone. He cleared his throat.

'Eileen is joining us, she has something to say,' he began.

Brian struggled from his seat. 'James, what are you *doing*? There's no point in asking her anything. I thought you knew that.'

'No one is going to ask her anything. She wants to say something. Here she is now.' Eileen came in.

Eileen was less of the Goldilocks now as she looked into six pairs of hostile eyes and the troubled face of Father Brian Flynn.

'Brian, I have to say something and it's not easy. I've had a troubled life and I am inclined to live in a fantasy world to make things better. So I pretend that I have a beautiful apartment instead of living in my parents' falling-down place in Mountainview Road. I pretend I have a lot of upmarket friends, but in fact I have a violent, drunken father who beats my mother. I have no trust fund or allowance or whatever I said. I steal clothes and fashion items. I am barred from most of the stores in Grafton Street and Henry Street so I have to go out to the suburbs now. I sell some of these things on . . .' She paused and looked only at the face of the priest.

'And then, because I didn't have anyone to love me, I made up someone to love me. I pretended that I was in a relationship with Brian. I see now what a dangerous, stupid, wrong thing it was to do. But I was so lonely. I tried to think of how comforting it would be. I made up all these stories. I watched him as he typed his password and then sent myself emails from the internet café. I borrowed his mobile phone from the centre and used it to send myself a message. I borrowed his key from Ania's handbag to get access to his flat.'

The silence was heavy. Their faces were stricken at the terrible things she had done.

'I'm very, very sorry, Brian. Can you forgive me?'

Brian was wordless. Literally without a word to say. Eventually he stuttered out, 'Why now? Now, after all this time?'

Johnny's voice was smooth and soft. 'Eileen had a great shock this morning when her mother had a fall. She realises that some things in life are more important than others. She now has got her priorities right. Is that it, Eileen?'

'Yes, that's it. I see now what matters and what doesn't.'

The big, generous face of Brian Flynn was about to welcome her back as a friend, but Johnny had plans for that.

'Since it's obviously too embarrassing for Eileen to be around people who know this part of her life, she is not going to be in the centre any more. She wants to say goodbye to Brian tonight and assure him in front of all us witnesses that if Brian forgives her and does not take her to court, she will not cross his path again.'

'Yes, that's what would be best,' Eileen said.

'But of course I forgive you,' Brian said. 'You are very courageous to have come here of your own accord—'

'She had to come,' Johnny interrupted Brian's speech. 'She is an ordinary, decent person who couldn't live long with such a deception and she knows that she will keep to this. It's the only thing she can do.'

And as Goldilocks walked out of Corrigans, and out of their lives, Ania noticed that she was not wearing smart boots as usual, nor her high-heeled, smart leather shoes, and the scarf was not one that would have been worn at the races. Ania also noticed that Tim was paying a lot of attention to Lidia and asking her what kind of music she liked.

Brian was wiping his eyes where tears of relief and happiness had begun.

'You are a very good druid, Father Brian.'

'A good *what*?' he asked her.

'Now I have to teach *you* English. It's an affectionate word for a priest.'

'No, it's not, Ania.'

'It is in Ania's world, but maybe you've had such a close call you might be prepared to get out of it and join the real world.'

'Ah, Johnny, Johnny, when all is said and done, what do you know about anything?' Brian asked, punching his friend cheerfully in the arm.

Chapter Six

Mountainview, despite its pleasant name, was one of the tougher areas of Dublin. Some of the big estates were home to drug dealers and it wasn't a place to walk alone at night. The school had its ups and downs but it was lucky enough to have a headmaster, Tony O'Brien, who could deal with toughness head-on.

Some of the older teachers found the change hard to take. Things used to be different, the place had been shabby but they had respect. The children came from homes where money was short but they were all keen to get exams. Today they only cared about money, and if someone's big brother was driving a smart car and wearing an expensive leather jacket, it was hard to get interested in having a job in a bank or an office where you might never make enough to have your own house or car, and a leather jacket was just a dream. No wonder so many of them joined gangs. And as for respect?

Aidan Dunne told his wife Nora all about it.

Big fellows would push past you in the corridor and sort of nudge the books out of your hand. Then they would laugh and say that sir must be losing his grip. Aidan remembered when they would rush to pick up the books. Not now. And they would call him Baldy, or ask him did he remember the First World War.

It was the same with the women teachers. If they weren't married some of the really rough fellows would ask them were they frigid or lesbian. If they *were* married they would ask them how many times a night did they do it.

'And what do you say?' Nora wondered.

'I try to ignore them, I tell myself that they're only insecure kids like always – it's just they have a different way of expressing it. Still, it doesn't make the day's work any easier.'

'And how do the women cope?'

'The younger ones are able for them, they say things like, "Oh, you'd never be able to satisfy me like my old man does," or else that, sure, they are gay because the only alternative is horrible spotty boys with filthy fingernails.' Aidan shook his head. 'By the time I get to the classroom I'm worn out,' he said sadly.

'Why don't you give it up?' Nora said suddenly. She taught Italian at an evening class and organised a yearly outing to Italy for the group. She had several other small jobs, but she had no interest in money or pensions or the future. She sat in one of the basket chairs she had bought at a garage sale and tried to persuade Aidan to join her in this carefree lifestyle.

But he was a worrier. It would be idiotic to leave his school now several years before retirement date. It would mean no proper pension; if he were to amount to anything he had to provide for Nora and his first family.

'Oh, you've well provided for them,' Nora said cheerfully. 'You've given Nell most of the money you got for the house, Grania is married to the headmaster of Mountainview School, Brigid has been made a partner in the travel agency. They should be providing for you, if you come to think of it.'

'But you, Nora, what about you? I want to look after you, give you some comfort and pleasures.'

'You give me great comforts and pleasures,' she said.

'But some *security*, Nora,' he pleaded.

'I never had security before, I don't want it now.'

'I have to finish out my time there.'

'Not if you don't like it. What about this lovely life we promised each other and we have mainly had?'

'It depends on my having a good safe job, Nora,' he said.

'No – it doesn't. Not if it's making you worry, and panic about these louts. We don't need it, Aidan. Not if it's affecting your health.'

'It's not affecting my health,' Aidan said firmly.

A week later Aidan and Nora were in one of their favourite second-hand bookshops; they were each browsing separately when she looked over at him suddenly. His hand was at his throat and he seemed to be having difficulty catching his breath.

'Aidan?' she called.

'Sorry, is it very stuffy in here?'

'No indeed – there's a lazy wind coming in from the canal.'

'A lazy wind?' he asked distractedly.

'You know – a wind that doesn't bother to make the time to go round you so it goes through you . . .' Nora smiled.

He didn't smile back.

She was alarmed now. 'Is there something wrong?'

'I don't seem to be able to breathe in,' he said. 'Oh, Nora, dear Nora, I hope that I'm not going to faint or anything.'

'No, of course you're not, just sit down there.' She was brisk and practical. First, she spoke to the shop owner.

'Where's the nearest hospital?' she asked.

'St Brigid's. Is there a problem?'

'I think my husband is having some kind of seizure. Taxi rank?'

'Don't bother. I'll drive you,' he said.

Nora didn't question it, there would be time to thank him later.

'Right, Aidan, Dara is giving us a lift,' she said.

'Where to?' he gasped.

'To somewhere that will help you breathe properly, my darling,' she said.

And he closed his eyes in relief.

At the A&E in St Brigid's the nurses moved him wordlessly into a cubicle. They had given him oxygen and the house doctor had been called.

'Take off his trousers,' the doctor said.

'What?' Nora was taken aback.

'Please, madam.' The Chinese doctor was very courteous. 'His lungs are flooded, we need to drain the liquid from him, we have to put him on a catheter . . .'

Nora explained this to Aidan.

'That's extraordinary – I don't feel as if I need to go to the loo at all,' he said.

The oxygen was helping. He was much calmer. Nora looked at a huge container and saw it filling up with what looked like gallons of fluid.

'How could that happen?' she asked.

'The heart is failing to pump,' the Chinese doctor explained. 'He is in heart failure at the moment.'

Nora felt all the strength leave her body. The good, kind man that she adored and who loved her too had a heart that had failed him. Life as they knew it was over.

In about an hour Aidan felt so much better he was ready to come home. He was surprised when he heard that they were getting a bed for him in St Brigid's.

'But I'm perfectly fine now,' he protested.

Nora went home for his pyjamas, dressing gown and a

sponge bag. She remained calm and reassuring on the outside, but inside she felt that she had lost the will to live.

The next few days passed in a blur: visits from teams of senior doctors, their younger assistants with clipboards, nurses, carers, cleaners, trolleys of food. Visitors coming in with anxious faces. And among them was Nora Dunne, tall, wild-eyed, with her long red hair with its grey streaks tied back with a black ribbon.

She sat beside Aidan's bed and they played chess happily together. If people had been watching them closely they would have noticed that they never talked about household things, bills, repairs, shopping. They didn't talk about neighbours or family or friends. They just lived for each other. And if people had been watching *very* carefully they would have realised that Nora was behaving like a robot. She was keeping the show on the road for Aidan.

Before he was discharged after a week they talked to him seriously about levels of stress in his life. When he told them about life up at the school, the cardiologist advised him seriously to give up the job.

Aidan wouldn't even consider discussing it. He would take his medication, he would take long rests each day. But he would not give up his job. It was the only thing he had to offer his wife, some stability. He had not been a good provider. There had been other calls on his finances. A previous family. No, in all honour he had to stay on until his pension was assured.

The medical team spoke to Nora too and found her hard to fathom. Over and over she said she wasn't remotely interested in possessions or pensions. They lived in a small and simple rented flat. She could easily go out to work and make the rent, their needs were not great.

'So will you encourage him to retire?' the cardiologist suggested.

'No, not if he doesn't want to, Doctor. Why should I stand between him and what he wants to do? Aidan always loved teaching, he would feel such a failure if we took him out of that school.'

'Could he not teach at home? Give private tuition, maybe?'

'No. Aidan doesn't approve of people having to pay for extra education. We couldn't ask him to go against his principles.'

'But you are such a strong personality, Mrs Dunne. I am sure that you could persuade him.'

'I'm sure I could if I tried – but it would not be honest to make him give up what he truly wants to do.'

'Even if it's killing him?'

'But he's going to die anyway, isn't he?'

'We all are, but with care he has plenty of life left.'

Nora's face was still empty. 'A life of fear and anxiety and thinking that choking will return.'

'We can help him make sure that it doesn't. As sure as can be.'

'Which isn't totally sure, is it?' Her voice was hard.

'No, any more than we can be sure that you won't both be hit by a bus on your way home. But we have a very good record in keeping people alive and well and in normal life after a heart attack. Your husband will be in that number. We have referred him to a heart failure clinic which he will have to attend regularly. It's a heart clinic attached to this hospital. Patients go there regularly to be monitored, to have blood tests, check their medication.'

'And why do you call it heart failure?'

'Because that's what their hearts are doing: failing to work at the optimum levels.'

'And Aidan has to come here every week, is that it?'

'To start with, yes, then as he progresses, less often. He will find it a great reassurance.'

Nora was silent.

'Truly he will, Mrs Dunne. All our research has shown that it makes people much more confident and positive, which is exactly what they need at this time.'

'And is it funded by a drugs company? Do they do experiments on the patients?'

'Absolutely not. It is operated under the aegis of this hospital and we are very proud of it.' He bristled with resentment at her suspicions.

'I'm sorry, Doctor. To you Aidan is a patient you are looking after, to me he is my whole life. I'm not thinking straight.'

'He will need you to think straight now more than ever before,' the doctor said. Clearly, this woman had to be brought on side. 'Go to the heart clinic with him, get to know the people there; you may both get a lot from it.'

For the first time, the tight, pained look left Nora Dunne's face. She was a handsome woman, the doctor realised.

'We'll give it a chance,' she said with a hint of a smile.

Barbara had visited Aidan in hospital to explain the system to him. Aidan listened to this attractive bouncy girl and nodded his understanding. It seemed to have everything you'd need: exercise class, blood pressure, weigh-ins.

There was an emergency phone number for them to call at night.

'Why would we not come straight in to Emergency?' Aidan had asked.

'Well, of course you could, but there might be a short cut. It could be a question of taking another diuretic. And then we would call you back in half an hour to see had the breathlessness disappeared. That's often all it needs, and it would save you all the business of coming in here again.' Barbara was cheerful and practical. 'You'll love the people there, Aidan, they're a great crowd,' she said.

It was an easy bus journey from Nora and Aidan's flat to the heart clinic. People were well wrapped up against the February chill and there was a mist coming in over the canal. Nora had tied a smart tartan woolly scarf around Aidan's neck before they set out. He felt perfectly fine again; it was only the shadow of all this happening again that hung over him.

The bus stopped outside the clinic's gate. Nora and Aidan both knew the story of how it had once been a storage depot, and had nearly become a car park until rescued by St Brigid's for this purpose. There was a big brass plaque outside saying *Heart Clinic*. Inside it was full of light and remarkably cheerful.

Nora and Aidan were shown around and introduced by a pleasant young Polish girl called Ania. Here was the exercise room: Johnny had a powerful handshake and a great belief that muscles could do anything. He showed them the various exercise machines and said he would look forward to building Aidan up on them.

Then Ania took them to meet Lavender in the dietician's room, and they got a food sheet and a list of the times that Lavender gave cookery demonstrations at which all were welcome.

Aidan recognised Barbara, the cheerful nurse, who in turn introduced Fiona, a beautiful girl. 'That's just in case you're unlucky enough to hit a day when I'm not here, Aidan, Fiona will do her best with you.'

'Don't take a blind bit of notice of her, Aidan,' Fiona said. 'You'll be ringing up secretly to know when Barbara is off, just like everyone else.'

And here was a young doctor called Declan, then an office manager whose name was Hilary who had all his details and files from the hospital; and finally the beautiful Dr Casey who ran the whole outfit.

'I'm Clara,' she said simply. She had notes in her hand from the hospital and when Aidan was borne away by Barbara to one of the treatment cubicles, Clara asked Nora to sit down. She glanced down at the hospital notes, which included a short scribble in the margin. *'Work on the wife,'* it said cryptically.

She was striking-looking, thought Clara. It was odd to see a woman in her fifties with long hair in what looked almost like alternate stripes of grey and red and realise that it had not been done in a hairdresser's, it was really due to nature.

Nora had a gift of being very still. She must be a restful person to live with. Clara wondered what she was meant to work on this woman about.

Soon it became clear.

Nora Dunne did not believe her husband was going to make any kind of recovery and now that was becoming a big part of the problem.

Clara gave her usual optimistic spiel about the clinic and its powers to keep people out of hospital. But she felt it was falling on stony ground. So she moved to a different tactic.

'We have found that those who come from a positive background, from a home where people really believe they will get better, *do* get better,' she said.

'Mind over matter, do you mean?' Nora did not sound convinced.

'Not really. Just affirmation, something to live for.'

Nora still looked sceptical. 'And I suppose you think religious people recover even quicker?'

'I have no idea. Possibly a firm conviction of faith might help, certainly. It's not something we can measure.'

'But you *can* measure a sunny, cheerful home atmosphere and what good it does?' Nora sounded very cynical.

'You have seen some of the facilities we can offer here at this clinic, Nora. You have talked to people who think that carefully and regularly checked medication, blood tests, monitoring, exercise and nutrition will all help to save and prolong lives. Why do you not feel part of this?'

'Because the quality of the life you are preserving and prolonging isn't going to be any good,' Nora said desolately.

'How amazing to be so certain!' Clara looked very angry. 'I have been practising medicine for years and I don't have your confidence in that judgement.'

'I am the least confident person you ever met,' Nora said sadly. 'I would do anything on earth to help Aidan get better. But you're asking me to believe in a fairytale. I find that hard to take on.'

'Do you believe in compromise?' Clara asked suddenly.

'Once I didn't, but in fact I do nowadays. Why do you ask?'

'I was going to ask you to give me six weeks where you pretend to think it's all working and doing him some good, and if after that you think it's only feel-good rubbish then go back to your principles.' Clara opened her diary. 'Why don't we choose a date in April when we decide what you feel. You're only investing six weeks. A month and a half? For Aidan?'

'How can I refuse?' Nora had a wonderful smile. Her cooperation was indeed going to be essential to her husband's recovery.

So for six weeks Nora Dunne kept her part of the bargain and spoke enthusiastically about the heart clinic which Aidan was attending.

She told her two sisters, Helen and Rita, who never showed much interest in anything. She met them once a week at the old people's home where her mother now lived. Rita and Helen made no secret of the fact that they thought their sister

Nora was eccentric and not to be trusted on any matter. After all, she had run away to Italy for years after a married man. When she had finally come home, run out of the place probably, she had dressed most oddly. Then taken a room in a very rough area and taught Italian in a tough school. She had 'married' a man who was a teacher in the school but of course it wasn't a real marriage since he was already married and divorced and it was one of these Register Office jobs. They sniffed as if to imply that a heart attack was the very least punishment Aidan Dunne might have expected for having committed adultery.

Nora and Aidan went to one of Lavender's cookery demonstrations and heard about how to reduce salt in everything and how to make little fish parcels. In front of everyone, Lavender took out squares of foil and on each one placed a small piece of cod; then she added sliced leeks, green beans and some cherry tomatoes. Then she sprayed everything with a low-fat spray and folded up the foil as an envelope. It took about twenty minutes to cook. While it was cooking she gave them helpful advice about shopping and asking for lean cuts of meat.

Lavender didn't assume that the audience had unlimited wealth: she was practical and helpful. Everyone tasted the cod when it was cooked and said it was excellent. Next week she was going to do low-fat desserts, she said.

Aidan was watching Nora's face to know what she thought of it. Nora said that it was all brilliant and imagine anyone wanting to buy all that fat greasy take-away when you could get this! Aidan seemed very relieved that she was enthusiastic and they went off happily to find a fishmonger.

Lavender had advised them to buy several pieces at a time and freeze the extra ones.

But Nora and Aidan didn't have a proper freezer so that wouldn't work for them.

'Never mind, it's good for us to walk to the shops each time,' Nora said as they left the heart clinic.

Clara overheard her and smiled to herself. This Nora was certainly keeping her part of the bargain.

Nora's great friend Brenda Brennan of Quentins restaurant visited that evening to know how Aidan was.

'What's happening to your gorgeous eating place tonight without you there to supervise?' Nora asked. Nobody could imagine Quentins without Brenda there, calm and in control.

'I'm learning to delegate, Nora,' she said. 'I have a leggy blonde from Latvia, impeccable English, great style. She's in there now and may well have taken the place over when I get back.'

'That's what I'm afraid of up at the school,' Aidan said. 'They have this bright young fellow in teaching Latin. Why would they want me back?' He looked worried.

'Because you know more Latin than that boy will learn in a lifetime.' Nora was loyal.

'I should be getting back there though. I'm feeling so well . . .'

'The headmaster said you were to take your time,' Nora reminded him.

'Yes, but the headmaster is my son-in-law,' Aidan said ruefully.

'Oh, Aidan, that has nothing to do with it,' Brenda Brennan broke in. 'I am certain of this much: I've known Tony O'Brien well over the years, if he says it he means it.'

'It's just that I feel such a waster.' Aidan was still worried about it all.

'You, Aidan? A waster? The very notion of it is ludicrous;

enjoy your couple of weeks, you'll be wishing you got more value out of your time off when you're back in harness.'

'But if I'm well enough to enjoy myself then aren't I well enough to go to work?'

'Aidan – take Nora out on the train to the seaside. It's lovely in Dunlaoghaire with the waves all crashing round. Winter is by far the best time to go. Or go on to Sandycove or Dalkey, go to one of those nice pubs that serve food . . .' Brenda could think of a hundred things to do. She provided the get-up-and-go that Nora lacked. Soon she had them making a list of twenty things they must do while Aidan still had his freedom.

'He's looking very well – the colour has come back to his cheeks,' Brenda said as Nora went with her to the door.

'The grey won't be long coming back to his face once he gets back to that school,' Nora said.

'Well then . . . ?'

'What do you think? He has this ludicrous macho feeling he must do it. Earn a living, get a pension. I can't stand in his way.'

'I would,' Brenda Brennan said. 'I'd throw myself in front of him and beg him not to go back there. That's what I would do if it were Patrick.'

'We are different, Brenda. You met when you were young. We were middle-aged, we respect each other so much, we neither of us wants to change the other.'

'I hope you know what you're doing.' Brenda didn't sound as if it were at all likely.

'Signora?'

Nora Dunne looked up, surprised. They all called her Signora, of course: it was a term of affection now. This time it was the school headmaster come to visit her after her Italian class.

'Oh, Tony, I didn't see you there. We had a grand turn-out even for a cold February night.'

'Aidan getting on all right?'

'He's fine really, Tony. His girls have been very good. Brigid is with him tonight and you know your Grania is coming tomorrow when I have to go and see my mother so he's not left alone. He's in very good form.'

'I'd go to see him only . . .' Tony O'Brien paused.

'I know, I know exactly, he'd think he had to hurry up and get back to work.'

'I don't want him to come back to all that rough and tumble, Signora. I'll try and sort out some kind of pension, allowance, whatever . . .'

'Ah, Tony, you know Aidan,' she sighed.

'Which is why I was hoping you might help,' he began.

'He's not a child in nappies, he's a grown man; everyone wants me to treat him as if his mind has gone rather than someone who has enlarged ventricles in his heart. His brain is still functioning and he is determined to go back to work.'

'And you're going to let him?'

'I'm not going to add even more to his stress by having dissension at home,' Nora said crossly.

'I could work things out,' Tony tried again.

'You know Aidan, he would smell pity and sense charity even when it didn't exist.' To Nora Dunne it was simple. Her husband had to go back to his job.

When Tony O'Brien went home that night, Grania seemed very excited about something.

He wondered had she seen some exotic Easter holiday that they could book. He hoped not. There was a lot to do in Mountainview over the Easter vacation.

She had the table set and a bunch of flowers. God – it

wasn't an anniversary or anything? No, no, of course not. He was good about that sort of thing. He looked at her blankly.

'Sit down, Tony,' she said.

He sat obediently.

'I have very good news,' she continued. 'We're pregnant. It's official, Tony, we're having a baby!'

And to his total surprise, Tony O'Brien began to cry. Huge sobs and heaving shoulders. The works.

'Aren't you happy about it?' Grania was anxious and wrapped her arms around him.

'*Happy?* I'm *unhinged* with happiness,' he sobbed.

Brigid had met a man, she told her father. Well, it was too soon to talk about seriously. But for the first time she had met someone that she wouldn't mind spending the rest of her life with.

Aidan was delighted.

She had met him at a press reception some months back and they got talking. They had both been working, she had been doing a presentation of their winter sports holidays and Kato had been in charge of the buffet supper. When everyone else had gone they stayed in the empty room and talked and talked. He was setting up a shop selling African objects. She had been out with him every week since then. They liked the same kind of movies and theatre and everything. It was nearly time to bring him home to meet her dad and Nora.

'And what does your mother think of him?' Aidan knew that the girls saw Nell from time to time.

'Oh, Mother hasn't met him,' Brigid said very firmly.

'Really? Why is that?'

'Kato's Moroccan, Dad,' Brigid said, as if it should have been obvious to everyone from the word go. 'Imagine introducing Mum to anyone from Africa.'

When Nora came in from her Italian class she was told the story.

'Where in Morocco is he from?' Nora asked with interest.

'Marrakech,' Brigid said, surprised.

Nora clasped her hands with pleasure. 'How wonderful. We'll go to see you there!'

'But Kato's going to live *here*. He has a shop, I told you.'

'I know, but you'll have to go and buy things there, and maybe your dad and I could go and you could show us round the Djemaa el Fna – it's this huge square in the middle of Marrakech where they have all kinds of things, a great market, snake charmers, musicians . . . It would be lovely to go with someone who knew it.'

Brigid was all smiles at the thought of this journey.

'And do you have a picture of Kato?' Nora asked.

'Of course I do.' She took out a packet of pictures where she stood with the arm of a tall handsome Moroccan around her shoulders.

'Isn't he handsome,' Nora said. Not a word about him being *foreign* and how there would be *many differences to get used to*. Just that he was handsome and that it would be great to go and see his country.

Aidan looked at Nora with affection. He was so lucky to have her. He must face those big bullies up in Mountainview School and get a proper life and pension for her. It was the very least that she deserved.

It was the exercise demonstration in Johnny's room. Nora and Aidan were sitting with the exercise sheet following, while Johnny went through the various movements. A man in a wheelchair joined in cheerfully for all the arm and neck exercises. He looked on enviously as Aidan did four minutes on the treadmill.

'I'd love to be able to do that,' he said. 'But I get out of breath after a few seconds so it isn't worth it.' His name was Bobby Walsh, he said; he had owned a big business once but after his heart attack he retired.

'Did you hate retiring?'

'I did at the beginning, but there are so many things I never had time to do before. It's hard on my wife, I think, having me under her feet all the time.'

'Is she with you today?'

'No, Rosemary has a hundred things to do, people to meet . . .'

Aidan felt lucky and loved because Nora had come with him. She was questioning Johnny about what kind of weights Aidan should lift. Johnny said everyone should have a couple of large tins of peas around the place.

'Did you have a son to take over the business?' Aidan wondered.

'No – Carl was never interested in it. Never at all. He's a teacher up at Mountainview – a tough place, but he's able for it; he says that a few of the older brigade find it hard going.'

'That's me for one,' Aidan said. 'I teach Latin there, that's when I can get into the classroom.'

'Oh, you're Aidan Dunne!' Bobby smiled with recognition. 'Carl often mentioned you, he said you make the kids love Latin – which is no mean achievement.'

'What's your son's name?'

'Carl Walsh.'

'Of course I know him, very nice young lad, teaches English, doesn't he?'

'That's right.'

'Well, I'll see him when I get back there, in a few weeks' time.'

'You're going back?' Bobby seemed surprised.

'Have to,' said Aidan Dunne.

*

Clara was pleased with the way Nora Dunne had given her support. So it might only be for six weeks but it was certainly whole-hearted. Nora Dunne was interested in everything. It was a great way to be, Clara decided.

She would take out her portable atlas and look at a map of Poland to find where Ania lived. She would take it out again so that Fiona could show her the little island in Greece where she had spent a summer. Nora would talk to the other patients and debate the merits of Jack Russells who barked their heads off with Judy Murphy. She would find Something New Every Day for Lar. She would discuss diets seriously with Barbara: Nora Dunne who was built like a lithe greyhound would puzzle over why celery soup was meant to be so good for you while a potato with a nice lump of butter on it was the devil incarnate. She would never be without entertainment and stimulus in her life and it was a gift far greater than money.

'Do you mind not telling your dad about the baby?' Tony O'Brien asked Grania.

'What?'

'I mean just at the moment.'

'But why? I was going to go over and tell them this evening.'

'I thought we could wait until Sunday lunch, they're coming here.'

'But Brigid is bringing Kato, she won't want us stealing all her thunder.'

'I'd say she and Kato won't mind a bit of the spotlight going off them at all.'

'I was looking forward to telling them!'

'This way is better, we might tie it in with asking them to baby-sit and maybe it would provide a way out of teaching for your father.'

'I wouldn't hold my breath,' Grania said. 'He's like you – lives for that bloody school.'

Nora and Aidan took a bus to the lunch party. They were looking forward to it; wasn't it great that Brigid had finally found a young man she liked. They had often thought she was lonely in her tiny city apartment. Grania would serve food without added salt and would make sure it was low fat. She would provide fresh fruit as an alternative to her great apple pie. It would be a happy afternoon.

Before they got there, Brigid was already starting to fuss.

'You mustn't mind if they say the wrong thing,' she said to Kato.

'The only wrong thing would be to say that I cannot see you,' he said.

'No, they won't say that,' Brigid said.

'Then we have no problems,' he said.

Kato stood in the hallway, a tall, handsome boy with a great warm smile.

'Mr and Mrs Dunne!' he said. 'How good to meet you at last.'

'And you too, Kato!' Nora kissed him on the cheek and Aidan shook his hand. Brigid stood beaming in the background. The introductions were over. The lunch could begin.

During the meal everyone except Aidan and Kato had a glass of wine. Kato poured more fizzy water for Aidan and said that they would be the only two with clear heads next day. Tony tinkled his fork against a glass and said that Grania had something she wanted to tell them. Brigid hoped it wouldn't be some further promotion at the bank for Grania; she didn't want to overpower Kato with all their successes at this first family meeting. Aidan hoped that Tony and Grania were going to move to another school in another town. Nora thought it might be a plan for a trip abroad to celebrate Aidan's birthday. She hoped not. He was still a little too shaky.

Then Grania told them the news. There was such an outburst of excitement and delight in the little town house that it was amazing the roof did not fly off. They were crying and hugging each other.

The best words were said by Kato as he wiped his eyes. 'Now I really know I am a member of this marvellous family, now that you let me be here for the sharing of this news.'

And Grania smiled at Tony. He had been right about that as about everything. It was the bit about Dad giving up teaching where he was going to run into some grief. Grania wished that it was over. They were going to lose anyway, best get it over with quick.

She didn't have to wait long. In the midst of all the excitement, all the wondering when they first knew and when it was confirmed and what date the baby would be born and would they want to know the sex in advance, Nora asked, 'Will you be giving up your job in the bank, Grania, to look after the baby?'

'Only for maternity leave. Then I'm going back,' Grania said cheerfully.

'So what will you do?' Brigid asked.

'Oh, I'm going to leave the baby every morning at your travel agency, you can file it under B!' Grania laughed.

'Yeah sure, we'd love that. But what *are* you going to do?'

'Well, we were thinking of asking someone to come in here, you know, an artist or a writer – they could have quiet, peaceful surroundings all day, just give a bottle and change a nappy. Shouldn't be hard to find . . .'

'But wouldn't they be a bit unreliable, bohemian?' Aidan said, looking concerned.

'Doesn't have to be a poet or a painter. It could be a teacher, say, someone who had a few private lessons to give.'

Aidan listened carefully.

'No, Tony,' he said.

'Hear me out. You'd be doing us a double favour, getting us out of two holes in fact. We could go off to work with a clear heart if we thought you and Signora were to be here.' Tony spoke right from the heart.

'I wouldn't have to tidy up especially for you,' Grania chipped in.

'There are lads in that school who need one-to-one tuition,' Tony said.

'I'll do it in the school, I'll stay as late as you like.'

'It won't work, Aidan, they're quiet kids, they're nervous of these gangs. They can't stay late, they go with the crowd for safety. It would really suit me to have a safe place to send them.'

'Good try, Tony, but no.'

'Dad, who would I feel safer with than you and Nora, it's a win-win set-up. You get the money you get to teach children who need it, our baby gets terrific people.'

'As I said, thanks, but no,' Aidan said.

'Signora, what do you think?' Tony asked.

'It's Aidan's call,' she said simply.

Tony looked at a loss. 'I don't want to upset a family do by pressing something further. But, Kato, do you have any wisdom to give to this?'

Kato looked from one face to another. 'Well, of course, the father of a family must do what he thinks is right, and from respect, none of us would want to change his opinion,' he said.

Aidan gave him a look which said he could marry his daughter Brigid tomorrow morning if he wanted to.

'I suppose you wanted me to say yes to Tony,' Aidan said when he and Nora got home.

'I want you to do what you want to do,' Nora said calmly.

'But you think it's a good idea?'

'I think we owe those young people something. They would be happy if we helped them out. They have been good to us over the years. Tony gave me the job as an Italian teacher, he put you in charge of evening classes. Grania always welcomed me, she and Brigid have been great; many other girls would have resented me stepping in there. I'd love to be able to help them.'

'No, Nora, don't make me feel guilty about it. It's just a ploy. It's just a scheme to find alternative work for me.'

'Oh yes,' Nora said. 'They knew in advance you were going to get a heart attack so they arranged to be pregnant at an appropriate time!'

'No, I don't mean that. They used the circumstances, that's all.'

'Oh, Aidan, stop thinking the world is a big conspiracy. You're not paranoid. Anyway I said I'm with you. Whatever you want to do, we do.'

'You'd *like* the two of us to look after that baby?'

'Well, we could be together there, we could get to know the baby, he or she would get to know us. Yes, there are ways in which I'd like it a lot.'

'Help me, Nora. I want to do the best.'

'Do the best for you, Aidan, not for me.' Nora went out into their little kitchen. 'We won't want much to eat this evening after all that marvellous spread, will we? How about an egg on toast later?'

'Help me, Nora,' he said again.

'Every step of the way – but you have your mind made up

to go back there. Why should I add to your stress?' She was calm and peaceful.

'But you would prefer if I gave it up?'

'One of the reasons I love you so much is that you never tried to change me. You never asked me to dye my hair, or wear more conventional clothes, or anything. I'm not going to do that to you either.'

'I'm looking for guidance . . .'

'No, my love, you are not. You are looking for my total support and you have it,' she said.

'I see Aidan Dunne in the waiting room,' Fiona said. 'He hasn't an appointment today.'

'No, but they might have come in for one of the demonstrations. Johnny and Lavender are doing their stuff this morning,' Barbara said.

'Right. Isn't Aidan's wife something else? She's a real character,' Fiona said.

'When we're old, will we be like that?' Barbara wondered.

'Well, if we had fellows who were as mad about us as Aidan Dunne is about her we'd be all right,' Fiona said.

'You *do* have someone like that . . .' Barbara was glum. 'The rest of us forgot to get thin so we don't.'

'Fiona, do you think I could have an examination today, I know it's not my regular day,' Aidan asked diffidently.

'Isn't that what we're here for?' Fiona was cheerful. She brought Aidan into the cubicle and sat him up on the bed.

'I'll take your blood pressure first,' she said.

'Is it okay?' he asked anxiously.

'It's a bit up on last week. Jump up on the scales here for me,' Fiona continued, relaxed and soothing. 'No, your weight hasn't changed, no sign of fluids here. Any stress or anything in the last day or two?'

'No – I learned I was going to be a grandfather, but that's all good.'

'You bet it is. Congratulations. Nothing to raise the blood pressure there.' Fiona was delighted for him.

'So I wonder why I don't feel so great,' he said anxiously.

'Is your wife here with you, Aidan?'

'You know Nora – she's always here with me; she's gone to talk to Lavender while I'm with you.'

'Suppose I ask Declan to have a quick look at you?' Fiona suggested.

'Great,' said Aidan.

Declan was calm also. 'BP is certainly a lot raised,' he said. 'Let's work out why that is.'

'Am I going to have another heart attack?' Aidan asked.

'I doubt it very much. It could be medication – or is anything else worrying you?'

'I *am* worried about something, but it's not enough to raise my blood pressure,' Aidan said.

'Could you tell me what it is and we'll decide whether that's right or not.'

Declan was frank and honest with him. But Aidan could not talk to this boy who was the same age as his children. He needed someone nearer his own age.

'Could I talk to Clara about it, Declan, it's a sort of middle-aged thing?'

'Of course – but you know Clara, that's not exactly the way to put it to her.'

'I'll be more tactful,' Aidan promised.

'Do you want Nora there?' Declan asked.

'Not really, if it's possible.'

'Leave it to me,' Declan said.

*

Clara took the consulting room and sat down with Aidan. Declan had meanwhile spirited Nora Dunne to talk to Hilary. They needed good pictures on the walls to lend some extra vision to the place. Could Nora help them about getting prints or posters?

'But Aidan?' she said.

'Is having his check-up,' Declan said very firmly.

'What is it about, Aidan?' Clara asked.

'How old are you, Dr Casey?'

'Aidan, I have asked you to call me Clara and you usually do and I am in my very early fifties, so I presume this is going somewhere?'

'I didn't feel at ease talking to Declan, he's too . . . well, young.'

'He's very good, Aidan.'

'Yes, of course. But he wouldn't understand about whether I should give up work or not . . .'

'Tell me about it,' Clara said.

She was a good listener; she nodded and encouraged and in the end the whole anxiety had been laid out. He *was* afraid of some of those thugs who had changed the face of the school where he had been so happy. He did get anxious and lose his self-confidence when they mocked him publicly. Yet he could not give up his career because of a heart problem.

He could not leave Nora without anything to live on.

He couldn't let a bunch of under-privileged sixteen-year-olds cut off his whole life. He would not accept charity and have his son-in-law wheeling and dealing, taking money from one pocket and putting it in another.

Clara listened with a sympathetic face but offered no solution. This was something that Aidan Dunne would have to sort out for himself. He needed something to happen that would help him make up his mind.

Rescue comes in the most unexpected way.

Frank Ennis had chosen this very moment to make an unexpected tour of the heart clinic to show to fellow board member Chester Kovac. Clara gritted her teeth in annoyance. How typical of him to barge in at the wrong moment. Not for him the courtesy of a phone call or the making of an appointment. Oh, no indeed. Frank regarded the heart clinic as a minor and unimportant part of his great empire. What could he want, bringing this philanthropist round to inspect the premises now, of all times?

Mr Kovac was a very charming man. He was full of praise for everything. He shook Aidan Dunne's hand and apologised for interrupting a consultation. Frank Ennis wouldn't have noticed that he was interrupting anything. Chester Kovac also spoke to Ania in Polish; his father was from the old country, he said. He said he had just met a most interesting lady called Nora and discussed pictures with her. He was going to take some of her ideas back to his own health centre in Rossmore.

'That's my wife,' Aidan said proudly.

'Really? And have you been long married? Do you have children?'

'No, we met late in life, we are not very long married, but very happily married,' Aidan said simply.

'Then we share something, Mr Dunne. We are both lucky men. I too married late in life and have a wonderful wife called Hannah. And has this clinic helped you, Mr Dunne?'

'I can't begin to tell you how much. Everyone here has been terrific, it's such a reassurance.'

'I see that in the reports. In fact I'm thinking of having something very similar in my own place in the country. It's not just city folk who have strain and stress you know . . .'

'No, but it can be tougher in the city, with the traffic, the gangs and the hooligans.'

'Don't I know? Why do you think I left New York? I only come to Dublin once a month for these board meetings in

St Brigid's. Sometimes Hannah comes too and we go to a theatre and stay overnight, but it's nice and peaceful to be home again.'

'Have you sort of retired, Mr Kovac?' Aidan Dunne asked.

'Yes, I think I have but I'm busier than ever. We had a great bit of good luck, two years back. My wife's niece Orla had a baby sort of unexpectedly, and there was a problem about raising her. So we gave her a room in the house and during the day Hannah and I look after the child while Orla goes to her classes in Rossmore. Then she comes home and takes her away.'

Clara looked very carefully at the floor. Across the room she could see the stocky figure of Father Brian Flynn who had come to collect his friend Johnny. She felt a great urge to go over to him and tell him that she was coming straight back to the Church this minute. There was a personal God and that personal God had intervened just at the right time.

Chester Kovac was talking about how he and Hannah and their dog Zloty would go for walks in the Whitethorn Woods wheeling the pram, and now that the little girl was old enough to toddle along with them it was better still.

'When you have so much happiness yourself it seems mean-spirited not to share it,' he said. Then something in Aidan's face made him stop. 'Here I am prattling on about things that aren't relevant to your life at all. Forgive me,' he began.

'No, please. It could be relevant. It could be very relevant. My daughter is going to have a baby, you see. She and her husband want us to look after it but I didn't think . . .' His voice trailed away.

'I know – I was the same way before little Emer was born. I thought it would be all little red puckered faces and screaming and nappies. But it's not – it's fascinating!'

'I was afraid we'd be too old . . .'

'So were we,' Chester said. 'But it makes us feel young.'

'I thought it was charity, finding us a job, channelling money at us.' Aidan had told Chester everything now.

'Believe me, it's you who will be doing the charitable thing, a member of the family giving love and care to a new baby.'

Aidan saw Hilary and Nora coming towards them. When she saw Aidan's face Nora knew at once that a decision had been reached. And that he was happy with it.

There were a lot of goodbyes, exchanging addresses and shaking hands with Chester, and heavy promising to go to Rossmore one day so that they could see for themselves. Nora had no idea what they were going to see, but she managed to sound enthusiastic.

Declan came out just as Nora and Aidan were leaving. 'Hey, someone should take Aidan's blood pressure,' he said.

'No need, Declan,' Clara said. 'I'd say it's perfectly fine now.'

'So we're into just guessing these days?' He laughed.

'Listen – if you'd witnessed what I just did you'd be down on your knees thanking the Almighty for keeping an eye on us,' Clara said.

'I knew this place was too good to be true,' Declan said. 'It's been a religious cult all along and no one ever told me.'

In the shopping precinct Aidan and Nora sat at the sandwich bar. They held hands and their coffee got cold as they talked excitedly about the years ahead. The child that would know them from the word go. The days free to teach children who really did want to learn Latin. A suitable place for Signora to give little conversation classes in Italian for executives. Grania and Tony could go out to work with a guilt-free heart every day.

Life couldn't get much better.

For the first time in their careful, frugal lives, Nora and

Aidan left unfinished coffee behind them. They were anxious to get the bus and go and share their great news with the baby's parents. They were impatient for the child to be born. How could they all wait until September?

Chapter Seven

Peter Barry had always been cautious and careful. It was essential as a pharmacist that you should not be slap-dash or reckless and he was proud that he kept all aspects of his life under meticulous control.

His daughter Amy had inherited none of these qualities. She was much more like her late mother: feckless, casual and unconcerned. Laura had been so hopeless about keeping records and having control of money that Peter had taken the whole thing over himself. He had immaculate accounts books. The bookkeeper and the accountant said that he didn't need anyone to oversee his figures, he had the whole thing under control.

Laura had been the arty one. She had known how to spread a piece of Indian cotton on the back of a sofa and make it look regal. She had always done the windows in the pharmacy for him. Laura had made beautiful clothes for Amy when she was a toddler. No other four-year-old had such dresses.

He looked back on the old pictures. Amy was like a little princess. But of course in recent years she looked like a terrorist or a member of the Addams family, with her matted hair and white make-up and black straggly clothes.

It was impossible to know what would have happened if

Laura had lived. Would they have been great friends and conspirators, the two of them ganging up on silly old Daddy? Or were his customers right when they said that teenage daughters hated their mothers even more than they hated their fathers? He would never know.

Amy was in her last year at school. But she had warned him not to expect any kind of good results. She hadn't been able to study because all they were offering in that school was 'pure crap'. If only her father could be in her classroom he would realise that it was rubbish, meaningless, nothing.

He had felt utterly inadequate and completely at sea when he went to the parents–teachers meeting. Her teachers, one after the other, told him that Amy was no trouble in class but paid no attention in any subject – she just stared out the window.

He suggested that she attend one of those sixth form colleges or cram colleges.

'For what?' Amy had asked. 'To learn more crap except at high speed?'

Everything was an effort. It was an effort to get up and go to school. An effort to wash her clothes in the washing machine.

They lived in a small apartment over the pharmacy. It had been part of the new mall's policy to mix housing with commercial zoning in an effort to make the place more human and avoid the empty-precinct syndrome. Amy grumbled because they didn't have a garden.

'Who would keep the garden if we had one?' Peter asked, not unreasonably.

Amy shrugged. She had a good line in shrugs. Expressive and defeated and then moving swiftly on to the next issue, which in this case was going to a seaside resort in Cyprus to celebrate the Leaving Certificate.

'But you tell me you have nothing to celebrate, Amy.'

'All the more reason to go and cheer myself up,' she said. But nothing ever cheered her up.

It was 8 a.m. and she was showing him a brochure about a holiday that cost some astronomical sum of money. Peter was adamant. He was not going to finance two weeks of Amy staying in a hotel, entering wet T-shirt competitions and partying all night.

'What are you doing it all *for*, Dad?' she asked him, her black-rimmed eyes looking at him as if she had never seen him before.

'Doing all what?' he asked.

'Oh – standing in a white coat looking at prescriptions and tutting over things and spending hours talking to reps from drugs companies.'

'Well, it's my work.' Peter was bewildered.

'Yes, but what's it for, Dad, if it isn't for me?'

'It *is* for you – but not for you to go to Cyprus.'

'Okay, that's your final word, is it?'

'Yes, it is, Amy. And I'm going to work now.'

'To make more money to give me when I'm too old to enjoy it.'

'People are never too old to enjoy it,' Peter said.

'Oh, they are, Dad,' Amy said. She didn't say any more but she obviously thought that her father was the perfect example of the point she was making.

She didn't really speak to him after that. She was polite but distant. She thanked him when he cooked a meal but announced that she was going out with a school friend. The next morning she read a magazine during breakfast, washed up her own cereal bowl and left at the same time as Peter did.

'This is silly, Amy. Where are you going?' He was worried. A silence had never gone on for twenty-four hours before.

'To get a job!' Amy called over her shoulder.

He saw her walking through the shopping precinct, her bag

over her shoulder. It seemed such a short time since he had held her by the hand at her mother's funeral and promised that he would look after her. He hadn't delivered on that promise. He had tried, but his own daughter looked at him with the eyes of a stranger.

It had been so simple when he was that age. His father had just assumed that his two boys would study pharmacy, and they did. Then, as now, it was very fiercely competitive to get a place on the course. Though chemists often told each other that they were just glorified shop assistants, they did have a pride in it all. They were people of authority.

Of course it had been so different in his father's time. A small town, one chemist shop, Mr Barry Senior was able to do so much more than Peter was nowadays. It wasn't said aloud but everyone knew that Mr Barry was as good as any doctor. He could give a child with a bad chest a course of antibiotics without needing to wait for a doctor's prescription; he could take a piece of broken glass out of a finger, or tell you if a weak ankle was a sprain or a break. He made his own elixirs which people came from far and near to get because they had such faith in them. And he had a cough medicine which worked pure magic.

His father knew there wouldn't be enough work for both boys in the shop. He was in an agony of indecision about which of them to take in, but as it happened Peter wanted to move to Dublin, and his brother Michael had gone to live in Cork.

Problem solved.

But not forgotten.

In Cork, Michael often bewailed the fact that he hadn't made a bid for the family business. In Dublin, when he came upstairs in his shopping precinct premises after long hours in the shop, Peter felt the same thing.

When his wife died, their father eventually sold the business to a young thrusting assistant who had turned it into a goldmine. Then Mr Barry Senior went to live in a bungalow in the west of Ireland where there was good fishing. He had taken up with 'a lady companion'.

Peter drove over to see him once a year.

The place was warm and comfortable. Ruby, his father's friend, had cooked a lovely meal, and had talked of their going on a cruise.

A cruise!

Peter and Amy had spent the night and as they drove home next day, there was some discontent niggling away inside him. A feeling that somehow his father had done altogether too well out of this deal. He even bragged about the old shop and spoke proudly about how many square feet had been added to the original premises.

Amy had looked out of the car window as they passed through towns and over rivers and past ruined castles on the way home.

'What are you thinking?' he asked her.

'I was wondering do those two old people still have sex?' she said.

And Peter found the image so unsettling he resolved never to ask Amy or anyone else what they were thinking. It was never good to know . . .

As he watched Amy go off to get a job he had no idea what was in her mind. Was she full of regret that she hadn't studied properly? Or resentment that she had no mother, only a crusty, mean-spirited father who didn't understand her need to go and get drunk for fifteen days in Cyprus? He wondered who would employ Amy, and as what?

He wished that he had a batty old friend like Ruby, someone he could speak openly with about Amy. But there was nobody.

Just at that moment, Clara Casey from the heart clinic came in.

'Peter, I've come with my begging bowl,' she began straight away.

'Right, what good cause is it this time?' He put on a mock-martyred look.

'Now, I never asked you for any money for *any* cause before, did I? No, it's your time, not your money.' She explained that they were going to have a series of lectures at the clinic for patients and their families as well as the general public. It was all part of trying to get a wider understanding of how the heart functioned. She would love it if he, as the local pharmacist, were to come in and talk about the different kinds of medication: beta blockers, ACEI medicines. If he could do it in lay-person's terms it would be much more satisfactory than doctors blinding them with science and long names. People trusted their chemists, they had faith in their pharmacists, Clara said flatteringly. It would come better from the man they saw in his white coat every time they went into the shop.

Peter was pleased that she thought so well of him. 'You've never heard me speak in public. I'm not one of the world's great orators,' he confessed.

'You're the person they'll be meeting, Peter; in fact you may even get more customers if you make yourself sound appealing and attractive and easy to approach.'

'Oh, well, if it's a matter of drumming up business then I have to go,' he said with a smile.

They fixed the date and the time and Peter said that he'd love to know more about the whole project. Possibly Clara might have dinner with him one evening? She paused for a moment and then said that would be lovely. But it *was* her hobby horse and she could talk for Ireland on the subject – so if he promised to insist on other topics as well then she'd be delighted.

'Where would you like us to go?' she asked.

He was going to say the café in the precinct, but that was more a snack-and-burgers place, not dinner as such.

'Quentins?' he heard himself say.

She smiled a big broad smile. 'Now that would be a lovely treat,' she said. So they fixed a date for that too and Clara went off to work.

Peter smiled to himself. The day had started well after all.

'Did you get a job?' he asked Amy that night.

'Yup, thanks,' Amy said.

'Could I ask what it is?' He knew he sounded lofty and superior and not like he should if he was trying to win her confidence.

'A bit like yours, I'm working in a shop.'

'I own my shop, Amy,' he said.

'Yup, and I may own a shop some day too.'

'And you'll be selling what, exactly?'

'Fishnet tights and stiletto heels.'

'And there are enough women out there to buy these things?'

'Who said anything about women, Dad? It's a drag shop, it's for TVs and fancy dress and the like.'

'Of course,' Peter Barry said, feeling slightly faint.

Clara was surprised that Peter suggested they should meet at Quentins around six thirty. It seemed very early. She would prefer to have come home to shower and dress before going out. It had been a long time since she had had a real dinner date. But he seemed to think that this was the right time, so she agreed. Probably he had to be home early, as he had a young daughter; anyway, she would take a change of outfit to the clinic and be ready to go when work was over.

During the day she wondered why she had said yes. Her usual response was to say that she had such an exhausting job she went to bed early, or to imply that there was a shadowy figure somewhere in her background that prevented her from accepting dates. But Peter had been easy-going, natural. And what the hell, a nice dinner at Quentins was just what she needed on a cool spring evening.

Brenda Brennan showed them to their table. There were a few tables occupied, and it was gracious and elegant: Clara looked around at her surroundings. She had been here twice before. Once with Alan shortly before she had found out about Cinta. He had left the table four times to make urgent phone calls. Clara had seen nothing unusual about it at the time.

Then she had come here with her friend Dervla on the night after Dervla's father, the wise Professor of Medicine, had died. Dervla had said that there would never be anything spontaneous and unexpected in her life again and Clara had suggested a posh dinner out. It had been very healing and well worth the cost.

Peter Barry had not been to Quentins before. He was still stunned at the thought that he had suggested such a top-of-the-range restaurant. There was something elegant and cool about Clara, something that called out for a place like this. He noticed immediately that she had dressed up in a smart brocade jacket and a black silk dress. She was enthusiastic about the menu, and settled for fresh sardines followed by lamb.

Their conversation was easy from the start.

He told her about growing up in a chemist's shop in a small town. About his father's late life romance, about how everything had changed. Not always for the better. His father had four chairs in the chemist's shop. Older people always liked to sit down. Today in his pharmacy he had one chair and that was just in case someone felt unwell.

He told her that his mother had been kind and self-effacing; she would be amazed if she had lived to see how many women pharmacists there were now. In her day it would have been highly unusual for a woman to qualify as a chemist.

'Lord, how nice it would have been, to have a self-effacing mother,' Clara said wistfully. 'Mine knew she was right about everything and still knows it.'

'And was she?' Peter asked.

'Not remotely,' Clara laughed. 'But then I think I'm right with *my* daughters too, and they don't take the slightest notice of me.' They talked easily about daughters and their difficulties.

Peter told how Amy had gone to work in a drag shop selling amazing red satin corsets and pointy shoes. Clara said that she wished her Linda would be as adventurous, or at any rate get a job: she seemed to think the world owed her a living. They talked about the heart clinic and how it had to be supported by a proper health education programme. About how pharmacies nowadays often depended on cosmetics for their profits. Peter said he hadn't studied long hours so that he could advise some mother about red velvet hair bands for her twelve-year-old's party.

Clara agreed and said it had been a long journey to where she was, and now that she had got there she spent an inordinate amount of time talking to Frank-the-Crank in hospital administration, who spent his working day trying to thwart them at every turn.

'He is so penny-pinching, so desperately the-letter-of-the-law rather than the spirit of it that we spend our time trying to think up equally petty ways to deal with him,' she laughed. 'Ania and Hilary and I have a ten-minute session every morning to fight him over who pays for the toilet paper or the tea bags. I don't care – it's so juvenile – I just want to get on with it.'

He looked at her admiringly: she was full of passion and enthusiasm. Just then he noticed that most of the people were leaving and the waitress approached their table.

'Would you like to have your coffees in the bar?' she asked politely.

'No, we're fine here,' Clara said before Peter had time to answer. 'Aren't we?' She looked at Peter for confirmation. But it wasn't there.

'The bar would be nice, I think,' he said.

'Whatever you say.' She seemed surprised.

'You see, I booked an Early Bird dinner, so they will need our table for the next sitting.'

'Oh, of course,' she said hastily.

'I mean, it makes sense, it's almost half the normal menu price,' he said defensively and somehow, some of the light went out of the evening.

'Dervla, is it too late?'

'Of course not, Clara, it's only nine thirty. I thought you were going out on a date.'

'I was and I did but I'm back home again.'

'That sounds like speed dating,' Dervla said.

'Yes, it does.'

'So – did you enjoy it?'

'I did actually – until the end when I realised he had taken the Early Bird option in Quentins just because it was cheaper.'

'Oh, Clara – that's not like you, judging people by what they spend. And anyway he'd have had to spend a fair whack in Quentins no matter which menu it was.'

'I don't know . . . I just felt it was a bit . . . I just don't know . . .'

'You didn't like him. Did he grope your knee?'

'No, I did like him, and there was no groping. I had been thinking of inviting him to Sunday lunch; the girls are rarely around at the weekends.'

'And did you ask him?' Dervla wanted to know every detail.

'No, I didn't. I thought I'd let it wait a while.'

'Just because he bought you a bargain meal?'

'I know it sounds idiotic, that's why I rang you.'

'Oh, invite him. Tomorrow. First thing.'

'Why exactly?'

'Because we always regret what we *don't* do, rarely what we *do* do.'

'Who said that?'

'I can't remember. Was it Mark Twain?'

'Shouldn't I get out now, quit when I'm winning?'

'But you're not winning, Clara, that's the point.'

'Oh Lord, Dervla, what would I do without you?'

'You might work yourself to death,' Dervla said and hung up.

'Was it a good evening?' Ania asked next day.

'It was very nice, Ania, very nice, beautiful food and very elegant . . .'

'But?' Ania said.

'That's just it, he was very charming, very polite. I'm just being silly.'

'It was that handsome Mr Barry from the pharmacy, you said?'

'Yes, do you think he's handsome? Really?'

'Yes – he is like a film actor, I think.'

'Yes . . . maybe.'

'And will you see Mr Barry again, do you think?'

'I think so – I am going to ask him to lunch on Sunday.'

'Oh good . . .'

'Why do you think it's good?'

'Because romance is always good,' Ania said simply. She thought about Carl and smiled to herself.

Clara reached for the phone before she could change her mind. 'Peter, thank you so much for last night.'

'Oh, good, Clara, I enjoyed it too, greatly.'

'Would you like to come to lunch with me in my house on Sunday? I could cook for you . . .'

'That's very nice of you – and will your daughters be there?'

'With any luck they won't. I'll email you my address. Is one o'clock okay?'

'Thank you so much, Clara,' he said and his voice was warm.

Dervla had of course been right. Now she was pleased to be seeing him again, instead of just sitting here grumbling about a date which had turned out to be slightly less than perfect.

'Dad?'

'Yes, Amy?' He was pleased that she had telephoned.

'You know the way you always complain when I don't tell you things?' She would ring, of course, when he had three people waiting for prescriptions.

'Yes, well what are we talking about here?'

'I'm going away for the weekend.'

'We could talk about this later.'

'There is no later, Dad. I'm going today. Back late on Sunday night.'

'Where exactly?'

'To London, they want me to see some of the shows that shops like ours do so that I could organise evenings like that in Dublin.'

'And who are you going with?' he asked weakly.

'That's right, Dad. So now you know. See you Sunday night.' And she hung up with the air of one who had solved everything and was now free to head off to England and explore the world of bizarre sex and fetishes.

Adi and her boyfriend Gerry were going on a protest march at the weekend, something about preserving trees, so that was one thing. All she had to do was to find out Linda's plans.

Linda said she wasn't sure of her plans. Nothing was firmed up.

'Well, can you firm them up now, please?' Clara asked.

'Why?' Linda sensed that she was being got rid of. She might settle for a posh lunch out if Clara were to finance it. 'I thought I might just stay here,' she said, testing the ground.

'Well then, whatever you buy for yourself perhaps you could have it in your bedroom,' Clara suggested.

'Buy for *myself*?' Linda was horrified.

'Well, yes, Linda, you haven't paid anything towards this household for two weeks despite our arrangement. I know you will get a part-time job and contribute very soon, but in the meantime you won't expect me to cook for you.'

'No, but if I don't have a job how can I buy food?' To Linda it was a mystery.

'Ah, yes, that's the trouble. It will sort of concentrate your mind,' Clara agreed.

'What are *you* doing on Sunday?' Linda said mulishly.

'I'm having a friend to lunch here.'

'As if I'd want to hear you and some other fuss-fuss old woman talking about the heart clinic.'

'Good – we'll take it that your plans have firmed up then, Linda.'

'All *right*, Mam, and by the way, there's no need to strip the fridge bare in case I drink *your* milk or eat *your* bacon . . .'

'I always think it's better to avoid any grey areas,' Clara said cheerfully.

*

Peter arrived with a bottle of wine.

'That's nice of you. Will you open it for us?' Clara handed him the corkscrew.

'I'm afraid it's a screw-top. They're on sale at the off-licence, but I gather they're very drinkable,' he said.

'Sure, personally I think all wine should be screw-top,' Clara said as she laid out some smoked salmon on brown bread.

'I think there's a lot of nonsense in the wine business,' Peter said. 'People buy just according to price; if it's dear it must be good. That's like the Emperor's New Clothes really. Some wines like this are very good and they're half the price of some of the so-called "good" wines.'

She wished he would stop talking about money. They were middle-aged, middle-class people. She was a doctor, he was a pharmacist, they owned their houses – they could afford a bottle of wine, for God's sake. But she knew she must beat down this small irritation.

Again the conversation was easy. He admired her home: it was bright and airy, and the garden was secluded and full of colour. She told him that the trick in gardens was to have big, colourful bushes that did all the work for you and needed no care. They took their glasses of wine and strolled around the small garden as she pointed out this plant and that.

'Do you grow them from seed?' he asked.

'No, I haven't got a greenhouse or cloche frames or any-thing you'd need to be in the whole of your health to get into that kind of thing.'

'But isn't it a fraction of the price?' he asked.

'Not if you had to buy a greenhouse and spend all day and all night pricking out seeds,' Clara said with spirit.

'No.' Peter was thoughtful. Friends of his had told him that having a garden was a great drain on your money, and he had consoled himself with this as he went upstairs to his apartment.

'If you come here again during the summer we could sit out and have our lunch in this corner,' she said.

'I hope we'll still be friends in the summer,' he said simply.

They had steak and kidney pie for lunch and cheese afterwards. Clara opened a bottle of red wine. When he asked her where she had got it and how much it had cost, she lied and said she didn't know, it had been a gift. She couldn't bear to tell him that she had gone into a wine shop and asked for something full-bodied and classy, a Burgundy perhaps, and had paid accordingly. Peter Barry would have found that a great sin, not a generous, hospitable gesture.

He talked about the reps from the drugs companies who came to sell their wares.

Clara told him that it was very encouraging to see people living so well with heart failure. Patients who had come in a few short months ago in a panic seeing the clinic as some kind of anteroom to the next world were now confident and able to manage on their own. He told her that they had had a drug addict in his pharmacy during the week. A boy totally out of his mind, demanding to be given access to morphine and anti-depressants. He carried the leg of a chair as a weapon; he was thin and covered with scabs. Peter had brought him into the back and shown him the safe and the locked drawers. He had told the boy that they needed three keys to open them and one of the staff was on lunch break.

'What did he do?'

'He believed me. He began to cry and shake. I knew the others had called the Guards so all I had to do was keep him there. I gave him a couple of tranquillisers and talked to him. He thought we were waiting for someone to come back from lunch – then the Guards came. It was very upsetting.'

'He's somebody's son, you mean?' Clara asked.

'Yes, someone had great hopes for him, gave him the full-cream milk at the top of the bottle. And look at him now . . .' He seemed genuinely concerned.

'I know, but we can't play God. I had a man in the other day, dizzy spells and irregular heartbeat, so Declan and I decided he needed to wear a Holter Monitor for twenty-four hours, to check on his heart rhythms. So we strapped him up and told him to come back the next day. When we printed out the report, we could see it had been turned off just before midnight. "Well, why did you turn it off?" I asked him. "I got lucky, Doctor, I picked up a fine dame and went home with her. You couldn't expect me to wear that bloody thing, she'd think I was a weirdo . . ."'

'Can't have been all that much wrong with his heart if he could score and bring someone back to his bed by eleven thirty!' Peter said.

'Yes, well, we don't know whether it did him any good or not. He took offence that we were so cross with him and he hasn't been back!'

'What will you do?'

'Declan is the diplomat, he'll find a ruse one way or another, believe me.'

They talked about their daughters. Amy off learning about bondage garments in London, Adi hugging trees and Linda sulking and mutinous. It wasn't what either of them had expected when they had first become parents.

'Will you come to the theatre with me during the week? There's a new play at the Abbey,' Peter asked suddenly.

'That would be great, I was just reading about it this morning,' she said.

Dervla rang her that night. 'Has he gone?' she whispered.

'Oh, hours ago,' Clara said.

'I forgot he was Mr Early-to-bed,' Dervla said.

'Well, it was lunch I invited him to.'

'Right, right – now the third date, has it been mentioned?'

'The Abbey Theatre, Wednesday,' Clara said.

Dervla gave a yelp of pleasure. 'So it's more than a whirl then?'

'I don't know.' Clara was cautious.

'And a fling? It's not really a fling.' Dervla was searching for a definition.

'I'm a bit old for a fling,' Clara said.

'Right – will we call it a thing? Clara is having a thing with Peter . . .'

'Really, Dervla, you are an idiot!' Clara said, but she laughed.

'It's a *thing*,' Dervla cried. 'It has now been officially designated a *thing* . . .'

Amy came in from the airport exhausted.

'Were they interesting, the clothes you saw?' he asked. He and Clara had decided they must assume some kind of enthusiasm for their daughters' lives or they would lose them altogether.

'Oh, Dad, *please*.' Amy seemed to think he was pathetic.

But he ploughed on. 'You're my daughter, Amy, you've taken up a new career, is it so bad that I be interested?'

Amy was still suspicious. 'You're only going to say what a waste, how I threw away my opportunities and all that.'

'Well, no, I wasn't going to say that, I was just wondering did you see things you might import? But if it annoys you, let's just leave it.' His voice was different somehow.

Amy spoke slowly. 'It was interesting, yes, but I think it might be risky spending big money on some of the things they have – a lot of leather, restraints, dominatrix gear, if you know what I mean.'

'I know.' Peter nodded gravely.

'It's not that there isn't a call for it, there is, but most of our customers almost *prefer* to go to London to be anonymous. That's what I think anyway, I may be wrong.'

'That's intelligent, to notice that; so it wasn't a wasted trip?'

'No, not at all. And I met a lovely guy on the plane coming back tonight. We're going out tomorrow.'

'Is he in the same line of business?'

'Ben? Oh no, Ben is an embalmer.'

'I'm sorry?'

'An embalmer, Dad. Even you must have heard of them. You know, when someone dies, formaldehyde and all that . . .'

'Oh yes, of course, that kind of an embalmer.'

'As if there were any other kinds.' Amy got herself a glass of milk and a biscuit. The hostility seemed to be over.

Clara was sitting reading when Linda came in.

'Your friend gone then?' she asked.

'Oh yes, long ago, we had a nice lunch. There's some steak and kidney pie left if you'd like to heat it up.'

'I thought I wasn't to be fed, some kind of new law.' Linda was obviously bruised by the injustice.

'Oh, I meant that you weren't automatically to expect you would be fed. I can always offer you something, can't I?' Clara didn't have to offer twice. Linda had the dish in the micro-wave already.

'Who was she, anyway?' Linda asked.

'Who?'

'The woman who came to lunch.'

'It was a man, Peter Barry, he's a pharmacist.'

'Oh, really. And what did Mrs Barry have to say about that?'

'Very little. She's been dead for twelve years.'

'A widower? Huh.'

'That's it.'

'A date, no less.'

'Not really.'

'Are you seeing him again, Mam?'

'Yes, on Wednesday, we're going to the theatre.'

'Don't you think you should let Adi and I meet him first?' Linda was wagging her finger and doing an imitation of the way Clara spoke.

'Finish that pie and wash the dish before the vegans come home and get upset.'

When Clara came in to the clinic the following morning, she saw Hilary already there, busy getting through the paperwork. She remembered their one-time jokey agreement that they were going to contrive a meeting between Clara's Linda and Hilary's Nick. The perfect marriage would result from it – but they had to do it on their own.

No point in talking to Hilary about anything like that now. She would look totally uncomprehending. Since her mother's death she had been like a stone, offering no conversation and responding as briefly as possible. Hilary still blamed herself entirely for her mother's death and the injury of an innocent driver. No amount of decisions and verdicts at the inquest satisfied her. She worked longer hours even than Clara did, but her soul wasn't in it. It was as if she was working to stop herself having to think about the enormity of what had happened.

Still, maybe she might remember the name of that hairdresser she had been to way back. The woman had taken years off her.

Clara would like to look young on Wednesday night.

Kiki looked at Clara's hair with interest. 'It's very thick and shiny for your age,' she said eventually.

'Thank you,' Clara said coldly.

'I mean, you were the one who wanted a younger style, I'm only saying that it's young enough.' She was obviously speaking the truth.

Clara smiled. 'Yes, but it's Office Hair, I want Evening Out Hair.'

'Are you going to a do?' Kiki brightened up.

'I'm going to the theatre,' Clara said.

'Are you going to be on the stage?'

'No, I'm going to be in the audience but I would like to look younger. Is that possible?' Clara knew there was an edge to her voice.

'You've got good ears,' Kiki said, 'have you nice earrings?'

'Yes, I do, as it happens.'

'Right, we'll make it short over the ears, change the shape a bit, that's all you're looking for, isn't it? A change?'

'I suppose that's right. Okay, go ahead, change me.'

Kiki shrugged. Older people were really quite mad these days. There was a time when they had a perm twice a year and that did them. Nowadays they wanted new images, make-overs, the lot. And as her boss always said, just as well for business that they did.

'I'll have you shampooed, madam,' Kiki said.

Later she brought a mirror so that Clara could examine the new style from every angle. It looked very good.

'Thank you, Kiki. And what exactly do you mean I have got good ears?'

'They're neat and small and stick to your head,' Kiki explained.

'But aren't most people's stuck to their head?' Clara lowered her voice nervously.

'Oh no, madam, you're so wrong, some of them who come in here have ears that look as if they're revving up for flight. Be proud of your ears, madam, show them off!'

'Thank you, Kiki.' Clara wondered why nobody had ever told her about her ears before. People were so unobservant.

Peter said she looked wonderful. 'Something different?' he asked.

'I got my hair cut.' Clara made it seem simple.

'What beautiful ears you have,' he said admiringly.

She had been about to make a joke, but she saw the genuine admiration in his face.

'Thank you, Peter,' she said simply and they went into their seats.

And so it went on for the next few weeks. Peter would ask her out twice a week and Clara would ask him out once a week. She took him to the zoo one day, and he took her to a circus. Since the lunch at her place, they avoided asking each other home. Too many inquisitive young people around. It would destroy the restful nature of their meetings. Nothing was promised, committed or even planned. It was just a relationship that suited them both very well.

The matter of sex would soon have to be sorted out.

The goodnight kisses were longer and more clinging. They were too old for this nonsense. They were both free agents. But neither wanted to be the first to suggest it lest everything change. And then Amy announced that she and Ben were going to a conference.

'An embalmers' conference?' Peter said.

'No, of course not.'

'A fetish conference?'

'We do have another life outside work, Dad; we're going to a creative writing weekend, if you must know.'

'That's great. And you'll be gone for the whole weekend?' He hoped she didn't hear the delight in his voice. This could be it. The weekend he invited Clara to stay.

'I won't be home on Saturday night,' Clara told her daughters.

'Ooh – is it the widower?' Adi asked.

'Is this *the* night?' Linda wanted to know.

'Don't be ridiculous,' Clara snapped. 'I am doing you the courtesy of telling you my plans. Next time I won't bother.'

'I've got good news, too, Mam,' Linda said. 'I've got a job so you get rent from next week.'

'That's great, Linda. Well done.'

'It's selling CDs and DVDs. It's not full-time work or anything.'

'No, of course not. Will you like that?'

'Well, it mightn't be too bad,' Linda said grudgingly.

'It's not actually using your qualifications,' Adi said primly.

'Yeah, a BA degree is meant to be a qualification. *You* wouldn't have a job if you hadn't added a teaching diploma to *your* qualifications.'

'At least I went out to work and contributed to this household,' Adi snapped.

'And I am now, so shut up.'

Clara thought it would be a great relief to get out of this place and be with quiet, undemanding Peter. She hoped that it would all work out all right. It had been so long since she had made love to anyone. They said you never forgot how to do it, and it all came back to you like riding a bicycle. But, hell, she had never made love with anyone except That Bastard Alan. She wished that she had accepted some of the offers that had been suggested over the past few years. It could have been a kind of rehearsal . . .

She packed a very expensive black lace slip instead of a nightdress. It was ridiculous to be so nervous at her age. But that's the way it was.

*

Peter had gone to great trouble with the flat. He had polished all the surfaces, and there were two vases of flowers on small tables. For dinner he had prepared smoked salmon, and a chicken tarragon. He had tried the chicken dish three times until he thought he had it right. He would serve wild rice and a salad. Fresh fruit and cheese to follow.

He looked around, pleased with what he saw.

When Clara arrived she left her overnight bag in the hall and came in full of compliments.

'What an ideal place to live, in the centre of everything,' she said.

He poured her a sherry, ice cold from the fridge. Clara could see how much trouble he had gone to. It was touching.

'Oh, I'm glad you like the sherry – it was half price at the supermarket but it tastes really good,' he said.

Why did he have to tell her that it was half price? It was the same with the chicken, the recipe said fresh tarragon but it was so expensive and most of it went to waste and the dried stuff was perfect and kept for ever. And, again, the same about the cheese. You could pay a king's ransom for a runny French brie, yet there was perfectly good Irish brie and all you had to do was let it ripen.

She wished with all her heart that he wouldn't pass these money-saving tips on to her. But maybe that was his way. She would offer him one as well. She had actually paid a lot for her leather handbag but she pretended it had been a bargain.

'I saw it in one of those "Today's Reductions" baskets,' she said to him.

His face lit up, he was genuinely pleased for her. He stroked the bag. 'It's perfect,' he said. 'Wasn't that wonderful of you to spot it. Well worth looking around for.'

Clara felt that she had earned brownie points for something so trivial and unimportant. Yes, she told herself, that's exactly what it was: trivial and unimportant. She would *not* let it ruin their evening.

And the evening ended very well and naturally as if they had been lovers for a long time. He told her she was beautiful, she told him he was exciting. He admired her beautiful black lace slip, she lay with her arm around his neck until they both fell asleep. In the morning she was surprised to find herself in the small bedroom in a bed that was neither a single nor a double but somewhere between the two. He brought her orange juice and coffee in bed and then they made love again.

They went to an open-air concert and bought a picnic. They walked around the railings of St Stephen's Green where the Sunday painters were exhibiting their work. Then they went back to Peter's apartment for yet another visit to the bedroom.

'I love you, Clara,' he said, as she left to go home on Sunday evening.

'And I love you too,' she said.

Did she mean it? she wondered as she drove back home in the sunny evening.

Probably, yes.

She had grown so used to *not* loving anyone after Alan that the term seemed unfamiliar. Peter was a good, warm man, he fancied her and admired her. He seemed to be happy to spend every moment, night and day with her. What was not to like about that?

She had better meet his daughter and he had better meet hers. And her friends. That's the way things happened. Yet there was a way that Clara felt it would be nice if they could keep it to themselves a little longer. A sort of escape, a restful place where the rest of the world didn't intrude at all.

When she got home, her two girls and the ever-present Gerry were sitting at the kitchen table.

'Did you have a nice time?' Adi asked.

'All loved up?' Linda wanted it confirmed.

'Yes, very nice time, thank you, and everyone here?'

'Dead interested in what you two got up to, Mam,' Linda said with a smile.

'Well, one sure thing I *did not* get up to, and that's pirating CDs like you seem to be doing.' Clara looked at the computer where Linda had been busy copying discs for herself.

'I wasn't exactly . . .'

'Not only is it illegal, but it's sure to get you sacked,' Clara said crisply and took a small jug of milk from the fridge to her room. There she made a mug of tea and called Dervla.

'I can't wait to hear,' Dervla said. 'Philip is furious with me. All day I've been miles away wondering how you were getting on.'

'Very well, in fact . . .'

'And did you . . . ?' Dervla paused.

'Did I what?' Clara was going to make her say it.

'Did you and he . . . do the bold thing?'

'Oh God, Dervla and we criticise our children for being juvenile!'

'Did you, Clara Casey? Yes or no?'

'Yes, we did, three times. Happy now?'

'Very relieved, I tell you. I thought you were going to become a nun.'

'I can't believe we are having this conversation,' Clara said.

'Neither can I. When are we going to meet him?'

Clara met Amy first. Peter asked her to come in for a drink.

Amy was surprised that her father had invited a woman in for a glass of wine. She wondered what the woman would be like. Serious, probably, grey-haired with glasses. She would talk about the importance of higher education. She would be shocked by Amy's job, horrified by Ben's work as an embalmer. Still, her dad had been good about Ben coming to the house even though he was nervous of him. Amy had better be polite to this woman.

She was astounded when she saw her. Elegant, groomed, well dressed. No grey hair and glasses, instead shiny, well-cut hair, and very good make-up. This woman was going out with her *father*? Amy was totally confused.

She had prepared some cheese canapés, but wished she had done something a little more fancy. They looked what they were, a processed cheese slapped on a water-biscuit. But Clara seemed delighted and ate several of them.

Clara was very interested in the shop where Amy worked. She said that she had a friend whose feet were very big, maybe she could get elegant shoes there; Dervla always complained that you could only get big shoes in the shape of a surgical boot.

Amy took it all seriously. 'Yeah, we'd certainly have something to fit her, but warn her that they'll have these endless stiletto heels. You see that your cross-dressing folk don't want to look like a vicar's wife, they need huge glamour.'

Clara nodded, and said it was wise to forewarn Dervla who was already very tall, and might well not be able to teeter round on stilettos.

Clara also spoke pleasantly to Ben as if she had spent most of her time talking to embalmers. They talked about the necessity of removing pacemakers if it was going to be a cremation. Sometimes people forgot to tell you that the deceased had a pacemaker, but Ben said he was used to looking for the incision where it had gone in. He explained that the general public always thought your hair and nails went on growing after you were dead, but that wasn't so, it was just that the skin retracted and the nails looked longer.

Peter was taken aback. He had never had a conversation this long and this amicable with Ben. Now it turned out that the boy was well trained in his strange craft and treated the deceased with respect and dignity.

Then Clara stood up to leave.

'I have to go now, I'm taking a colleague to the cinema,' she said.

'Can I come?' Peter asked, slightly sheepishly.

'No way – my friend Hilary has been very upset recently about her mother's death, we are going to a very girly, sugary movie. You'd hate it, Peter, really you would. I'll see you some time during the week.' And she left them all gaping as she ran down the stairs and out into the precinct.

'I'm inviting my friend Peter to supper on Saturday,' Clara announced. 'I'll be cooking a salmon, I'd love you all to come.'

'Will there be an announcement?' Linda asked.

'I don't think so – unless you have something to tell us, Linda?'

'Very droll,' Linda said. 'Just wondered, that's all.'

'Is Gerry invited?' Adi asked.

'Of course. Gerry is part of the family.'

'There will be things he can eat, *we* can eat?'

'Yes, there will, and the rest of us can have salmon.'

'What will we call him, Mam?' Adi asked.

'Peter, that's his name.'

'Not "Daddy" then?' Linda wouldn't let it go.

'No, Linda, not "Daddy"; you manage to remember Cinta's name when you go to see your dad. It would be nice if you remembered Peter's.'

'Will he be overnighting, Mam?' Adi asked.

'No, Adi.'

'Do we have to dress up?' Linda wondered.

'No, Linda, just be there around seven and make him welcome . . .'

Their jaws dropped when they saw Peter. He was so much better-looking than they had thought. A pharmacist? A chemist? He should have been old and stooped. Instead he was tall and handsome. A very cheerful smile.

He asked Adi about teaching, he talked to Gerry about organic vegetables, and he even got Linda to promise to show him how to use an iPod. They questioned him closely and he answered openly. He had been a widower for a long time, he had one daughter who thought he was an old fogey, he didn't travel very much but this year he was hoping to go on a short break to Italy, rent a car, drive on the wrong side of the road and have a great time.

'Will you be involved in this, Mam?' Linda asked.

'Oh yes, indeed,' Clara said, as if it were the most natural thing in the world.

When he came to leave, he kissed Clara on her cheek and said that he had had a delightful evening and would see her tomorrow as arranged.

They waited until they heard the garden gate closing then they all went mad. He was terrific, he was like a film star, he was great fun. How had Mother managed to trap him?

And Clara went to bed well pleased.

The worst was over. They had met each other's children, everything else was going to be plain sailing.

Clara's mother was the first to hear.

She had called around unexpectedly to the house on Sunday and the girls told her that Mam was out with a real looker, a guy in a velvet corduroy jacket. Apparently it was a fully fledged Affair.

'You didn't tell me any of this?' Her mother's sharp disapproving tones came down the line.

Clara had a busy day but she knew better than to cut her mother short.

'No, I was waiting until we could have a nice lunch with plenty of time to talk about it rather than rushing it all on the phone,' she began, pulling her diary towards her. She would *have* to meet her mother now.

'Where had you in mind?' her mother snapped.

'I thought Quentins would be nice.' Clara looked to see which afternoon wasn't too bad – Friday maybe? 'Friday, Mother, and I'll tell you all,' and she hung up with a heavy heart.

'Are you all right, Clara?' Hilary asked.

'Not really, I have to have lunch with my mother while she interrogates me about my sex life.'

'Will she?'

'Not directly of course, you know what mothers are like . . .' Clara could have bitten her tongue off. 'Oh, Hilary, I'm such a fool. Forgive me, I wasn't thinking.'

'Don't think of it, Clara. It's not important.'

'But it is, I know what you'd give to be able to have lunch with your mother again.'

'Maybe not. This could have been one of her bad days, she might think I was her aunt or the postman or someone about the drains.' Hilary laughed ruefully.

Clara thought that she seemed to be getting a little better about it all. Not much but a little. 'Thank you, Hilary. I don't deserve you.'

Hilary noted she had written Quentins on the diary page for Friday. 'My, you're sure pushing the boat out for your mother! Quentins no less!'

'I'd better not tell Peter then, he'd go mad at the expense.'

'Careful, is he?' Hilary asked.

'*Sensible* is what he would call it,' Clara laughed.

'You look happy,' Hilary said admiringly.

'I'm almost afraid to say it but I think I am,' Clara agreed.

Alan called about thirty minutes later. 'Did I hear congratulations are in order?' he asked.

'That's such a cliché, Alan, what are you trying to say?'

'I'm trying to say that the girls told me about your young man and I'm glad for you, that's all.' Alan sounded injured.

'Thanks, Alan. Is this it or is there more?'

'Well, I thought you'd tell me something about him, when did it happen, where is it leading?'

'And why in the name of God do you think I should discuss these things with you?'

'We're friends, Clara—' he began.

'We are *not* friends, we are contesting almost everything.'

'That is because you are being so unreasonable.'

'Goodbye, Alan.'

He called back immediately. 'Don't you hang up me, this is intolerable.'

'That's right, it *is* intolerable – I am trying to do a day's work, I will not tolerate your whingeing and whining about this and that just because *you* have nothing to do.'

'No, please, listen to me.'

'I have a line of people waiting to talk to me, Alan. You will have to excuse me.' She felt nothing as she replaced the receiver.

Peter had certainly done that for her, he had chased the big, overpowering shadow of Alan Casey away.

Clara met Peter's brother and sister-in-law and some of his colleagues. They were invariably pleasant and welcoming towards her. In turn she introduced Peter to her friend Dervla, and to Hilary and Ania and Declan from the clinic. Everyone got used to Peter calling to collect Clara after her work or even to bring her a packed lunch to share. People knew that they were going to Italy together and there was a general air of approval about it all.

Her mother was characteristically downbeat.

'Too long on his own, too set in his ways, I'd say,' was her verdict, as her mouth opened and snapped closed over oysters in Quentins.

'Only time will tell, Mother,' Clara said wearily.

'Oh no, common sense would tell, but I am afraid you're not well stocked in that department.'

'Isn't this a lovely restaurant?' Clara said.

'And it ought to be at these prices.'

'Would you like to meet Peter or not?' Clara asked.

'Common courtesy would suggest that you might introduce us but then . . .'

'But then I wasn't well stocked in that department either . . . is that what you were about to say?'

'Clara, dear, do stop frowning, if this young man is so charming he won't want to see such a crosspatch.'

'Right, Mother, big smile coming up . . .'

Unfortunately she nailed the smile to her face just as Frank the Crank, the hospital manager, spotted her across the room and thought she was smiling at him. He came straight over.

'The lovely Dr Casey,' he said, holding out his hand.

She couldn't have been more annoyed. Her mother looked up.

'Are you Peter?' she asked.

'No, madam, I'm Frank.'

'Lord – another one!' Mother said, astounded.

Clara clenched her teeth. 'This is my mother. Mother – Frank Ennis. Frank runs the hospital single-handed with a fist of steel.'

'Not exactly,' Frank smiled, letting it be assumed that that was precisely what he did.

'Lovely treat to give your daughter,' he said to Mother.

Could Mother leave well alone? No, of course she couldn't.

'Oh, dear me, Frank, it's Clara's treat, she's rolling in money – I'm a poor widow lady.'

Frank looked at Clara, pleased. Now he had something on her. Clara had fought him euro by euro, cent by cent for her salary, her staff and her expenses and here she was being described as rolling with money. Clara felt an unreasonable desire to give her mother so hard a slap that it would knock her off her chair. But life was about keeping up appearances, so it was a temptation that she managed to resist.

Clara and Peter were serious about going away for a few days and they were looking through the travel brochures and the map of Italy when Amy came in. She talked cheerfully for a while and seemed interested in their plans.

'I'll be away at the time myself. Ben and I are going to Cyprus,' she volunteered.

'That's terrific,' Clara said, and they got the map to see where Ayia Napa was.

'Do you know what, Clara?' Amy looked out from under her great fringe of long fuzzy hair.

'No, what?'

'If you would like to spend nights here in this flat with my father, that's fine with me.'

Peter turned a dull brick red. Clara knew she had to rescue the situation.

'That's most generous and welcoming of you, Amy. I do appreciate it, and if it's too late to go home some time, I'd be very grateful, but at the moment it's not a big issue.'

'Okay, not at the moment, but when you come back from Italy you might feel different, what with being used to sharing a room. I just wanted you to know that it's cool with me.'

The holiday was a huge success. They spent a couple of days in Florence, a couple of days in Venice and then a lazy weekend beside a big lake. On the last day there, Peter asked her to marry him.

She hadn't expected this.

'Do you mind if I wait a little while before saying yes?' she asked gently.

He did mind, she could see that, he had hoped she would say yes at once. She could hardly bear to see his face. It had crumpled. It was hard for this man to change the habits of a lifetime, a man set in his ways as her mother had guessed. But she was not going to say yes under an Italian pergola of flowers by a blue lake. She had to come home and think about the life they would live together. That night she saw him getting up and go to sit at the window, his face sad and his shoulders stooped. They didn't mention it on the homeward journey.

And once back in Dublin, Clara said that she would need to go back to her own place to get her clothes into order for work.

'That's not important, you're running away from me.'

'Oh no, I am *not* running away from you. You have asked me a wonderful question and now that we are back in the real world I promise you that I am going to think about it very carefully.'

'When will you have thought?' he asked.

'Soon, Peter, truly.'

'But can't we even talk about what's holding you back? Is it where we live, is it our work? Is it the children?'

'No, it's none of these things. I just have to get used to it as an idea.'

'You must have known how I felt.'

'I didn't think it would involve marriage.' She spoke truthfully and he could see that.

'I know that you were a bit bruised the first time round . . .'

'No, that's not it, that's long over and done with.'

'So what is it, I beg you, Clara?'

'Soon,' she said.

'Will we take Dimples on an outing?' Fiona suggested to Declan.

'Where were you thinking of? Across Europe on the Orient Express?' Declan asked, smiling at her affectionately.

'Maybe one day, but we should break him in gradually. Suppose we said a walk along Killiney Beach for starters?'

'How would we get out there?'

'On the train. Come on, let's go – Saturday?'

'I was going to catch up on paperwork.'

'I'd make us a gorgeous chicken sandwich – and one for Dimples, too. *Please?*'

'Well, that's it then, I can't stand between a dog and a chicken sandwich.'

'You're very agreeable, Declan Carroll – will you be a very nice old man?'

'Any day now,' Declan promised.

They looked a happy little family, the red-haired doctor, the beautiful girl and the big floppy Labrador dog, as they looked out the window of the little train. Dimples loved Dalkey, which was where they got out. It was full of interesting smells and people with small dogs. They strolled along together looking at the houses and gardens.

'Imagine Bobby Walsh and Rosemary living out this way for all those years,' Declan said. 'You'd think it might have made her nicer just being here, but no . . .'

'That woman hasn't a nice bone in her body,' Fiona agreed. Then they saw the sea and Dimples barked enthusiastically.

They climbed down the rocky path to the beach at White Rock and walked along Killiney Beach. The mountains ringed the bay beautifully and other dog walkers throwing sticks had chosen to make the same outing. They greeted each other cheerily. Then they found a rock and ate the sandwiches. Dimples saw a bird and followed it to the shoreline.

'God, that was a near thing. He could almost have caught it.' Fiona had her hand to her mouth in dismay.

'No, not Dimples; anyway birds are very fast and very clever. They always escape.'

They watched Dimples barking over-excitedly at the edge of the water. The bird swooped by again, maybe to have a laugh at the sight of the fat Labrador. So Dimples ploughed determinedly out to sea in pursuit. Then suddenly, he was in trouble: the waves wouldn't let him in, he was floundering and beginning to panic.

Fiona had her shoes off and was into the water immediately. She shouted at Declan not to consider coming into the sea, that it was all under control. It didn't look under control. She was nearly up to her waist in sea water by the time she caught Dimples' collar and dragged the dog in to safety.

Dimples showered everyone around with his almighty shakes. And then he sneezed eight sneezes in rapid succession.

Declan hadn't even got his feet wet.

'I did nothing,' he confessed. 'I can't swim.'

She had struggled to help Dimples, she was indifferent to the fact that she was soaked to the skin, she was protecting him. Declan had never loved her more, and never felt more useless.

'You saved Dimples,' he said.

'Well, I thought up this cracked idea – I couldn't let Dimples perish, could I?' She was shivering and then totally unselfconsciously she peeled off her jeans, her socks, her pink frilly pants and wrapped herself up in the rug they had intended to sit on. She tied it around her waist with the belt of her jeans, sat down on the pebble beach and drained the half bottle of wine that had been part of the picnic. 'I think I can say I deserved that,' she said cheerfully.

'Fiona?'

'Yes?'

'Fiona . . . It seems an odd kind of thing to say just now . . . but . . .'

'But I shouldn't strip off like that on the beach. I won't again, I just wanted to get out of the wet clothes.'

'No. That's not what I was going to say. Not at all.'

'So what was it?' She looked at him, her eyes squinting in the weak sunshine, already warm and dry from the rug that wrapped her up.

'I was going to ask you would you marry me?' he said in a rush.

'*Marry* you, Declan?' She was utterly astonished.

'Well . . . yes. There's nothing in the world that I want more.' He was almost afraid to meet her eye in case he saw pity or ridicule or a wish for a kind way to let him down gently.

She said nothing.

'I'd be very good to you and look after you. I love you, Fiona, with all my heart.'

'Married?' she said. 'You mean married, married like grown-ups?'

'Please say yes. Please.' Declan was looking at Dimples' tail thumping on the beach. He was still afraid to look Fiona in the eye.

'Declan,' she said in a low voice.

He looked up. She was smiling.

'I thought you'd never ask me. I'd *love* to marry you. I'd love it with all my heart.'

And he leaped up and dragged her to her feet, and kissed her for so long that Dimples was concerned and began to circle them with anxious barks. And if anyone had been watching the little tableau they would have seen the rug around the girl slip down and the two young people grab it as if their lives depended on it.

Back in the clinic, they told Clara she looked wonderful. Tanned and rested.

'And like a demon for work,' she threatened. 'Come on now, tell me what's happened.'

They told her stories.

There was of course only one real item of news: Declan and Fiona were going to get married.

They had tried to say nothing but everyone knew that something was afoot. Eventually Barbara had more or less beaten it out of them. Had they made plans or had they not? When they shuffled and said sort of, the place had gone mad.

In vain did Declan and Fiona try to protest that no ring had been bought, no date had been fixed. It was the first home-grown romance and everyone was milking it for all they could. Ania had rushed out and bought sparkling wine, Lar had a few choice facts about weddings for people to note down and remember. There was a card, too, which Clara must sign: they had been waiting for her to come back. Hilary had been wistful, she remembered being young and in love. Bobby Walsh had said it was enchanting news and that Rosemary would be delighted, which nobody really believed. Johnny managed *not* to say that no good would come from it all; and Lavender offered to make the wedding cake and said they should tell her in good time when they set a date.

Then Bobby Walsh had taken a turn and been back in intensive care, and everyone there said that he was brilliant because he knew all his medications. Blinded them with information. He was on the mend again and coming in every week.

'That's thanks to Declan,' Clara said.

Kitty Reilly had discovered a new saint called St Joseph of Cupertino who apparently was the last word on curing people. She had leaflets about him which she distributed to everyone in the waiting room. Fiona had said as a joke that poor Padre Pio must be up in heaven feeling very left out now that Mrs Reilly had moved on, so Kitty had got a whole new stock of Padre Pio medals for fear of causing offence.

Lar had taken to asking the people in the waiting room to learn one new fact per visit, which was irritating them. One of Judy Murphy's Jack Russell terriers had broken his paw when a gate slammed on it and poor Judy was on her way carrying him to the vet when she met Declan who put it in a splint for him. And the vet said afterwards that he never saw a better job, and that if Declan tired of dull, boring, bad-tempered human people, there was always a job for him with dumb animals and man's best friends.

Lavender had got a famous celebrity chef to come and give a cooking demonstration on one of their Evenings of Getting to Know the Heart. Johnny had got a once-weekly slot on television doing cardiovascular exercises. Tim the security man had fallen in love with Lidia who was Ania's flatmate and she was bringing him back to Poland to meet her family.

'And what about you, little Ania?'

'Nothing new with me, I still work hard and I still say thank you to Our Lord every night for making me meet you and change my life so much.'

'And are you still saving for your mother's house?'

'You wouldn't believe how much I have saved, Clara. I work in Declan's mother's launderette, and I do some clean-ing in that nursing home where Hilary was thinking of taking her mother. They are so nice there . . . Mrs Cotter is a little like you, I think.'

'That's good,' Clara said. 'And does Carl Walsh still give you English lessons?'

Ania looked down at the ground. 'Yes, yes,' she said. 'But there is no hope in it. No hope, I fear.'

'Hey, but your English is *great*!' Clara said.

'Oh yes, I am learning the English. That's fine, that part of it,' Ania said.

And then Clara realised she meant there was no hope for her with the handsome Carl Walsh. Clara would not like to have taken on the formidable Mrs Walsh herself. Bobby would have been a pussy cat but Mrs Walsh – why, you'd need nerves of steel for her.

'On a level playing-field you might have had plenty of hope.'

'Please?'

'It's an expression, it means . . .'

'I know what it means – it means if all things were equal,' Ania said.

'That's exactly what it means. But because of his mother they are probably not.'

'It's pleasing, anyway, that you think there might have been hope,' Ania said.

Clara had never been one to talk out her problems with girl friends, analysing them to the bone. She *did* like a good gossip with Dervla O'Malley, but apart from that she kept her difficulties to herself. She had discussed with no one the fact that she was going to marry Alan Casey. Perhaps she should have. And why was she speaking of Alan and Peter in the same breath? Even to herself? They were so utterly different . . .

Dervla was a good confidante and very astute.

'Did he ask you to marry him?' she asked. They were having a lunchtime coffee in Dervla's golf club. It was one of the few places they would be sure of not being disturbed.

'Yes, on the last night,' Clara admitted.

'Am I going to have to beat it out of you? Are you going to tell me what you said?'

'What do *you* think of him, Dervla?'

'He hasn't asked *me* to marry him and somehow I don't think Philip would like it if he did.'

'Seriously, though, what *do* you think?'

'I think he's so suitable it's as if we invented him.'

'I don't have this breathless feeling.'

'Well, God, Clara, look at the age of you! If you were going round with teenage palpitations then it really would be something to worry about.'

'So you think I should?'

'Are you mad? Advise you? Advise *you*, Clara? But, all right, I think if you settle for Peter, you will have a pleasant, happy, good-tempered companion who loves you. What's wrong with that?'

'The words "settle for", I think that's the flaw,' Clara said.

'Lord, the devil wouldn't please you, Clara Casey.'

'Did you settle for Philip?'

'You know I did. I couldn't have the hopeless guy I fancied, he needed to marry money and so he did. And later I met Philip and I bless every day since then.'

'But no *zing zing*?' Clara probed.

'I don't know what *zing zing* is!' Dervla laughed.

'You *do* know what it is,' Clara insisted.

'Well, I know what it *was*, certainly, but I think it runs out after the age of twenty-five.'

'So after that we just settle for people?'

'It's very comfortable, and a lot less lonely and it's less likely to end in tears,' Dervla said.

'You may well be right,' said Clara and they didn't talk about it again.

That afternoon she found herself talking to Nora Dunne, the tall, competent wife of Aidan Dunne who had done so much to help her husband regain his health and strength.

'Dr Casey, I have come here to thank you for being so helpful,' she said now. 'I should have trusted you from the beginning. Aidan and I have a whole new life. I also want to apologise for wasting your time with my worries and complaints.'

'No, no, please, you were in shock.' Clara was soothing.

'It's just that he is the love of my life. I think of him from the dawn every day until I go to sleep that night. I wonder what *he* thinks of this and of that, I store things up to tell him. I think I went a little mad when I heard the words "heart disease".'

'It's very controllable nowadays. We don't pretend that it has gone away, vanished completely, but with regular monitoring, great things can be done.'

'I know that now, Dr Casey, but I'm afraid the possibility of a life without Aidan blew everything out of my mind. You see I met him so late in my life, the only thing that made sense was if I were to have him for a good many years now.'

'I know, I know.'

'I believe you do know, these people here at the clinic told me that you too had a new love recently in your life and that you had gone to Italy with him. Don't be cross – you see I was so anxious to apologise to you personally. I had them driven mad. They told me you were on vacation . . .'

'There's no need for any apology, Mrs Dunne. I am surprised though that they told you I was holidaying with a man friend. It's quite true, as it happens, but they usually never say anything. About my private life.'

'Oh, that's my fault entirely, please don't blame them. I kept pestering them. I think I wore them down.'

Clara looked at her. Nora Dunne was like a woman in the grip of some great passion. Eventually Nora spoke again.

'I was so glad when I realised that you too had a great love in your life, then you would know the terror of loss, the need to be with someone that makes you almost insane. If anything happened to Aidan, I would not want to live. I think my own heart would stop beating in sympathy. I couldn't bear a day or a night without him now and without seeing his dear face. And if you, Doctor, were in La Bella Italia with a man you love, then you would find it in your heart to forgive me.'

Clara looked at her – but she didn't see the woman in front of her. Instead she looked through her. She saw a life of *settling for* Peter, a life of bargains and special offers and cut-price goods, a life with companionship and no loneliness and no risks and no free spirit any more.

'You have done me a great favour by coming here today. I had something to do which I was putting off, but now it's clear, and it will be done this evening,' she said.

Nora Dunne looked after her, confused, as she left the building and got into her car.

Peter answered the buzzer when she rang the doorbell of his flat. He sounded delighted to see her.

She went up the stairs with a heavy heart.

'Will I open some wine to celebrate?'

'No – unless you want to celebrate being free of me,' she said gently.

For a moment he was too shocked to respond. Then he sprang to his feet. 'But *why*, Clara, *why*? We get on so well – Amy loves you, I love your girls.'

'Peter – do you know what I mean by *zing zing*?' she asked.

'No. No, I don't know, what is it?'

'It doesn't matter.'

'I could learn,' he said hopefully. He was so nice. She was completely mad. Like she had been mad to marry Alan.

But it *did* exist – mad, passionate love. She had seen it in her clinic not an hour ago. It was there somewhere. There would be no settling for anything. There would also be no rethink. Peter said they should wait before making a decision, but Clara's mind was made up.

'Can we be friends and occasional lovers?' he asked.

'No, that won't work,' Clara said. 'Sit here and think of all the good things there are about this, Peter, there are many. And I'm glad we went into it rather than just fencing around; we always regret what we don't do, rather than what we *do* . . .'

'Maybe you'll regret not marrying me then?' he said.

'You will marry someone, Peter, and you'll be a great husband.'

'And you?'

'I think not. I'm too fond of being a free spirit.' She hugged him as you might a brother as she left the cheerless apartment.

She was down the stairs and out in the busy precinct before he could say any more. In the jeweller's on the corner they had a lot of rings discounted. She knew without having to ask that he must have been in there already and maybe even chosen one. But she put her shoulders back and walked on with more purpose than she had for a long time.

Chapter Eight

When Vonni went to collect her mail, she saw that there was a letter from Fiona. It was odd, she had only heard from her last week. She had been full of news about this boy Declan Carroll who was a doctor in the heart clinic and who had a car crash but was recovering very well. Perhaps this one was saying that they were engaged. Vonni hoped so.

Her little craft shop was empty. She sat down and poured herself a cup of thick sweet Greek coffee and opened the letter. It was not about an engagement, even though it said the romance continued as wonderfully as ever. Fiona wanted to tell her that these really eccentric seventeen-year-old twins would love a job of any kind for the spring break.

She said that no amount of genealogists and historians could explain who they were. They possibly had real parents somewhere and they were originally from some toffee-nosed family but for years Muttie and his wife Lizzie had given them a home in St Jarlath's Crescent.

They were bright and funny. The boy was hoping to go into law and the girl was going to be a teacher. They were agreeable kids and they would be well able to carry boxes of things or go with Vonni to market. They could do washing-up for Andreas as well. They didn't want to make real money, just to pay for a holiday and get some work experience.

She ended up, *'I hope you'll be able to find something for them, Vonni. Despite all my mad dramas and disasters there I just love the place, and I always think of it and you all with huge affection. Love always, Fiona.'*

Vonni thought about it for only a moment, then she took out her writing paper and began a letter.

Dearest Fiona,

Send me the twins, I'd love to meet them. The hens died of old age and I hadn't the energy to replace them so the hen-house as you used to call it is empty. We'll have it cleaned up and put two beds in it and they can stay here. Tell them to come on a night ferry – Aghia Anna looks glorious in the dawn – give them directions to my place and I'll look after them . . .

She would go now and put it in the post box. But the bell on the door jangled and she looked out to see who it was. It was Takis, her lawyer.

He walked into the shop and looked around. 'Are we on our own, Vonni?'

'You sound as if you had secrets of state to tell.'

'No, but it is private business.'

'Fire away, Takis.'

'Your son is in jail on remand in England.'

'My God – what for?'

'Some VAT fraud or other.'

'And what's going to happen now?'

'He can't get bail. It's quite high you see, they're afraid he'll skip.'

'And how do you know all this, Takis?'

282

'Well, since you made your will a while back leaving everything to him, I had to keep an eye on where he was. In case you died and I had to get in touch with him. No matter how I feel about this it *is* your wish . . .'

'And Stavros asked you to get in touch with me?' Her face was full of hope.

'No, Vonni, he doesn't even know that I am aware of his circumstances.'

'He didn't ask for me?'

'No.'

'But I will organise his bail, of course I will.'

'I was afraid that's what you might want.'

'Afraid?'

'My contact says that he will skip.'

'Well, if he does, he does. He must get that chance. I owe him that.'

'You owe him nothing.'

'So you say, but I know different. I was drunk and out of my mind all through his childhood. I owe him more than can ever be repaid.'

'It's a lot to take on, Vonni. You may have to go to England, they won't accept anonymous funds from abroad.'

'I'll go, of course I'll go,' she said.

Takis bowed to her and left. He would have given the boy a boot up the arse. But mothers were different.

Fiona went to see the twins with the letter from Vonni.

'It's an unusual name,' Maud said.

'For an Irish person,' Simon filled in.

'I think it was Veronica originally,' Fiona explained. 'She's from the west of Ireland.'

'You must have said we were great if she's taking us on and giving us a place to stay.' Maud was a bit overwhelmed by it all.

'It's only a hen-house, but you're right, I did say you were very reliable.'

'How do you know we'll be reliable?' Simon wanted to know.

'Because the chief of police out there, Yorghis, is a great mate of mine and he'd lock you up quick as look at you if you weren't reliable.'

'Oh, well then,' Simon said.

'Then we have to be very reliable,' Maud agreed.

'And when you get out of jail, that's if you ever do, I will come round to your house and beat you both with a stick until you bleed for letting me down.'

'Lord!' said Simon.

'Heavens!' said Maud.

'Is Declan very frightened of you?' Simon asked.

'Oh, I do hope so,' Fiona said with a smile. 'How are you getting there?'

'We got a cheap flight to Athens . . .'

'And you say the ferries go two or three times a day . . .'

'So we take the bus to Piraeus . . .'

'And the boat to Aghia Anna . . .'

'And walk up the 26th of March Street . . .'

'And Vonni's shop is on the right as you go up the hill . . .'

Fiona looked at them in bewilderment. She wondered what the people of Aghia Anna would make of them.

Vonni and Andreas were having coffee by the harbour.

'I may have to go away for a short while soon,' she said.

He knew better than to ask her why. She would tell him, or she would not tell him. He talked on easily about his son Adoni who had come back from Chicago to help his father in the taverna. Now of course he wanted to buy up half the town. Andreas shook his head. Nothing was enough for young people nowadays. They always had to have more, more and still more.

'I know, Andreas, I know only too well.' She was very silent then.

He wondered if her trip had anything to do with that son of hers.

'So you want me to keep an eye on the Irish children for you?'

'If I have to go when they are here I would really appreciate it. Just a fatherly eye on them to make sure they're not bringing riff raff into my hen-house, which by the way is lovely. Please thank Adoni again for lending me his men to clean it up.'

'I was glad to see him do that rather than open a fifty-bedroom hotel. Really and truly.' Andreas was appalled at such daring and risk-taking.

'I spoke to Fiona, she phoned me last night, and said they were looking forward to seeing us. Imagine – to be their age and seeing this beautiful place for the first time . . .' She smiled around at the view of the harbour and the purple mountains. 'Fiona says her young man has asked her to marry him. She's very happy. He sounds like a good man.'

'When you go away, Vonni, don't stay away too long,' Andreas said.

It had been good advice to tell them to arrive at dawn. Maud and Simon stood leaning over the rail of the ferry boat as they came in to the harbour next morning. They pointed out the various landmarks that Fiona had told them about. That big long low white building must be the Anna Beach Hotel; the huge building high on a cliff must be the hospital.

Muttie had said they should bring Vonni a bottle of Irish whiskey. Fiona had said absolutely not, it would be the last thing she would like to see. So instead they had brought a porter cake in a tin.

They were slightly fearful of meeting Vonni. Fiona was quite frightening enough but this woman was much, much older, and probably mad and had painted a hen-house for them to live in.

Fiona said that they must do whatever she told them to do; it might be choosing wool for blind people, or carrying plates from a hillside market. Maybe Vonni might want them to give leaflets about her shop to day-trippers. Fiona had warned them again that she would know every heartbeat of it all because she would be in regular contact with the chief of police, Yorghis.

They hardly dared to say his name so fearful did they feel about him.

It was fantastic in the harbour as the old ladies in black clothes carried their cages of hens and baskets of shopping off the ferry. There were families meeting and greeting each other. There was music coming from a café.

'Do you know, it's straight out of . . .' Maud began.

'Central Casting!' Simon finished happily for her.

And together with their back packs they walked up the 26th of March Street and found Vonni's house. They knocked at the door wondering what kind of person would appear.

She was very small and wiry, with long hair twisted in a braid behind her head; she had heavy lines on her face but a bright smile.

'You look as if you need a good breakfast. What would you like?' she asked.

'*Avga* if that's all right . . .' Simon said.

'Or indeed anything at all,' said Maud politely.

'*Avga* indeed, you've been learning your Greek.'

'So far, I just learned ten words, food things, things we might be able to afford,' Simon admitted.

'Ah, if only you had been here when my magnificent hens were laying, you would have had beautiful *avga*,' Vonni said. 'But we'll do the best we can with shop eggs instead.'

'Can we help you at all?' Maud wanted to establish how helpful they would be.

'Not at all, haven't you been up all night on that boat. Go out and put your things in what I must stop calling the hen-house.'

'It might be a hen-house again when we've gone,' Maud said reassuringly.

'No, I don't think so, my friends tell me that I should use your room to let next year. I'm getting slower and there are other craft shops. Bigger and better than mine.'

'We'll help you as much as we can . . .' offered Maud.

'And restore you to your rightful position,' Simon said.

Fiona had been right. They were like some marvellous, mad double act.

Muttie called on the Carrolls' house in St Jarlath's Crescent. Declan was just leaving for work.

'And will you tell that nice fiancée of yours that she did a great job settling our Maud and Simon in. They rang to say they got there safely and this Vonni is great altogether.'

'I'm so glad to hear that.' Declan was pleased to be able to report such good news.

'They said the place was like paradise – maybe you and Fiona will go there on your honeymoon?' Muttie suggested.

'She hasn't agreed to set the date yet, she keeps saying there's plenty of time.'

'She's a very sensible girl,' Molly Carroll said approvingly. 'You were blessed the day you laid eyes on her I tell you.' She spoke with a sense of satisfaction, as if she had personally gone out into the highways and byways and found Fiona herself.

'And what took Fiona out there in the first place?' Muttie was interested.

'It was a few years back – she went with a group of friends,' Declan said. He knew from Fiona that there had been a boyfriend and that it had all ended badly but she seemed edgy and ill at ease when they talked about it, so he had let the subject fade into the background. He felt that wherever they went on honeymoon it would not be Aghia Anna, scene of many good friendships and solidarity, but also a scene of too much drama and pain.

Fiona was very pleased that the whole Greek adventure was going so well. It brought her mind back to the island and all the friends she had made there. She sent two postcards. One to David in England, David the gentle Jewish boy who had been so wonderful that summer and whose father had died so he had eventually persuaded his mother to sell the business that he had never wanted to run.

> *Dear David,*
>
>   *I have two seventeen-year-old friends who are 'working' with Vonni and having the time of their lives. They say the hen-house has been refurbished and there are five cafés by the harbour now. All our other friends are there. Wasn't it magical?*
>
>   *I have fallen in love, properly this time and it's the real thing. He's asked me to marry him and I've said yes. Have you done anything like that?*
>
>   *Love,*
>   *Fiona*

Dear Tom and Elsa,

I can't stop thinking about Aghia Anna because I have two teenage friends out helping Vonni for a couple of weeks and I remember those great days and nights we had out there. I am sure California is just as wonderful.

I have met a marvellous man, a doctor in the heart clinic where I work and we're going to get married. I suppose it's like knowing the real thing when you've only known phonies before. Anyway, when we set a date for the Big Day you'll be invited . . .

Love,
Fiona

'I don't know what I did before those twins came here,' Vonni said to Andreas and Yorghis. 'They are so quaint and old-fashioned and yet they're willing to do anything at all. I took them up to Kalatriada and we saw all these boxes of things going from a place that was closing down. Much too many to carry on the bus, so Simon took the bus back here, found Maria and brought the car up, and we had the whole lot home by nightfall. Much too bright a lad to be a lawyer.'

'Don't let Takis hear you say that,' Andreas laughed.

As it happened, Takis was passing by taking his little evening stroll around the village.

'Don't let me hear what?' he asked.

'She was speaking ill of your profession,' Andreas and his brother Yorghis laughed.

'Ah, Vonni, you're just the person I was hoping to meet. Remember those papers I was talking to you about. Shall I bring them round to your house tonight?'

'No, Takis, I have two Irish children there, can I come up to you instead?'

'Certainly,' he said and continued his walk.

Andreas and Yorghis exchanged glances. This had something to do with Vonni taking a trip away. But she wasn't going to tell them and they weren't going to ask.

'So what happens now?' Vonni asked Takis that night.

'I have let them know that the money is available for bail.'

'You didn't say who it was?' She looked anxious.

'No, but this is the point, they can't just accept a lump of cash from somebody without knowing where it came from. It could be laundered money or drugs money. So we have to say who you are.'

'What a fuss about nothing, it's *his* money – I made it over to him,' Vonni said.

'They have to do things by the book. And Stavros didn't know that he *had* that money, you see, so they are bound to be suspicious when it appears out of the blue.'

'Yes. I suppose. So what do I do?'

'There are a few formalities.'

'Do I get to see him?'

'Um . . . no . . . not while he's still on remand, but of course when you bail him out you can see him then. I mean, he'll want to thank you.' Takis spoke doubtfully.

'I don't need to be thanked,' Vonni said. 'It's what any mother would do.'

Vonni told the twins that she had business in England.

Simon went down to a computer in the Anna Beach and booked her a cheap ticket from Athens. 'Will you want to go to Ireland since you are over that way?' he asked.

'No, thank you, Simon, just England will do,' Vonni said.

'Better wait until we are in Ireland to make you welcome,' Maud said reprovingly. 'And you'll come for Fiona and Declan's wedding, won't you?'

'Yes, but Vonni might have friends and relations of her own there.'

'Not to speak of.' Vonni was crisp.

'Will I help you pack?' Maud suggested. 'I could do some ironing or whatever you liked.'

'No, I'll just take a couple of things. Hand luggage. What you could do, which would be a great help, is to go and buy my ticket on the ferry for me, and go up to the hospital and say I'll be away for a bit but that you will give them a hand.'

'And will we say how long you'll be away?' Simon wanted to be prepared.

'Just a couple of days. I'm not exactly sure . . .' Vonni began.

'So we'll just say . . .' Simon said.

'That you'll stay for as long as it takes . . .' Maud finished and Vonni smiled at them gratefully. It was much easier to go away now that the twins were there looking after her business and her home.

They went down to the ferry to wave Vonni off. Andreas was there too, in his big leather boots. He had brought a little parcel of cheese and olives in case Vonni forgot to have lunch.

'Go well, Vonni, be home soon,' he had said.

Maud and Simon watched with interest.

'Do you and Vonni have a special friendship?' Maud asked.

'Yes, that's what it is, a very special friendship.'

'Did you ever think of getting married to her?' Simon wondered.

'Yes, I did, but it was the wrong time. I should have thought about it and asked her earlier. It was too late when I had the thought.' The old man's face was far away for a moment, but then he cheered up.

'I have a good idea – my brother Yorghis is coming to dinner tonight, when he closes the police station, maybe you could come too and meet him?'

'Yorghis?'

'The head of police?'

'Your brother?' The twins sounded like international criminals on the run.

Andreas looked from one to the other. 'Yes, like me he is on his own, we often eat a meal together and look down on the lights of the town.'

'Oh, please, Andreas, we haven't done anything wrong!'

'The time we knocked the orange stall over, we spent *hours* gathering up all the oranges and dusting them for him. He was very happy and . . .'

'. . . and when we went swimming in the harbour we didn't know it wasn't the right place because of the boats and we said sorry over and over and the harbour master said *To Pota* which means it doesn't matter . . .' Simon was anxious to explain.

'So please don't call Yorghis,' Maud begged.

'We don't want him to hear about us,' Simon added.

'And Fiona would kill us; she said she would beat us with a stick until we bled all over the place!' Maud's eyes were enormous.

'Fiona said this? *Fiona?*' He seemed taken aback.

'Yes, do you know her?'

'I do – she was here one summer – but she didn't seem the kind of person who would beat someone to death. Rather the reverse . . .'

'Really?' Maud was very surprised. 'She always seemed fairly frightening to me.'

'And Declan who is the son of Muttie's friend seems fairly anxious to please her.'

Andreas had long lost control of the cast of thousands who figured in the twins' conversation. 'So – Yorghis will be here about eight,' he said, going back to something he did understand.

'If you don't mind . . .'

'We'd really prefer . . .'

'We'll be more careful in future . . .'

'About orange stalls and harbours.'

'I have no idea what you're talking about,' Andreas said eventually. 'Just be at the taverna at eight o clock.'

Dear Fiona,

This is just to explain that we met your friend Yorghis, the chief of police, socially last night. We want to stress it was a social meeting. He turns out to be the brother of Andreas who owns the taverna. We had dinner there last night and Yorghis was very pleasant and not at all interested in the orange stall incident. The harbour master had said nothing about our swimming in the wrong place so I'd say that there are no problems there.

We are having a wonderful time here and cannot thank you enough for telling us about this lovely place. It's hard to believe that the hen-house was ever a hen-house: it has a window in the roof and paintings and plates on the wall. They must have been very comfortable hens.

People say that you were very quiet when you were here. But then maybe we all change. They are all pleased to hear about your engagement.

You have nothing to worry about. Our meeting with Yorghis was just social and he sang songs for us after dinner which he wouldn't have if anything was wrong.

Vonni has gone to England on business so we are looking after the shop. Maria, who is a young widow, comes in to work every day to speak real Greek to people, but mainly we are in charge.

Thank you again.

Love,

Simon and Maud

Fiona had completely forgotten having threatened the twins with serious beatings and the wrath of the police chief out in Aghia Anna, so she was mystified as she read their letter. And like almost everyone who came in contact with Simon and Maud she felt the world tilting slightly. One thing only puzzled her. Vonni gone to England on business? Vonni didn't have any business in England. What business would take Vonni to England?

They were very welcoming in the bed and breakfast where Vonni stayed. She told them she had never been in England before.

'Imagine! When you think how near it is to Ireland! But early in life I married a Greek and went off to the Mediterranean. And England didn't figure very much.'

The couple who ran the place were interested. 'What an adventurous life!' they said in awe.

'It can be too adventurous,' Vonni said sadly.

'Well, we can point you in the direction of some nice scenic attractions,' the wife said, sensing a sadness here.

'No – the only scenic attraction I need to be pointed at is the prison,' Vonni said.

And so they told her there was a bus which went right past their door and they asked her no more. They just refilled her mug of tea.

Restful people. She had been lucky to find this place.

Next morning, she stood at the bus stop and watched ordinary people doing ordinary things. Girls were going to work in shops, women were taking children to school, men with worried faces were looking at their watches.

These were people with families, men, women and children who lived normal lives. They weren't going with a briefcase full of certified cheques to see a son now estranged for decades with the intention of bailing him out of prison. Their hearts were not heavy with anxiety as hers was. They knew what the day was going to bring while she had no idea what was going to happen.

The heart clinic was going from strength to strength. Frank Ennis called by to tell them that there had been a wonderful article in a US newspaper about the place. Apparently they had treated the wife of an American journalist who was spending three months in Dublin and had gone into heart failure and been exceptionally well cared for. Frank Ennis kept stabbing at the paper and saying that you couldn't buy this publicity for any money.

Clara had been pleased but unimpressed. This was what they tried to do for everybody. It was of no more value because it had been done for a columnist's wife.

'At least he said the place was clean, airy and well equipped, Frank!' Clara said. 'If you had it your way it would have been a poky dungeon . . .'

Hilary was watching Frank's face: it seemed to fall a little. Hilary was beginning to think that Frank's interest in Clara was more than professional. She had told this to Clara who pealed with laughter at the very idea.

'*Frank!*' she would cry in horror. 'I would rather be a nun for the rest of my life.'

Hilary stuck to her belief. 'He rings up to know are you going to be there, and he doesn't bother coming if you're not.'

'You'll need more skills than that if you are going to set up as a private detective or a psychologist!' Clara laughed.

Kitty Reilly was passing by, full of religious fervour. 'I think there's too much laughing in this clinic,' she said disapprovingly.

'We never laugh about our work, Kitty,' Clara apologised.

'But in your free time, you could have said ten prayers while you and Hilary were laughing there – and think what good that would have done.'

'I know, Kitty, you're probably right, but *after* prayers a good laugh is all right, don't you think?' Fiona had her hand to her mouth to control herself.

She was regaling Barbara with the story in the treatment rooms.

'This place is better than working in a circus sometimes,' Barbara agreed. 'What are you frowning about now?'

'I can't think what Vonni is doing in England. She doesn't know anyone in England except David. I wish I knew what she's doing there.'

Stavros shared a cell with Jacky McDonald from Scotland. Jacky was there over a misunderstanding as well. They had little in common apart from the unfairness of their imprisonment and the lack of anyone to post bail for them. So it came as a shock to them both when Stavros heard that there was a serious possibility that the funds were coming for his release.

'Who could it be? Your da?' Jacky asked enviously.

'It must be – but where he got the money I don't know. Maybe my grandfather died, he owned some barber shops. There could have been money there, I suppose.'

'You don't know if he's dead or not?' Jacky was incredulous.

'No – how would I?'

'What about your mother?'

'God, no, she's a hopeless drunk, probably dead from drink now. Anyway, if she did get her senses back she wouldn't help me.'

'Why not?'

'Well, I got this awful drooling letter from her, way back, apologising and saying she loved me. Jesus!'

'And what did you say?'

'What anyone would say. I said, "You live your life and, please, let me live mine." No, it couldn't be her.'

Through all the formalities, they were very polite to Vonni. She even saw signs of sympathy in fairly impassive faces. They were making it easier for her and she was grateful.

'And will I get to see him?' she asked.

'We had instructions not to tell him who it was from. The lawyer in Greece was very adamant about that,' a fatherly man told her gently. He was the kind of man who would never have understood the years of history between Vonni and her son.

'Yes, that's right,' she said.

'So now that we have checked the legitimacy of the funds, as we had to, we are just saying they arrived from Greece.'

'Yes, yes, of course,' Vonni said.

'So once he's bailed he'll probably get in touch with you.'

'Not necessarily. It's just that I live in Greece, and now that I'm actually in the place where he is, I thought I might see him.'

'If you want to talk to him first and tell him you are putting up the bail . . . ?'

'No – that would be blackmail. That would be saying that he must be grateful to me, he *must* see me.'

'And would he not want to see you anyway? His mother?'

'I was a bad mother,' Vonni said simply.

'We're all bad parents. There's no training for it, you see, like there is for a job.'

'I'm sure you did all right.'

'Not really. My son wanted to be a musician. I forced him to go and get a proper qualification. I thought I was doing the right thing. He met a girl, she got pregnant and they married. He's still in a job he hates and it's all my fault.'

Vonni looked at him open-mouthed. The English were meant to be reticent, and yet this man was telling her his whole life story. This man knew Stavros – maybe he was saying something to prepare her for disappointment.

Vonni was touched.

'I will leave the address and phone number of the B&B where I am staying, with you. When he asks, perhaps you could give them to him.'

'*If* he asks,' the official said.

'You think he might not ask?'

'You never know.'

'Well, when it's all gone through, give him my address anyway . . .'

'Certainly,' the man said, and put the piece of paper in a letter rack on his desk.

'You mean it's all signed and delivered?' Jacky looked at Stavros in disbelief.

'I know, isn't it fantastic? I'm sorry it didn't come through for you too,' Stavros said.

'And who was it?'

'I didn't ask – you know what they say about not looking a gift horse in the mouth.'

'Yes, but it's a hell of a lot of money.'

'All the more reason to keep shtum about it. I'm just going to disappear.'

Jacky looked at him in confusion. 'That's what you're going to do?'

'Well, of course it is. Why, what would you do?'

'But you said it was a misunderstanding?'

'Sure it was, but am I going to reform the courts of justice all on my own? Good luck, Jacky . . .' And he was gone.

At the desk he was given the address.

'Who left this for me?' he asked.

'A lady.'

Stavros looked at the name and the phone number.

'Boy, if you had known her back then you wouldn't have called her a lady . . .'

'She looks fine now.' The older man's mouth was a thin line of disapproval.

'Whatever . . .' Stavros tore the paper in half and threw it into the wastepaper basket.

Back at her B&B, Vonni waited.

And waited.

After two days a man rang and asked to speak to her. She knew that it wasn't Stavros, it was an older man. A kindly voice that she had heard recently.

'It's not my job or my business, but I thought you should know that your son didn't take your address.'

'But why did you not give it to him?'

'I did try but there was a sort of a mix-up.'

Vonni knew that she shouldn't ask but she had to know.

'What sort of a mix-up? Did he leave it behind when he left?'

'Sort of, yes.'

'How?'

'He just didn't take it with him, madam. I didn't want you to be sitting there waiting. After all you did for him . . .'

'And did he say anything? Anything at all? You can tell me . . .'

'No, madam. Nothing.'

'Thank you. That's a relief anyway.'

And Vonni packed her little bag and went out to the airport. Simon had told her how you travelled standby on a plane, it was much cheaper. And now, of course, that she had no money at all she would have to take such things into consideration.

'If Vonni can go to England, maybe she could come to Ireland to our wedding?' Declan suggested.

'Sure she could.' Fiona was casual. 'And when we get round to organising one we'll certainly invite her.'

'Which might be sooner rather than later?' Declan suggested.

'Or which might be thought out carefully rather than rushed into,' teased Fiona.

Sometimes Declan found it worrying that she didn't want to set the date right away. He wanted to marry her tomorrow, but he wouldn't put her under pressure. He would wait until she was ready. They had their whole lives ahead of them.

His father's friend Muttie had an address for Maud and Simon so Declan sent them a fifty-euro note.

> *If you see something nice and maybe typical of the area that's not too heavy to carry, I'd love you to bring it home as a present for Fiona. It will be a surprise for her so don't tell her. She tells me that you are practically running the place over there. Well done!*
>
> *St Jarlath's Crescent is much the same: we are having a good spring, but of course it's nothing to what you have out there. I'm back into the swing again and I only use the stick a little, so I'm as good as new, which was never all that great to begin with. Good luck, and give our best to Vonni. Why did she go to England do you know? Fiona said she never went anywhere these days.*
>
> *All the best,*
> *Declan*

Maud and Simon read this letter carefully.

'A necklace,' Maud suggested. 'They have nice filigree ones up in Kalatriada.'

'Yes, but they're not really *of* this area. Maybe it should be some Aghia Anna pottery?' Simon was struggling to obey the message in the letter.

'We'd break it, it's such a long journey home, Simon.' Maud was practical.

'If Vonni comes home, we could ask her of course,' Simon said.

'I forgot to tell you – I met Yorghis, and he says she's coming tomorrow.'

'Did he say . . . ?'

'No and I didn't ask . . .' Maud finished.

'Sure it's her business,' Simon agreed.

They planned how to welcome her.

'I keep thinking we should get some wine or champagne even,' Simon said.

'Yes, but she's like Mother, it doesn't agree with her.' There wasn't an ounce of disapproval in Maud's voice. 'We'll just get in eggs and mushrooms, bread and honey. I imagine she's coming on the morning boat. So Yorghis says.'

'We'll be there to meet her,' Simon said.

There were five men and two women waiting for Vonni. Andreas, his brother Yorghis, Dr Leros and the lawyer Takis, and Simon. Maria was there and Maud.

When Vonni came into harbour she saw them from the deck of the ferry boat and waved, delighted. They decided to have breakfast at Mesanihta. They all searched her face for some hint of how things had gone for her in the few days she had been away.

But since they didn't ask any direct question they could not complain that they didn't get any answer.

Andreas wondered were the English people friendly? Very, very welcoming, apparently. Yorghis wondered were they loud? Some of them had ended up in his cooling-off rooms when they had been obstreperous over the years. No, Vonni hadn't found anyone loud. Rather the reverse.

Dr Leros came nearest to saying what was in his mind when he wondered had she been worried about her health – gone to see a specialist? Vonni was taken aback by this. No, no – her health was perfect.

Maria asked what kind of clothes the women wore in England and Vonni said she didn't really know, she hadn't really looked. Takis the lawyer asked had her business turned out as she had hoped. Vonni looked at him vaguely and said it had all been done as had been planned. He got nothing more.

Maud and Simon asked no questions at all. They told her that everything had gone very well. There had been very good sales of the little blue mugs. They had put them in the window and people came in especially to look at them. They had been up to the hospital and chosen the wool for blind people. They had done some baby-sitting at the Anna Beach Hotel and had been paid. They had put the money aside for Vonni to cover their board and lodging. They were learning ten words of Greek a day and they had learned a little Greek dance. Their blond hair was shining in the morning sun and their skin was golden. They looked a lot healthier and less eccentric than when they first arrived.

Vonni smiled at them with pleasure. Not everything worked out well. But some things did.

This was what she had to hold on to.

Simon and Maud carried Vonni's little bag home for her after all the warm bread and honey at the Mesanihta.

'Is it good to be back?' Maud asked.

'To your real home?' Simon defined.

'Yes, very good.' Vonni looked around her, happily greeting people here and there.

'We got lots of shop *avgas* in case you'd like an omelette,' Simon said.

'I could murder an omelette,' Vonni said with a tired smile. She went in to change her clothes while the twins got the food ready.

They were so kind and attentive and totally undemanding.

'Well now, you two,' she said to them later. 'I can't have you working for your entire stay here. I want you to enjoy yourselves, take a few days off. Take the money you earned and go and see more of the island.'

'But we thought we could repay you a little,' Simon said.

'No need, aren't we all doing fine the way we are? I'd love you to see all the beautiful places, the gorge and the caves and the beautiful empty beaches up in the north of the island. When you are busy professional people, a lawyer, a teacher – you will always look back and remember it. That would give me huge pleasure . . .'

'If you really mean it . . . ?'

'If you're totally sure . . . ?'

Vonni looked at them thoughtfully. The few euros they had earned minding children at night in the Anna Beach would go a long way to seeing them around the island. 'Please believe me. And another thing?'

'Yes, Vonni?'

'Why do *you* think I was in England? I notice you never tried to find out. What do you think it was about?'

They paused for a moment and looked at each other.

'Go on, say it – I wouldn't ask otherwise.'

'I think someone died,' Maud said.

'Yes, I think you went to a funeral,' Simon agreed.

'Why do you think that?'

'Because your eyes are very empty. Different somehow.'

'And even if you're smiling you seem sad.'

*

303

The time flew by, the holiday was over and it was time for a bronzed Maud and Simon to go back to Ireland. Vonni had helped them to choose Declan's gift for Fiona, a beautiful hand-painted scarf.

'Will you come over for Fiona's wedding?' Simon asked the night before they left.

'No, Simon, I'm too old to travel now,' she said.

'But you went to England?' Simon was always remorselessly logical.

'That's because it was an errand of mercy,' Maud reminded him.

'An errand of mercy,' Vonni repeated wonderingly.

'Was that the wrong thing to say?' Maud was distressed.

'No, it was a lovely thing to say. Do you think you two learned anything here, anything that will stay with you for life?'

'Well, we learned a little Greek. Not enough, I know, but some,' Simon said.

'And we learned that you don't have to have lots of money to make you happy,' Maud added.

'That's for sure. Where did you learn that?'

'Well, everywhere, I suppose. Up in the mountains where they have hardly anything. And here with you. You don't have a lot but you don't ever seem to want a big income or anything. You just get on with life, fine the way you are. No matter what happens.'

Vonni was surprised. 'But you two don't think money buys happiness, do you?'

'No, but we meet a lot of people who do.'

'Do you know, I think you two are pretty good at getting on with life no matter what happens,' Vonni said. 'You're managing just great.'

'Please come to Ireland, we'd love to show you things,' Simon suggested.

'We'll take care of you like you took care of us,' Maud offered.

'Let's wait until Declan and Fiona fix a day, we'll see then,' Vonni said.

'People always say "we'll see" when they mean "no",' Simon grumbled.

'You're very observant, Simon, you'll be a good lawyer,' Vonni said. She felt a great closeness to these young people. It had been a while since she had let herself get close to people in this way.

Later that night, Takis called.

'Where are the Irish kids?'

'Down catching some *buziuki* in the harbour front. Andreas and Yorghis and I will join them later – do you want to come?'

'No. I want to talk to you.'

'Oh dear.'

'Oh dear, indeed. Well, he's gone, left Britain, though he's not meant to. He didn't turn up to check in as he was supposed to, probably went on a day trip to France and didn't come back. You've said goodbye to your money.'

'It was his money, Takis, you know that. His to do what he liked with.'

'He never met you, did he, never thanked you.'

'How do you know that?'

'The authorities there were in touch with me. I spoke to that man – he remembers you going to visit.'

'It's not important.'

Takis sighed heavily. 'There was never any use talking to you.'

'There's more, isn't there?'

'Oh, Vonni, you can read faces like a book. Why could you not read the face of your own son?'

'I told you, it didn't matter, it was his money to spend when and as he liked. What more have you to tell me?'

'He shared a cell with a Scottish fellow called Jacky, and Jacky asked the people to forward a letter to you. They sent it to me and I'm afraid I opened it.'

'Really?'

'I was afraid it might be a begging letter.'

'And was it, Takis?'

'In a way, yes. But I thought you should see it.'

'Very generous of you, considering it was addressed to me.'

'Just read it, Vonni.'

She did.

Dear Mother of Stavros,

I shared a cell for many weeks with your son. He was so happy to be released thanks to your generosity. I suppose I was just hoping that you might be a wealthy woman and that you might be able to put up my bail too. It's much less than for Stavros. I would work forever to get it back to you, I would be so grateful I would do anything on earth you wanted.

Stavros is not a bad lad, but he is very confused. He sees things as black and white, he doesn't know the world is grey. He said you and he had a lot of problems when he was a child. It only seemed to be drink when he got down to it, which we all had in our homes, but he is very unforgiving.

Stavros telephoned me once since he was released. He wanted an address of someone. I asked him had he seen you and he said no. I asked him why he was not grateful and he said you must be as guilty as sin about your past otherwise you would never have raised that money for his bail. He said that he had been beginning to wonder had he been too harsh on you, but this proved that you knew you had ruined his life and caused him to be the way he is.

I only tell you this because I would be so different. Please,

Mother of Stavros, believe me, I would be so grateful and I would look after you when you get old.

Yours,
Jack McDonald

When she looked up, Takis was looking out the window, over the rooftops which led down to the harbour. He did not want to meet her eye. He tried to arrange his body so that it did not scream the words 'I told you so' at her. Everything she had been left was gone as she had been warned.

'Well, thank you, Takis. Now we all know where we are.'

'Yes, that's true,' he said.

'And I think we are on our way to the *harbour*, don't you?'

'You can go to a party after that? You are a remarkable woman, Vonni.'

She smiled at him as she smiled at her friends all around this island: the smile of someone who felt lucky and free and who tonight had been proved to have paid all her debts. She didn't want sympathy, she wanted solidarity.

'*Pame*, Vonni. Let's go,' he said.

'*Pame*, Takis, let's go to the taverna,' she said.

Chapter Nine

Linda Casey wished she had lived at another time. A time when her talents would have been appreciated. She could have been a royal mistress, or a kept woman in a luxury apartment or even a wife to some gentleman landowner who encouraged her to have a small town house in Dublin.

But no, she was of the here and now, in a world where everyone, men and women, had to go out and work for a living. Were they meant to thank the Women's Lib people for this? A world where relationships were full of compromise, where marriages didn't last. And a world that said you should be grateful day and night because you had a place to live, an education and were young and reasonably good-looking.

Linda didn't think that was nearly enough.

But try telling that to anyone and see how far you got. Not very far with her mother. Mam seemed to have transformed herself into some kind of advertising campaign for how a well-groomed, middle-aged woman should live. She had seen her mother sponging jackets with lemon juice, putting shoe trees in her shoes to keep their shape, polishing her handbag, and creaming her neck with some heavy unguent. And for *what*? Mam was still a sad, driven person. So what if she looked good? Inside, she was like everybody else, a mess.

Linda couldn't really remember when Mam and Dad had got on well. Her sister Adi, who was two years older, said she could, but then Adi was so sentimental: trees had feelings and we shouldn't sit on leather sofas because an animal had died to make a covering for us to sit on. And as for Adi's boyfriend Gerry . . . He was a total nutter! Adi had made herself into a complete doormat for him.

Linda would never put on an act like that for any man, no matter how wonderful he was. But she hadn't met many wonderful men. Or any wonderful man, to be honest. Wherever they were, they weren't in Dublin.

She had been out three times with this fellow called Simon, which by Linda's standards was almost a life commitment. Simon was attractive. He had a rich daddy, a doting mummy and a job in his uncle's estate agency where he had very little to do. But Simon was accustomed to going out with women who paid their way. They didn't actually halve the price of meals or anything, but sometimes these girls would host a couple of hours' drinks in a hotel or take half a dozen people to lunch in an Italian place. Linda hadn't a hope of being able to keep up with that pace.

'You're basically a daddy's girl, Linda. You're looking for someone to look after you,' he had said, before heading off to new conquests.

He was so wrong. She was *not* a daddy's girl. She called her father 'Alan' for heaven's sake. That showed you how little she thought of herself as his baby daughter.

He had been selfish and childish always.

Her mother had been *mad* to stay with him for as long as she had. Linda would have thrown him out much earlier. Dad was so immature. He wasn't going to stay the distance with Cinta, the one they called the 'bimbo', especially now that there was a new baby imminent. It was so gross to have a baby step-sister or step-brother. And Dad would expect lots of ootchy-kootchy gurgling once the baby was born. He would eventually lose interest in it as he did in everything.

Linda's mother had once said bitterly that Alan's philosophy was 'yours till death do us part or something marginally more interesting comes along'. Mam could be quite funny sometimes. Most of the time, of course, she was like a sergeant major running the household as she did her clinic.

She had recently gone on an economy drive. There was hardly anything to eat in the fridge. And also there was this emphasis on Linda getting a job. That had never been important before. She had intended to take a year off and travel the world before looking for a job. But her mother had been very forceful about it. Either Linda went off and saw the world, leaving her room ready for her mother to let to someone else, or else she stayed and contributed to the household.

There *was* no decision. Linda didn't have any money to travel the world and neither parent was going to donate anything to the trip to Thailand, Cambodia and Australia that she had been hoping for. She didn't want to get a job in the civil service or a bank or an insurance office. She wasn't like her mother, with a passion for medicine in general and cardiology in particular. She didn't want to teach like her sister Adi. She was so different from her sister that Linda often wondered if she might be adopted. Adi was so easily pleased with everything and she loved all those screeching children in the school. She gave a portion of her salary to Mam every month and then put some towards Saving the Whale or whatever.

Adi and Gerry were saving to go to some desperate place to protest about clubbing seals or frightening deer or something. Imagine! They were *saving* to do that! Linda wouldn't have gone if someone had paid her to go. And if she had any money at all she was out to buy shoes or to go through a thrift shop. She had found the sweetest little fox tail thing, which of course she had to keep well hidden in case the two 'Friends of the Earth' saw it and brought a pack of baying protesters around her. She had hidden it from her mother also. It wasn't Clara's kind of thing and anyway she would undoubtedly wonder aloud how it was that Linda had money to buy this kind of nonsense but not enough to contribute to her keep.

But now she had a part-time job in the record store, so at least her mother couldn't grizzle as much as she used to. Sometimes there was even cooked ham or a casserole in the fridge, which Linda was allowed to share.

And of course Mother had been very good-tempered because of this sort of dalliance she had with Peter, the handsome chemist man. A dalliance was a good way to describe it. They went to the theatre, on picnics and entertained each other to meals. They even went on holiday together, to Italy. Adi and Linda had thought he was perfectly fine but then it had all ended suddenly. Probably because Mother was pushing for an engagement ring. But even if she *had* been dumped, Linda's mother was in remarkably good form. She was very hyper about some ghastly fundraising thing at the clinic. Linda had referred to it as a cake sale and her mother had been apoplectic.

'It is *not* a cake sale! It's a serious attempt to raise money that the hospital should have given us in the first place. We want to publicise the lecture course and so we're inviting the media and all the movers and shakers in the medical world and business people. Everyone in the clinic is giving their all to it and I will *not* have you dismiss it as a cake sale!'

Linda had been startled. 'Sorry, I wasn't listening. I got it wrong.'

'You never listen. You care about nothing and nobody, except yourself.'

'Hey, Mam, that's a bit strong.'

'Don't "Hey, Mam" at me. You're an adult, Linda. Stop putting on that baby voice.'

'Right, I'll stop calling you "Mam" altogether. I'll call you "Clara".'

'I don't care what you call me. Just have something intelligent to say!' Clara banged out of the house and revved up her car.

Linda watched from the window. She had really annoyed her mother for some reason. She shrugged. No point in trying to work out why. The old were impossible to understand.

Clara came into the clinic with a brisk step.

'You're in a bad mood,' Hilary said.

'Oh boy, are you right,' Clara said.

Ania had seen it, too, and hastened in with the coffee.

'Have we anything terrible this morning?' Clara asked.

'Frank is coming in for what he calls a chat at eleven,' Hilary said.

'As if that man ever had a chat with anyone,' Clara sighed.

'Well, it's about the money that poor Jimmy from Galway left us in his will,' Hilary explained. 'He sees a problem.'

'Of course he does,' Clara agreed, 'every time he looks in the mirror, he sees the main problem around here.'

Ania giggled.

Clara sighed. 'Right, hit me with what else there is,' she said in a resigned voice.

'Isn't today one of Lavender's cookery demos?' Hilary asked.

'Yes, it starts at eleven thirty. We must all put in an appearance to support Lavender.' Clara was adamant. 'So let's try and get the dreaded Frank off the premises before she starts. Let's try to bring his little chat to an amicable end. He's going to go mad if he gets a whiff of Lavender grilling mackerel.'

'Is that what she's doing?' Hilary was interested.

Clara nodded enthusiastically. 'Yes. She runs all the recipes past me. It sounds nice. Maybe we should have an early lunch and eat it all.'

'You know I never cooked mackerel in my whole life,' Hilary said.

'*Makrela?* That's what it's called in Polish too. Is it a good fish?' Ania asked.

'It's a forgotten fish,' Clara said. 'My grandmother used to eat it four or five times a week. Then people went off it. I suppose when they could afford meat and chicken.'

'I learn so many things from you, Clara.' Ania went off about her work, pleased to have new information.

'Lord, isn't *she* a nice child! Why couldn't I have had a daughter like that, rather than an obstinate, bad-tempered mule like Linda, who refers to our big reception here as a "cake sale".'

Clara was so indignant that Hilary had to laugh. 'Sorry, Clara, but if you could see your face! Maybe we should refer to it as the cake sale from now on, it might calm us down. What else has Linda done?'

'You don't want to know, believe me. She shrugs so much I think she has dislocated her shoulders. She has no get-up-and-go, no plans, no life plan.'

'You're being very harsh about this girl who is going to be my daughter-in-law one day,' Hilary said.

Clara had totally forgotten that she and Hilary had plotted to get Nick and Linda together in a way that did not include any possible involvement on the part of their mothers. It was good to see Hilary so recovered that she could think of discussing it again.

'We'll have a planning lunch about that,' Clara said. 'But tell me first, apart from the mackerel demo, good, and Frank chat, bad, what else does the day offer us?'

'Bobby Walsh's grisly wife says that one of the drugs we've given Bobby has been withdrawn in the United States.'

'Did she say which one?'

'She did. I looked it up. No mention of it. I even asked Peter at the pharmacy. He said he would have heard and there's nothing.'

'Oh, God, is she coming in?'

'At 10 a.m. . . . on the grounds—' Hilary began.

'On the grounds we get the lousy ones over with early,' Clara finished for her.

Mrs Walsh came in with a clipping from a magazine that said that a medication, which was in the ACE inhibitor range, was being examined by the authorities in America.

Patiently, Clara explained what the drug needed to do, which was to reduce increased heart muscle thickness. She pointed out that there were dozens of these medications on the market and that they were checking one particular brand for side effects. It wasn't the brand that Bobby Walsh was taking.

'If I could explain exactly what ACE inhibitors are,' Clara began. 'It's Angiotensin Converting Enzyme inhibitors . . . and—'

'Kindly don't patronise me, Dr Casey.' Mrs Walsh had a voice like an electric saw.

Clara longed to tell her to get out of the clinic and to stay out, but this wasn't appropriate. It was Bobby Walsh's heart she was looking after. That's where her duty lay. She mustn't get sidetracked by this monstrous woman.

'I have no intention of patronising you, Mrs Walsh. I'm just telling you and Bobby that there's no cause to be alarmed. The main side effects of such drugs could be dizziness or a dry cough. Bobby has neither. So now, can you please tell me what additional help I can be?'

'I don't like your smart-aleck attitude, Dr Casey, and believe me, this *will* go further.'

'You are concerned with your husband's health, so, please, go as far as you like to reassure him and you.'

'Oh, Bobby isn't worried. He thinks you're all great here.' Mrs Walsh's voice was withering in her scorn.

Clara stood up to show the meeting was finished. 'That's good to know, Mrs Walsh. And if there's anything else?'

'*You* will be the one to hear if there's anything else. I have a personal introduction to Frank Ennis who is on the hospital board. I'm sure he'll want to have a chat with you about all this.'

Clara was bright and positive. 'Well, he's coming here in about forty-five minutes anyway for a meeting, so if you'd like to stay I can introduce you to him myself and then you can have your little chat.' Clara relished the thought of setting this terrible woman, with her grating voice, on poor old Frank Ennis.

'No, that won't be necessary.'

'But *do*, Mrs Walsh. We can make the consultation room available to you and I won't be in the area. I'll be going to Lavender's healthy heart cookery demonstration.'

Mrs Walsh practically ran out the door of the clinic. Clara and Hilary did a high five in the air.

'Get the lousy ones over first,' they said happily.

Frank was adamant. The late James O'Brien had left his money to the hospital. The hospital was named in the man's will. The money would go to the charitable and fundraising department of the main hospital. It would be spent wisely. Clara fought him strenuously.

Jimmy had come regularly to *this* clinic. He knew nobody in the main hospital, except the people he had met in A&E on his first visit.

'Well then . . .' Frank began, triumphantly.

'And because he was a man who took privacy to the point of madness, he refused to give them the name of his family doctor in the west. He went to a bed and breakfast when he was discharged and because A&E had to pass his care on to *someone*, he was referred here. He loved the clinic. He said so in his will. He thanked them for making his heart disease seem under control. That money is being used here, Frank, if I have to take you to the High Court or further.'

'There isn't any further,' Frank said in a sulky tone.

'Yes, there is. This could go to the Court of Human Rights!' Clara said, her eyes blazing.

'We could see that a proportion of it comes this way . . .' Frank began, and Clara knew she had him on the ropes.

'This is where he wanted his money to go. It comes *here*,' she said.

'The art of the deal is knowing when to compromise,' Frank said.

'That's balls,' Clara said pleasantly. 'Something is either right or it's wrong. I don't look at a patient and say his arteries are all clogged up and he needs angioplasty, but then, on the other hand, I don't feel able to do all the paperwork so we'll compromise and I'll ask him to come back in three months and we'll get it started then. That's not the way things work in the real world, Frank.'

'I'm sorry, that *is* the way.' He went on to raise his offer from one-third of Jimmy's estate to half. He met nothing but a shake of Clara's glossy head.

'It's not a fair comparison,' he blustered. 'You took an oath to help people. It's different for you.'

'I did take an oath and I'm keeping to it.'

'I didn't take any such oath,' he said.

Clara laughed aloud. 'Oh, yes you did. You vowed you would make life as difficult, as penny-pinching, nitpicking and bureaucratic as it could possibly be. You promised your-self that the spirit of a hospital should never be considered when the real thing, the letter of the law, can be brought into play. But you picked the wrong one in me, Frank, I'm not going to lie down and roll over.'

'I didn't pick you at all. I was landed with you!' Frank had some spirit at least. 'And I would remind you that this clinic didn't exist before and may well not exist after your time. You refer to it as if it were an important entity in its own right instead of very small potatoes, which is what this place is.'

'It's what this place *was* and would have still been if you'd been allowed your way. But it's not now and it's going further and Jimmy's money will bring it to the next stage.' She was very angry now.

'The place is funded by the hospital—' he began.

'If you think, Frank Ennis, that I am going to waste one more minute of time arguing with you about whether we rent chairs for a lecture or buy them and store them, if you think that I will ever again go through the humiliating experience of pleading with you to pay what are very low fees to visiting experts for this series of lectures . . . If you think that I am going to spend hours talking to you and your bonehead colleagues about the feasibility – God, I hate that word, feasibility – of having a youth programme so that school kids could come in and learn about their bloody hearts and how to keep them beating properly—'

'You never mentioned having children come in here!' Frank could see a thousand problems already.

'I didn't because I am weary to the soles of my feet dealing with you on any subject and so Jimmy's money will buy us time and freedom to set this up on our own.' She actually sounded weary.

'But you can't—'

'I can and I will, Frank. And now I'm going to a cookery

demonstration. We have over fifty people waiting in Lavender's room, the dietician's space which you said need only be a desk and a chair.'

'She's not cooking with a live flame, is she?' Frank said, horrified.

'I very much hope so, Frank. She has a two-ring gas grill and a big mirror behind her set at an angle.'

'And who paid for the mirror, if I might ask?'

'You might ask, even though it's actually none of your business. Hilary and I bought it at an auction. Johnny and Tim put it up on the wall for us. It cost you and the money boys and girls precisely nothing!'

Clara was moving purposefully towards the cookery demonstration. Frank could see other people in the clinic heading in the same direction. That sandy-haired doctor who had been in the bad car crash but had made a miraculous recovery. The two pretty nurses Fiona and Barbara, the muscle man Johnny, who looked as if he should be a bouncer outside a nightclub rather than working in a medical setting. Also that rather silent security man Tim, who had been appointed here in a very high-handed way by Clara instead of taking part in the hospital's general security system. This whole place had become dangerously like a family or even a province that was about to declare independence and call itself a nation. He had better go and see what horrific liberties she was taking with health and safety at this demonstration. He was disconcerted by the buzz of conversation. These people *had* formed a little community. It would have to be watched carefully.

Lavender was a born performer. She could have had her own television programme. Clara's mind raced ahead. Maybe Lavender could have a slot on someone's talk show, 'Five Minutes for your Heart'.

There was a small lecture on salt and the Irish obsession

with spreading a salt shaker over all food. Lavender suggested having no salt on the table. If you thought up enough other harmless seasonings there was no need. She took fillets of mackerel, showed them to the audience. You could buy packets of fillets or else ask a fishmonger to fillet them for you. In a glass you mixed the juice of an orange, a lime and a lemon and a spoonful of vegetable oil, and you brushed the mackerel with this and then grilled them.

They smelled terrific and as she passed the plate around for people to taste, Lavender was busy grilling more. Everyone would want a taste and some people were taking far too much. There was an easy salad that went with it and Lavender said that their hearts would thank them warmly for such food.

In spite of himself, Frank was impressed. The bright cheery room, the no-nonsense Lavender, the general air of hope and of being in control of their own lives. When this clinic had been first considered that was the mandate, the mission statement; and for all her annoying ways, Clara *was* getting it done.

When the demonstration was over, Clara got a message to call her daughter Adi.

'Sorry, Mam, I was talking to Linda about something else and she said we're both to call you "Clara" from now on. Is that right or is it just Linda being cracked?'

'It's Linda being cracked. *She's* calling me Clara. I said that was fine with me if she had something worthwhile to say. Do you know she said that the grand reception we're organising here was a *cake sale*?' Clara's face got red with anger again.

'Yeah, she knows that was a mistake. She doesn't listen, Mam, that's all.'

'She'll need to learn to listen some day,' Clara said.

'She's sorry. She's cooking a dinner tonight to try and make it up, buying the things herself. It's so rare, Mam, I think we should sort of be there.'

'I don't want to sit and watch Linda mess up my kitchen and then say I'm organising a cake sale.'

'She'll never say that again, Mam.'

'I don't want to go. Honestly, I don't *feel* like it. And look at all the times Lady Linda has done or hasn't done things because of how she feels!'

'Oh, Mam, I'm having a bad day too, *and* I had to persuade Gerry to come.'

'Well, exactly.' Clara felt a surge of affection for the silent Gerry.

'No, that's not it, Mam. How will there ever be peace of any kind unless four people can sit down to a one-off meal made by Linda?'

'She'll have things that you and Gerry won't eat,' Clara countered.

'No, she won't. She checked with me. It sounds lovely: chickpeas and tomatoes and garlic and things.'

'Terrific,' Clara said.

'And she's getting you a fillet steak. And Gerry and I aren't to start wrinkling up our noses at it and talking about dead animals and we've all agreed to that.'

'I don't *want* steak. I'll eat her bloody chickpeas!' Clara roared as she slammed down the phone.

To her annoyance she saw that Frank Ennis was watching her from the door with a smile on his face. 'Sorry, Frank, a bit of a domestic,' she said, trying to make light of it.

'No, no, please. I'm just glad to see that you lose your temper with other people as well as with me,' he said and left.

'Take no notice,' Hilary said. 'He's just trying to get at you.'

'I know,' Clara said.

'Ania's gone out to get us a nice healthy lunch.'

'I don't want a nice healthy lunch. I want a plate of French fries followed by an ice cream and washed down with a huge gin and tonic.'

'Kindly remember where you are, Clara. You'll get a salad sandwich on wholemeal with a piece of fruit.'

'It still won't bring down my blood pressure,' Clara said. 'The drug that could combat Linda Casey hasn't been invented yet.'

Clara brought a bottle of wine to the feast.

Linda looked very pleased and said there was no need, but she opened it immediately, so it was obviously better than what she had bought herself.

She had to admit that Linda had made an effort. There was a bowl of crudités on the table with a series of dips. Linda had chopped all those vegetables up herself. She had warmed up some healthy, stone-ground bread. She bent, flushed and worried, over her casserole. The main course was surprisingly good and she had made coffee to serve with the fruit platter afterwards. Nobody, not a cardiologist nor two vegetarians, could have anything but praise and support.

Clara was about to tell a story about Hilary at the clinic and then she remembered that if their plot was to work Linda and Nick must never know that the two women were friends. So instead she asked about the record shop and was surprised to hear that Linda had been promoted and asked to expand a section on jazz.

She had been about to say, 'I never knew that you knew anything about any kind of music.' Instead she said, 'That's good. Nice to see your interests being rewarded.' And she saw her elder daughter smile at her approvingly. Peace had been created, for a time anyway, in their kitchen.

After dinner there was an unexpected call from Alan. Clara had been expecting some calls about the reception so she answered the phone.

'Oh, hello, love. Are you on your own?' he said.

'No, Alan, we're having a family dinner.'

'Family?' he asked, startled.

'Yes, Alan. Our two daughters, Adi and Linda, and Adi's boyfriend Gerry. You *do* remember them, I hope?' She could hear the others giggling behind her.

'Don't be such a bitch, Clara!'

'Sorry?'

'So smart-arsed,' he said.

'No, I mean sorry, Alan, did you want something?'

'I did, but no, not with you in that mood.'

'Right, another time then.' She was about to hang up.

'Clara, please. Please!'

'What, Alan?'

'Can you come and meet me somewhere?'

'Not tonight, as I said. Another time.'

'I need to talk tonight.'

'I can't tonight. The evening isn't over yet, and anyway, I've had some wine so I can't drive. Give me a ring at work one morning.'

'She's thrown me out,' he said.

'Cinta? Never!'

'Yes, I'm afraid.'

'But the baby, it must be nearly due now?'

'In two weeks. But she's giving it away to her sister who can't have children.'

'But, Alan, that's *your* baby too.'

'Do you think that's making a blind bit of difference? She says that I didn't get divorced in time to be married for the child's birth and so I have no say.'

'But that's not fair. You started the divorce proceedings once you knew she was pregnant.'

'Yes, around then. More or less.'

'So are you going to let her give your child away?'

'What choice have I, Clara? She holds all the cards.'

'And has she found somebody else?'

'No. No way. She's going to study, she says, and needs her freedom.'

'And did this all come out of a clear blue sky?'

'To me it did,' Alan said sadly.

'Well, to whom did it not?'

'To my friends, *our* friends, anyone who knows her. There was a bit of a misunderstanding about something a couple of weeks back, but I thought it was all done and dusted. Apparently she was brooding about it. How was I to know?'

'Poor Alan.' She was actually sorry for him.

'So I was wondering . . .'

'No, Alan.'

'We are still man and wife. It's still my home.'

'Nonsense, Alan, there was a separation agreement. The divorce will be through shortly. You have no more right to come here than you have to go and stay with the President of Ireland up at Phoenix Park.'

There was a silence at his end.

'I wish you luck,' she said.

'I have nowhere to go, Clara.'

'Goodnight, Alan.'

The girls were looking at her with curiosity. Gerry had tactfully started doing the washing-up.

The questions hung in the air. Clara knew she must answer them somehow. He *was* their father: she mustn't be too flip and dismissive.

'It's complicated,' she began. 'Your father doesn't change.'

'So he was caught?' Linda suggested.

'Apparently,' Clara said.

'Will you take him back, Mam?' Adi asked.

'No, Adi. No, I won't.'

'And his baby?' Linda asked.

'Is being given away to the bimbo's sister.'

'And Dad isn't . . .' Adi could hardly believe any of this.

323

'No, darling, he isn't. It was different with you two. He really loves you both. Yes, in his funny, mad, complicated way he *does* love you.'

'And does he love *you*, Mam?' Adi asked.

'He loves the memory of me. He loves what I was twenty-something years ago. It's a kind of love.'

Linda spoke. 'Clara's right. Alan is who he is. The sooner we all accept that then the sooner we can all move on.'

Clara stood up. 'Talking of moving on, I suggest we have a liqueur as my treat. I think we've all earned it.' And she closed the curtains in case Alan drove by and looked in the window. He was a fool but she didn't want to make his life a misery seeing what really had turned out to be a happy family dinner taking place in the household he had walked out of, causing so much pain and upset all those years ago.

'More cheerful?' Hilary asked the next day.

'Much, thank you. I'm sorry for being like a bear yesterday.'

'No, you were like a cabaret. Was the meal bearable?'

'It was great. Alan rang up in the middle of it to say his bimbo has thrown him out and is giving away their baby. And, as it happens, Linda made a huge effort to be normal and almost succeeded. I enjoyed it.'

'Well now!' Hilary was surprised.

'So much so that I think all that's wrong with her is she hasn't met the right man yet.'

'*Clara!* You and I are the old guard: we've spent years saying that we mustn't be measured by the man that we happen to have caught. What's happening to the sisterhood if you weaken?' Hilary was outraged.

'I'm not weakening for the sisterhood, only for Linda. Let's have dinner in the Italian place tonight and we'll plot the whole thing.'

'Tonight?'

'Go on, it's not as if either of us has anything else to do,' Clara said.

'You really have a way of making a girl feel special,' said Hilary, then they got down to work.

Alan rang during the day and Ania took the call.

'Hold on, Mr Casey, and I'll see if she's free. She *was* in a consultation.' Clara shook her head. '*No*, I'm sorry it's going to go on for some time. Shall I tell her that you called?'

'Don't bother. She doesn't care. If she had cared about anything she would have called *me*. Goodbye,' he said.

Ania repeated it slowly to Clara.

'Sorry, Ania, to involve you in such childish behaviour from people who should be well past that.'

'Oh, Clara, if you knew how important I feel here. To be able to be a part of everyone's lives. It gives me great . . . wait . . . wait . . . I know the words . . . self-esteem.'

'Your English has come on so well. They wouldn't know you back home!'

'Yes. I met somebody from home. He could not believe it. He knew nothing. It was very satisfying.'

'Was he a boyfriend?' Clara asked.

'One time, yes, I think, or maybe he never was a boyfriend. Maybe it was all in my own mind. But now it's over. You know when something is really over, don't you?' She looked enquiringly at Clara.

'Yes indeed, you do. The trick is not to feel sorry for the person.'

'No. In my case this would never happen,' Ania said very seriously.

Clara hoped she was equally certain. She had been feeling something dangerously like sympathy for Alan since last night.

She wondered where he had slept. And what he had done that Cinta had discovered.

'So, let's approach this like a problem in the clinic. Something that has to be solved before Frank gets wind of it.' Clara opened the discussion at the Italian restaurant.

'Nick is a bit of a dreamer; very easy-going, *too* easy-going. You'd need to light a fire under him.' Hilary put her cards on the table. 'He has no get-up-and-go. He plays in this club. He wouldn't go to university, said it was too expensive for me, and so he taught kids the piano and the guitar and then has played forever in this dead-end club.'

'Is it dead-end or is it just somewhere you and I wouldn't go to in a million years?' Clara asked.

'I think it's dead-end. They're always worried that they won't be able to keep up the lease. There are no crowds. No breakthroughs, or whatever people have in the movies, yet he turns up there night after night. He's very vague when I ask him how many people are there. He says there were plenty and they liked the music. He gets what they call a percentage of the door, which means, I think, a fifth of what they take when people pay five euros to come in. But it's never very much. He makes up the rest by teaching.'

'And now to be truthful about Linda. Even though she was terrific last night, she is a very self-centred little madam. She thinks a pair of shoes that costs a week's wage would be good value. Good value! Where is she coming from? She thinks the world owes her something. Maybe we shouldn't unload her on your boy!'

'He's been well able to let other girls disappear from his life. We needn't worry about him being overwhelmed.'

'But how could they meet?' Clara puzzled.

'If we introduce them, it's over before it begins,' Hilary agreed.

'So *how* can they get together?' Clara wondered. 'Suppose Linda were to get free tickets for Nick's club?'

'No, she wouldn't go. She'd smell a rat. Or if she did go, she wouldn't necessarily meet him,' Hilary objected.

Clara was not going to give up. 'What can we do then?'

'Could we get Nick a voucher for the record store where Linda works?' Hilary asked.

'Wouldn't work. He could go to the wrong assistant or it might be a day she wasn't on. You'd actually need a degree in some kind of higher mathematics to work out her shifts,' Clara said, still mystified by her daughter.

'There has to be a casual way? Could we ask them to come to the clinic, do you think?' Hilary said.

'And then they'd see the two of us old crones cackling with laughter and they would both leave in disgust,' Clara said.

'But suppose they *didn't* see us? Suppose they came and we weren't here and they had to talk to each other,' Hilary persisted.

'Ah, come on, Hilary, how could we get them to the clinic and not be there? Think of a way and if you can then I'll buy it.'

'What if we were to invite them to the reception . . .' Hilary began.

'No. They'd regard it as a chore.' Clara was definite.

'But suppose they were the only kindred spirits there. They might fall on each other.'

'We can't introduce them,' Clara said.

'I know, of course, it can't be you and me, but suppose Ania did it?'

'She wouldn't carry it off,' Clara said.

'If there was only something that could get us out of the scene there,' Hilary said.

'I know. We'll get drunk,' Clara said, eyes shining.

'Now?' Hilary was alarmed.

'No, you clown, at the reception.'

'Excuse me, did you say that you and I should get drunk at this reception, which has been breaking our hearts for weeks? *Drunk?* Is that what you said?'

'Not really drunk. Not *drunk* drunk. Just pretending.'

Hilary emptied her glass of wine. 'That's a good idea, you think, to pretend to be drunk at this, our big showpiece night? Drunk in front of people like Frank Ennis, like the whole hospital board. In front of whoever the Minister of Health sends. In front of the cardiologists. In front of the media. Clara, are you insane?'

'No one will see,' Clara said cheerfully. 'Everyone else will think we are sober. Only Nick and Linda will think we're drunk.'

Hilary attracted the waiter's attention.

'Can we have another bottle of Pinot Grigio? Things have taken a turn for the worse here.'

Linda was pleased with the way the dinner party had gone. Clara had been very pleasant. She had produced a bottle of Cointreau and four little glasses. She had coped well with Alan on the phone. She had told them funny stories.

If only she could be like that all the time, it might be bearable to live at home. Odd that she had been so interested in the record store and how they had asked Linda to be in charge of the jazz section. She had been really surprised by that and wanted to know more. And the dreaded Gerry had been helpful and did the washing-up, which was useful when Mam, well, Clara as she now was, wanted to tell them their dad loved them. Maybe he did in his own mad dad-like way.

'Nick, you know this big reception we're going to be having at the clinic?' Hilary asked.

'Of course I do, Ma. Have you talked of anything else?'

'It's important. Sorry to go on about it.'

'No, that's fine. I just wonder why this Clara person doesn't take more interest in it. It's meant to be her show, isn't it?'

'Oh, she does work at it, in her own way,' Hilary said.

'Do you *like* her? As a person?'

'I don't know her very well. She's very efficient, certainly,' Hilary said, stifling her sense of disloyalty.

'Yeah, like Attila the Hun.' Nick grinned.

'I suppose.'

'So what were you going to tell me about the reception?' Nick asked.

'Oh, it was nothing really.'

'Ma! What was it?'

'I just wanted to tell you the date and I wanted a small favour.'

'Say it.' He was such a good-tempered boy. She hated all this subterfuge.

'Well, on the night I'll have to socialise with people and have a glass of wine with this one and that one. I shouldn't take the car and, Nick, I was wondering if you could come and pick me up at about nine o'clock?'

'Sure I will,' he said agreeably.

'It's just that would make me feel much better,' Hilary said.

'I'll be there, but where's the problem? Couldn't you just have called a taxi or something?'

'I *could* have but it makes me look a bit lonely and sad. I'd love my nice son to come and pick me up.'

'I'll be there, Ma.'

'I'm not interfering? Upsetting a date or anything?'

'You know me, Ma. It'll have to be a very speedy girl to catch me,' he laughed.

'I mean it. We all hope to meet someone we like. I don't want to stand in your way.'

'You don't, Ma. You never did. Maybe I'm not the kind of guy anyone would fancy long-term.'

'Oh well, we'll see,' Hilary said.

'Adi, should we do something about Clara's reception?' Linda asked.

'What can we do?' Adi wondered.

'Well, we could show a bit of solidarity. It's hugely important to her, as I know to my cost.'

'She's forgiven you about the cake sale.'

'I know. I want to do something. Could you and I offer to be waitresses or something? Save her money?'

'We could ask her, I suppose,' Adi said.

They offered but Clara said no. She thanked them but said she would be too edgy and nervous that night. They wouldn't see her at her best.

'But we never see you at your best,' Linda said, a little too honestly. 'I mean, we see you ranting and raging about nothing here and we survive it.' Something about her mother's face made her make a hasty addition. 'I mean of course you see *us* in bad situations too. Like Adi being soppy and soft in the head and me being . . . well, I suppose a bit confused.'

It didn't calm the troubled waters quite as Linda had hoped. But Clara hadn't taken offence about it, which was a relief. In fact she seemed touched and surprised at Linda's self-knowledge.

'You're both very good to offer to help and if there *is* anything nearer the time I'll certainly call on you,' she said. 'But I have lots of people lined up to help.' She had to remember not to say that without Hilary the whole project would have died long ago. It was hugely important that Linda never knew how much of a friend Hilary would always be.

*

On the day of the reception they were all at high doh in the clinic. They had set up tables for wine and soft drinks and coffee at one end of Lavender's room and another where food would be displayed at the other end. They lined the wall with chairs for those who needed to sit down. The doors were opened into the other parts of the clinic, with Johnny's equipment pushed well back, but his exercise charts prominently displayed on the walls. The treatment cubicles had been changed into a highly acceptable cloakroom with rails for people's coats, and two girls from a nearby school would hang up each person's coat and give them a coloured ticket.

There had been huge competition to do this job as it was rumoured that two pop stars, a well-known actor and several television personalities were going to be among the guests.

The patients had been invited too, and all the members of the board.

'What do we have to do?' Mrs Reilly asked suspiciously. Everyone knew what Mrs Reilly *would* do. She would tell them that her improved heart condition was entirely due to the personal intervention of some saint and hand out leaflets about the curative powers of the said saint. The clinic would not feature in her praise. But they couldn't leave her out. Mercifully, she decided that she had other fish to fry that night.

'Our Holy Mother must have explained to Our Lord that Mrs Reilly would be better not at the clinic,' Ania said cheerfully. Clara and Hilary looked at each other. They had often said that the marvellous, pious, Polish people who had come to Ireland had done the great service of making Irish Catholicism look modern and liberal by contrast. But they said nothing, apart from nodding gravely in agreement.

Other patients might be more supportive, like Judy Murphy who would tell anyone that the clinic was essential to those who wanted to live independent lives. Or that great woman Nora Dunne, with her piebald hair and her burning eyes, whose husband Aidan had regained his will to live. She was such an advertisement for them, particularly since she was a convert, with all the zeal that a convert brings. She had been so sure that the life with her gentle husband was over when he had his heart attack and now they seemed to feel immortal as a couple.

Even Lar, with his obsessive wish to make everyone learn something new every day, would be a good ambassador for what they were doing. Lar was remorselessly cheerful. If anyone asked him how he was, he always said that he was fighting fit and that a lot of rubbish was talked about heart failure. All you had to do was control it. If they had hired a PR firm to send out the message, they could never have come up with anything as good as Lar.

Ania had made them all name badges in big clear writing: green ones for patients, red ones for the staff and yellow for the guest lecturers.

'You haven't done a label for yourself,' Clara said, surprised.

'Oh, I wouldn't be worth a label,' Ania said. 'What would I know if somebody asked me about the clinic?'

'More than most people. Do the label, Ania, this minute, or else I'll do one for you!'

'That's very kind of you, Clara.'

'And Johnny has a friend who is a photographer who's going to do a staff picture before it all begins, all of us with our names on us. There'll be a copy for everyone and if we like it we'll put it up on the wall here.' Clara was full of enthusiasm.

'I can send a copy to Mamusia, to my mother. She will be so proud to see me as part of a team over here.'

Clara swallowed hard. There was something about this girl that made people feel protective about her and ashamed at the same time. Ashamed that they weren't more grateful for all they had compared to Ania. Clara had bought a new jacket for the night. A cream-coloured brocade, piped with red. It fitted her perfectly. She had been back to Kiki the hairdresser and looked as good as she had ever looked. She did a fashion parade in the kitchen before she left.

'You don't look as if you should be parking your own car. You should be drifting out of a limousine.' Adi was full of admiration.

'You know, you could be in your fifties,' Gerry said admiringly.

'I *am* in my fifties, Gerry.'

'Early fifties,' he said, 'forties even . . .' His voice tailed away.

'Are you on the pull, Clara?' Linda asked with interest.

'Sorry?'

'I mean are you after some man there tonight?'

'No. I'm after many men, and many women, too. What I'm after is getting recognition and support for work which I think is important.'

'But you're all dressed up like a dog's dinner,' Linda said.

'I have to try and sell the whole concept of this to people who are successful and they wouldn't listen to me if I went in a cardigan, with my hair in rat's tails and wearing some kind of a pillow case!'

She looked so totally different from this image that they burst out laughing.

'Oh, and do you know what I'd really like, Linda? If I get over-excited and have a glass of wine too many, could you come and collect me?'

'Sure,' Linda said. 'Don't get too bladdered now and spoil the whole effect.'

'No, I'll try not to get . . . er . . . bladdered,' Clara said and left for the clinic.

'I shouldn't have said she looked in her fifties,' Gerry said.

'No, honey, it's fine. She knew what you meant,' Adi consoled him.

Linda rolled her eyes to heaven and said nothing. It was absolutely terrifying what people did for love. Adi used to have a sort of a mind of her own. Once.

They had the group picture taken.

Johnny's friend Mouth Mangan was a kindly man who understood that this was *the* picture of the night for the people involved. He had arranged it in such a way that the smaller members would be standing on a step and the others not. They would look very equal, which was the purpose of it all.

Mouth said they were all to look over his left shoulder as if they had seen something amazing there and say the words 'beer mat'. This made them all laugh and he took the picture at once. Then they were to say the word 'sympathy' and they all looked more serious. That was it. Over and done. Mouth had taken away his tripod and was setting up his other camera to take pictures of the celebrities.

'Do you do weddings?' Declan whispered to Mouth.

'I'm great at weddings,' Mouth Mangan confided, 'I can do all the officials in eight minutes flat!'

'Officials?' Declan was bewildered.

'You know: Bride, Bride and Groom, Bride and Groom and attendants, Bride's parents, His parents, *all* parents. Makes it easier and quicker if there are no divorces, remarriages and second families?' He looked at Declan questioningly.

'No, nothing like that.'

'Then I mix and merge among the guests and give you a contact sheet and you order what you want and put what you want on a website. When is it? The wedding?'

'We haven't set a date yet,' Declan said a little wistfully.

'Well, she'd better get a move on.' Mouth was practical. 'I

don't have too many Saturdays free in the next year and a half.'

The place was filling up. The staff with their red badges introduced themselves to everyone. Frank Ennis watched, surprised, as they swung into action.

'Do I get a red badge too?' he asked Barbara.

'Wouldn't say so, Mr Ennis, you're only the hospital, aren't you? It's not as if you were a member of the clinic here,' Barbara said.

'Or even a friend to it,' Clara said sweetly.

'You look very lovely tonight, Dr Casey,' he said.

'And you scrubbed up well too, Frank. Nice tie. Did your wife choose that for you?'

'Sadly, Dr Casey, I am not blessed with a wife,' he said.

'You mean you're *available?*' she said in mock excitement. 'Lord, I wonder do the many unattached ladies coming here tonight know that?'

'I didn't say I was available,' he said loudly.

And Hilary covered her mouth to stop laughing aloud.

Bobby Walsh arrived with his wife and son. Carl was pushing his father in the wheelchair. Mrs Walsh's hard eyes ranged the open-plan clinic with some surprise. They showed even more surprise when she saw some well-known faces there. Surely that was . . . ? And that woman was definitely a television celebrity. What was *she* doing here? A well-known businessman was talking to an actor. How had that shrewish woman who ran this place brought them all together? The bad-tempered Clara Casey was looking extraordinarily well tonight. Probably had a face lift. Rosemary Walsh wished she had dressed more carefully herself. She hadn't known it was going to be so smart.

She saw Ania, the clinic's Polish maid, nearby so she took off her coat and handed it to her.

'Make sure it's put on a hanger,' she said.

Clara had seen. 'How *good* to see you, Mrs Walsh. Looking for the cloakroom, are you? Just down there at the end.'

'I thought . . . ?' Rosemary Walsh began.

'Yes, I thought everyone could read the sign easily, but apparently not. Next time we must make it bigger. Come with me, Ania, I want you to introduce me to Father Flynn.' And they moved off, leaving Rosemary Walsh more fuming than she had ever been in her life.

The speeches were short and to the point. Frank Ennis, who had of course insisted on speaking, was actually quite good. He was even rather gracious about the clinic and its elegant director, Dr Casey.

Then the formalities were over and when everything seemed to be going well, Clara rang Linda.

'Sorry, love, it's Clara here.'

'And you're pissed!' Linda said, proud to have identified the situation.

'I wouldn't say that, but then us hopeless drinkers always say that, but I think I'm beyond driving.'

'Okay, will I come down now?'

'Yes. Come in and have a glass of wine.'

'How's it all going?' Linda remembered to ask.

'Amazingly well, and you should see the style,' she added.

'You don't sound too pissed,' Linda said grudgingly.

'You know what it's all about. Holding it all together.'

'I'll get a bus there now,' Linda promised.

'Take a taxi. You don't want to be parading your finery in the bus. Take a taxi. I'll pay.'

'Oh, I'm to get dressed up too?'

'Well, I know you won't come in your jeans,' Clara said. She dared not say any more or Linda would be suspicious. But

336

she knew her daughter well enough to realise that she had sent enough messages about smart attire.

Clara introduced Bobby to a man who had once played rugby for Ireland; he was animated in the conversation. She noted too that Ania was deep in conversation with Bobby's son Carl. Rosemary Walsh stood on her own, her mouth set in a fury. She reminded Clara of someone. Then she remembered. Rosemary Walsh's face was like Clara's own mother's face. Ready and willing to disapprove of whatever presented itself.

Clara's mother had not come. She'd been invited but said she had a bridge game and that she couldn't be expected to support every lame duck cause that her daughter came up with. It was a relief that her mother wasn't there.

It would also be a relief if Rosemary Walsh would collect her coat from the cloakroom and leave now. But life didn't work like that.

Clara fixed the smile back on her face and introduced Rosemary to a bank manager.

'You're never a heart patient?' he said gallantly. It was exactly the right thing to say to Rosemary, so Clara joined in to reinforce it.

'Mrs Walsh's husband, who is much older than she is, is one of the people who has done very well here at the clinic. Hasn't spent a day in hospital since he came to see us first. He's a great supporter, and he's here tonight, over there with his son.'

The bank manager was impressed, and Rosemary looked less beached than she had.

Clara had also introduced the good-tempered priest Father Flynn to a millionaire with the instructions that he wasn't to divert the millionaire's money entirely to his own centre.

It was going better than she had dared to hope.

Nick arrived first. Clara saw him talking to his mother and

337

had to steel herself not to go over and greet him. She watched as Hilary got him a glass of wine and introduced him to a couple of colleagues. He was tall and relaxed, as at home there as he would be anywhere. Would he be right for her troubled Linda?

Linda came in then. Clara saw her looking around the roaringly successful party in wonder. Clara felt a wave of pride at being able to show this to her over-critical daughter. Cake sale indeed!

She saw Hilary move Nick into Johnny's physiotherapy room and so Clara headed that way too with Linda.

'You need to look at these amazing exercise plans he has on the wall,' she said. 'I'll try not to be too long.'

'You're great at hiding the signs of drink,' Linda said grudgingly. 'I thought you'd be on all fours.'

Clara waved her wine glass around airily. It was her first drink tonight but Linda must never know this. 'Oh, I fear I'm well over the limit,' she said. 'I'm glad I sound all right. I have two or three more people to talk to.'

'Take your time, Clara.' Linda was cheerful about it all. At least she wasn't going to have to carry her mother to the car. She was glad she had put on her black and white silk dress. It looked good on her and she had extremely uncomfortable shoes which went with it. She had dropped her sneakers into the boot of the car as she passed by. She would never be able to drive in these shoes. Linda looked around at the people there. She recognised one or two faces from the television. She saw politicians whose faces were familiar. Ah, God, why had she called this a cake sale? She wondered where this awful man her mother hated called Frank was and she'd love to met this boringly angelic Polish girl who seemed to be everything a mother wanted wrapped up in one small hardworking parcel.

She noticed a pleasant-looking man across the room

studying the exercise charts. He wasn't wearing a badge. He must be a visitor like herself. She thought he had looked at her admiringly when she came in. But then she must stop thinking things like that. Usually people weren't fancying her at all, just looking with a passing interest at someone with long legs. It had been her downfall thinking that people were admiring her when more often than not there was no admiration at all.

It was Fiona who introduced them in the end. Clara told her to do it.

'Just say this is Nick Hickey. This is Linda Casey. Please, Fiona, now.'

'Why don't you or Hilary do it?'

'I'd tell you, but then I'd have to kill you, so it's better you just go and do it,' Clara urged her.

'Ooh, is it a touch of matchmaking? Are we going to be talking about two weddings soon?' Fiona joked.

'If you mention anything like that, even remotely, I will take you to one of those treatment beds and skilfully remove your entire heart and transplant it into someone else,' she said, with such intensity that Fiona backed down.

'Yeah, sure, I get the message.'

'This conversation is over and did not take place,' Clara said.

'What conversation? You'll have to excuse me, Clara, I have a couple of things to do.' Fiona escaped to Johnny's room and did the job.

She was very beautiful, Clara's daughter. She didn't need any mother trying to find her a fellow. And as far as Nick was concerned, he was so easy-going he didn't look like Last Chance Saloon either. Still, this was her mission.

'I came to pick up my mother because she's drunk,' Linda said.

'So did I, in a way. Snap!' he laughed.

'Who is your drunken mother?' Linda asked.

'Hilary Hickey,' he said, 'she's the office manager.'

'My mother is Clara Casey,' she said grumpily.

'Oh, the head honcho,' he said. 'I see.'

'She looks quite sober though.' Linda felt defensive now. She didn't want to let this office manager hear that Clara was a dipso or anything.

'Better to be sure though these days,' he said approvingly.

'Are you involved in the clinic here?'

'Not enough,' Nick said ruefully. 'I didn't realise exactly how much they had all done here. I must say I'm impressed.'

'Me too,' Linda said. He hadn't said what he did for a living. Well, that was okay. She hated those people who immediately pinned you down and classified you by your job. Her ex-boyfriend Simon said that you should always ask someone what they did for a living the moment you met them so that you wouldn't waste any time with nobodies and losers. But that was very Simon. Not necessarily anything you'd want to live by.

This Nick was nice. And he revealed his job himself. He said he didn't get much exercise as he taught music, which was a sitting-down job, and he played in a club which involved sitting around and then standing up to play in an intense atmosphere.

Linda said she worked in a record shop and told him where it was.

'They're terrific,' Nick said, 'they're starting a whole new jazz section.'

'And I'm in charge of it,' Linda said proudly.

'Never!' He was very impressed.

'Yes, I have a rack of Count Basie, Duke Ellington and Miles Davis already, and they've given me funds to get more.'

'Will you have Artie Shaw,' he asked, 'and Benny Goodman?'

'Sure I will. I was going to get going with jazz women. You know, Billie Holiday, Ella . . . ?'

'And Lena!' he cried. 'You'll have lots of Lena Horne.'

'Oh yes, yes. My favourite, Lena is. "More Than You Know".'

'Mine is "At Long Last Love",' Nick said.

The guests were all leaving. Clara and Hilary, the two ostensibly drunken mothers, were peeping around the door.

Linda and Nick were oblivious to it all.

All the scheming ladies had done was to speed it up a little for them. And now they must stand back and hold their breath and never ever, as long as they lived, admit this little plan to either of the young jazz fans who stood in their own world in the middle of Johnny's exercise room.

Chapter Ten

F iona was invited to come to supper in St Jarlath's
Crescent. The twins were going to cook a Greek meal
and they had asked Molly if she'd mind.

'And did she?' asked Fiona, knowing how proud Molly
Carroll was of her cooking skills, her roasts and her casseroles.

'Apparently she's delighted. She's talking meatballs and
kebabs with them as if she grew up on a Greek island.'

'She's one dote, your mother,' Fiona said affectionately.

'You made her what she is now. When I went to the hospital she was so difficult. I dreaded you ever having to meet
her. Now you're the best of pals.'

'Well, why wouldn't we be? Aren't we both mad about
you?'

'So, when do you think we should give my mam a day out?'

'She has plenty of days out,' Fiona said. 'Weren't we up at
the zoo, the pair of us, last week? She told me it had been years
since she was there and I loved it too.'

'You know full well what I mean,' Declan said.

'Oh, a *wedding* day!' Fiona said, with a laugh.

'Yes, sweetheart, a *wedding* day . . .'

'Haven't we all the time in the world to arrange that?' Fiona
said. 'Would Wednesday be okay?'

'To get married?' He looked up gleefully.

'To go to supper with the twins at your house, you eejit.'

Bobby Walsh told Declan that he and his wife were having a ruby wedding party. That was forty years married. He sighed with pleasure about it, though Declan couldn't see why. That sharp-tongued, restless, impatient Rosemary! Imagine being married to her for four decades. But maybe she hadn't seemed like that when they started out.

'So, we're having about seventy people to the house and I was wondering, would you and Fiona like to join us?'

Declan was taken aback. 'Well, that's very nice of you, Bobby, but you don't want to be bringing dreary old doctors and nurses in on top of all your friends.'

'On the contrary. I owe you everything. I wouldn't be here planning to celebrate if it hadn't been for you all. And there *was* a bit of a misunderstanding between Rosemary and Clara.'

'Ah yes!' Declan looked calm and understanding. He had heard all about the 'misunderstanding' from Clara. It had, in fact, been a shouted attack from Rosemary – but better let sleeping dogs lie there, he thought to himself.

'So, it's on the twenty-first, but I'll send you a proper invitation. That's really great, now. I'm so happy you'll be there.'

And indeed he sounded happy, Declan thought.

'Rosemary with you today?' he asked, as they completed the blood tests and the chart filling.

'No. She's out talking to caterers. Carl brought me. He has a day off from the school.'

'He's a great son, you must be delighted with him!' Declan said.

'Yes, he is, he's a great boy and he loves that teaching job. Of course Rosemary thinks it's not nearly good enough for him, tells everyone he's doing an MA, but there'll be white blackbirds before that lad goes back to university. He'll go on at that school until he's drawing his pension.'

'Great to have found something which makes you happy,' Declan said, as he helped Bobby on with his coat.

'If he finds as good a woman as I did, then he'll be a lucky man,' Bobby said.

Privately, Declan hoped that young Carl would find a much better woman than Rosemary, but his face showed nothing of this.

'We'd been waiting for him for over ten years. We'd almost given up hope. And then he arrived.' Bobby was so good-natured and cheerful about everything, including his bad-tempered wife. It was fortunate that the boy they had waited so long for had inherited most of his father's characteristics rather than his mother's.

'Fiona will be thrilled,' Declan said, as he shook Bobby's hand.

'And when are you two . . . ?' Bobby began.

'Don't ask,' Declan whispered. 'It's like not mentioning the war, everything functions fine if you don't start looking for a date for the Big Day or whatever. If you do, all hell breaks loose.'

'You're a wise man, Declan,' Bobby said. 'It will all turn out absolutely fine. Believe me.'

Declan found it hard to believe anything from a man who was pleased to be married to Rosemary for forty years, but he smiled his thanks, as he did so often. It was easier than gut-wrenching confrontation. Sometimes, he wondered, might he be a bit dull?

Ania knew that Clara and Hilary had a secret, but she didn't know what it was. Sometimes they giggled like schoolgirls. Other times they sat, heads together, making lists. But they never told her. She didn't mind. She hadn't told them all about Marek coming over and how she had got over him in just one minute, standing there in that restaurant when he was assuming she would dance naked for men to make him money.

Maybe it was about Hilary's son and Clara's daughter, who had got together at the big reception. That had been a lovely night, Ania remembered wistfully. Carl had admired how well she looked. He had said her English was coming on by leaps and bounds and he had laughed at her fondly when she paused to write down leaps and bounds. It was a lovely phrase, reminded you of a hare in the grass, leaping and bounding ahead.

He had even kissed her on the nose as he left.

'You are so sweet, Ania, and so clever. I wish I had students like you in my class.'

'I am not clever, Carl. Truly I am not.'

'Excuse me. From where I stand you are very clever. And look, you can turn your hand to anything.'

'That's only because I need to work hard to make money. I just have to try many things.'

'This is what I mean. One moment you're running a laundry, the next you're running this clinic . . .'

'I would not say that! Working here, yes.'

'I have listened to you all evening. You're such a good ambassador for the work that is done here. Then you work in a jeweller's—'

'I just clean there!'

'*And* in that international centre. *And* you mind children. *And* you go round to people's houses and clear up after their dinner parties.'

'That *was* a good idea. I thought of that myself.' Ania's eyes were shining. 'It is nice for the hostess that she can go to bed and come down to a nice clean kitchen.'

'Yes, but when do you sleep, Ania? How many hours are there in the day for you?'

'Not enough,' she had said seriously. 'I would need forty hours in the day if I were to earn enough to give my mother the life she deserves.'

'Maybe she just wants you to be happy,' he had said. He wouldn't say all that unless he liked her a little. Would he?

Father Brian Flynn was having what he thought was an exhausting run with his friend Johnny, who thought it was a casual walk. They had taken the little DART train that went south from Dublin, out to Killiney on the coast, and then they climbed what Father Brian thought was a mountain and Johnny said was a slight incline and looked down over Dunlaoghaire harbour, where the boats came in from England and the rich yachtsmen moored their craft; then they descended from the mountain, or *incline*, to Dalkey, drank two pints in a friendly pub, after which they'd take the DART back to Dublin.

Brian was always knocked out by it. Johnny, who must have had different muscles and sinews, felt no pain at all.

They sat in Dalkey and discussed the world. Brian was having the odd problem about financing the centre. He had been told to make it self-funding. How could he do that? He'd already roped all his friends in to paint the place. He'd asked Ania to make curtains and tablecloths for him. He couldn't increase the prices they charged – these young people sent so much money home already they had barely anything left to live on.

If only there was a way of making money out of the premises. It was a big hall with a few little rooms off it where people held meetings. They served tea, coffee and soup and sandwiches in the hall. Attached to it was a small chapel. After mass on a Saturday night or Sunday morning, Brian

346

welcomed the various young Europeans, still a little lost in the big city, and glad to have a place for coffee and a chat. He couldn't charge them high prices to make the place self-funding.

'Can you do a dance or a nightclub or something?' Johnny suggested.

'Aw, come on, Johnny, it hardly goes with the wholesome image, does it?'

'I didn't mean a strip club.' Johnny was offended.

'No, I know you didn't, but judging by what nearly knocks my eyes out going along that street, we wouldn't be out of place.'

'There must be *something*,' Johnny said, refusing to be beaten.

'Lord, it was nearly easier back in Rossmore, where people would say that we should all go up to the Holy Well and ask St Ann what to do.'

'But I thought you left to get away from all that?' Johnny was puzzled.

'I did, but like everyone, I'm beginning to wonder was there something in it? They all came back from that mad well delighted with themselves.'

'She told them what to do?'

'She planted the seeds in their heads, apparently. Don't get me started.'

'And what does Father Tomasz think?'

'Ah, Father Tomasz. Nicest man that ever wore shoe leather. Mad about the bloody well. It's going stronger than ever. People want to get married there and all!' Brian stopped talking. 'God Almighty!' he said suddenly.

'What is it?' Johnny thought something was wrong.

'God – that's the solution. We can have weddings at the centre. I'll marry them first in the chapel, or Tomasz can come up and do the Polish ones, and then we give them a wedding breakfast in the hall. What a fantastic bloody idea!'

Clara was holding her breath about Linda. She had been to Nick's club twice. He had been to her record shop almost every day. He had said she was a genius and what's more he had told the boss that he was mad not to take her on full-time.

Linda had thought about it for six minutes and said that was fine with her. A proper salary and a budget for promotion.

'What will you promote?' the boss had asked her, not unreasonably.

'Your store and its fine support for Irish or visiting jazz artists. You could even have a happy hour on Thursdays at late opening, get somebody to play, bring in the punters.'

The boss listened with interest. He had thought she was a silly, brainless blonde with long legs who would stay for three weeks. Now she was planning on running an empire.

Hilary was also holding her breath. Nick had got a haircut. He had smartened himself up considerably. He had asked Hilary did she know of any hall he could rent; a place to give a music class. Lovely as home was, it wasn't the place to hold a big class with twenty people. He had been talking to somebody who had said it made more sense to teach twenty kids four chords all at the same time for a series of six Saturdays at an agreed fee. Somebody had also told him that he was nearly thirty and it was time he made people aware of how good he was. Since Hilary had been telling him the same thing for twenty years, she gasped in disbelief to think that *somebody* — who happened to be Clara's daughter — had been able to make him listen.

Linda had stopped wearing those ludicrously short skirts and high boots. Nick had bought a sweater that wasn't full of holes with threads running loose. Linda didn't talk much about Nick at home. Nick didn't speak of her to his mother. But at the heart clinic two middle-aged women talked about them all the time and were once even seen doing a little dance around Clara's desk.

On the Wednesday of the Greek feast, the twins came round early to Molly Carroll's.

'A lot of it is in the presentation . . .' Maud began.

'The way you lay the dishes out,' Simon added.

'We brought these little pottery plates . . .'

'So we can display the meze . . .'

'And we are giving the plates to Fiona . . .'

'And you and Declan too . . .'

Molly felt dizzy listening to them. You had to turn your head left and right as if you were watching a tennis match. But they were completely delightful and chattered on as if she was their oldest friend.

Their conversation was filled with people she had never heard of: this Vonni, and Andreas, and Andreas's brother Yorghis and the local doctor, Dr Leros, who had taken bits of broken plate out of Simon's feet when he had danced too enthusiastically in a restaurant. And all the time they talked they were decorating the table with bowls of olives, flat pitta bread, plates of hummus and taramasalata and things like squid that Molly wondered if she would ever be able to eat.

They had made what looked like an ordinary shepherd's pie but called it moussaka and filled it with evil-looking purple vegetables; a Greek salad of tomatoes, cucumber and feta cheese stood on the sideboard and a dessert which looked like sheets of brown paper with almonds and honey.

Molly sighed. She could have done such a good joint – nice normal food – not all these silly little bowls. Paddy would have given her the best loin of lamb or rib of beef from the butchery department where he worked. But these children's uncle or grandfather or whatever he was, Muttie, was important in Paddy's life and they had become obsessed by this celebration.

Molly was getting better about sitting back and letting other people get on with things. It hadn't been easy. For years she had been running this house herself as well as working in the launderette. Every morning she had ironed one shirt for Paddy, one for Declan. She had been home to welcome them with their supper. But everything had changed.

Declan spent most of his free time with Fiona now. And she was such a good girl, too. Totally mad about Declan of course, and good for him too. He had much more confidence these days. And Fiona made everyone laugh. She went off with Paddy and Muttie and drank pints in their pub; she had taken Molly herself off to the zoo for a great day and Fiona had talked to everyone and they spent hours looking at the exotic birds and went nowhere near the lions.

So, if Fiona liked all this greasy food served in tiny dishes, then why not? Molly would join in. She was wearing her smart new tartan dress and tried desperately to understand the ramifications of the people the twins were talking about.

'Of course Adoni says our tomatoes are wrong for the *horiatiki* salad but . . .'

'But Vonni said that Irish tomatoes are fine if you brush a little honey over them . . .'

'It's a kind of creative thing to do, making a meal . . .' Simon seemed surprised by the thought.

'Molly knows this. She's been making Paddy and Declan meals for years.' Maud was more tactful.

Molly let it all wash over her until she heard the key turn in the lock. Declan and Fiona were home. They had picked Paddy up at the pub. The feast could now begin.

The twins carefully explained every dish as if they had invented it. The Carrolls listened, entranced, as the twins told of the midnight café, the market in the square, of the crowds that came up every night to Andreas, how Simon and Maud had worked there at night as well as in Vonni's shop during the day. Adoni had even organised a truck that left the square every hour to ferry people up and back.

'Oh, they're not nearly as tough now as they were in my day. We had to haul ourselves up there all by ourselves!' Fiona said.

'Was your day a long time ago?' Simon asked.

Fiona waited politely for Maud to finish the sentence, but Maud was uncharacteristically looking down at the tablecloth.

'Oh, yes, sorry, we weren't to talk about *your* day,' Simon said, remembering.

'It's just that Vonni said it wasn't the best of times for you,' Maud said.

'No, it wasn't, but the place was terrific and even though I was being very foolish over a fellow at the time, I met a lot of good friends, and I'm thrilled that you met some of them too.'

So it hadn't been a disaster after all. Simon let his breath out slowly. 'Oh, they were wonderful people and we'll never be able to thank you enough for introducing us,' he said.

'I heard you were great workers and great company. She misses your chats,' Fiona said.

'We showed her how to text but I don't think it's going to be her thing.'

'No, I can't see her doing it,' Fiona agreed.

'But she *is* thinking of coming to your wedding,' Maud said.

'We haven't actually set the date yet,' Declan pointed out.

'We said it wasn't definite . . .' Simon said.

'. . . but it would probably be before the end of the summer . . .' Maud explained.

'. . . while the good weather is still here . . .'

'. . . and the days are longer.'

'Great,' Fiona said, laughing. 'You seem to have covered all the main points, and do you think she'll come?'

'She wasn't going to and we told her that you considered her a great friend . . .'

'. . . and that friendship should never be one-sided . . .'

'. . . and she saw the sense of that.'

'She does know how to get cheap flights online . . .'

'We went down to the Aghia Anna Beach Hotel and showed her how to get online. The manager says he'll boot her up.'

'So there shouldn't be any problem.'

'And of course, it sorted out our career,' Simon said.

'We know now what we want to do,' Maud said.

'And what's that exactly?' Declan asked.

'We are going to be in the catering industry,' Simon said proudly as if he was about to open his restaurant that night.

Fiona told Ania all about the Greek feast the next day as they were getting the treatment rooms ready.

'They sound wonderful,' Ania said.

'It's better than being at a play, watching them. They've decided to go into catering and they're going to do some kind of night lectures and then learn all that can be taught while actually on the job. Their cousin-in-law runs this company, Scarlet Feather, and they're going to get some practice there.'

'Scarlet Feather! It is the catering company that is doing the food for Carl's parents' ruby wedding!' Ania was pleased to be part of things.

'Well, you might even meet them there or maybe it's too important a do for them to let Maud and Simon loose on it.'

'Oh, I haven't been invited,' Ania said.

'But you will be. You're Carl's girlfriend.'

'I am Carl's friend, yes, and I am a girl, yes, but I am not a girlfriend,' Ania said. 'I do not want to raise my hopes too high.'

'But he comes in to teach you English once a week. He always talks to you when he's here with his father. You and he have been to art galleries and museums and the theatre.' Fiona was confused.

'That's only to make me less stupid. Less thick,' Ania said.

Fiona suddenly wished that Declan hadn't said that they would go to this bloody party. If Ania wasn't there it would be like an act of betrayal. Then on her way out to lunch, Fiona saw Carl Walsh coming in. She debated asking him whether or not Ania was being invited to the ruby wedding. But suppose the answer was no? Anyway, she mustn't try to play God. It wasn't her business.

'What will people give to your parents as gifts on their ruby wedding day?' Ania asked Carl.

'Red glass, apparently. Some of them are getting together in groups. There's going to be a Bohemian glass decanter and six wine glasses – that's from one group. Red coffee cups from another. And another are getting two huge salad bowls. It's all nonsense really – they have enough dishes and glass to last them the rest of their lives.'

'Perhaps their friends want to celebrate,' Ania suggested.

'You live in a happier, more honest world,' Carl said to her. 'This is all to show off the house, the caterers, the view, everything.'

'But people will have a good time? Yes?'

'Er . . . well . . . *you* will have a good time, I hope . . .'

'I am to be invited?' Ania's eyes were bright with excitement.

'Of course. You're my great friend, aren't you?'

'I will receive an invitation, like the other guests?'

'Yes, if you want one, Ania, but I always assumed you were going to come. I can't do it without you.'

'Thank you so much, Carl, I was afraid, well, you know . . . I didn't really think . . .'

'Just think how miserable I would be there if I didn't have you to talk to.'

'But you will need to be talking with your parents' friends, passing the drinks, making the conversation.'

'Just making conversation, not *the* conversation . . .' He always corrected her gently and she tried hard to remember each time.

'It will be wonderful,' she said happily. 'I will make good conversation to people and I will dress well to do you credit.'

'You couldn't *not* do me credit,' he said and he looked at her for a long time over their tomato sandwich until eventually he broke the moment and got out the English grammar book to carry on where they had left off last time.

The days passed quickly then. Ania got yet one more job. She needed extra money to pay for her dress. Not one cent of her savings would be taken from the fund she was building up for her Mamusia.

While clearing tables and collecting glasses, she came across a Chinese man who was offering a boy the chance to work four hours a week helping to weed and replant window-boxes in a big apartment block. The boy said the hours didn't suit, so Ania offered to do it. She was astounded at the luxury of these sea-view apartments as she went in and out of the lavish places. It wasn't far from where the Walshes lived. In fact she passed their house every time she went out that way to the tree-lined roads of the coast.

She wore cheap cotton gloves and covered her hands in Vaseline. Yes, it was a job, and a good one, but she didn't want to go to this great party with rough hands full of earth and soil. The Chinese man, whose name was Mr Chen, was silent and helpful. She learned quickly, turning the soil, feeding the plants and replacing those that had been allowed to die of neglect. She also had a tin of white paint to touch up the window-boxes where they were showing wear and tear.

Ania looked in wonder at the stylish furnishings in the apartments: the elegant chairs and the padded window seats, where the owners could sit and look out at the sea. It was a different world from her own. When she woke up in her flat she saw rooftops from the small window. There were no window-boxes, no wide marble stairs with great fern planters on the landings. But Ania hadn't any sense of envy. All these people, or at least their parents, must have worked hard to get such great wealth. It was open to anyone who might work.

And then Barbara and Fiona took her to their favourite thrift shops to find something to wear for the party. They moved confidently through the rails of clothes, offering a garment here and there. But Ania shook her head. They were too short, too tight, too revealing. Too much like the clothes that Marek had wanted her to wear in the Bridge Café to attract the clients to come and dance. She just shook her head.

'God, if I looked like you, I'd wear that,' Barbara said, looking admiringly at a black leather dress with metal decorations.

'Why don't you wear it?' Ania asked.

'Because I couldn't squeeze my huge bosoms into it.'

'I would so love to have huge bosoms,' Ania said.

'It's a known fact that no woman is satisfied with the size of her breasts,' Fiona said sagely.

'But you, Fiona? You don't want different bosoms surely?' Ania was startled.

'Indeed I do, and so does everyone in this shop. But the main thing is not to spend any time worrying about it. What about this red dress? It would look terrific on you.'

'It has no sleeves and I have arms like the little matchsticks.'

'Do you know what would be lovely?' Barbara was thoughtful. 'If we could just find someone who can sew, they could put lovely lacy sleeves on to that red dress and it would be perfect.'

'Sew? I can sew,' Ania said.

And soon they had found an old lace blouse which Ania said would be child's play to unpick to make sleeves for the dress.

'We'll knock that awful Mrs Walsh's eyes right into the back of her head,' Fiona said, triumphantly.

'No, no. Don't say that. She has been kind. She invited me.' Ania would not be brought down. This had been a wonderful visit. The cost had been tiny. Ania still had money for a hairdo. Things were really looking up.

Dearest Mamusia,

It is 1 a.m. and I am sewing lace sleeves on to a red dress. I wish I were with you and you could show me how to make the best use of the material I have.

You know this nice young man called Carl who helps me to learn English, I have often written to you about him, his father is a patient here at the clinic; well, his parents are forty years married which is a ruby wedding and they have invited me to their house, which is a big white mansion near the sea coast. And I have been asked to the celebration. It's very exciting and I will tell you all about it. Say a prayer for me so that I don't do anything foolish and silly.

Father Flynn is doing up the hall where I made the curtains and tablecloths. He thinks we might have weddings there. A Polish priest will come to do the marriage service and we will provide the food and entertainment. Perhaps if one day I marry an Irish man, the wedding will be there and you

and Mrs Żak and everyone can come from Poland to dance at
the wedding feast. But I do not think it will happen soon.
  I love you always and think of you every day.
  Your fond daughter,
  Ania

Cathy and Tom looked around the house. It was as airy and elegant as they would have expected from the outside. But they were more interested in working out the technicalities: where to park the catering vans so that they were not too obvious; where they would set up the bar; would the guests have their drinks out on the big balcony; which room to set up the coat rails. They checked the power points and the cloakrooms.

Mrs Walsh was a sharp-faced woman with a slight whine in her voice. 'How many staff will you have?' Her husband was in a chair with a stick beside him; he was so full of smiles and enthusiasm, it almost made up for the wife.

'We will both be here with a barperson and a waiter and also you will be glad to know we have two trainees, excellent young people, so they will be here as back-up.' Cathy managed to be both calming and efficient, but Rosemary Walsh was determined to find fault.

'We thought we were paying for a *professional* service.' The whine in her voice had become more pronounced.

'And indeed we will offer you a *highly* professional service, Mrs Walsh. The Mitchell twins will be here to observe: they will stay in the background, take coats, help with parking. Very often a hostess likes extra hands to pass around canapés at the start of an evening to break the ice. We thought you would be delighted to have two extra people at no extra cost.'

Rosemary Walsh felt she was being corrected, very politely, but it annoyed her.

'Yes, well, it's just this is the last big party we will have,' she began.

'Oh, never say that, Mrs Walsh. There's the golden wedding, and then you might have a wedding in the family, a christening. There's always a reason for a party.'

'I doubt if we'll see our fiftieth, Ms Feather, and we only have a son, so any wedding will be his bride's department – *if* he ever finds a bride. So let's concentrate heavily on the party in hand.'

'Indeed, and it will be a pleasure to help at such a happy occasion,' said Cathy Feather, soothingly. She wondered over and over how it was that women like this often ended up with kind men and huge houses and enough money to host a party for seventy people. In several years of catering, it was a thought that had crossed her mind more than once.

Simon and Maud tried on their uniform: the shirts with Scarlet Feather on them; smart black trousers. They were told they must have very clean nails and Maud's hair must be tied well back. They stood and watched in the kitchen as the canapés were assembled. Over and over they repeated what each one contained.

'This is a shortcrust pastry boat with asparagus and a hollandaise sauce,' Maud pronounced.

'These are choux pastry with a slice of rare beef and served with a horseradish and cream sauce,' Simon said.

'Suppose someone asks you what's in a Kir Royale?' Cathy asked. They looked at each other blankly.

'I'd say we'd ask the barperson,' Maud said.

'I'd say it was a mystery ingredient,' Simon said firmly.

'Wiser to *know* what it is,' Cathy suggested. 'Here, look at these bottles: this is Crème de Cassis, and this is an inferior champagne.'

'But we don't *tell* them it's inferior, do we?' Maud asked.

'No, indeed, you do not. I think you two will be great. Tom and I will have to watch out for our own business when you get started . . .' And the twins grinned at the compliment.

On the day of the ruby wedding, the weather was perfect. A warm day with a little breeze coming in from the sea.

'Didn't we make a wise choice all those years ago, Rosemary?' Bobby Walsh said as he gave her a ruby necklace.

'Yes, we did, Bobby.' And for once her voice was soft.

Carl was coming to take them both out for a light lunch in a smart place. These catering people seemed to know what they were doing, even though that woman had a bit too much attitude. Rosemary's hairdresser was coming to the house at three o'clock. It was all going according to plan.

Other people were getting ready for the party too. Fiona and Declan were doing a fashion parade for Molly. Declan was wearing his very smart jacket, dark green and well cut. Fiona looked very chic in her own outfit. It was a very bright orange and red silk dress worn with a demure black jacket. Ania had been able to make her a matching silk flower to pin on the jacket. It looked like a designer outfit.

'The shoes will crucify me but it'll be worth it,' she said.

'Why not wear ones you're more comfortable in?' Declan suggested, but his mother and girlfriend didn't even dignify this with an answer.

Then their taxi arrived and they set off to pick up Ania. She said she would be standing on the corner of her street.

When the taxi drove around the corner they saw a little crowd. Johnny was there; a priest, whom they had met briefly, was part of the group; Ania's friend Lidia and Tim the security man. She was getting a great send-off.

She looked stunning with her shiny black hair, her dancing eyes and the red dress which fitted her like a glove. The long lacy sleeves looked as if they were part of a high-fashion statement. This girl shouldn't be scrubbing floors, Fiona thought, she was so talented. *Please* let it be a good night for her. Let the awful Rosemary not say anything unforgivable.

Nick and Linda were going to be on a radio talk show on the night of the Walshes' party. Clara had invited Hilary to supper. Since the young lovers would be safely in the radio studio, the women could afford to have an evening together without arousing any suspicion.

They tuned the radio to the right station and Clara grilled them some salmon and served it with green beans.

'Lord, wouldn't Lavender be proud of us,' Hilary said.

'Yes, she would, until she saw the rum babas in the fridge for dessert,' Clara agreed. They were on the coffee stage when their children came on air in a discussion about great jazz classics. They talked easily and unaffectedly, sharing their enthusiasms and firing people up to go to jazz clubs and visit record stores.

Linda spoke easily about the live performances on Thursday nights, and mentioned that Nick would be playing some evergreens at the store next week.

'That's cosy,' the interviewer said, 'is that how you two met?'

'We would always have met,' Nick said with certainty.

Clara and Hilary looked at each other in shock. They would have met anyway? Like hell they would.

But again the two women vowed that they would never reveal their secret.

That night, as Brian Flynn, Johnny, Tim and Lidia waved Ania off in her finery to the party, they knew that one of them would suggest a pint. It turned out to be the priest.

'I have something which needs to be sorted,' he said.

They followed him willingly into Corrigans.

'What's the problem?' Tim asked.

'I am. I am always the problem.' Brian Flynn was gloomy.

'Go on out of that, Brian, you're usually the solution rather than the cause.' Johnny was strong in defence of his friend.

'Not this time. I was so thrilled with the notion of having weddings to pay for the centre, I went at it like a bull but there are all sorts of problems. You need a licence for this and a permit for that and Health and Safety. The whole thing is a nightmare. There's people leaping out of the woodwork shouting "*no way*" before you even get to first base.'

He looked like an injured bloodhound as he gripped his glass, lines of disappointment etched into his face.

'Can't you rent it out privately? Wouldn't that get round it?' Tim was trying to help.

'No, there's a book full of rules about that, and a heavy shadow of insurance looming over it all. We couldn't ask people in to have their wedding if we weren't insured.'

'Remember your friend James, the calm person?' Lidia asked. 'When we had that other problem he was terrific. He brought out a pad of paper and put down all the possibilities.'

'We could do that I suppose,' Johnny suggested.

'We're not good at it, we get distracted,' Tim said.

Brian took out his mobile phone.

'James, I know life would be easier for you if I quit the Church entirely, but we'd love you to come and have a pint and help us see things clearly.'

'Another stalker?' James asked.

'No, nothing like that, but we need the cool approach.'

'Usual pub?'

'Yeah, at the back.'

'I'll be there in thirty minutes,' said James.

'Let's raise a toast to Ania,' Lidia said.

'She'll be fine,' said Johnny, who couldn't understand why

Ania was getting dressed up and braving the horrific Rosemary Walsh in her lair.

The first people they saw when they went into the party were Simon and Maud, immaculate in their Scarlet Feather uniform and holding trays of canapés.

Maud stepped forward as if she had never met Declan and Fiona in her life. 'Might I offer you a quail's egg? There's a little celery salt for dipping.'

'Or perhaps some artichoke heart with a cheese sauce?' Simon added.

Fiona wanted to laugh out loud, but she knew they all had to play roles.

'Thank you so much, it all looks quite superb,' Fiona said, but she managed a wink and a thumbs-up sign as well.

'Isn't this an enormous house,' Ania whispered to her.

'Far too big for the three of them,' Fiona said.

'But it's their family home.' Ania was defending Carl's family. She was clutching the beautifully wrapped gift of a little red glass jam dish. A perfect gift for the occasion.

Fiona hoped that Rosemary would be gracious and thank her properly, but hadn't much hope. She had tried to persuade Ania to leave her gift in the front room with the other parcels, but no, she was determined to hand it over herself. 'This place is so unsuitable. It's full of stairs and steps. Bobby needs somewhere flat for heaven's sake,' she couldn't help observing.

'Maybe one day,' Ania said.

'Lady Rosemary leave this palace? Never. Come on, Ania, let's explore.'

'I don't like to push myself forward.'

'Have one of those quail's eggs, Ania, it will be a long time before any of us sees those again. Then we'll go out on to the balcony and look at the view.'

Declan was talking about rugby to a man in a corner and

seemed well settled in. Carl was on the other side of the room. He waved to them but implied that he was stuck where he was for a while. Fiona gently guided Ania out on to the broad balcony where patio heaters dealt with the evening breeze coming up from the huge bay below them.

Groups of middle-aged, well-dressed, highly vocal people were pointing in wonder at the various landmarks they could see. That was the church, that was the town centre. The harbour was around the corner where there was a luxury liner moored in the bay. What a place to live. Rosemary Walsh's heart must have been gladdened by all the admiration and envy.

Rosemary was moving towards them.

Suddenly Fiona wanted to be miles from here. She couldn't bear to see this woman talking down to Ania, dismissing her beautiful dress, barely thanking her for the little red glass jam dish.

'Look at those apartments over there. I do their window-boxes,' Ania said. 'I go there with Mr Chen and last week we put in lots of bedding plants. I can almost see them from here. I must tell him.'

Everyone else was wondering how much the Walsh house was worth and whether they would get planning permission to build a block of apartments in their grounds, but Ania was pointing proudly to her work, tending window-boxes.

Fiona slipped across the room. Ania was happy to look out at the view. Imagine, Carl had grown up here and known this all his life.

Rosemary hadn't recognised the girl in the striking designer dress standing in the sunset on the balcony. She must be somebody's daughter. She approached and realised it was Ania. She looked at her, dumbfounded. This was the Polish maid from the clinic.

'Ah, Mrs Walsh, may you and Bobby have many returns of this day. I have brought you a little ruby wedding present.'

Rosemary steadied herself from the shock by holding on to a small table.

'I hope it will be useful to you.' Ania's face did not reveal that she had spent a week's earnings on this gift.

'How good of you to come, Ania,' she said in a slightly choked voice.

Ania saw, with disappointment, that she had taken the gift then put it down on the table and showed no sign of opening it. Possibly Fiona had been right: she should have left it with the other presents in the front room.

'What a beautiful house you have, Mrs Walsh.'

'Thank you, yes. Well, it was very good of you to come. You're a very helpful girl, they all tell me.'

'That's nice to hear!' Ania felt her face go pink with pleasure.

'So I suggest you give them a hand in the kitchen,' Rosemary Walsh said.

'The kitchen?' Ania was startled.

'Yes, out that way, towards the back.' Mrs Walsh was shepherding her out.

Ania didn't want to leave the little glass dish on the table. 'Your present, Mrs Walsh?' she said, trying to reach for it.

'Go on, dear, don't keep them waiting. They're dying for some help.'

'Help?' Ania was bewildered.

'Washing up, dear. Hurry now.'

This couldn't be right. She had a printed invitation. Nobody could have thought she was coming to do the washing-up. Is this what Carl had meant when he said that naturally she would be at his parents' party? That he couldn't do it without her? He had meant she would be working in the kitchen?

She felt she had no choice but to do as she was told.

There was nobody in the kitchen. The waiters were all out serving the buffet. Some glasses had been brought back and the coloured plates and trays which had held the canapés were on the table.

Sadly, Ania filled a sink with soapy water and began to wash the glasses. She was polishing them by the time a tall young woman came in.

'Hi, I'm Cathy,' she said. 'Who are you?'

'I'm Ania,' she said in a low voice.

'And what are you doing washing the dishes?'

'I am helping you.'

'No, no. We stack all these in racks and put them into our van, they get washed back at base.'

'But Mrs Walsh said—'

'Mrs Walsh is a horse's ass!' Cathy said.

'A what?'

'It doesn't matter.'

Just then a tall, handsome man came into the kitchen. Cathy spoke to him. She sounded very angry.

'Tom, this is Ania. That cow sent her in here to do the washing-up.'

Ania was upset to have caused all this trouble. 'You see I thought I was a guest but actually I was the help,' she said.

Tom and Cathy exchanged looks.

'We'll get you back into that room at once!' Cathy said.

'No, *please, please* don't upset Mrs Walsh any more. I have already annoyed her by coming here. Her son invited me and I must have misunderstood.'

'Where's the son? I'll find him.' Tom was all action.

'I beg you not to,' Ania said. 'Really, I am begging you on my knees. It would make everything so much worse. Just let me stay here. I can put the plates into the racks if you show me.' She was holding Cathy's arm as she spoke.

'But her son? Your friend?' Cathy said.

'. . . would think I am even more stupid than I am. I am happy to help here and then I will go away.'

Her beautiful lace sleeves were all wet and soapy from washing up.

'This is all wrong,' Tom said.

'Sometimes that's the way things are. All wrong,' Ania said.

Fiona looked around for Ania and couldn't see her. She must have gone to the Ladies room or maybe she had found Carl. But no, Carl was there chatting away to a group. He came to greet Fiona.

'Where's Ania?' he asked.

'I left her out on the balcony,' Fiona said and they went back out together to look. But there was no sign of her.

'She's looking terrific. She could be a model,' Fiona said.

'She's very beautiful, yes.' Carl was straining to see where she could be. Suddenly Fiona saw the small, unopened gift on a side table.

'This is where she must have been standing after I left her. I'll take the parcel in case she wasn't able to deliver it properly. Let's find Declan and go and see if we can find her.' But Ania was nowhere to be found.

Eventually Carl and Fiona went into the kitchen. Tom and Cathy were supervising the lobster and salmon buffet and preparing to wheel it into the main room. The twins were carrying the trays round. The bar waiter was opening two kinds of wine and the waitress was laying out the plates and cutlery.

The party was in full swing.

There would be no speeches and no cake. Rosemary had read that such things were vulgar and nouveau riche. Bobby had wanted to tell everyone how happy they had been but she had won that battle. Much more sophisticated to let people *see* their happiness rather than braying about it.

'Can I help you?' Cathy had quite liked the young man at first, but now she felt only scorn for him.

'I was just looking for a friend,' he said.

'Ania?'

'Yes, yes,' he answered quickly. 'Is she all right?'

'I think so. Yes.'

'But where is she? I've been looking for her all over.'

'She's gone home,' Tom said.

'But was she sick? Is she okay?'

Cathy shrugged. 'Not particularly now. She ruined her dress doing the washing-up.'

'What the hell was she doing the washing-up for?' His face was very angry.

'Your mother asked her to help us. It wasn't necessary but then a taxi came with more ice and we sent her home in that.'

'*No*, no. She can't have gone home. My mother surely never asked her . . .'

'Oh, she did, Mr Walsh,' Cathy said. 'And Ania didn't want us to call you,' she added.

'I am going to go into that room and punch Rosemary's lights out!' Fiona said. 'Okay, Carl, so she *is* your mother, but this really is going too far.'

His face was like stone. 'No need. I'll do it myself,' he said.

'Carl?' Fiona was nervous now.

'Not physically. Relax.'

'There are still people there. Maybe you should sort of wait.'

'Go home now, Fiona. Take Declan with you. Make a big fuss about how late it is. That's what would help.'

'Don't forget that your father—'

'I won't forget that. Please, Fiona, go.'

She and Declan stood in the hall shouting goodbye to

people until finally the remaining guests realised that the party was over.

The Scarlet Feather vans had been stacked and were revving up to leave. Maud and Simon waved excitedly from the front seat. Declan's taxi was waiting.

'Was it a good night?' the taxi driver asked.

'No, it was shitty, actually,' Fiona said.

'Oh well, you can't win them all,' the driver said, shrugging.

This smartly dressed young couple, going to a party at a house that was worth at least three million and they *still* couldn't enjoy themselves. That was life in modern Ireland for you.

Ania was so grateful to the kind catering people who had got her out the back door so quickly and without fuss. Apparently there had been some misunderstanding, where *they* thought the Walshes were arranging the ice, and the Walshes thought that Scarlet Feather was doing it. Cathy had cut through any problems by ordering a taxi to deliver four bags of it.

It hadn't been the only misunderstanding that night.

How *could* she have been so foolish, Ania wondered, as she sat in the back of the taxi. Carl was just being nice giving her an invitation. They had always meant for her to come and help. Her face burned with the shame of it all.

The taxi pulled up in her street and she got out. 'Are you sure I don't have to pay you?' she asked fearfully.

'No, they pay by the month. You're all right.'

Please may there be no one around, Ania prayed. Everyone in the café knew she was going to this party. She had shown them her outfit only a few hours ago. She managed to slip through the door and up the stairs without catching anyone's eye. The flat was dark and quiet. Ania lay down on her bed and let the tears come. She sobbed until her ribs ached. Then she stood up and took off her new dress. She put it on a hanger, the sleeves, of course, totally ruined. When she felt strong enough she would take them out, but now she had other things to do.

She dressed in her jeans, sweater and anorak then took out a big plastic wallet of money from under her mattress. She looked through the bundles of euros with unseeing eyes.

The last guest had gone. Carl helped his father get up from his armchair. Carl looked at the long, curving staircase. It would be a challenge.

'Would you like to sleep downstairs, Dad, rather than facing that journey up?'

'You know, I would, son.' Bobby Walsh had a sofa-bed in his small study den, near the kitchen. It seemed very tempting.

'I'll run up for your pyjamas and dressing gown.'

Rosemary Walsh was touring the house, peering behind objects in case glasses or cutlery had been overlooked. She examined the kitchen carefully. They had been true to their word these caterers – everything was left in pristine condition. The unused food had been wrapped, labelled and installed in either fridge or freezer. She jumped when Carl spoke right beside her.

'Mother, can you come into the front room, please, I want to talk to you.'

'Can't we talk here?'

'No, Dad is sleeping in the study and I don't want to disturb him.'

'You shouldn't encourage him to take the easy option. He'll never get better if he doesn't make an effort.'

'The other room, Mother.'

Rosemary shrugged.

Carl sat on a tall chair.

'That's not very comfortable.'

'I don't feel very comfortable,' he said.

'What *is* it, Carl? We're all tired. Can't it wait until to-morrow? The party went well, didn't it?'

He said nothing.

'I mean, they were expensive, those Scarlet Feather people, but they did deliver. And I suppose they were polite to the guests, even if a little lacking in charm to those who actually pay them.'

'They brought enough staff then?'

'Yes, they had two odd young people who were apparently trainees. We didn't have to pay for them, and do you know, they turned out to be relations of the Mitchells, the law family.'

'So there were plenty of hands on deck?'

'Yes. I think it worked fine. Don't you think so?'

'So there was no need for anyone else to help?'

Rosemary hadn't got the drift. 'No. Why?'

'I was just wondering why you asked Ania to go into the kitchen and help with the washing-up?'

'Oh dear, is she bleating about that? I just asked her to give them a little hand.'

'Why did you ask her to do that?'

'Because she would have felt more at ease in the kitchen, darling. Carl, I know you're very much for all people every-where being equal, but she's a little Polish maid. She's here for a couple of years to make a few euros then go back. That's what she is, she *knows* that's what she is. She was perfectly happy to lend a hand with the washing-up.'

'But you didn't ask any of your other guests to help in the kitchen?'

'Carl, please, be sensible.'

'I am being sensible. She was a guest. *My* guest. I never got to see her because *you* had her out there working for you when you admit that you had plenty of people working there already.'

'Listen, she was out of place.'

'She was *not* out of place. She had a beautiful dress. She had a new hairstyle. She had spent over a week's wages getting you a present . . .'

'Oh, God, she *did* give me a package. Where is it? I don't know where it ended up.'

'And your thanks for all this was to send her out to the kitchen because she would feel more at home there.'

'Come *on*, Carl, I was being kind to her.'

'No, Mother, you were never kind to anyone. You were never kind to Dad or to me, and particularly never kind to anyone that you thought you might conceivably be able to boss around.'

'I know you have kindly feelings towards her, Carl, but this cannot be. She's from a different world. They work very hard, I know, but they're not like us.'

'Please stop, right now!'

'I mean it. You have so many friends, you could have so many more. This girl is nothing to you.'

'I am very fond of her. In fact, I believe I love her.'

'You believe!' his mother scoffed.

'Yes, I believe, because *I'm* not sure. I'm not at all sure about love. Father loves you deeply. I don't know why. So I've learned nothing about love from him. You only love possessions. You don't love people, so what could I have learned from you?'

Rosemary looked alarmed. 'You can't *love* this girl, Carl. You're sorry for her. You must know that. She would hold you back totally.'

'From what?'

'From a normal social life like tonight. She wouldn't be able to cope, learn our ways.'

'And your way to help her cope with what you call "our ways" was to order her out of your party, to which she had been *invited*. Would you just listen to yourself for once?'

'I just didn't want anyone being embarrassed. That's all.' Rosemary was mutinous.

'I am very embarrassed, Mother, more so than I have ever been in my life.'

'Carl, this is all nonsense. Let's go to bed.'

'I am never sleeping another night in this house,' he said.

'Look, it's just the drink talking.'

'I didn't *have* any drink. I was too busy being polite to your friends. People who are old enough to remember going to England when there were signs in the windows saying "No Blacks, No Irish". I was talking to a man whose mother was a maid in Boston and she was sent away from the family where she worked because she wasn't humble enough. She married a bank official and helped him climb to run a bank of his own.'

'That's a totally different—'

'It's exactly the same, except it's worse for us. We have plenty. We have so bloody much in this country and we should be delighted to see all these new people coming in to join us. But no, it's a pecking order, isn't it? Even for us, who were at the bottom of the pecking order until not so long ago.'

Rosemary blazed with anger. 'It's easy for you to have such high ideals living in a house like this. You've had everything!'

'Not any more, I won't.'

'Oh, *stop* being so petulant, Carl. If you go now you'll just be back here tomorrow. Let's not go through the whole silly process.'

'I will not be back, Mother.'

'Come on, where will you live? You earn practically nothing at that school. How will you make a living, for God's sake?'

'I earn a teacher's wage. I pay a quarter of it into a bank

account for you and Dad. I have done since I began work. I won't do it any more when I don't live here. I'll survive.'

Rosemary looked at him. He seemed to mean it.

'What do you think your father and I are *doing* all this for?' She waved her hands around the elegant house. 'It's all for *you*, Carl. Don't throw it back at us! What more do you want?'

'I could have asked you not to throw my friends out of this home, had I ever known that it would even cross your mind to do so,' he said.

'Carl, please . . .'

'I'm sorry for you, Mother, I really am.'

He moved to leave the room.

'That's right. Go to bed. We'll all go to bed. It will feel different in the morning.'

'I don't know how it will feel for you in the morning and I couldn't care less,' Carl said. He took his car keys from the drawer in the hall table and ran down the steps.

As Rosemary looked out into the dark she saw him get into the car he had insisted on buying for himself. She shook her head. He could be very tiresome, but by this time tomorrow it would all be over and forgotten.

It was a noisy part of Dublin where Ania lived and even though it was late at night, there were still cafés and clubs open. People spoke in many different languages.

Carl didn't even plan what he would say when he found Ania. There was no need to rehearse how he would apologise for his appalling mother and explain that he had left home. Maybe she might even let him stay with her. The important thing was to find her and to hold her and to stroke her lovely face and hair.

He knew the address. He hadn't been to her flat but he had eaten a couple of meals in the restaurant. She had told him about the different kinds of sausage and they insisted he have a selection on his plate so that he could choose which he liked best.

He went into the restaurant and asked, 'Is Ania at home, do you think?'

'No, she has gone to such a fancy party. She was dressed like a film star,' said one of the brothers who ran the place.

'She left. I was wondering if perhaps . . .'

'There's Lidia. She will know.'

Lidia was on her mobile phone. She seemed very agitated.

'But of course I'm worried, Tim, she just left a note saying not to fuss. She would be in touch. But the bad thing is that she has taken her passport.'

Chapter Eleven

Molly Carroll had a phone call at 8 a.m. to say that there were three customers standing outside the launderette and nobody had opened up.

'But Ania's there at seven to open the place up.' Molly was full of concern.

'She's not there today, Molly.'

So, clucking with disapproval, Molly Carroll left breakfast set out and bustled off to open the launderette. They depended on early morning people, knowing they could put in a bag of clothes in the morning and collect them later the same day. It was so unlike Ania.

Hilary was listening to the overnight messages on the clinic's answering machine. They all had to do with being sorry. A woman had chest pains in the night and had called the emergency number, but it turned out to be a thing of nothing. She was sorry for upsetting everyone. A man, who had got the wrong number, kept explaining that he was sorry to have missed the appointment but would make it up in spades on another occasion. And one from Ania saying that there was a bit of a crisis. She was very sorry indeed and would explain everything in a few days. She had left the keys to the clinic in an envelope in the restaurant under her flat. Johnny could pick them up.

A crisis that was going to last a few *days*? Ania? Hilary was very startled.

Lidia and Tim hadn't slept a wink. Where could Ania have gone? She gave no indication at all.

'I *know* all her friends,' Lidia said. 'I've tried them all and no luck.'

'What about Father Flynn?'

'Not a word. He's asking everyone at his centre, but no word yet.'

'She can't have gone to the airport. It was too late,' Tim said, mainly to reassure Carl Walsh who was almost mad with worry and claiming that it was all his fault because he hadn't been there to meet her and welcome her in. Lidia hadn't understood the full details of what had gone on at the party and tried to calm him down.

'It can't have been your fault. She was so pleased to be invited. And did your mother like her gift?'

'Don't talk to me about the gift!' Carl cried, his face distraught. 'There must be *someone* we haven't thought of!'

Fiona came by to tell Declan the news that Ania had disappeared and together they sat and ate the grapefruit Molly had left out. It was better than the two fried eggs, sausages and fried bread she would have insisted on if she'd been there.

They had been talking on the phone to Lidia, Carl, Hilary and Father Flynn. There was the slight possibility that she might turn up at the heart clinic but they didn't think it was likely. They were alarmed when Hilary told them about the message on the answering machine.

'So should we get the Guards?' Fiona asked.

'She specifically asked Lidia not to make any fuss,' Declan said.

'But she must have been so upset.'

'I know, Fiona, but what's the point of asking your friends not to make a fuss if you can't trust them to do what you ask?'

Fiona looked at him, surprised. 'What kind of a doctor are you going to be, Declan Carroll?'

'One who takes my patients' wishes seriously.'

'How far would you go down that road?'

'Only time will tell. Time and the knowledge that I will have a good, wise wife beside me to mark my card. What are you doing on Saturday? I thought then we might go and look at rings. I was wondering, would you like an opal?'

'You're not to spend too much on it, Declan. Please – anything would do me. Honestly. I don't need an expensive ring – just to know you love me is enough.'

'It's your birthstone. I thought that was important. Now let's go and look after sick people. That's what we do.'

He looked so devoted, she felt almost weak. What had she done to deserve all this love?

Father Brian Flynn discovered a girl who had seen Ania waiting for an airport bus.

'But there are no planes to Poland at night,' he said.

'I think she was going to London first.'

'But there wouldn't have been planes there until the morning.' Brian Flynn couldn't believe that the level-headed Ania had disappeared into thin air.

'I do not know, Father.'

'Of course you don't. I'm just worried, that's all.'

'You would have been more worried if you saw her last night. She was like a person who had seen something terrible.'

*

377

Bobby Walsh came into the kitchen for his breakfast.

'Didn't they leave the place immaculate?' he asked his wife as he helped himself to tea and toast.

'Yes.' She spoke sharply.

'Where's Carl?'

'He went out last night and he didn't come back.'

'So, he went straight into the school then?'

'I think not. They called here looking for him.' Rosemary finished her coffee.

'So where is he?' Bobby was alarmed.

'Being deeply silly,' Rosemary said and left the house.

He heard her car starting up and leaving. The car sounded as angry as she had looked.

Bobby Walsh suddenly felt very lonely in the big house by the sea.

Clara looked up when Hilary brought in the mug of coffee. 'Where's Ania?'

'Nobody knows,' Hilary said. 'She left an odd message.'

They puzzled over it. Anyone in the clinic could have called in sick. But not Ania. She would have crawled in, if she had breath in her body.

'Is it love, do you think?' Clara asked.

'Well, yesterday she was all sunshine. She was going to a ruby wedding at Bobby Walsh's. She's very fond of Bobby's son Carl.'

'I wish her luck dealing with that Rosemary.'

'No. She was mad about Rosemary. Rosemary had sent her an invitation, apparently, and Ania had bought a lovely little red glass dish for her.'

'Maybe the Walshes know where she is.'

'I don't fancy making the call, Clara.'

'All right, cowardy-custard. I'll do it.'

*

'Hello, Bobby. Clara Casey from the heart clinic here. No, no, nothing to do with your tests, you're doing fine. No, oddly it was something else entirely. I was wondering if you had seen our Ania? You see, she was going to your house last night to an anniversary party. No? Oh, I think she was there. No, of course, with so many people. I wonder, would Mrs Walsh recall? Oh, she's gone out? Right . . . Sorry for bothering you, Bobby. See you next week, as usual. Yes, right, of course we'll let you know.'

Hilary looked at her questioningly.

'That man Bobby Walsh should be canonised in his own lifetime. He says he's very sorry, he didn't see Ania last night. He'd love to have talked to her. No one told him she was there. We're to let him know when she surfaces.'

'*If* she surfaces,' Hilary said.

Fiona was passing the desk when the phone rang. She picked it up absently, her mind still on buying an opal ring and what on earth could have come over Ania. It was Rosemary Walsh.

'Is that Clara?'

'No, Mrs Walsh, it's Fiona.'

'It was actually Ania, the Polish girl, I was looking for.' She gave a tinkling laugh to underline the unexpected nature of her call.

'We are all looking for her, Mrs Walsh.'

'What do you mean?' Mrs Walsh sounded alarmed.

'She hasn't been seen since she was sent into your kitchen last night.'

'Er . . . yes. She's a most helpful girl – she offered to help with the washing-up.'

'No. I think you *asked* her to do the washing-up. She thought she was a guest.'

'Oh, that's all been cleared up by now.'

'No, it hasn't. She hasn't turned up for work. She's left her flat. Father Flynn has been looking for her. Carl has been on the phone every few minutes. I don't think it's been cleared up at all!'

'Kindly don't take that tone with me, Fiona.'

'I'm not taking any tone, Mrs Walsh, I'm just telling you that the Guards are being called and they will be here shortly.' Fiona had the great pleasure of hearing Rosemary Walsh gasp. It wasn't true about the Guards. But oh, it was worth it just to hear that intake of breath.

When Ania's bus pulled into her village she got out and went into Mrs Żak's shop.

'This is a surprise, Ania, does your mother know?'

'No, Mrs Żak – may I make one quick call to Ireland, please?'

'I was sure you would have a mobile phone like all these young girls are getting.'

'They are too expensive, Mrs Żak. I will pay you for the telephone call.'

Mrs Żak watched astounded as Ania seemed to speak in perfect English into the telephone. She couldn't understand what the girl was saying but it sounded very fluent. Little Ania, who had been afraid to lift her eyes to anyone until she met that troublesome boy Marek. *Now* look at her! She was speaking a foreign language as if she were a professor.

Ania spoke to Clara. 'I am so sorry to do something so un-expected as to run away. You see I made a big mistake. Per-haps Fiona told you?'

'She did, Ania, and you're not the only one who makes mistakes with Rosemary Walsh. Her life is one long history of mistakes.'

'But I embarrassed everyone. Carl must think I am a fool.'

'He is so worried about you, Ania. Every few minutes he

rings to ask have we any news. Perhaps you could telephone him. He'll be so relieved to know you are all right.'

'No, I can't do that. Please, Clara, perhaps you could ask Fiona to do it?'

'And when will I say that you're coming back?'

'I have only just got here, Clara, I haven't been to see my Mamusia yet. I do not know.'

'All right, Ania. Don't sound so worried. Everyone will be so happy that you are safe. You have many friends here, all very concerned about you.'

'Thank you, Clara. I am sorry I was such a poor choice of a worker.'

'You're the best worker we have here. You've been here for months. You'll always have a place here when you need it.'

Two big tears came down Ania's face. Mrs Żak looked at her over her glasses. The girl was probably pregnant. Why had she come back to upset her mother with further bad news?

The word spread quickly that Ania was back in Poland having a rest. Clara phoned Carl first and then Frank Ennis in hospital administration. They would need a temporary replacement.

'Did she give you adequate notice of her trip to Poland?'

'It was an emergency.' Clara was crisp.

'Well, I'm not expected to find temps in trees,' he said.

'Right, will we appoint our own then?'

'No.' Frank wanted nothing more to escape his grasp.

'Good. We'll see a temporary replacement for Ania tomorrow.'

'For how long?' Frank asked.

'You will be informed,' Clara said.

'We don't *really* need a replacement for Ania. We'll all pitch in,' Hilary said.

'Where is your solidarity and sense of self-worth?' Clara was shocked. 'If Frank thinks we can manage without Ania then we'll be managing without her forever. This is just to save her job.'

'Bobby?'

'Are you home, Rosemary?'

'Yes, of course I am. Is everything all right?'

'I've had nothing but phone calls all day, Rosemary. That little Ania from the clinic has disappeared. The last anyone saw of her was here, apparently.'

'I'm sure that's not right.'

'Why didn't you tell me she was here, Rosemary? I'm very fond of her.'

'You're not the only one,' his wife said.

'What do you mean?'

'Your son has been sniffing after her too.'

'I'm not sniffing after her, Rosemary.'

'No, no, of course you're not. Sorry . . . I would have paid her, Bobby.'

'Sorry? Paid her for what?'

'For working in the kitchen.'

'I thought she was a guest. That's what Clara said. What Carl said. What Fiona said.'

'When did all these people say these things?' Rosemary looked drawn and frightened.

'On the phone. Today.'

'She wouldn't have done anything silly, Bobby? Anything really silly? Would she?' Rosemary looked very worried.

'Why would she have done anything silly?'

Rosemary breathed more easily. He hadn't been told the whole story.

'Europeans,' she said. 'Very unstable.'

*

Declan went to a library and looked up opals. There was some bad luck attached to them, but then there was bad luck attached to all stones. He found a story about the Spanish King Alfonso who gave someone an opal and she died, and everyone who got that opal died. Declan, who was practical, thought they would have died anyway. People had such a short life expectancy in those days. He wasn't going to attract Fiona's attention to it.

He went to the jeweller's and told him the upper limits of his spending power. The jeweller said he would make up a tray and see him on Saturday.

The temp they sent was Amy Barry, daughter of Peter, the pharmacist. Clara looked at her with interest. Amy looked up from under her dark fringe.

'Oh, it's you,' she said to Clara, without much enthusiasm.

'Very nice to see you again,' Clara said.

'Don't suppose I'll get the job now, I mean, knowing I worked in a bondage shop. Not much chance for me here.'

'Why not?' Clara seemed to think working in a fetish shop was fine preparation for a clerical job in a heart clinic.

'Why didn't you marry my dad?' Amy asked with interest. 'He was mad about you.'

'We were too old and set in our ways. It would have been too much adjustment. Your own romance going well?'

'Fine thanks. You know I always liked you,' Amy said, refusing to be deflected.

'And I liked you too,' Clara smiled easily.

'But not enough to give me a job?' Amy's fists were ready for the fight.

'Of course you can have the job, just tell me why you left the corsets and bondage, and that you do know that when Ania comes back we have to let you go.'

'The corsets and bondage are bankrupt, and I do understand about this being just a temp job,' Amy grinned.

'Right. You can start straight away.'

'That's great. Have you any hints for me?'

'Yes – we are united in our hatred of Frank Ennis,' Clara said. 'You should regard him as the natural enemy of this clinic and you won't go far wrong.'

Carl Walsh was staying with Aidan and Nora Dunne. They were very easy company and asked him no interrogating questions. If they wondered why a man whose parents owned a seaside mansion wanted to stay on the sofa of a poky little flat like theirs, they never made any reference to it. There was such affection in these small rooms compared to the icy-cold life his mother ran in her mansion. Carl could hardly believe it was all in the same city.

Aidan and Nora were planning a Sunday lunch party for Aidan's birthday. Again, Carl was stunned to see how little money they had and how things had to be considered carefully before they were bought. A revulsion for the showy anniversary party came over him. His mother hadn't one ounce of decency in her. He realised that now. Up to this, he had blinded himself to her ways, thinking that his father just needed an easy life. But now Carl realised that he must have been in denial. Someone should have stood up to Rosemary Walsh a long time ago.

'Will you join us for the lunch, Carl?' Nora was ever welcoming.

'No thank you, Nora, I'm not much company these days, and I will have to go home and collect my things some time. I'd better do it this weekend.'

'You might even make peace with your parents.' It was the first time that Nora had mentioned any friction.

'I have always had peace with my father,' Carl said.

'Yes, but women are complicated. We twist things. Get things wrong . . .'

'*You* don't.' He spoke simply.

'No, but I see it's upsetting you and I don't like to see you so down, Carl.' Nora's voice was full of sympathy.

'I am down because I was so stupid. I met a marvellous girl and I let her get away.'

'Did she like you?'

'I thought so, but I'm such a fool. I'd do anything to have that night all over again.'

'And where is she now, this marvellous girl?' Nora wanted to know.

'In a village in the south of Poland. She doesn't want to talk to me.'

'And when will she be back?'

'They don't think she is coming back.'

'I'm sure she will, Carl. You're a good lad. They're not easy to find.'

'I'm not a good lad, Nora, I'm a clown.'

'We're all clowns from time to time, believe me. I'm only sorry you're spoken for. I had such high hopes of you and Aidan's daughter from his first marriage. Ah well!'

Ania walked up the hill with a heavy heart.

She didn't really believe Clara that lots of people missed her. But she was back home now, with a bag full of money for her mother. Hardly an hour had passed when Ania had not been working. It would all be worth it when she saw her Mamusia's face take in the amount of the gift.

She hoped that Mamusia would not cry. Ania felt that if she herself started crying again she might never stop.

Fiona and Declan bent over the rings and tried them on her finger.

This one had a lovely setting. That one had huge colours in

it whichever way you turned it. Eventually, they picked one which had three little opals in a line.

'That was the very first one you went for, always a good sign,' said the young man who sold stones all day and was very good with the patter.

'And when will the great day be?' he asked, as he polished the opals one more time.

'Not for ages and ages,' Declan said hastily.

'The end of this summer,' Fiona said.

'That's right, girl. You nail him down,' said the young jeweller, enchanted with it all.

They went to lunch at Quentins and showed the ring to Brenda who said all the right things and brought them a glass of champagne.

Then they rang Fiona's parents and told them that the ring had been bought. There was huge excitement and they invited the Carrolls to come for a Chinese take-away that evening. Fiona wrote emails to Tom and Elsa in California, to David in England and to Vonni in Greece.

She said she was very happy and that she wanted them all to meet Declan.

'Why did you change your mind about the timing?' he asked.

'I think because I saw the mess poor Carl and Ania made of it all and I didn't want us to get into a scene like that.'

'Where's Carl staying?' Declan asked.

'Don't know. Amazing it took him so long to see through his mother.'

'He was keeping the peace for his father's sake,' Declan said.

'You always have the kind word,' Fiona said adoringly, twisting her finger to admire the ring again.

Dear Fiona,

How great that you are getting married – congratulations, and of course I'd love to come. It will be a great chance for a holiday.

When I sold my father's business my mother was upset, but now she thinks it's all for the best. I am going to open a business of my own importing pottery. Maybe I will find some marvellous Irish things when I am there. You must point me in the right direction.

It will be magic to see you again and share in your wedding day. Let's hope Vonni, Tom and Elsa can come too.

Love,
David

Fiona,

Only for you would I take my old bones back to Ireland. I swore never to go there again, but what you tell me about this man Declan sounds too good to miss. I did ask Andreas to come with me, but he says no. He will see all the pictures.

Those great twins have invited me to stay in their house with people called Muttie and his wife Lizzie. Is this for real? They also tell me they're in catering and they hope they might even do your wedding. You don't know this now – I thought I'd forewarn you.

Now that I have decided to go I am quite excited.

Thank you for keeping in touch – you are a good friend.

Love,
Vonni

Dear Fiona,

We can't come for the most amazing reason. We are pregnant!

Elsa is having our baby and it's due just that week: I thought for years I would never have children, but we went

*for AI treatment and we're expecting a daughter the very day
you will be married. I wish we could be there. But we will
come and see you as soon as our little princess is old enough to
travel.*

*Bill is delighted. Even Shirley is enthusiastic, so life
couldn't be better.*

*Didn't we all have an amazing time that summer. I can't
bear to think we will miss Andreas and Vonni and David.
Please take lots of pictures and we will want to hear every
detail.*

Love from us both,
Tom

Simon and Maud were learning that catering was utterly exhausting.

'I think we may well be burned out by the time we're
twenty-five,' Simon said.

'Cathy and Tom survived it,' Maud said, not ready to give
up yet.

'Yes, but they were mad about each other,' Simon grumbled.

'Well, *we* get on all right.'

'But we're not *in* love like they were.' Simon worried at it
like a dog with a bone.

'God, Simon, suppose we were to get partners that we were
in love with? Would that make it all right?'

'It would get us over the worst bits, I suppose.'

'I think we should try to attract business. That's what we
should be doing.' Maud was very firm.

'Like what?'

'Like Fiona and Declan's wedding. We could present them
with a buffet choice and give them a price.'

'But where would we *do* it, Maud? We don't have any
venues, as Tom and Cathy call them.'

'We could look for them. Tired tennis clubs? Old schools? There must be *something*, Simon.'

'And if we did find a venue?' Simon was anxious.

'We just come up with a menu.' Maud was confident.

'Brian?'

'James?'

'You've been running this hall already as a café, haven't you?'

'Yes, you know I have.'

'So, what's the problem?'

'What do you mean?'

'If Health and Safety say it's okay as a café, it should be okay for a wedding.'

'But the alcohol?' Brian asked.

'You're not selling alcohol, Brian. You don't have a liquor licence.'

'That's what I mean.'

'And couldn't these people bring their own?'

'I don't think it works like that,' Father Brian said.

'It works the way you want it to work. How are you to be blamed if a whole lot of Poles turn up with their own fire-water?'

'James, it won't work.'

'*My* advice, on very good authority, is to try it and to plead total ignorance, *if* the matter ever comes up.'

Molly Carroll said she really liked Fiona's parents. Maureen and Sean Ryan and Fiona's two sisters had made Molly and Paddy very welcome: they were level-headed people with no airs and graces.

She had thought it odd that they didn't have a roast to entertain their future in-laws, but then it turned out they had only heard about the engagement very late in the day. And that Chinese food had been very tasty.

They had all agreed to stay out of it and let the young people make their own arrangements. Lord knew what kind of ceremony or wedding breakfast they had in mind.

Simon and Maud had met Father Brian Flynn when they heard he was looking for someone to prepare a christening party for some Slovaks.

'It's just eastern Mediterranean food,' Simon said.

'No problem. Heavy emphasis on aubergines, stuffed peppers, courgettes, olive oil,' Maud agreed.

'There's a problem about alcohol,' Father Flynn said.

'Oh, we know all about that, Father,' Simon said reassuringly.

'Our mother was the very same way.' Maud patted him on the hand.

'Not *me*,' Brian Flynn said crossly, 'it's the law, you see. Rules about selling drink.'

'Oh, I see,' Simon said. 'I thought you had a problem yourself. So they just have to bring their own, is that it?'

'Yes, I gather that's within the boundaries.'

'Fine. We could provide pitchers of fruit juice and whatever they have on or under the table isn't down to us.'

'Yes. That would work, wouldn't it?'

'From what we hear around the place, that should cover everything,' Maud said. Wise beyond her years.

On the way home from the centre, Simon said suddenly, '*That's* where we could have Fiona and Declan's wedding. We've found our venue.'

'You know that you and Fiona are going to be married this year?' Simon asked Declan anxiously.

'Yes, Simon, I *had* remembered that.'

'It's just I wondered, could you tell me is it going to be a religious or a civil ceremony?'

'Oh, well, a bit of a church wedding first, to please the old folk.'

'Yes, but what kind of a church?' Simon seemed very anxious. Declan wondered if he were some kind of zealot.

'Um, well, an ordinary church, I imagine. You know, a Catholic church somewhere.'

'So you haven't anywhere actually planned?'

'No, not yet. Simon, could I ask you, exactly what is this all about?'

'We thought of a terrific place for you to get married.'

'Did you?'

'We did.'

'Why am I nervous about this?' Declan asked.

'There's no need. It's a real church, a real priest and everything.'

'And what's the snag?'

'There isn't one.'

'There always is. Come on, tell me.'

'You have to bring the drink into the place . . . in paper bags.'

'It's a speakeasy,' Declan said.

'It's nothing of the sort!' Simon was indignant.

'So, what is it?'

'It's a lovely hall, down near the Liffey. It's beside a church. It's where new Irish people come. Polish people; Latvians; Lithuanians. I thought you'd love it.'

'And we might well love it,' Declan said. 'You haven't booked it or anything, have you?'

'Sort of,' Simon admitted.

*

Ania's mother had been wonderful. It was so good to have Ania home, she said, over and over. Such a lovely surprise when she had walked through the door.

But there were no pleas to stay. Her mother had more courage than Ania remembered. Nothing much had changed her, while Ania's whole life had altered.

Mamusia asked questions about Ireland. The nice man, Carl, who had taught her English? He was well? Yes, he was well. And his parents' fortieth wedding anniversary, that had been good? Yes, fairly good. Not great, but good.

Ania sat with her mother and took out the money she had worked so hard for. This would pay for all the changes in the little house. The changes that would make it into a real business and not a cottage industry. One of Ania's brothers-in-law would do the building work. It could begin any day now.

The light faded and it started to get dark. Mamusia pulled the curtains and turned on the lamps; Ania sat there wondering why she had ever left. Was this whole busy life in Dublin some kind of dream? She was very tired. She hadn't slept since she had fled from Carl's home. She'd been up all night waiting for the first flight to London and then the flight to Poland.

Her mother saw her nodding off and pulled a rug over her knees. She slept on and dreamed that Carl had sent her a big bunch of flowers with a card saying: 'I love you, Ania. Come back to me.'

When she woke at four o'clock in the morning, she was very sad it was just a dream. And she went to her bed with tears in her eyes.

'How sure were you when you married Dad?' Linda asked her mother.

'Too sure as it turned out,' Clara said.

'No, I mean what did it *feel* like when you decided you'd hitch your star to his?'

'We didn't put it that way then, Linda.'

'I'm just asking for honest information.'

'Okay. This is the truth. I fancied him. I fancied him rotten. When he said "Marry me", I thought of getting away from my mother who, as you might recall, is pretty difficult. I didn't think people said "I love you" and didn't mean it. I was there like a shot from a gun. Now, is that all right?'

'Not really. Nick and I are wondering if we should get a flat together. But we're nervous. I mean, we both have perfectly reasonable mothers. I wished you liked Hilary more, by the way.'

'I *do* like her,' Clara said.

'Yes, but only in that sort of head-patting way. And we wonder whether we should get a place of our own in case it sort of exposes all the weaknesses in our relationship.'

'How wise of you both,' Clara said.

'You sound pissed off over something, Clara.'

'No, I don't. I had another lovely day at work. Ania has run away back to Poland because her boyfriend's mother thought she had come to her party as a maid. Frank Ennis has made my life hell on wheels again. Peter Barry's lunatic daughter turned up looking for a job, and I gave her one. Fiona and Declan have decided they are going to get married in an immigrant centre on the Liffey. I wrongly thought I was coming home to a nice bowl of soup, and I find you booted and spurred and wanting to discuss the meaning of life. Not even vaguely pissed off!'

'You're not the worst, Clara,' her daughter Linda said.

High praise indeed.

Fiona and Barbara went to have a look at the hall in Father Flynn's centre.

'It's a *bit* basic,' Barbara said.

'But we can do something with it – and we can afford it. We can't run to the wedding palace where Declan and I rise up in a swirl of dry ice . . . And anyway, you know that's not what I want. I just wonder is it worth everyone's time coming up here, you know, cousins from the country, David from England, Vonni from Greece?'

'They only want to see you happy and have a rake of food and drink. And this Vonni, and this David, would they think less of you because it's not all chrome and glitter?' Barbara persisted.

'Of course they wouldn't.'

'So, last thing, is it grand enough for Declan?'

'Barbara, you *know* Declan.'

'Right, so all we have to do is make sure those twins don't poison us all. Let's go and make Father Flynn's day with a booking.'

Rosemary heard voices in the kitchen when she got back home. Bobby was talking to someone. Her heart lifted for a moment, thinking it might be Carl. The silly boy couldn't keep this up forever. She would be gracious and courteous to him. Show him that she could rise above his petty behaviour. But it wasn't her son. It was that imperious Clara from the heart clinic.

'Imagine, they entertain you in the kitchen, Dr Casey!' Rosemary sounded shocked. Her look at Bobby was intended to say that he would suffer for this later.

'I called because Bobby didn't come for his appointment this morning and I was in the area anyway.'

'Oh, and what exactly has you in this area?'

'Concern, Mrs Walsh. Concern that Bobby didn't turn up to his appointment. There was no reply when I telephoned.'

'Really, Bobby.'

'I know. Sorry, love, I couldn't make the phone, I was very out of breath.'

'And also I'm looking for a Chinese gardener who services some of these blocks of apartments nearby. Our Ania, from the heart clinic, has gone missing. I wondered if he had anything to say.'

'And had he?' Rosemary asked.

'Not really, except that he wanted to give her some money he owed her and said there was plenty more work if she needed it.'

'And where *is* she?'

'She's in Poland. She got upset about something and took herself off the day after your party, apparently.'

'Rosemary would have paid her, whatever the going rate was. I know she would,' Bobby said suddenly.

'Sorry?' Clara hadn't understood what he was saying.

'Shut up, Bobby,' Rosemary said.

'No, it's not fair that they should think any of this was *your* fault,' Bobby said, his face burning with the will to make everything right.

'I'm off now,' Clara said. 'Will Carl bring you into the clinic tomorrow, Bobby?'

'Carl's left home,' Bobby said.

'Yes, well, a taxi then?'

'I can bring him in,' Rosemary said.

'Any time tomorrow morning is fine, Bobby. We'll always make room for you,' Clara said and swept out. She paused and looked at the view of the yachts out at sea and the purple Head of Howth across the bay. This house was the last word in terms of a desirable property. But it hadn't brought much happiness to the three people who had rattled around in it. What a terrible waste.

*

Fiona was in the bus on her way to her parents' house. She hoped they would be enthusiastic about this hall. The great thing was they could have it any time and Father Flynn said he would be delighted to marry them.

Someone had left an evening paper on the seat so Fiona looked at it idly. There was the usual celebrity gossip: film stars visiting Ireland and news of soccer teams in England. Then she saw a small paragraph. A young man had been found dead in a city squat, most probably from a drugs overdose. There was no identification and the Guards authorities were anxious to trace anyone who knew him. He was about twenty-five to thirty, small build, the only clue lay in a watch. It was engraved with a date and the words 'Love always, Fiona'.

Shane?

Dead from an overdose in a Dublin flat?

Fiona thought she was going to be sick. She staggered to the doors and got off the bus still holding the newspaper. There was a number to contact. But wait, she didn't want to get involved. She hadn't thought about Shane for months, years even. Why bring it all back?

Why meet his mother under these circumstances? But she couldn't turn away either.

He deserved a burial, a mother, someone to identify him. She sat on a bench beside the bus stop and considered her options. She could ring the Guards and give Shane's full name and address. She could find his mother and warn her of what was in store. She could do nothing. If she hadn't found that newspaper she would never have known.

But it was clear to Fiona what she had to do. She called the number printed in the newspaper. 'I think the dead body is a man called Shane O'Leary. If you were to ring the police station in a place called Aghia Anna in Greece they would give you the phone number of the police station in Athens that

396

booked him three years ago. They will have his fingerprints and details. Who am I? I am nobody. Really, I'm not important. It's just to help you and maybe his mother, if she's still alive. No, I have no more to say.'

Then she closed her phone and waited for the next bus.

That night, as she was going to bed, Fiona realised that she had no feelings at all about the dead Shane. She had hardly any memory of their time together or why she had loved him so much. It was impossible to remember why someone could love so madly, so one-sidedly. It must mean that she had been insane for a whole part of her life.

Father Flynn was showing off his hall proudly. He was explaining to a young Polish couple that his first wedding would take place at the end of August, a marriage between a young doctor and a nurse from the heart clinic and they had given permission for this couple and another pair to come to the wedding and see if they liked it all.

'They must be generous people.' The couple were surprised.

'They are good people, yes. And the caterers are marvellous. You'd love them.'

'They might be very expensive.'

'No, I think not. They did a great buffet for a Slovakian christening. Unpronounceable char-grilled vegetables – none of the people had ever seen them before, but in the end everyone was delighted with it.'

'And perhaps we can make some decorations for the hall. You have nice curtains, but not many pictures.'

'We had a lovely Polish girl, Ania, who worked here with us but sadly she's gone back home.'

'Maybe she is very happy there,' the young couple suggested.

'Maybe . . .' said Father Flynn, who had heard a fair

amount of the story from Johnny, Declan and Fiona. Wherever Ania was, he didn't think she was very happy.

Ania was, in fact, in discussion with Lech, one of her brothers-in-law. They were going to remodel the shop for Mamusia. They would make a big, long window here and put two garments in it. A friend would write the sign.

'You worked very hard to make all this money, Ania.'

'She deserves it. I disgraced her.'

'That's all in your mind. You weren't the only one that Marek fooled. He's in jail now. Did you know?'

'No, I didn't know.' She was startled that she didn't feel anything at all at this news. Neither relieved nor upset. Just indifferent.

Lech had his metal measuring tape out and was writing down figures in his notebook. Ania looked out and prayed that this would work. She hoped so much that ladies who wanted a spring outfit would come up this hill and consult with her mother. Everything would have been worth it then. Yes, even all her mistakes.

There was somebody coming up the hill as she watched. A man with a bag on his back. He paused now and then to look around him, to take it all in. She looked again.

It was.

It was Carl.

Amy said that she liked working in the clinic. There was a good atmosphere. 'I hope that this Ania *never* comes back. I hope she meets a rich Pole there who owns a dozen restaurants. Then I can go on working here until I die,' she said to Clara.

'I wouldn't bet on it, Amy,' Clara said. 'I hear that her fellow went out there after her. We could look up any minute and she might be right there, at that door.'

'The nonsensical things people do for love,' Amy said.

'I know! Isn't it just? Are you still with your fellow, Ben, the nice embalmer?'

'Yes, I am as it happens. Fancy you remembering.'

'Oh, I remember. I liked him.'

'I suppose you and he being vaguely in the same business, you had quite a lot in common,' Amy agreed.

If Clara was disturbed to be considered in the same line of business as an embalmer, she showed nothing.

'Does your dad get on with him?'

'I don't think he knows what to talk to him about. He's always afraid that Ben will start to talk about dead bodies, which he rarely does. Anyway, Dad's all caught up with your woman nowadays.'

'Your woman?'

'You know, Mrs Thing, from Lilac Court.'

'Claire Cotter! Never!'

'Is she awful?' Amy asked eagerly.

'No, she's marvellous. Ideal for him actually.' And Clara was relieved to find that she actually meant it.

'Okay, if you say so. I'll look at her with warmer eyes.'

Fiona listened as Bobby said Carl had taken a few days off school unexpectedly and he hoped the boy was all right.

'You know, Bobby, I never met a fellow that was more all right than Carl. I wish I had had a teacher like him when I was at school.'

'It's just that he's probably taking time off to think about his life. You know, he's at the age he should be having his own home. Like you are, Fiona.' Bobby admired the opal ring.

'Like I am,' Fiona said in an oddly quiet tone.

'Will we go shopping for wedding outfits?' Fiona's mother suggested on Thursday, the late opening day.

'I'll go and look for something for you, Mam.'

'It *is* customary for the bride to dress up too,' her mother said.

'Ania will make my dress. It was all arranged.'

'But isn't she . . .'

'Yes, she is, but she'll be back,' Fiona said.

Fiona received a text message from Ania who had borrowed a mobile phone: 'Mamusia and I spent a long time thinking about your wedding dress. I know what will look wonderful on you. Will you trust us? You will be the most beautiful bride in Ireland. I am happy in my heart. Love, Ania.'

Barbara was going to lose fourteen pounds for the wedding.

It was realistic, she said, as she ate an egg sandwich filled with butter and mayonnaise and that two pounds a week was the recommended weight loss.

Molly Carroll and Maureen Ryan were going to a place called Big Day that specialised in Mother of the Bride outfits.

They were now firm friends and had urged each other not to go to town, not to be too fussy, not to be over the top.

Their husbands knew this was only a rallying cry to go completely mad.

They were discussing getting shoes dyed, coordinating handbags and having a professional make-up person on the day.

The twins were sick with excitement. They begged Cathy and Tom for some help.

'Why should we help you to do a rival gig?' Tom asked jokingly.

Cathy knew that you never joked with Maud and Simon. 'Sure we'll come along and look at the place,' she said.

'It's not really a rival operation . . .' Simon began.

'They wouldn't be able to afford you two ...' Maud agreed.

'The groom spent all the money on an opal ring.' Simon was censorious.

'So there's not a lot left over for the catering, you see.' Maud wanted there to be no grey areas.

'Show us the place and we'll tell you what you need.' Cathy cut across the ever-increasing complications of any conversation with Maud and Simon. 'Show us the venue, kids, and bring a notebook,' she said.

Vonni had booked her ticket to Ireland. She showed it to Andreas.

'Come with me, old friend,' she entreated.

'No. You won't marry *me*, why should I go halfway across the world to be your escort at a wedding party?'

'Andreas, we would be *mad* to get married. I need you, Andreas. I might go back on the drink unless you're there.'

'No, you won't. You didn't drink in Ireland before. Why would you start now?'

'I might become unhinged.'

'No. It was my country and my countrymen that unhinged you. You've recovered now.'

'We never really recover.'

'Well, you're as near to it as anyone I know,' Andreas said, patting her on the hand.

David Fine's mother was surprised that he was going to Ireland to a wedding.

'Was that the girl who came here when your father was diagnosed?' she asked.

'That's right, Mother. Fiona.'

'I thought at the time that you two were sweet on each other back then.'

'Oh no, not at all. She was in love with a madman back then but fortunately she got over him,' David explained.

'So she's not marrying the madman then?'

'No, marriage was the last thing *he* had in mind.'

'Will it be a Catholic wedding, do you think?'

'Almost certainly.'

'You'll need someone to mark your card, David, when to stand and sit and kneel.'

'Oh, I'll watch the others,' David said airily.

'And will it be a fancy wedding, do you think?'

'I have no idea. She's marrying a doctor. He's got red hair and is very kind. She sounds highly excited.'

'Of course she's excited,' David's mother said, 'isn't she marrying a doctor?'

'We should send flowers to the wedding,' Elsa said.

'Imagine. Vonni going back to Ireland for it,' Tom said.

'I wish we could be there. Where will we send the flowers, do you think?' Elsa asked.

'She mentions a church near the Liffey. I guess the florist would know,' Tom said.

'Or we have her home address.'

'I'm glad she's happy,' said Tom. 'This fellow sounds a much better bet.'

'Almost anyone in the world would be a better bet than Shane,' Elsa said.

Bobby Walsh knew more about what was going on than most people thought. But he didn't confront Rosemary with this information. Instead, he arranged to rent a flat for his son. It was nearer the city and would be handier for Carl going to the school where he taught. Nearer for Ania too. Little by little he had pieced it all together from what this one and that one said. And mainly from what people didn't say.

Johnny, in the exercise room, had told him most. And that new girl, Amy, who was dressed so oddly and doing Ania's job, she had revealed that the Polish girl had gone home in a rage because some old bat had thought she was the hired help at a party when the son of the house had invited her as his guest.

Bobby's face burned with shame, but this wasn't the time to face Rosemary down.

And Bobby knew something that nobody else knew. He knew that Carl and Ania were coming back on Saturday.

He had already texted Carl about the apartment. It was furnished. They could walk straight in when they got back. It was theirs for a year until they had decided where they would like to go.

Then Bobby would buy them a place. He was going to sell that big house by the sea. There were far too many steps. The estate agent was looking for a mews. He hadn't told any of this to Rosemary yet but he would when the time was right.

The time was right on Friday.

Rosemary came home with some mackerel.

'I thought we'd make that bloody woman's recipe,' she said.

'She's not a bloody woman. She's called Lavender and she's a helpful, kind person who's showing us how to eat *properly*.'

'Okay, it's only a form of words.'

'Not a very good one,' he said.

'Don't come after me, Bobby. I've had a tough day.'

'So have I.'

'*You've* had a tough day? What have you done? You don't even go upstairs any more!'

'True.'

'So tell me about your tough day.' She looked very angry.

'Well, I looked through what seems like a thousand flats on a laptop before choosing one to rent for Carl. Then I went through a tedious amount of description about this house with the intention of putting it on the market.'

'You are never thinking of selling this house!'

'Yes, that's exactly what I *am* going to do.'

'Without consulting me?'

'I was waiting for you to come home, Rosemary, before going ahead finally. Now that I've told you, I can call them.'

'Bobby, have you gone completely mad? You can't get a flat for Carl. We don't even know where he is.'

'I do, Rosemary, he's in Poland.'

'He's where?' She looked ashen.

'Yes.'

'He went after that little tramp. I don't believe it. It's impossible. He must *see* that.'

'She's not a tramp. She's his girlfriend.'

'Well, I may have spoken a bit in haste.'

Silence from Bobby.

'And I am prepared to admit this to Carl when he returns to his senses.'

More silence.

'So is all this silly protest over?'

'There's no silly protest.' He spoke slowly.

'So why wasn't I consulted about this?' She looked at him, horrified.

'Because you're not involved in this any more,' Bobby Walsh said.

'Why?' Rosemary begged.

'You must know why by now,' her husband said sadly.

A couple of days later Fiona saw in the papers that the body of the young man had been identified as that of Shane O'Leary. The deceased had apparently taken a lethal dose of drugs and was identified by his mother due to a tip-off to the Guards.

His father had died some years ago as a result of an accident in the construction industry.

Mr O'Leary had been travelling on the continent in Europe. His family hadn't been aware that he'd returned to Ireland. He was the eldest of four boys and the premises where his body was discovered was a vacant flat in a house that was in need of renovation. It wasn't known how the deceased had come to be there.

Fiona read the short item over and over.

She hadn't known that Shane had any younger brothers. He had told her nothing about his father being killed. He said the old man had gone off to England and abandoned them all.

What had his mother thought when the Guards came to her door?

His brothers must still be young, at school even. How had they felt at the death of their absent brother?

She was puzzled that none of these questions meant anything to her. She didn't care about the answers. It was as if she was reading about a total stranger. Yet this was the man she had left home with to tour the world. The man whose child she was expecting with joy.

Shane had hit her and she had miscarried, but even then she had believed he would come back to her and that they would spend their lives together. Had she been insane?

Although Fiona had not one feeling left for Shane O'Leary, she still had a lot of questions that needed answering.

Questions about herself. Like was she capable of having any normal relationship with any man whatsoever? She twisted her ring around and around on her finger. Nothing seemed real any more.

She hoped that neither her mother nor Barbara would see the item in the newspaper. She didn't want to talk about it or even think about it any more.

*

Father Flynn decided that he couldn't go through with this shebeen mentality about people smuggling drink into his hall. Either he was responsible enough to run a function or he wasn't. A wedding day was too important to let any question mark hang over it.

He read the terms of the recent Health Acts. All it involved was that he applied for a licence to the HSE, the Health and Safety Executive. They would grant it and then there would be no hole-in-the-wall behaviour. Not everyone agreed with him.

Johnny said it would halve the price of drink if they got it on sale at a supermarket. James said that you never knew where you were with those guys. Brian might meet the bureaucratic official from hell.

Father Brian tried to discuss it with Fiona, but he could sense she wasn't interested. Her mind seemed to be far away and she was looking through him without seeing him at all or listening to what he said.

Molly and Maureen had got very satisfactory outfits in Big Day. It had been a great outing: very nice staff with tea and sandwiches on the premises. They could have stayed there all day. They *had* more or less stayed all day. And the outfits weren't silly. They could be worn again and again at whatever functions turned up. Like a christening, maybe. They giggled happily.

At Big Day the owner had said they were very relaxed compared to a lot of brides' mothers and grooms' mothers. She wished that all her customers were so easy to deal with. So Maureen and Molly bought more and more and said it was the best day out they ever had.

But try as they might, they couldn't make Fiona interested in the garments they had bought.

Her mind seemed to be a million miles away.

*

Ania came into the clinic on Monday.

She looked for a long time at Amy, who was passing around mugs of coffee.

'You must be St Ania, the Polish girl,' Amy said eventually.

'And you are Amy, Peter Barry's daughter,' Ania agreed.

'So, you're back. I go. Right?'

'I'm not St Ania. I am just so lucky that they will take me back.'

'Aw, go on. They're mad about you!'

'Did you like it here?'

'Yes, I did.'

'I came in through the hospital this morning. They're looking for people to work in A&E, taking records and notes to leave the nurses free to cope with what they should be doing.'

'Is that part of Frank Ennis's territory?'

'Yes, in that everything in the hospital is a bit.'

'But isn't he our natural enemy?' Amy asked.

Ania laughed. 'I think I got back here just in time. You have nearly taken over already.'

Ania and Carl couldn't believe the new apartment that Bobby had arranged for them.

'We can't take this, Dad,' Carl said with tears in his eyes.

'And what did I work hard all my life for, if it wasn't to give you a place to live?' Bobby beamed with pleasure.

'But it's too much. Specially since you're going to sell the house and buy somewhere else. You don't want to have to shell out for this place as well.'

'We can pay the rent, Bobby,' Ania said. 'I will just get a few more jobs. It's not difficult.'

'No, child, you continue to send your earnings to your mother. That's what you came here to do.'

'Oh, she's so pleased with everything, Bobby; if you could

see what they're doing to her house! Even my sisters are pleased with me too. Which usually they are not.'

'Did you meet them all, Carl?'

'I did. They were very welcoming. At least I *think* they were. I couldn't understand a word anyone was saying!'

'Oh, they were, Carl, very welcoming indeed.'

Bobby cleared his throat. 'Rosemary is very sorry about the misunderstanding . . .' he began. He saw Carl's face harden, but Ania laid her hand on his arm.

'Please tell her that it's all forgotten. In many ways it was all helpful. It forced us to do what we all wanted to do.'

'I'm not sure that Rosemary wants to move house, but it's going to happen. And she will get used to it. It's most generous of you, Ania, to see things so positively.'

'I have a lot to be positive about,' she said.

'Carl, I was wondering?'

'No, Dad, not yet. I don't have a lovely positive soul like Ania.'

'You could grow one,' Ania said.

'Yes and I might one day.'

'Or maybe soon, Carl, so that your father could enjoy more peaceful days in these busy stress-filled times.'

'Maybe,' Carl said. But he had no intention of speaking to his mother.

Ania bought the material for Fiona's wedding dress in a market. It was a cream and yellow Indian silk. It would be beautiful.

Fiona stood like a statue raising her arms to be measured and for Ania to pin a kind of underslip that would act as a pattern for the real thing. She hardly said anything. She didn't ask Ania about the trip to Poland, about the new apartment, about what Carl had said when he arrived at her mother's house.

Normally Fiona would want to know every detail.

She didn't talk about her own wedding either. All the conversations that Ania started seemed to run into the ground. Yes, it was great to be getting married by Father Brian. Yes, the centre sounded a terrific place for a wedding breakfast. Oh indeed, many of the friends were coming from abroad. And certainly, the two mothers were having a good time.

Ania put down her box of pins. 'Fiona, be honest with me. Do you want someone else to make your wedding dress?'

'No, Ania, how can you even think that?'

'So what is it then?'

Fiona looked at her stricken. 'I can't marry Declan,' she said suddenly. 'I'm not a person who has any judgement about men. I can't go through with it.' She began to cry, heavy sobs.

'And what does Declan say?' Ania asked.

'He doesn't know,' Fiona wept.

'Well, you must tell him.'

'I can't.'

'You'll have to. I'm right in the middle of making him a waistcoat trimmed with the material of your dress. He *has* to know, Fiona. For heaven's sake.'

Carl had invited his friends Nora and Aidan Dunne to supper in the new apartment. Ania had cooked some salmon for dinner. Carl had brought her flowers. Life could not be better.

They were so nice, the Dunnes, and so fond of each other. You could see it immediately, the way they listened to each other's stories, touched each other's hands. Aidan was a patient at the clinic so Ania had already met them there, but she had had no idea what interesting lives they had led. She sat and chattered happily as if she had been accustomed to entertaining like this all her life. At nine o'clock there was a ring at the door.

Ania went to answer the buzzer. Who could be coming to

call at this time of night? She looked at the little screen. It was Carl's mother.

'Please excuse my not telephoning, but I know Carl doesn't want to see me.'

'It's not that, Mrs Walsh, it's just that we have people here for dinner, you see.'

'It will only take a minute. I have something to say to you. I need not bother Carl.'

'Perhaps this is not a good time, Mrs Walsh.' She could see Carl roll his eyes up to heaven.

'Tell her to go away,' he mouthed.

But Ania was too kind. 'Come in, Mrs Walsh, but it can't be for long. I hope you will excuse us.' She buzzed the entry-phone.

Ania returned to the table. 'We'll offer her a glass of wine.'

'She deserves a boot up the arse!' Carl said.

Ania smiled apologetically at the guests. 'Bit of a long story,' she said.

'We know a lot of it,' Nora said. 'Should we leave?'

'No, please, no. I will take Carl's mother into another room and talk to her.'

'You don't have to do this, Ania. She behaved so badly.'

'You were polite to *my* mother when you could not understand one word she was saying. I will be polite to yours.'

Ania ushered Rosemary Walsh into the bedroom where Fiona's wedding dress was hanging on the wall.

'And is this going to be . . . ?'

'For Fiona.'

'I see.' Rosemary didn't attempt to disguise her relief.

'Won't you have a chair?' Ania sat on the bed.

'One bed,' Rosemary Walsh said.

'That's right. I brought you in a glass of wine,' Ania said.

'I don't want any wine, thank you. I wanted to say that my

words to you on the night of the party were wrong. I should not have said what I did. You were Carl's guest. I knew that. I behaved very badly.'

'You must have had your reasons.'

'No, looking back on it, I can't think what my reasons were.' Rosemary Walsh was at a loss.

'So that's all right then, Mrs Walsh.'

'No, it's not all right. I want you to tell my husband Bobby that he cannot sell our house. That you will come and live there with Carl and help with getting Bobby bathed and upstairs and everything.'

'I think that is something you should discuss with Bobby and Carl, not with me.'

'But if you say that you'd be a back-up, a carer, you know, then they'd agree.'

'I don't think so. Bobby is very set on a new place. He was showing us brochures, advertisements.'

'That's only because he thinks Carl won't be around for him.' Rosemary looked almost beseeching.

'I think Carl is happy here and Bobby is happy for us to be here, Mrs Walsh. So I will not say anything at all to change things.'

Rosemary looked at her long and hard. 'They're right. You *are* intelligent. You're sharp. I made a mistake. I apologise for that as well. At what must have seemed rudeness.'

'It was a misunderstanding, Mrs Walsh. It's over now.'

'You are very clever. I see that. Too late.'

'It is not too late.'

'It is. I'll go now, Ania.'

'Are you sure you would not like some wine?'

'I'm sure. Thank you.'

There was laughter from the next room.

Rosemary looked at the door. 'Carl never brought any friends home to dinner when he lived at home.'

'Well, maybe he needed a place of his own.'
'Goodbye, Ania.'
'Goodbye, Mrs Walsh.'

Fiona wanted to tell him something. Declan didn't have to be Einstein to know this. Even Dimples the dog seemed to know. He lay quietly examining his paws and making no sounds. Declan's father Paddy was off with Muttie and their associates in the pub.

His mother Molly was talking finery with Fiona's mother Maureen.

'Declan?'

'There's something wrong, isn't there?'

'You feel it too?' She seemed relieved.

'I feel that you are upset about something certainly.'

'I can't marry you,' she said.

'You've met another fellow.' He smiled at her indulgently.

'You know that's not true.'

'So it's me then? You've gone off me?'

'As if, Declan Carroll.'

'So, what is it then, pet?'

'It's a long story,' Fiona said.

'We have all the time in the world,' said Declan and folded his arms to listen to the most complicated rambling tale of which he understood hardly a word. Except that because of bad judgement, in fact, worse, *no* judgement, Fiona wasn't going to marry anybody.

Ever.

Chapter Twelve

Fiona thought that more marriages must have taken place because people didn't want to upset the arrangements than between people who really *should* have got married. She understood it only too well. Look at all the people she was upsetting by this decision. She didn't even dare to think about her parents and Declan's parents and her sisters who would not now be bridesmaids. The fallout from that would last a generation. Then there were all the cousins, aunts and uncles on both sides who had ordered wedding outfits and even, in some cases, had already sent wedding presents. They would be incensed.

And Vonni coming to Ireland for the first time in decades. David coming over from England for his first ever visit. The whole staff at the clinic, who had been so excited and supportive. Father Flynn, whose first wedding it would have been in this centre by the Liffey, would feel like a fool. The twins, Maud and Simon, who had told almost everyone in Dublin that this was the start of their career, would be crushed. Ania, who was happy and smiling again, and who had made a beautiful dress, would not now see her creation walk down the aisle.

It was easy to see why other women had given in over the

years rather than alienate half the planet. But then other women hadn't known the great insight that had become clear to Fiona.

The day she had read that newspaper item, which summed up Shane O'Leary's short life and sordid death, Fiona realised that she had, at one period of her life, been prepared to marry this man. She was expecting his child. She had been distraught when she had miscarried. She had *longed* to hear him propose marriage and suggest that they live by the sea in Aghia Anna and bring up their child there.

How could she be capable of making *any* decision?

She would go far away from here and all the people she had let down. She would go abroad and find herself. *Do* something worthwhile rather than getting swept along in some insane project which had now become completely out of control, with opals and buffet feasts, and decisions on who was to make what speech.

Had Declan really understood, really understood that it was over? That the wedding was not going to happen. He had been too calm. He had said that of course she should just do what she wished to do. He would be broken-hearted all his life and he would never marry either. There were ways in which it would all be a giant waste.

But if that's what she wanted, then that's what would happen.

No, he wouldn't hear of taking back her ring. She must get it made into a brooch or a pendant. And he wanted one week before they told people.

'A week? But people will be busy making their plans, Declan. We *have* to tell them now.'

'But it's about *me*. I haven't got used to making *my* plans to live without you. Give me just one week,' he asked.

'This isn't some awful, devious scheme?'

'No,' he said sadly, 'if I had an awful, devious scheme that might work, I would have one, believe me.'

'All right then.'

'Yes and we tell nobody. Nobody at all.'

'But they'll go on making arrangements.'

'Let them. It's only for a week. Then we tell them. Okay. Swear.'

'I swear.'

'Not even Barbara?'

'Not even Barbara,' she agreed.

'Good girl,' he said.

Fiona noted that he hadn't tried to argue with her, change her mind, tell her that she was wrong. All he had asked was a week's grace, and that she should keep the opals. He must have known in his heart that it would have been doomed.

Clara was surprised to see Frank Ennis standing at her desk.

'A rare and unexpected pleasure,' she said.

He came straight to the point. 'Can you give that girl Amy a reference?'

'Yes, she was fine. If we had a job for her, we'd give her one.'

'That's all right then. She looks a bit weird.'

'But then what a mistake it would be to judge people by their looks,' Clara smiled.

'Sure. So the wandering Pole has returned?'

'Yes, Ania's crisis is over, I'm glad to say. Everyone was delighted to see her back.'

'And I gather you have a wedding coming up?' Frank said. Clara wondered how on earth he could have known that.

'Absolutely. Declan and Fiona. Big day out. *And* we have loads more romance going on. Ania is together with the son of one of our patients. My daughter and Hilary's son have fallen in love. All I need is to get a young fellow myself and we can say the objectives have all been achieved.'

He was almost sure she was joking, but not quite.

'I thought you were already spoken for, with the pharmacist in the precinct?'

'Oh, Frank, that's old news now. Peter is history. He's actually involved with the lady who runs Lilac Court, the nursing home.'

'Well really!' Frank Ennis was dumbfounded.

'And how did you know about Declan and Fiona's wedding?' Clara wondered.

'Well, I'm invited, as it happens.'

'*Invited?*' Clara was taken aback. Fiona and Declan had invited the Enemy to their wedding? Never.

'Well, more or less. I'm a plus *one*,' he said. 'Fiona's cousin, who's a social worker, was invited and her invitation said plus one, so that's me.'

'Well, well, well.' Clara was, for once, without words.

Fiona and Declan would scream with laughter over this.

'So you'll have to save me a dance, Clara,' Frank said.

'I wouldn't want to step on the toes of Fiona's cousin,' Clara murmured diplomatically.

'No, no, you wouldn't be. That's not an affair or anything, not even an understanding or anything. Just a casual friendship. I think she just thought it would be a nice day out.'

'And it will be, Frank, it will be,' said Clara.

'And you can tell me all about your plans and where you go after here,' he said.

'After here?'

'When your year is up,' he said.

Clara had quite put it out of her mind that she had only been hired for a year, at her own heavy insistence at the time. 'Ah yes, when the year is up,' she said vaguely.

'I'm sure you have your plans. Your career plan.' Frank was eager to know.

'You wouldn't believe me if I said I had nothing planned,' she smiled at him.

She had been right. He didn't believe her. Clara Casey without a game plan.

Please.

Clara sat at her desk when Frank left. What an extraordinary year it had been.

Alan's bimbo becoming pregnant. Alan asking for a divorce, then asking if he could come back home. Adi and Gerry planning to go and save a rainforest. Linda having a change of personality since she'd met Hilary's son Nick. Then there was the episode with Peter Barry the pharmacist, who had wanted to marry her.

But most of all there was the clinic. That's what amazed her. It was bigger in her mind than all the other life-changing things that had happened. They *were* making a difference. They were managing to keep people out of hospital. They had restored confidence and given new hope to people with heart disease and they had made it part of ordinary life.

It had been well worth doing. She was in no way ready to move on.

Ania was in charge of the collection for Fiona and Declan's wedding present. She had felt odd about it at first: it was a difficult situation. But then nothing had happened since Fiona's outburst. There was no announcement that the wedding was cancelled. Everything seemed to be going ahead. It was going to be all right.

It hadn't been difficult to get donations and arrange for everyone to sign the card. The question was what to get them? There was no wedding list registered in a store. There were no helpful hints and no mention of a colour scheme for the new flat they were hoping to buy. And yet the money was flowing in. They had enough for Ania to buy a really good present.

Ania brought up the subject casually. Whether crystal-ware was worth the expense or did Declan prefer simpler glasses? Was silver old-fashioned now or did young people still like it? Was it possible to buy a work of art for someone else?

Declan brushed Ania's careful detective work aside with a laugh.

'Ania, we don't want *anything* and if people are going to give something, then maybe a CD or a book or a vase. *Please, Ania.*' Which had been no help at all.

On the other hand, it was a lot better than what Fiona had said this morning.

Ania had asked if in Fiona's opinion cast-iron casserole dishes might be a good gift? She had tried to make it appear as if she was thinking of cast-iron casserole dishes in entirely general terms as a gift for unspecified people.

Fiona's eyes had filled with tears.

'Do you have a list of who gave you what, Ania?' she asked unexpectedly.

Ania didn't know what to answer. 'Um . . . well . . .' she said.

'It's just that you'd need to know what to give back to people if, for example, the wedding did *not* take place.'

'*Fiona!*' Ania cried.

'I have said nothing, nothing at all. You must remember that. I said nothing except that if you *are* collecting money for anything, you should always write down what people give you.' And Fiona was gone, wiping her eyes.

Ania realised that she had to keep quiet about this. It was hard when Carl was asking her what kind of a suit he should wear for the wedding and when Fiona's mother and Declan's mother were busy trying to discuss the corsages Ania was going to make for them to wear with their new outfits and when Maud and Simon were on the phone to her regularly about table decorations and when Barbara was starving herself to fit into a kingfisher-blue dress which was a size too small.

Fiona and Declan really might *not* be getting married. Should all these people be warned? Ania had a headache that wouldn't go away.

Brian Flynn called into the heart clinic to pick up Johnny. They were going to go south on one of their marathons. Or little strolls, as Johnny called them.

'Will you come with us, Declan?' Johnny suggested. 'The DART out to Bray and a few runs up and down the esplanade there, filling your lungs full of good, fresh, sea air.'

'God, it sounds very healthy,' Declan said. 'Wait till I put on better running shoes.'

'Then filling our gut with pints of good, fresh beer,' Brian added.

'That does it, all right,' agreed Declan.

'Afterwards, you can brief me about my duties as best man,' Johnny added. 'I'm not sure—'

'But you're totally sure we can all yomp these miles and climb these peaks,' Brian grumbled.

'Stop complaining, Brian, you know it's good for you,' Declan said, glad that the subject had been changed.

'I thought you'd be up to your neck in arrangements,' Brian said, still hoping to have an ally, any ally who might slow Johnny down.

'No, I leave all that side of it to the women,' Declan said. No need to tell Brian and Johnny that Fiona refused to see him in the evenings.

She said she was keeping her part of the bargain by behaving as if nothing had changed during the daytime, but it would be pointless going out in the evening and going over old ground again and again. She had explained her position and said she was sorry. What more was there that could be said?

Fiona said she would like to take Dimples for a good long walk. Molly and Paddy approved – Dimples was running to fat.

Fiona and the large Labrador set off together. They walked into the centre of town and went towards Trinity College. Fiona remembered a school trip which had taken them by Sweeney's Pharmacy, the old chemist shop mentioned in James Joyce's *Ulysses*, which didn't look as if it had changed at all in over a hundred years. And she paused at the hotel where James Joyce had met Nora Barnacle. Now *there* was a love affair that shouldn't have worked and yet it did.

Fiona didn't know if they allowed dogs in there, but she didn't ask. Dimples looked entirely at home anywhere, so no one was likely to stop them.

She found herself looking up at the old buildings which had been there since the first Elizabeth was on the throne of England. She saw the lines waiting to go and see the Book of Kells. Imagine monks decorating that, nearly seven hundred pages of it, instead of getting on with things. But maybe they weren't doing anyone any harm.

Fiona wondered, was she in danger of becoming very bland and dull?

They came out and walked around Merrion Square. Fiona showed off the various landmarks to the dog. Where Oscar Wilde had lived; the statue of the same Oscar with his one-line witticism engraved on it; the Georgian fan windows over the colourful doors; the foot-scrapers; the different door knockers. She had seen them all many times before but somehow this was different. She realised she was printing it all in her mind.

Next week, when she and Declan told people that the wedding was off, she would work out her notice, repair as many broken fences and crushed dreams as she could, then she would go away. Far away.

What she was doing tonight was saying goodbye to Dublin.

An elderly American couple stopped her to admire the dog.

'That's Dimples,' Fiona said sadly.

'And have you had him long?' they asked, playing with Dimples' ears.

'He's not mine, he's my fiancé's.' Fiona looked at the opal ring and bit her lip.

'Oh well, same thing.' The lady found some chocolate in her bag and gave it to Dimples who loved it and held up a huge paw to thank her.

'Not really,' Fiona heard herself say.

'So, are you going to live in a place where they don't allow dogs?'

'No. We're not going to get married,' Fiona said, and it all came out in a gush. How she was a person of no judgement. It wouldn't be fair. She had to go away, miles away.

The couple looked at each other, mystified.

'And is everyone upset about this?' the man asked eventually.

'Nobody knows,' wept Fiona, 'nobody knows except us. It was a ludicrous promise he made me make, to keep it all secret for a week.'

'How much of the week is left?' The American woman was very interested.

'Four and a half days, but nothing's changed.'

'No, of course not. Look, it's pretty simple, isn't it? Do you think he loves you?'

'Yes, yes, he does,' said Fiona through her tears.

'And do you love him? Because if you don't, you mustn't marry him. But if you do . . .'

421

Brian Flynn couldn't believe that they were going to do two more laps before they had their pint. He thought he was going to die on the spot.

'We'll revive you,' Johnny said unsympathetically.

'It's *good* for you, Brian,' said Declan, a veritable Judas Iscariot who turned out to love exercise too.

Finally they got the pint.

'You're curiously calm for a condemned man,' Johnny said to Declan.

'It's all an act,' Declan said truthfully.

'And how's Fiona?' Brian asked.

'Oh, wouldn't it be great to understand the mind of a woman.'

'They're usually more focused than we are. Certainly about weddings.'

'It would be much better if you could look at some of these properties, Rosemary,' Bobby Walsh pleaded.

'What for? Haven't you said that you're buying one anyway? What does my approval mean one way or another?'

'I just want somewhere all on one floor. I can't make stairs any more. We have many good years left.'

'Shuffling around in a crowded apartment? I don't think so.'

'If we're together isn't that all that matters?'

'We're together *here*,' she said.

'I live in a bedsitter here, Rosemary. I can't manage the steps up to the hall door. Let's choose somewhere *you* like.'

She said nothing, just stood there like a mutinous child.

'Then *I'll* have to choose for you. There's a very nice place I've been told about. It's got a little garden. There's a block of thirty just going on the market. If we offer the estate agents the chance to sell this place, then they'll give us our pick of the new apartments. The corner one on the ground floor looks the nicest. You can see the sea from the window, and they have a swimming pool in the complex.'

'Where is this place you've set your heart on?'

He named the posh area and saw her eyes widen a little. She would have no trouble selling the idea of this move to her snobby friends. If he played this properly it might be plain sailing from now on.

'It wouldn't hurt to see it,' she said.

Hilary Hickey was coping with two painters. They had come to touch up some neglected areas of the clinic – at the request of Frank Ennis. That was surprising enough. Then it was even more odd to see Rosemary Walsh come alone to the heart clinic. It wasn't a day when Bobby had an appointment. She hoped Mrs Walsh wasn't here to make some kind of trouble. Fortunately Ania had gone for her lunch so there wouldn't have to be a confrontation there.

'I wonder is there anyone who could give me some advice about Bobby's heart condition?' Rosemary Walsh began.

'Well, Clara is up at the hospital just now.'

'Not Clara,' Mrs Walsh said.

'Declan's here.'

'Yes, Declan.'

She was imperious still. But she seemed to be readjusting her face somehow so as to turn on the charm.

'Ah, Dr Declan, and we're getting near the big day.'

'Indeed, Mrs Walsh. Looking forward to seeing you and Bobby there.'

'And what kind of a *gift* would you like?' Rosemary managed to make the word 'gift' seem somehow beneath her.

Declan smiled wanly. 'Just your being there would be enough, but if you do insist, then we would love a CD, some nice music that meant something to you and Bobby perhaps?'

She looked at him witheringly. 'What I really came for was to know about Bobby's heart. Would it increase his life expectancy if we were to live somewhere on one floor?'

'You know it would, Mrs Walsh, we've been over this many times. Clara and I showed you both the results of his stress test. Gentle exercise, a swim if possible, but no stairs.'

'So I suppose I have to do it then,' she sighed heavily.

'Do what?'

'Give up my lovely house by the sea and move to a cramped flat. Bobby has his eye on one,' and she named the development.

'Hardly most people's idea of a cramped flat,' Declan said. 'Most of Ireland would love to be able to afford a place there.'

'Compared to what I was used to,' she said coldly. Then changing the subject abruptly, she said, 'And could Johnny come round and do exercises with him there: try and build him up a bit?'

'No, Johnny works here and in the hospital. He could give you a list of exercises, however, or the details of some other physiotherapist that you might like to employ personally.'

'You mean he won't come to a sick man's house?'

'Johnny works here for the Health Service. You and Mr Walsh are lucky enough to be able to afford a private physiotherapist. And indeed, Johnny can write out the exercises for you, and you could do them with Bobby.'

'You're asking *me* to do exercises?'

Something snapped in Declan's head. The strain of the last few days, of keeping up an act, pretending everything was all right when he wanted to howl at the moon – all of it crashed around him in the face of this dreadful woman.

'Listen to me, Mrs Walsh. If I thought I could help Fiona's life by doing exercises, by cooking her low-salt, low-fat meals, if I thought I could give her one more day in this world with me, I would do everything I could. I would stand on my head

424

if I thought it would help. And so would Nora for Aidan Dunne, and so would Lar's wife, and so would so many of the relatives who come here. You may not feel like that. We're all different.'

'Are you criticising me, Dr Carroll?'

'No, Mrs Walsh. Now can you tell me what exactly you wanted me to say to you when you came in here?' He turned away so that she wouldn't see him shaking with rage and annoyance.

'Please, Dr Carroll—' she began.

'Just tell me, what did you hope for?'

She was so shocked by his voice that she answered him truthfully. 'I suppose I hoped you would say it didn't really matter. That Bobby wouldn't improve, no matter where he was. Then we could stay where we were.'

'That's what you hoped to hear?' Declan was trembling.

'Yes, since you asked me.'

'May you get what you deserve, Rosemary Walsh,' he said and turned away. He closed his eyes and tried to do measured breathing. 'May you get what you deserve in life,' he said and walked away. He was halfway down the corridor when he heard the crash and the screams.

Hilary was already on the phone for an ambulance when Declan burst back into the room.

Rosemary had pushed her way past the workmen's ladders and knocked one of them down. The ladder was supporting a long plank of wood where two painters stood working away. They had been thrown to the ground in a welter of paint pots and falling timber. Right on top of Rosemary Walsh.

Declan knelt beside them. Was this all his fault? Where the hell was Ania? The one time they really needed someone to speak Polish.

425

'Ania!' he called out helplessly. Fiona appeared at the door and took in the situation at a glance.

'She's got a new mobile phone. I'll call her,' Fiona said. It was done in seconds. Ania was running back from the sandwich bar in the precinct.

'Rosemary?' Fiona said.

'Unconscious. She has a pulse. I want to move the guys first.'

Ania ran and knelt beside them. Declan barked questions and Ania, holding their hands, translated quickly. Declan saw confidence coming back to their faces as they were being addressed in their own language.

'Tell them they're fine,' he said.

'I already have,' Ania said.

Fiona suggested that Ania sit with the Polish men until the ambulance arrived. She took her place kneeling beside Declan.

'She's breathing,' she said.

'Barely,' Declan said.

They knelt there looking at Rosemary Walsh, her face cut from splintered wood and her legs at a very odd angle. She might have a fractured spine. Declan ran his hands up and down her.

'Broken arm. Broken leg. Her neck feels okay, but I don't want to risk moving her.'

'What would you do if there was no ambulance coming?' Fiona asked.

'What I'm going to do now. I'd start to resuscitate.'

'But . . .'

'Her breathing is very shallow. We could be losing her,' he said. And in front of Hilary, Lavender, Ania, Fiona and the two groaning Polish boys, Dr Declan Carroll began a mouth-to-mouth resuscitation of Rosemary Walsh, undoubtedly the least likeable person that any of them had ever met.

*

The ambulance men were full of praise. If it hadn't been for the young doctor, they said . . . and shook their heads. They had her in the hospital in no time. She was badly injured but she would live. Someone would have to tell her next of kin.

'I'll tell Carl,' Ania said.

'I'll tell Bobby,' Declan said.

By the time Clara got back, Hilary had spoken to the Guards who were called to investigate the incident and told them in her clear voice how Rosemary Walsh had walked directly into the ladder and caused the accident.

'And why did she not see the ladder?' the young policeman asked.

'She was in a stressed condition,' Hilary said diplomatically.

'Where's Declan now?' Clara wanted to know.

'Out in the leafy suburbs, breaking the news to Bobby.'

'And why didn't Fiona go with him? I saw her as I came in.'

'Search me, Clara. I don't think all is well in that area. I have a feeling that you and I will be wearing our new gear to our own children's wedding sooner than giving it an outing for Declan and Fiona's big day.'

'Yes, I think you're right. Pity. They are so suited. And I imagine it means we'll lose Fiona.'

'But why?' Hilary asked. 'Declan will be going anyway. His time here is nearly up.'

'Fiona won't want to hang around. Not if it's all over. She'll move on somewhere.'

'I wonder what it's all about?' Hilary said.

'Something utterly unimportant. These things usually are. We'll never know,' Clara said with a sigh.

*

'Bobby, it's just Declan Carroll.'

'Declan, how good to see you. How did you get in?' Bobby was in his little bedsitting room.

'I let myself in. I'll sit down here beside you.'

Declan had in fact taken Rosemary's keys from her handbag.

'Rosemary left the door open? That's so unlike her.' Bobby was distressed.

'No, no.' Declan was soothing.

'Let me get you a cup of tea.' Bobby was always the polite host.

'Let me make it. I make great tea.' He made them a mug each with a lot of sugar.

'I don't really take sugar,' Bobby began.

'You do today, Bobby. Rosemary had a bit of an accident. She's perfectly fine now, but she'll be in hospital for a while. Ania and Carl want you to go and stay in their flat. I'm to take you there now.'

Bobby's face was drained of colour. His questions came tumbling out.

'Believe me, Bobby, she's going to be fine. I'll take you to see her. Please, Bobby, drink your tea.'

'Oh, poor Rosemary. Where did it happen? Was she in the car?'

'No, nothing like that. She was walking down a corridor and she bumped into a ladder and a great plank and tins of paint and two men who were painting all fell down.'

'And how was she hurt?'

'A lot of grazes and scratches. And she's a broken arm and a broken leg.'

'*No!*'

'But it's all under control. She has a great young surgeon and she'll be going into theatre tomorrow.'

'Rosemary in an operating theatre, she must be so frightened.'

'She's sedated. She's very calm.'

'And does she know you've come to see me?'

'I told her, but she may not have taken it in,' Declan said. 'Bobby, can you direct me? I'll pack a bag for you and we can meet Carl and Ania at the hospital.'

'Carl is coming to the hospital? To see her?'

'Yes, indeed.'

'Oh, she will be pleased. They had a silly misunderstanding, you know.'

'People have forgotten all about that,' Declan said cheerfully.

Just as well Bobby didn't know what an uphill struggle Ania was having asking Carl to go and see his mother. He was resisting it as hard as he could.

Fiona was sitting in a bar looking out over Dublin Bay. It was so beautiful.

Declan used to say that they were so lucky to live in Dublin: a big roaring city and then the sea only ten minutes away and the mountains twenty minutes in the other direction. She noticed that she was thinking Declan *used* to say. After next week it really would be the past. She looked up as a shadow fell across the table.

'Barbara, what on earth are you doing here?'

'Once upon a time it was "Oh, Barbara, isn't that great. Sit down and have a drink." '

'We're ten miles from Dublin. You're not here by coincidence.'

'You're right. I'm not. I followed you.'

'You what?'

'Yes, I followed you. You don't come home to our flat. You don't talk at work. You're not at your mother and father's house. You're not up at the Carrolls' house. Am I not entitled to know where my friend is going and what's wrong?'

'Nothing's wrong.'

'Yeah?'

'No, seriously, Barbara, that's not fair. You're worse than any of them. Can't you understand that I just want some time by myself?'

'No, I can't.'

'Well, you should learn. That's what people want from friends. They want support and understanding. Not a load of detective work and following people out on trains.'

'Tell me, Fiona.'

'No, I won't. I can't.'

'Why can't you? We used to tell each other everything. I told you about the first time I ever went to bed with a fellow and he was so appalled by all the safety pins in my underwear it nearly turned him off. And you were great. You understood.'

'I know, but this is different.'

'And you told me about Shane and I understood. Why can't I understand now?'

'It's about Shane. It's all about bloody Shane.'

'But he's *dead*, Fiona. You must know he's dead.'

'How did *you* know?'

'I saw it in the paper.'

'And you said nothing to me?'

'I waited for you to say something to me and you didn't, so I thought you just didn't want it mentioned.'

'I felt nothing about him when I heard. I was the one who identified him to the Guards.'

'You actually went to see his body? Oh, my God!' Barbara was shocked.

'No, I phoned the Guards.'

'And what did you feel?'

'Nothing. Nothing for him. I didn't care if he lived or died.'

Barbara's kind face was stricken.

'Oh, sit down, Barbara, for God's sake, sit down and have an Irish coffee.'

'I haven't had an Irish coffee in weeks. Remember the kingfisher-blue dress, a size too small.'

'Forget the bloody kingfisher-blue dress. There isn't going to be a wedding.'

'Then I'd like a large brandy,' Barbara said.

'Mother?'

'Is that you, Carl?'

'Yes, Mother. You're going to be fine.'

'I'm sorry, Carl.'

'What for, Mother, it was all an accident.'

'Yes. I'm sorry for not just dying there and then and leaving you all to get on with your lives normally.'

'Mother, you're going to be fine and we are all delighted that it wasn't too serious.'

'I'm sorry for what I said.'

'We all say things we don't mean.' He patted her arm.

'I didn't wish to be hurtful,' she said.

'Neither did I, Mother.'

Rosemary closed her eyes. Carl left the room.

Outside the open door his father sat in a wheelchair pushed by Ania.

'Thank you, son,' Bobby said, with tears in his eyes.

'No, Dad, it's the truth. We all *do* say things we don't mean,' Carl said. But his face was cold. They all knew that Rosemary Walsh had meant exactly what she said.

Declan was cleaning his shoes in the kitchen at St Jarlath's Crescent.

'Mam, will I do your shoes for you? I'm doing my own.'

'No, Declan, but you could do something for me?'

'What is it, Mam?'

'Could you tell me what's wrong between you and Fiona?'

'What do you mean, what's wrong?'

'She came back here the other night with Dimples. She'd walked about ten miles around Dublin and back and she had been crying her eyes out.'

'And did you ask her why?'

'I didn't like to. I thought you and she might have had a row.'

'No, we didn't,' he said simply.

'If you could have seen her! She just handed Dimples back to me and walked down the crescent. She was bent over, as if she were in pain.'

Declan had stopped brushing his shoes.

'It will all be sorted out by Monday,' he said, speaking like an automaton.

'Oh, Declan, if something needs to be sorted out why for the Lord's sake wait until Monday?' Molly Carroll asked.

'That was what was agreed.'

In Dunlaoghaire, ordinary people with ordinary lives enjoyed the summer evening by the coast. They went for long, healthy walks the length of the pier. Some of them got into yachts and went out into the bay. Others settled into small restaurants.

Only Barbara and Fiona seemed out of touch with the gentle summery feel of it all.

'Tell me again,' Barbara said. 'You feel nothing over Shane. You love Declan, but you can't marry Declan because you don't trust your judgement? Is that it?'

'Well, that's a way of putting it.'

'I've listened to you for half an hour, Fiona, and I'm on my second large brandy. I can't understand *what* you're saying. I've tried to sum it up. Am I right or am I wrong?'

'Basically right.'

'Then you are quite totally mad,' Barbara said.

'Why? I made one bad call. I might be making another. What's so hard to understand about that?'

'Well, where do I start?' Barbara said. 'I could start by saying that Shane was a snivelling loser. A drug addict who hit you. Who dug deep and found the victim side of you. That's Shane. Declan is Declan. Mad about you, funny, good, kind, wise. You have never been so happy and positive since you met him. You could take on any job. He builds up your confidence. Look, why am I telling you all this, trying to sell him to you? I bet he doesn't *know* any of this.'

'I tried to tell him, but he said the past was over. I don't think he understood – he made me promise not to say anything more until Monday.'

'Because he's normal, that's why. Who could understand your rantings and ramblings?' Barbara called for the bill. 'You're going to talk to him now!' she said.

'No, he said Monday. That's what was agreed.'

Barbara took Fiona's mobile phone. 'Hi, Declan, Barbara here. Fiona and I are in a pub in Dunlaoghaire. Can you get here?'

Fiona looked like a guilty child.

Barbara continued, 'It's important that you know *she* didn't tell me. I guessed. She's still bleating on about doing nothing until Monday. Monday! God, Declan, we'll all be dead by Monday. Could you come out here quickly? I'll try to hold her down until you get here.'

Barbara stood and watched as Declan and Fiona joined the groups of ordinary people walking in the evening sunshine. She knew that neither of them could see the sea or little boats bobbing up and down. They weren't aware of the other people: the man selling balloons; the children eating huge ice-cream cones. But they walked close together and seemed to be talking to each other. Barbara sighed.

It was going to be all right. They had just looked at each other and said nothing when they met. That was a good sign.

Oh well, she would walk some of the way home. She had to get rid of three hundred-plus extra empty calories she'd drunk. It looked as if the kingfisher-blue dress might be needed after all.

'My legs feel a bit wobbly,' Fiona said, 'could we sit down?'

Declan guided them to a stone seat. He sat there and held her hand.

'You do know what it's all about?' she said after a while.

'No, I don't, to be honest.'

'But I *told* you. I explained for hours.'

'I didn't understand it fully.'

'What did you think it was?' she demanded.

'Nerves,' he said simply.

There was a silence.

'I don't *have* nerves,' Fiona said eventually.

'Good. Because neither do I. I am so sure we'll have a great marriage.'

'We can't marry.' Her voice was very level and calm.

'Why not exactly?'

'Because I once made a very stupid choice and fell in love with the idea of getting married and roaming the world. I'm afraid I'm doing it all over again.'

'But we're *not* roaming the world. We're going to settle down here. We're meant to be putting a deposit on a flat this week.'

'No, Declan, too much has happened.'

'And did it all happen since we agreed to get married?'

'In a way, yes. Shane died.'

'Shane?'

'The fellow I went off with to Greece. Remember I tried to tell you . . .'

'And I said what had happened in our past wasn't important.'

'But it *is*, Declan, it's what shapes us.'

'Well then, I was poorly shaped. I hardly *had* a past.'

'And I had Shane.'

'This fellow you fancied way back? Were you upset because he died?'

'I swear I couldn't have cared less.'

Declan's honest face was almost at the end of trying to understand all this.

'What has this to do with us? We don't have a difficult relationship. We want the same things or I thought we did. Where's the similarity?'

'I might be making an equally mad decision. In a few years' time I might care nothing about *you*. It's just the way I'm made. My mad personality.'

'It's up to me to make you keep loving me,' Declan said.

'No, if it were only that simple. I'm a mad, damaged person, incapable of making decisions. It's better that I don't make any ever again.'

'You've got to help me here, Fiona. I'm focusing. I'm concentrating, but I still don't get it.'

'I'll tell you the whole story again then,' she said.

'Will you tell it slowly this time? *Please*, Fiona?'

She actually smiled. 'I will,' she said, 'and if I go too fast, slow me down.'

And the telling did take a long time, but the talking took even longer.

And so everything was back on track. Nobody had been told anything of what went on out by the sea, what was said, what was not said and what was patted down.

The wedding dress fittings were cheerful. The waistcoat was made. The hall was decorated. Brian Flynn was duly licensed to serve alcohol. The twins brought tasting menus to the Carrolls' house so that everyone could decide what they liked and what they didn't. The two mothers brought their shoes to be stretched. Ania managed to wrestle from Fiona that if she were at a *theoretical* wedding, and she were the *theoretical* bride, she would love some heavy cut-crystal tumblers or a cut-glass bowl and Ania ran off and bought both as there was enough cash in the fund.

Declan suggested that Fiona find out where Shane's grave was.

'It's making too much of him,' she said.

'You loved him for a while. He deserves some kind of goodbye,' Declan said.

His mother had no idea who she was.

'There were so many girls,' Shane's mother said on the phone, 'and for what, in the end?' But she told Fiona where the grave was and she and Declan went to see it. The headstone was not yet up. Just a simple cross and the number of the plot. Fiona laid flowers on it.

'I'm sorry you didn't have a better life,' she said.

'May you sleep in peace,' Declan said.

And oddly, she did feel better as they left the big city graveyard. Somehow peaceful.

Rosemary Walsh was very bruised and battered, but recovering.

Bobby came to see her every day. Ania had offered to wash her nightdresses, but Carl had been adamant.

'You're going to be her daughter-in-law, not her carer,' he said.

'But a good daughter-in-law would be happy to care for a sick woman.'

'Dad can take the nightdresses home and Emilia can wash and iron them or they can be sent to a laundry.'

'It would be such a little thing,' Ania said.

'To me, it would be a big thing,' Carl said.

He went to see his mother once a week and helped his father organise the move.

On one of his hospital visits he brought an inventory of what they had in the big house looking out over the bay: furniture, paintings, glassware, ornaments.

'You can take about a fifth of this, Mother,' he said.

Immediately she began to complain.

'Dad says he doesn't mind what *he* takes but that possessions are very important to you. You collected them over the years. So just let me know and I will arrange that they be transferred.'

'But it's not at all certain that we really *want* to move. We might rent something.'

'Dad has bought it, Mother. And you can't go back to the old house. You couldn't manage the steps either.' He spoke as if her injuries were of no remote interest to him.

'Will you always hate me, Carl?' she asked.

'No, indeed, Mother, I don't hate you at all,' he said in a flat voice with no tone of reassurance in it.

Frank Ennis came to discuss the accident with Clara.

'Will we sue Mrs Walsh?' he said.

'I think not, Frank. The woman could have broken every bone in her body. Her husband has serious heart failure. Hardly likely to be helpful to him.'

'But she did knock it down.'

'Oh, I know she did, but not deliberately.'

'That's not the point. They will have plenty of insurance.'

'So have we.'

'But we're blameless. There was even a sign warning people. I checked.'

'Leave it, Frank. We're well covered. I checked that too.'

'You don't know how to save a no claims bonus,' Frank said, shaking his head.

'No, I'm glad to say I don't,' Clara agreed.

'What are you wearing to the wedding?' he asked suddenly.

'A moss-green dress with a black hat with ribbons of moss green around the hat.'

'Sounds lovely,' he said.

'It's not bad, certainly. And you, Frank, what will *you* wear?'

'Well, it does say "Dress Smart Casual". I wish I knew what that means.'

'I think it means no jeans,' Clara said.

'That wouldn't be an option,' Frank said seriously. 'But I was wondering about wearing a blazer.'

'A blazer? Like with brass buttons and everything?'

'No. It has ordinary cloth-covered buttons,' he said. He looked very unsure.

Clara was touched, despite herself, and decided to be kind. 'And light-coloured trousers?' she suggested.

'Exactly. I thought of pale grey and an open-necked shirt and a cravat.'

'God, Frank, you'll be beating them off you with a stick!' she said.

Vonni arrived three days before the wedding.

She looked older than Fiona had expected. Or maybe it was that this was Vonni in unfamiliar territory. If she had been back in Aghia Anna among all the people she knew, greeting everyone and busy about her work, it might have been different. Here, she was in a totally changed Ireland, in a capital city she hadn't seen for decades. Her only friends were Fiona,

438

Maud and Simon. She looked bewildered, which was something Fiona had not seen before.

Fiona had arranged for Vonni to stay with Muttie and his wife Lizzie, where the twins lived. It had been touching to see how eager they were to see her again and show her their city. And proud that she would be at their first professional wedding engagement.

Maud and Simon had gone to the airport to meet her and chattered the whole way back to St Jarlath's Crescent where Vonni met Muttie and Lizzie, and then Declan and his parents, and finally Fiona. Fiona had arranged to take Vonni out for a meal to catch up.

They went to the Early Bird meal at Quentins, where Vonni almost fainted at the prices. It was all so expensive, this new Ireland, compared to the country she had left. They talked long and affectionately of Tom and Elsa and the new baby. Who could ever have foreseen any of this? And of David, who now got on well with his mother and was finally doing what he liked to do with his life. They were surprised that some woman hadn't pinned him down. He would be ideal husband material.

They talked of Andreas back in Aghia Anna, and his brother Yorghis, and how Andreas's son Adoni had taken to the business so well. How he was going to marry Maria, the widow of Manos, who had been killed in a boat accident.

'The same Maria that David taught to drive!' Fiona cried.

'The very one,' Vonni agreed.

And Fiona touched lightly on the forbidden world of Vonni's son. A blank look came across Vonni's face. So no change there then.

'I'm not trying to pry, I just wondered if there was anything at all?'

'Nothing of significance. No.'

So they left that and Vonni touched gently on the closed subject of Shane.

'Did he ever come back to Ireland?' she asked.

There was a silence.

'Sorry,' Vonni said, 'I shouldn't have mentioned him.'

'No. No problem. He *did* come back to Ireland. To die.'

'Merciful God,' said Vonni.

'Yes. He died in a dirty bedroom from a drugs overdose.'

'What a waste of a young life,' Vonni said.

'Yes, I suppose so.'

'You're not upset then?'

'No, in fact I'm shocked at how un-upset I am.'

'That part of your life is over. That's why it hasn't any power to hurt you any more.'

'I believe that now. Declan convinced me.'

'You told him about Shane?'

'Yes. Declan is remarkable.'

'You're very lucky, Fiona. He *is* special, just like you wrote to me when you met him first. You'll be very happy.'

'I don't deserve it.'

'Yes, you do. You had guts when you needed them. You are kind to people. Don't be so quick to put yourself down. That was one of my faults too.'

'Are you better now?'

'I think so, yes. I've stopped blaming myself that my sister doesn't like me. It's not *my* fault any more.'

'You're not going to see her while you're here?'

'No. I don't think we'd have anything to say to each other.'

'I could go with you on the train tomorrow if you like?' Fiona offered.

'Two days before your wedding! You have a million things to do, Fiona.'

'I don't, as it happens. We could have lunch with her and come back that evening.'

'No, Fiona, honestly. It's a long way to travel to have two old ladies sit and look at each other with disapproval. No, we'll give it a miss. I'll just continue with the Christmas and birthday cards.'

'And does she . . . ?'

'Not any more. She used to send postcards from places, just showing off that she visited Rome or New York. But she doesn't even bother now.'

Vonni was resigned and Fiona changed the subject.

'Right, we'll take you on a tour of Dublin instead. There's a get-on get-off bus we could try.'

'Correct me if I'm wrong, Fiona, but isn't that what *all* buses are? You get on them, you get off them?'

'No. This is a *tour* bus. We can stay on it all day if we want or get off and explore something and get back on another. It's a great way of seeing Dublin. I'm going to suggest David does it too. Maybe we could go together, the three of us, and the twins, if they're ever going to take any time off again.'

'Fiona, what do people *earn* in this country to be able to pay prices like this? Look at what they charge for coffee!'

'Why do you think we're all racing out to Aghia Anna?' Fiona laughed and patted the old, lined hand on the table.

When David arrived the next day, Fiona met him and took him to his lodgings in Barbara's flat.

'She won't mind?'

'No, this is my room when I stay here. I've been wandering around for the last few weeks: Declan's house, my parents' house and here. She'll be glad of the company.'

David gave her another hug.

'I'm so pleased to see you so happy after . . . after everything.'

'And you too, David. I'm taking you off on a bus tour of Dublin right now. We're meeting Vonni at the start point.

And the twins. But I won't even begin to explain who they are exactly.'

'It's all like a dream, Fiona. And the sun is still shining, like when we waved goodbye to the others at the Café Midnight in Aghia Anna,' he said, taking out his notebook and pencil for the journey.

She had forgotten just how much she liked David. Wasn't he just great to have come over for her wedding?

The two days before the wedding were busy for everyone. Vonni had been invited with Paddy Carroll and Muttie Scarlet and their associates to have a drink in their pub. She explained that she didn't drink herself due to early excesses, and they all nodded gravely as if that could have been their own problem had things not been different.

Barbara had taken David to a pottery exhibition where he met a lot of craftsmen and women who invited him to different parts of Ireland.

Clara's daughter Adi had left for South America with Gerry to save some forest. Linda, on the other hand, had got a major arts programme on television to cover Nick Hickey playing alto sax at a jazz evening in the record shop. Clara and Hilary had been in the audience bursting with pride over the two of them.

Peter Barry and his new lady friend Claire Cotter had sent a wedding gift of a half-dozen linen table napkins and had already taken two dancing lessons so that they wouldn't look foolish on the floor.

Father Brian Flynn had invited his Polish priest friend Father Tomasz from Rossmore to attend the wedding in the hope that he might send more weddings their way and that it might also distract him from St Ann's Well which he had become altogether too fond of.

The twins had practised so well that they were sure it would work. Their nerves had calmed down.

Lavender had seen the wedding menu and told her patients that if they stayed with the smoked salmon and salads they couldn't go far wrong.

Johnny had said there was no better exercise than dancing and had shown some of his stiffer patients how to look and feel more limber. He had to borrow a tie for his role as best man.

Tim, the security man, who was coming to the wedding with Lidia, thought privately that the place was a fire hazard and that those twins would probably burn it down on the day. So he quietly installed more fire extinguishers and fire blankets just in case.

Ania had delivered the wedding dress to Fiona's parents, delivered the waistcoat to Declan and the wall hangings to Father Flynn.

She had made a moss-green silk flower for Clara, arranged flowers for the two mothers and done buttonholes for Johnny and Carl.

'What are you wearing yourself?' Carl asked.

'I haven't thought,' Ania said.

'You know the dress you wore to my parents' party?'

'Ye-es.' She spoke doubtfully.

'I never saw it properly.'

'It isn't much to look at now. The sleeves had to be removed. It looks a bit sad now.'

'Could you make new sleeves?' he wondered.

'I'd need to get lace,' she said.

'Let's go and buy some lace.'

'You mean new lace in a shop?' She was overwhelmed by such extravagance.

'That's what I mean,' Carl said affectionately.

Frank Ennis tried on his outfit. He was afraid he looked like a mad old sailor. Maybe the blazer wasn't a good idea. He wished he'd said no to the invitation, saying that sadly he would be elsewhere. He would be hopelessly awkward and out of place.

Lar and Judy and Mrs Kitty Reilly were all gearing up for it. Kitty Reilly had now discovered St Ann's Well in Rossmore and was praying that the place be made the new Lourdes or Fatima. Her children were very impressed that she had been invited to the wedding of a young doctor. That was class. They were less impressed by the venue. An immigrants' church in the back streets of Dublin. A hall where these people ate their foreign food.

The Walsh family were going together. Carl was going to push his mother in her wheelchair and Ania was going to wheel Bobby. Ania knew the church and the hall. She knew exactly where they would be settled.

The house move had taken place. Rosemary would be coming to live in the new apartment in a couple of weeks' time. She was only on day-release for the wedding.

She was very different now. She was grateful for suggestions, instead of scorning them.

Ania had said that she might want to wear something smart for the wedding and that Bobby should ask her to choose from her outfits. Rosemary said that this was very thoughtful of Bobby and she would like a long cream skirt and a brown velvet top. She fussed about what gift they should send until Carl begged Ania to ask Fiona what they wanted and to tell them quickly before everyone went insane.

Fiona said that she and Declan would just love a picnic basket so that they could go up the Head of Howth or out to sit in Killiney Strand. Rosemary rang the top stores and ordered the last word in picnic baskets.

Fiona and Declan had stared at it dumbfounded when it arrived. They had only meant an insulated bag that would keep beer cool. This was a huge basket with leather straps and brass buckles and proper cutlery *and* plates *and* glasses and even napkins. They could hardly wait to take it on its first outing.

By the wedding morning, Barbara and David had become great friends. They had been to the theatre together. They had walked by the Liffey and they had taken the DART out to the seaside where Barbara pointed out the houses of pop singers and actors.

He was interested in everything – including Barbara.

She told him about the dress and the fear the zip might split.

'Why don't I sew you into the dress?' David suggested.

'Are you serious?'

'Totally. I can make big loopy stitches, give you room to breathe. Dance even?'

'*Dance?* David, if I get down that aisle, I won't move again for the rest of the day.'

'Wait till you see the stitching job I'll do,' David promised. 'You'll be dancing until dawn.'

The two mothers were congratulating each other on getting this far.

'I think it was your talking to Declan that did the trick,' Maureen said.

'No. You knocked some sense into Fiona.' Molly was anxious to give equal praise.

'I don't think I did that much, Molly. We've always been terrified of Fiona.'

'She's the sweetest, gentlest girl I ever met,' Molly Carroll said, and not for the first time Fiona's mother wondered at the different faces of ourselves that we showed to different people.

*

Fiona woke on the day to find her sisters standing by the bed.

'We brought you scrambled eggs and toast,' said Ciara.

'And fresh orange juice,' said Sinead.

'Thank you so much. I'm going to miss you,' Fiona said.

'We never did this before,' Ciara said anxiously.

'No, that's not true, but it's still very nice. What time's Barbara coming?'

'She's downstairs having coffee with Mam. She's looking terrific.'

'Is she dressed?'

'Yeah, she's all glammed up. She says you're to take your time. Have a shower and she'll come up and help you then.'

'If I eat much more of this, she'll have to sew me into my dress.'

'That's what your friend did to her apparently. David. He sewed her into her dress. She was telling Mam.'

Fiona shook her head. Her sisters were both daft. They never got the right end of any stick in their lives.

There was a crowd outside the church when Fiona and her father arrived. Father Flynn had encouraged everyone to come and cheer on the wedding. There were even photographers and journalists asking where the bride and groom were from. They were disappointed to find out that they were both Dubliners. They were hoping this would be more exotic, maybe even a celebrity wedding.

'Thanks, Dad, for everything,' Fiona said at the church door.

'I can't tell you how happy your mother and I are today. Like when we think . . .' he stopped.

'Let's not think about things like that, Dad. Not today,' Fiona said.

'How did you get to be so bloody serene all of a sudden?' Barbara hissed at her.

'How did *you* get into that dress?' Fiona hissed back.

'David sewed me into it this morning. He's a peach, David. Why didn't you ever tell me?'

'I did tell you.' Fiona was stung. 'That's why I got you to give him a room.'

'Girls!' Fiona's father was very firm. 'Enough of this, the music is playing. We have to walk the walk.'

And as the sun shone through the windows of what had once been a biscuit factory, Fiona heard the music begin. If her life had depended on it, Fiona could not have identified what they were playing, even though she had chosen it herself. She saw everyone in the church stand up and they got a nod from Father Brian on the altar.

They were off.

At the altar, Declan turned around. Walking slowly towards him was the most beautiful girl in the world. She looked dazzling in her Indian silk dress, she carried yellow and white roses in a bouquet. The dress was plain and classic, letting the fabric speak: it was like some designer creation, yet Declan knew it had been made by Ania, helped by her mother.

The church was crowded, but Fiona never once looked around her to take in the surroundings: she walked on towards him, her face one big radiant smile. She was going to be his wife in a few moments from now.

Declan closed his eyes for two seconds at the wonder of it all.

Hilary didn't care who saw her crying; she didn't even bother to wipe her face.

Clara felt a tear coming out of the corner of her eye; and to her astonishment Frank Ennis passed her a tissue.

There might have been fifty such scenes in the congregation – but Declan and Fiona saw none of them.

Nothing could take their eyes away from each other.

*

Father Flynn had asked only one favour, that the speeches be kept brief. He had been told by a very wise person that there was one rule to remember. You can never be too short or too flattering. He told this to Fiona's father who might easily have been long-winded. He also mentioned it to Johnny, who as best man would certainly have felt it necessary to make some risqué jokes; but he saw something in Father Flynn's face that made him lose the original script.

The photographer, Mouth Mangan, was as good as his word and remarkably speedy. There was no endless hanging about. Father Flynn took his business card in case they should need his services again.

The hall was a delight. The huge buffet tables were so welcoming and a legion of Simon's and Maud's friends were doing what was called work experience: passing drinks around and helping people to fill their plates.

Everywhere Fiona and Declan looked they saw friends and well-wishers. Fiona felt bathed in such happiness she could even be nice to Rosemary Walsh.

'Thank you again for the really wonderful picnic basket,' she said. 'It was *such* a generous gift.'

'Good, good. You wrote a very nice letter. One does try. It's such an *odd* thing to want. Bobby and I thought the only thing to do was to try and get you a top-class one.'

'And you did, Mrs Walsh. It's quite splendid. Can I introduce you to anyone? My mother? Declan's mother?'

'I don't think so, dear. Who is that lady with the lined face and the coloured skirt? The one who looks like a gypsy.'

'That's Vonni. She came from Greece specially.'

'And *is* she a gypsy?'

'No, not at all. She runs a craft shop there.'

'And is she Greek?'

'Irish.'

'Heavens! She does look interesting.'

'I'll bring her over to meet you,' Fiona said and made her way over to Vonni's side. She clutched Vonni's arm and whispered, 'Only one really poisonous person here and she said she'd like to meet you. She was the one who behaved so badly to Ania. Remember, I told you?'

'Lead me to her,' Vonni said, with a gleam in her eye.

'Gently, Vonni,' Fiona warned.

'Like silk,' Vonni promised.

Everyone said the speeches were a delight: short and warm. What more could you want?

The food was delicious and Fiona had asked for three cheers for the caterers whose first official function this was. Only the cake and the dancing remained.

Vonni had love-bombed Rosemary Walsh almost out of her wheelchair with her praise and delight for the new Irish, and how they had arrived just when the Celts needed them. Rosemary had never met such a forceful argument and found herself stammering agreement.

Linda and Nick told their mothers that they didn't want to upstage Fiona's day, but they thought they might well get married in this church and have the reception in this hall.

'You're getting *married*?' Hilary and Clara spoke in unison, their mouths round in shock and pleasure.

They had hoped and plotted that the two young people would get together, but actually getting married? It was beyond their wildest dreams.

Ania kept an eye on the wheelchairs so that she could give any assistance if it was needed.

'Ania?'

'Yes, Mrs Walsh?'

'I wanted to ask you something.'

'Of course.'

'It's a bit awkward.'

'Do you want to go to the bathroom, Mrs Walsh? I can take you there easily.' Ania was ready to be helpful as usual.

'No, no, nothing like that. It's about what I said to you and to Carl. I am *so* sorry.'

'But that's all a long time ago. It's long ago. Forgotten now.'

'Carl hasn't forgotten. His face is cold and hard. He is my only child. If you and he were to marry you would be my only daughter-in-law and your children my only grandchildren. I can't bear to think that I have lost all this with my stupid remarks.'

'No, no, believe me, Mrs Walsh.'

'Could you call me Rosemary?'

'No, that would be difficult. Look – Carl must take his own time to make his peace. Me? I have made my peace with you. I will always be your friend. I love your son. I hope to make him happy, but I don't want to do anything to force his hand. Is that the expression?'

'That's the expression, Ania. You are very bright. I am just a blind person.'

'You are a person who needs some wedding cake. I will go and get you some,' said Ania.

Rosemary watched her in her elegant dress go across the room talking to this person and that. She realised that only a few weeks ago she herself was doing that at her ruby wedding party.

And look at her now.

Tom and Cathy Feather came in at the cake stage to see how their protégés had fared. It all seemed to have been a glorious success. They had followed all their training too about leftovers. These had been sealed in plastic bags and put into the freezer.

The dancing had started. Bride and groom danced to the music of 'True Love'.

Then the parents and their spouses. The best man went over to ask the maid of honour, but she was already dancing with David, so Johnny asked Ciara, one of Fiona's sisters, instead. Then Declan's uncle asked Hilary to dance. Carl and Ania were out on the dance floor. Linda and Nick danced close together, planning their own wedding. Tim and Lidia danced. They had their plans too. They were going to buy and renovate a house out on the coast. Bobby reached over and took Rosemary's hand.

'That's what I have for you, Rosemary "love for ever true". That's the way it feels to me,' he said.

'Thank you, dear Bobby,' she said.

It had been a long time since she had called him 'dear Bobby'.

Clara looked up as Frank Ennis approached her. He looked very well, almost roguish, in his outfit.

'You promised me a dance,' he said.

'And I'm delighted you remembered.'

'You're the most stylish woman in the room,' he said as they danced together.

He was lighter and less blundering than she might have expected.

'Thank you. You look pretty racy yourself. What about the lady you're meant to be escorting?'

'She's having an affair with a bottle of wine,' Frank said.

'Right, no guilt then.' Clara smiled at him.

'Are you properly divorced and everything?' he asked as they negotiated a corner.

'Yes, I will be shortly,' she said.

'Good,' he said.

'What has this got to do with the hospital board?'

'Nothing. It's me. I won't see you at work any more and I want to see you socially.'

'Why won't you see me at work any more?'

'Your year is up next month,' Frank Ennis said.

'Oh, balls, Frank, I'm not leaving. There's far too much to do. Far too many battles to be fought and won. You know that. I know that.'

And he said nothing. Just put his arms around her more closely as the whole heart clinic and their friends and relations danced to the music of 'Hey Jude'.